The Magazine

HUGO AND KASIA MORENO

*Dedicated to our parents, for their love and patience,
and to Leora, for being herself.*

CONTENTS

PART ONE

Dear daughter 'neath the sun

FRIDAY, JUNE 13, 1997

10:06 a.m.

Rebecca Morgan tensed as she looked up, startled by the soft knock on her half-open office door. She could never get past the expectation that all messengers bore bad news. Abigail, the editor in chief's assistant, leaned in through the doorway, one hand tucking a stray strand of gray behind her ear. The thick violet frames of her huge eyeglasses gave her the look of a kindly insect.

"Did you get my message?" Abigail asked. "Or see the email?"

"No, why? What's wrong? I was just polishing up this profile before I file it..."

Rebecca glanced guiltily down at her phone. The little green light was on, showing a caller had left a message. Abigail's, no doubt. Rebecca knew the light had been on for half an hour, but she hadn't yet psyched herself up to retrieve the voice mail. She often marveled at the perversity of her career choice: a reporter who was terrified of phones. Sometimes she would sit paralyzed at the ominous ringing, then watch the little green light come on. She would stare at the light with awe, contemplating its potential for random doom.

"Nothing's really wrong, or at least not for you," said Abigail. Although she sounded perfectly composed, as always, behind her flashy glasses her left eye twitched with a nervous tic that Rebecca had seen only a few times before. "There's going to be an announcement at the bottom of the spiral staircase at eleven, and Roberts wants to make sure you'll be there. It's really important to him."

11 a.m.

The eighty-two writers and editors who worked out of *The Magazine*'s New York office waited at the bottom of the spiral staircase, buzzing with

2

curiosity and jostling one another in front of the receptionist's desk. This annoyed the receptionist no end, until she finally got up and stalked away, muttering something about an extra-long lunch.

"What's this whole thing about?" Billy the Bully asked Abigail impatiently. "Stupid meeting, I don't have time for this shit, I'm having lunch with Steve Rattner. I need to do some work this morning."

Abigail sighed.

Rebecca, standing a few feet away, turned toward Helen Caswell and rolled her eyes, then did her trademark Billy the Bully impression, assuming an expression leaden with self-importance while impatiently tapping her foot. Helen had to struggle visibly to suppress a snicker. Rebecca noted that Billy shut up instantly when Roberts appeared, with Bob Llewellyn, the owner of *The Magazine,* at his side.

Llewellyn looked at Roberts, and after getting a go-ahead nod, moved a step forward and started into an obviously well-rehearsed speech:

"This is a momentous time for *The Magazine*, a time of change. After forty years at the helm, Greg Roberts has told me it is his deepest wish to retire. Though I tried to dissuade him…"

Just like that.

Usually, when employees retired from *The Magazine* they were feted with a full-scale party in the Llewellyn galleries, with booze and a buffet with chocolate-covered strawberries and fancy hors d'oeuvres. But Roberts had always detested parties. And though he was eighty years old, Rebecca was certain he wasn't ready to retire. After forty years, he was getting the boot.

Rebecca struggled to digest this development. Roberts was cranky but talented, and utterly dedicated to his work. Over those forty years, he had made *The Magazine* what it was. For the past two decades, he had worked even harder—demonically, in fact—despite his personal tragedy. No, she corrected herself, because of it. That car wreck on the Long Island Expressway had not been his fault—a drunk driver had lost control and jumped the median—but it had cost Roberts his wife and daughter, leaving him nothing to live for but work. Leaving him wracked by survivor's guilt and the pain of his shattered hands, hands that had required extensive surgery and months of agonizing physical therapy. She knew the pain returned whenever he typed for more than a few minutes, knew it had grown worse the past several years. The pain inflamed his customary anger at sloppy writing. He would pepper stories with comments that sometimes slipped over the line between brusque and cruel. A Roberts edit was not for the thin-skinned.

Some of the tougher writers, Rebecca among them, appreciated Roberts and considered his comments badges of honor. But many others were tired of the grumpy old bastard.

11:20 a.m.

Toward the end of the meeting, before everybody started to disperse, Rebecca looked up and blinked, uncomprehending, as Abigail approached her once again. She had been right, the news was bad. Apocalyptic. She hadn't felt so disoriented since the end of the Cold War. No, this was worse, this was personal. Almost like…

Suddenly ashamed at her self-involvement, she realized what this must mean to Abigail. After thirty years as Roberts's right hand, Abigail would see her life change dramatically, one way or the other. Rebecca wondered whether Abigail would stay on under a new boss.

Now Abigail leaned close, looking solemn. "Rebecca, are you okay? Listen to me, Rebecca, listen carefully." She grasped Rebecca's arm firmly, held her gaze and whispered forcefully, "Roberts wants to see you in his office at noon, it's important."

"Okay, Abigail, I'll be there."

She stood for a moment, staring blankly into space. But the sight of Abigail catching hold of Helen's elbow and leading her into a corner snapped her back into focus. She was almost sure she overheard Abigail say, "Twelve-fifteen."

Rebecca continued to watch, tracking Abigail's progress through the crowd. Trying to look distracted, Rebecca wandered among her colleagues, vaguely in the direction of the staircase, which kept her trailing in Abigail's wake. Bruce Buccino stood in a shadowed corner, lurking at the edge of the crowd. Abigail walked briskly up to him, leaned close and said something, then scurried away without waiting for a response.

12:00 p.m.

Rebecca stepped tentatively into Roberts's office, expecting to find the man subdued, depressed, perhaps even nostalgic. But she saw at once that he was in his usual dictatorial mode.

Roberts hurled a fountain pen onto his desk. She watched it smack against the blotter and bounce. Roberts always threw a pen down on a desk or table just before passing judgment on someone's idea, exclaiming, "What's this crap?" in his high-pitched cackle, a demented voice of damnation. Or sometimes it was: "It's great, let's go with it, let's get on it as soon as we can."

Rebecca hung suspended in the moment, wondering which it would be this time, good or evil, yin or yang.

His cackle was excited: "Let's do it, let's see to the future of this magazine. Let's decide who should take over. I got Llewellyn to agree to promote someone from within, you know. Don't want some outsider coming in and fucking things up."

Elation. He wanted to consult with her about the next editor in chief.

But Roberts didn't pause to elicit her opinion. Instead he launched into

4

his own checklist: "Preston? I don't think so. Lacks spine. Too close to the Llewellyn family. As an editor he's too slow, too intellectual, kills color...doesn't realize magazine articles should be short enough to be read on the toilet.

"Bruce—got a chip on his shoulder. Thinks he's smarter than everyone else. So he comes on like a steamroller. Sometimes you need someone who knows how to use a stiletto." He paused and fixed her with his gray, inscrutable stare.

Rebecca chuckled nervously.

He continued without comment. "Who else out there is really editor material, eh? They're all too crazy or too drunk or have their heads too far up their asses. You know who I mean, too. So who is there? Helen?

"She doesn't really like to get dirty. Too proper at heart, I think. I know you two are friends, what do you think? I'm right, aren't I?"

"Well..."

"She'd make a fine manager, but as a journalist, does she have the stomach for it, what it takes to be a great one? The nerve, the cunning?

"It could be you, Rebecca. It should be you. Just give me one last bullet, one more great story. If you could do it for this next issue, that would be ideal. Our lineup so far just isn't exciting. That would give you, oh, a good ten days. Don't bother working up a pitch. Surprise me."

She felt unsteady in her knees. Her vision fogged, and for a second she was afraid she would faint. Editor in chief. Editor in chief. For several seconds her brain refused to process anything but those words, an echo in her skull.

As the initial shock subsided, her eyes cleared. Objects sharpened. The feeling in her legs crept back, and she realized that she was still standing. Her mind suddenly seemed keener than ever, as if compensating for this momentary lapse.

She was ready to talk. She wanted so much to hear his thoughts about running the magazine.

But she could tell that he had already dismissed her. Once he was done, he never bothered to wait for a person to respond. He didn't say, "Thanks, that's all I needed," or even wave someone away. He simply tuned out.

Rebecca still stood in front of him, but he refused to acknowledge her presence any longer. He reached for a pile of readers' letters on his desk and started leafing through them.

She stood her ground for several more seconds, hoping that this one time would be different, that this was some sort of test, that he would look up and talk to her. But no.

12:36 p.m.

She sat in her office, still stunned, trying to think.

She had already taken steps to clear her head and work through the shock. After Roberts had dismissed her, she had wandered back toward her office on autopilot. Somewhere in the maze of gray cubicles she had suddenly halted, bummed a low-tar cigarette from one of the reporters and made a beeline for the stairwell. She had smoked half the cigarette as she walked around the block before the dizziness became unpleasant, ducked into a cafe for a large latte to go, then returned.

Now Helen slipped through her door, closed it behind her. "He asked you for a story, right? A great one."

She nodded.

"For the editorship."

She nodded again.

Helen sighed. "Yeah, me too. He's setting up a competition. Looks like a four-way, you, me, Bruce and Preston."

"I see. Well, good luck."

"Yeah, same to you." Helen hesitated. "You know, I won't mind if you win. Even Bruce, I could live with that. Just not Preston."

12:42 p.m.

Rebecca locked the door to her office. Had to barricade herself in and think. She didn't have much time.

She felt a twinge of unease at the prospect of flinging herself into a head-on competition with Helen and realized she'd have to just set that emotion aside. Sometimes friends had to compete, but it was possible to be friendly rivals, wasn't it? Besides, she suspected Roberts was right about Helen: She could be, well, squeamish wasn't the right word. Genteel, that was it. Nothing wrong with that, but sometimes the journalistic calling demanded other virtues. As for herself, Rebecca knew she was capable of summoning up her inner ruthlessness. And now was the time to use it.

Focus. She sat at her computer and stared blankly at the screen. She had a few ideas for stories, of course, but not fleshed-out ideas. More like notions. Half-baked hunches. She couldn't afford to waste time on dead ends.

Her fingers fluttered across the keyboard. She printed out a number of SEC filings, paused to scan them quickly. She zipped through several investment Web sites, buying a few analyst reports along the way. More printing, more scanning. As she scanned, she dialed the phone, left voice mail messages. It was lunchtime, but she was checking with sources she used regularly and trusted. Some analysts, some hedge fund managers. They'd call back promptly.

By 2:30 that afternoon she was sure she'd caught the scent of a story. The conversations she was having were all background, off the record, but they all seemed to confirm her hunches. It would be a kickass story, too, if she could nail it down in time. That was the rub. This was the kind of story she would normally spend months on, patiently stalking her quarry. She had a week to bag this one. Alpha/Omega was a big company with notoriously opaque financials and a complex structure: Although most of its revenue came from pharmaceuticals, it was organized more like a conglomerate than like a typical drugmaker. The CEO, Ron Popitz, was infamously secretive, and most analysts who covered the firm lived in terror of him.

That was the next thing to line up. Popitz would be key. Even if all he did was deny and obfuscate—certainly that was what Rebecca expected—an interview would be central to the story.

Luckily for her, she had a way in, or so she hoped. She had written a cover story on Popitz a few years back, when he first became CEO. It had been positive overall. She thought it had been downright flattering, but Popitz could be a prickly son of a bitch. Still, at least she could evade the usual channels through the PR department.

She flipped through her Rolodex, praying Popitz hadn't fired his old executive assistant. What was her name? Yes, Stephanie. She dialed, held her breath. Jackpot: Stephanie's soothing voice on the line.

Rebecca identified herself, reminded Stephanie of the flattering story, turned the charm on full. Within seconds, they were chatting like long-lost friends. Before she could wear out her fragile welcome, Rebecca segued smoothly into her pitch. Undertones of urgency. Dark hints of weakness in the company's financial state. Rumors of trouble. A story that might turn negative unless Popitz himself cleared things up. She was offering a sympathetic ear.

Stephanie put her on hold. Of course, Rebecca was bluffing. She didn't have squat, at least not yet. But she couldn't wait. Besides, sometimes a really emphatic denial could set you on the right track. Four minutes. Five minutes. She was beginning to think she'd been cut off when Stephanie's voice returned.

"Rebecca? Listen, middle of next week he flies to California for a couple days, and his schedule's a bit hectic before that, but if you could do something early Monday morning…"

Rebecca barely restrained herself from whooping into the phone.

SATURDAY, JUNE 14, 1997

8:17 a.m.

Rebecca stuffed her dirty jeans, some underwear and a dozen T-shirts into a laundry bag. She always wore jeans and T-shirts while working in the office so she didn't have to waste any time thinking about clothes. She slung the nylon bag over her shoulder and hiked two blocks to the local laundromat. While waiting for her clothes to wash and dry, she read that day's business section of *The New York Times*, the previous day's *Barron's* and three days' worth of *Investor's Business Daily*.

After dropping her clean laundry off at home, she dashed to the dry cleaners to pick up her two suits—she planned to take them both to the office on Monday. When she needed to dress up for a work interview or a meeting, she chose from one of the two suits she usually kept hanging on the door of her office—a Banana Republic black pantsuit and a gray J. Crew suit, both of which Rebecca had selected for their unpretentious simplicity. To go with the suits, she had three simple collarless blouses—she considered collars pointless, just useless excess—in black, white and gray. Each blouse looked good with each suit, and she could thus create several different combinations and not seem to wear the same clothes all the time.

That was usually enough clothing for one story's important interviews. She interviewed scores, sometimes hundreds, of sources for a single story, but many interviews—with analysts, for instance—took place on the phone. After she completed a round of interviews, she had her clothes dry-cleaned again, so they'd be ready for the next story.

On the way back from the dry cleaners, Rebecca stocked up on supplies—two huge bottles of Diet Pepsi, frozen diet desserts and hot dogs. When she got hungry at home she would eat cold hot dogs, and when she craved sugar she indulged in the intensely sweet chemical edge of diet desserts. She gulped down bottles of Diet Pepsi to stay awake while working through the night.

She kept only these bare necessities at home, since she ate most of her meals in the office. The pace of her work could vary radically from day to day, but she tried to order her hectic life with fixed routines. She usually picked up the same things every day from the greengrocer around the corner from the office: a bagel with butter for breakfast; a plastic container of readymade sushi for lunch; and another plastic container of tuna salad, which she mixed with cottage cheese from the salad bar, for dinner. Sometimes, when she was busy writing or preparing for an interview, she skipped a meal or two.

She felt both fortified and purified by this monotonous, unbalanced regimen. It dovetailed with her sense that bad food was a ritual necessity for people who worked hard. After several days of cheap sushi and tuna, her stomach rebelled. She welcomed the familiar discomfort—the vague, persistent nausea, the bad taste in her mouth. Like a gastrointestinal badge of honor, it signaled that she had been working hard enough. It was time to switch to bland muffins for a couple of days.

When interviewing someone over dinner in a restaurant, she usually ordered a green salad and salmon. Most restaurants had those items on the menu, so she avoided the food decision—one less distraction. She had eaten that same dinner in all the most expensive restaurants in New York City, and she supposed she should be a connoisseur of salad and salmon by now, but she never really paid enough attention to feel competent to compare dishes. She'd never understood that whole foodie thing, people studying their Zagat guides and discussing hot restaurants. Food was fuel.

Sometimes she thought she should have been a nun, but in the Middle Ages. Perhaps abbess of some extreme, fringe order. How comforting that would have been, to be surrounded by women who understood discipline and the art of self-denial.

1:36 p.m.

She dealt with the ex's books. Jason had left several hardbacks in her apartment. When they had broken up a couple of weeks before, he had made a point of asking for them back, and she had assured him she would FedEx them to his office. Now she fit them into a small box and carried the package across the street to the Mail Boxes Etc. store. She wanted to make sure Jason didn't call asking about the books. She didn't want to hear his voice again and start thinking about their three months together.

Rebecca's boyfriends usually lasted about three months. Typically, she went to bed with them on the first date, disregarded any lingering attachments to former girlfriends, took them out to dinners, talked to them about work, lent them money if they wanted, and saw them as often as they felt an urge for sex with her. When they left, she was temporarily stunned, and wept at unpredictable moments for several days.

9

She was done crying over Jason by now, but not yet indifferent enough not to be distracted by him. And for this next week she couldn't afford any distractions.

5:11 p.m.

She descended into the stack of printouts she'd brought home from the office, feeling herself sucked into a vortex of numbers and officialese until she lost her bearings and found it hard to breathe. Still, her sense that she was onto something was hardening into conviction. She had examined the quarterly cash flow statements going back two years, had done the math. Free cash flow was drying up even as earnings were rising—a sign of trouble, possibly some sort of sleight-of-hand in Alpha/Omega's accounting. Inventory turnover was slowing—products were sitting in warehouses too long. She checked the numbers for accounts receivable: steadily rising. It seemed the company was having trouble collecting unpaid bills.

Suddenly, about 11 p.m., a couple of murky connections became clear. She felt as if she were coming up for air.

She stood, stretched, grabbed an oversize sketch pad, carefully tore out four sheets and taped them together. Now she had a paper rectangle five feet by four. Marker in hand, she crawled across the paper, diagramming. Circles, boxes, arrows, question marks. By midnight it resembled an alchemical formula, but it represented the more mundane mysteries of corporate structure. Holding companies, subsidiaries, offshore entities. She would map this territory yet.

SUNDAY, JUNE 15, 1997

7:33 p.m.

Every surface in her living room was covered with paper. Diagrams and documents.

Rebecca stood in her tiny kitchen, gazing absently out her window and across the neighboring rooftops as she brewed another pot of Earl Grey. It was that hour of summer twilight when the city turned luminescent. She thought it beautiful. Still, she missed the distinctive golden light of evening in Brooklyn, a magical light she'd never seen in Manhattan. Well, by this time next Sunday she would be in her father's garden. The story should be written by then. If it was, it could be the happiest evening of her life. If not, if it turned out she didn't have a story…she didn't know. She missed her father's easy company.

The story she was working on touched on Madsen Laboratories, the company that had employed her father for thirty years, but only in passing. Madsen was one likely beneficiary of the troubles of her main subject, Ron Popitz's company, Alpha/Omega. If the rumors of a cash flow crunch and disappointing clinical trials proved true, then rival Madsen could steal market share from Alpha/Omega. But she didn't see a real conflict of interest. Her father was a well-respected researcher toiling in the labs, not senior management.

Besides, she didn't plan to talk to her father while she was working on the story. She was even skipping her usual Sunday dinner with him in Brooklyn—something she had never done before. But this was about her entire career, her life—she couldn't spare the time or energy for dinner. She had emailed him at work Friday afternoon with the news that she couldn't make it, and had added that she was immersed in a big story and couldn't talk for the next week, but would see him the following Sunday. He had acknowledged the email, and she was grateful for that—she loved her father devotedly, but he was one of those people who seemed incapable of cutting a phone call shorter than twenty minutes. Especially when talking to Rebecca. That was the real reason she planned to avoid speaking to him. She couldn't afford twenty minutes.

In her imagination she already saw herself a week into the future, in his garden. Every Sunday evening since she had graduated from Mount Holyoke and rented her first New York apartment, a tiny studio three blocks away from *The Magazine,* she had traveled to Brooklyn for her dinner with Dad. He always cooked, and she always brought wine.

In the summers they ate in his brownstone's tiny backyard garden. He barbecued steaks and hot dogs on an old-fashioned Weber charcoal grill—a bulging bulb on three legs, which Rebecca called R2D2. It was the same old grill he had bought the first summer after her mom had died. That was the summer that had inaugurated their barbecue tradition.

That same summer they had also started planting flowers. After years of driving Mom to the clinic or the hospital for chemotherapy, and spending hours trying to decipher piles of cryptic medical bills and insurance statements, which grew even faster than weeds, it seemed like the first moment in their lives when they had any time for the garden.

They planted perennials in June, and every day the flowers surprised them with something new. After the first blue blossom suddenly appeared, they would run to the window every morning, expectant, to check on their garden's progress. They wanted to see what else might have bloomed during the night, and which areas were the most desperately threatened by weeds. They deliberated where they should move some yellow blossoms that they had mistakenly planted in the middle of a red and purple patch, where the yellow flowers—though the healthiest and brightest ones—simply didn't belong.

That little garden was the most important and beautiful thing they had that summer, and it kept them alive.

Now it was summer again, the twenty-fifth summer since Mom had died, and Rebecca was going back to her garden. Next Sunday.

MONDAY, JUNE 16, 1997

8:07 a.m.

Rebecca left her apartment building and walked down Broadway to 65th Street. The crosstown bus would take her across Central Park to Madison Avenue. She was meeting with Ron Popitz at 9:30, at the Carlyle Hotel. The bus ride shouldn't take more than ten minutes, but she couldn't risk being late. That morning she was wearing what she considered her most professional combination—the black pantsuit and a white collarless blouse.

8:42 a.m.

She arrived at the Carlyle forty-eight minutes before the meeting and perched on a sofa in a corner of the lobby. The Carlyle's lobby hardly looked like a lobby at all. It felt more like the living room of an old-money Park Avenue apartment. The Persian carpet seemed well broken in, as was the upholstery on the sofa Rebecca sat on.

The Carlyle was different from every other hotel because of what it didn't have—the vulgar enticements of Sheratons, Waldorf-Astorias, Bristols and Savoys. The Carlyle was small and subdued by comparison, purposefully un-hotel-like. A small front desk was the lobby's only concession to its function. There were no artificial flower arrangements, no arrows leading to conference rooms or ballrooms, no notices advertising the hotel's business center.

And no people noise. No bellboys and maids running busily around, faking interest in satisfying the guests' every whim. When Rebecca came into the Carlyle's lobby and sat down in the corner, the aging concierge pretended not to notice her. He looked like a venerable English butler. Rebecca would have bet twenty bucks that his name was either James or Jeeves.

She took out her notebook and started going over her questions for Popitz.

9:30 a.m.

No sign of Popitz.

Rebecca wasn't surprised. She didn't expect him to appear on time. Way early, just possibly. Way late, very probably. But never on time. He would want to start out with the upper hand by making her wait.

Alpha/Omega was a huge, and hugely profitable, company. But Rebecca saw vulnerabilities. A lawsuit was about to strip its major antidepressant of patent protection three years early. Its blockbuster allergy drug was also threatened by generics. Everything depended on what was coming down the pipeline, and the pipeline was full of ominous, rumbling echoes. Rumors of blockages and leaks, of dead-end clinical trials. Rebecca suspected the pipeline had turned into a big clogged artery.

And Popitz was facing an invigorated rival in Madsen Laboratories. Madsen had always been a respectable number two or three in its markets, playing Avis to Alpha/Omega's Hertz. But things were changing now: Billionaire money manager Tom Richardson had bought a stake in the company that gave him effective control. He had seized the helm of the board of directors and was driving Madsen aggressively, firing and hiring, cutting costs, transforming the firm into a cutthroat competitor.

It was bad timing for Popitz. He couldn't afford a determined rival with deep pockets. Rebecca had heard rumors that whispered of a cash crunch buried in those convoluted financials, as well as the pipeline troubles. There were even hints that many of Alpha's senior managers—tired of being bullied and humiliated by Popitz—were ready to bolt. Some might defect to Madsen.

A lot of this would be difficult to confirm. Rebecca anticipated scores of fruitless phone calls that week, and if she got lucky, a few liquid lunches with disgruntled former employees and embittered competitors. This story would require every ounce of charm she could ooze, and it would still be hard to get much on the record. Even people who had retired or made career moves into completely different industries remained terrified of Popitz. Some former employees liked to say that even the dead were afraid of him.

9:45 a.m.

Rebecca approached the concierge and asked him where the house phone was. She wanted to call Popitz's suite.

James/Jeeves stared down his long, aristocratic nose at Rebecca from what seemed to her a great height. "Is there anything I could help you with?"

"Yes. I was supposed to meet Mr. Popitz at 9:30." She glanced pointedly at her watch. "I just wanted to make sure that he's in the hotel, that he hasn't forgotten about our meeting."

"I will take care of it," said the concierge. He turned and disappeared down a long hallway.

9:57 a.m.

She stood up at the concierge's return. He walked up to her and announced, "Everything is fine," in a tone that brooked no argument or elaboration.

"But..." Rebecca started to protest.

"Everything is just fine," he repeated politely but sternly.

Rebecca was usually impervious to people's attitudes toward her, but something about James/Jeeves made her feel socially inadequate. Vaguely embarrassed, she stared down at her own shoes. Just for a second or two.

When she looked up, he was gone.

10:32 a.m.

The elevator pinged. The doors slid open. Popitz emerged, chomping on a huge unlit cigar. He ignored Rebecca and strode directly across the lobby to the concierge. Sitting just a few feet away, Rebecca listened intently.

"You know me, I've been living here for the last 18 years, and there were never any problems. It's all her, she's impossible. Everything is a catfight with this woman. She complains about the whole staff. She can find something wrong with everything. Yesterday it was the maid, and the day before that her breakfast wasn't delivered fast enough. As if she could afford room service before she married me. That's what I get for mixing with white trash from Queens. Now you'll just have to help me handle the bitch until I can get rid of her."

"It's going to be fine..."

"You always say that. I bet you I'll have to move out of here because of that skank....Goddammit, I'll never move out of here, I'll divorce the bitch before I even think about it. Eighteen years in this hotel. I don't need this bullshit in my life. I have no time for this kind of crap...."

"Sir, you know I'll do everything in my power to smooth the way for you. Let me play with it for a while and see what I can work out. Everything is going to be just fine."

10:36 a.m.

Popitz spun around and walked over to Rebecca.

She scrambled awkwardly to her feet and extended her hand. "Hello, it's nice to see you. Thank you for agreeing to talk to me."

"What time is it, lady?" he barked at her. "If you worked for me and showed up late to meetings I would fire you. I should fire you anyway..."

Three men in three shades of navy blue, dapper yet serious in their beautifully tailored suits, appeared in the lobby. Popitz abruptly cut off his tirade and rushed over to greet them, abandoning Rebecca. She felt stranded, washed up in the lobby like flotsam.

"Ernest, but how are you, so great to see you. And Howard!" Popitz was saying as he bestowed handshakes and backslaps.

Popitz and the men, still exchanging loud greetings and did-you-hear-abouts, sashayed right past Rebecca and disappeared up a narrow stairway. The concierge followed them.

10:45 a.m.

The concierge rematerialized in the lobby. To Rebecca he seemed annoyed, even somewhat taken aback, that Rebecca was still there.

He spoke to her in that definitive tone: "Mr. Popitz has booked the conference room for several hours. His meetings with these gentlemen usually take quite a long time, and I know that after the meeting Mr. Popitz's driver is taking him somewhere for the rest of the day. I don't think it would be advisable to wait for him."

Rebecca felt like throwing up. She had to talk to Popitz. She didn't really have a story yet, just a set of hunches and rumors. Not that she expected Popitz to spill his guts to her, but even some outright denials would help. If she could get him to address certain issues, it would anchor the story. Also, people surprised you sometimes. They slipped up.

She needed this story. She couldn't let Roberts down.

She wouldn't give up, whatever it took. Even if she had to camp in this lobby and wait forever.

Her legs felt weak as she slowly lowered her body back onto the sofa. She couldn't think.

The concierge spoke again. "I really cannot in good conscience advise you to wait…"

10:55 a.m.

The elevator door opened and a young woman stormed into the lobby. She charged at the concierge and demanded, "Where is he? James, you absolutely have to tell me where he went."

Even through the haze of her despair, the name registered, and Rebecca almost laughed out loud. James. It really was James.

The woman—no, not so young, Rebecca corrected herself, well-kept but now approaching the fortyish zone—had clearly sprung out of bed in a hurry. She wore flip-flops and a tiny tank top, the kind young girls like to sleep in. She was still angrily fiddling with the zipper of her jeans, which seemed stuck or caught on something.

"James, please," she half begged, half demanded, "this is important." She shook her head, and an untidy mass of dark red hair danced across her face. Rebecca guessed she had run a quick brush through her hair upon rolling out of bed—a few strokes, no more. The woman reached up automatically and pushed the hair back from her face. No makeup. She wore a huge ring shaped like a ladybug studded with diamonds and rubies. A gaudy bauble, thought Rebecca. One that no doubt had cost twice Rebecca's annual salary. At least.

James started speaking to her in hushed tones and flashing guarded glances toward Rebecca, clearly embarrassed by this inelegant commotion. But the woman seemed to have no emotional stake in the concierge's overriding imperative: to uphold good manners in the lobby of the esteemed Carlyle Hotel. Just the opposite, in fact. The more desperately James tried to calm her down, the louder and angrier she became.

"I don't care who else is here, I want you to tell me right away where my husband went. And don't pretend that you don't know where he is. I know you're covering for him, like you always do, and I know that he pays you pretty well for that." She suddenly seemed to run out of steam and lowered her voice a notch. "Not that I blame you. Better to sell your loyalty. Most of his spineless yes-men are just too scared to cross him. But you—I respect you, James. Once bought, you stay bought."

"I am sure that you will find your husband soon enough, Mrs. Popitz, and everything will be fine." James pointedly kept his expression blank, his voice neutral.

Mrs. Popitz. Rebecca sat up straighter. Her brain began to function again, quickly spun up to full speed, alert for an opportunity.

"Oh, James." The woman smoothly switched tactics, no doubt sensing that throwing a fit would be a waste of energy. She must have noticed James's discreet but repeated glances at the clear outline of her breasts. She shoved her right hand, which finally seemed finished fiddling with the zipper, deep into her jeans and arched her body slightly backwards.

"We were supposed to go apartment hunting," she whined, like a hurt little girl. "I have a real estate agent all lined up, she's the very best. I want to live in an apartment in the city like a real person, not cooped up here in this institutional bachelor pad. I want to have something of my own. I want to buy chairs and a bed. I want to make breakfast in my own kitchen. I'm a fantastic cook, you know. Cooking is how I relax. I have to be able to cook again.

"I just want to feel like I'm at home." Simultaneously, she tossed back her hair and wriggled her fingers inside her jeans. "James, you have a home, I'm sure you can understand a girl who just wants to have a real home, like everybody else. Can't you help me find him?"

James—was he ever-so-slightly flushed?—managed a blank stare and repeated his mantra. "Let me see what I can work out. I'm sure everything is going to turn out just fine."

At this, she snapped.

"Oh, shut up, you're worse than he is. I might as well talk to the fucking wall."

Mrs. Popitz spun around and stalked through the lobby, back toward the elevator.

As she passed Rebecca, she gave her a quick, angry look and then stopped short, as if remembering something.

Rebecca ventured tentatively, "Mrs. Popitz?"

"Hey, you wouldn't be that journalist Ron was supposed to talk to this morning? He blew you off too?"

Instantly, Rebecca was on her feet, smiling warmly. "Yes, I'm Rebecca Morgan, from *The Magazine.*" One last heaven-sent chance. She couldn't let it slip away.

James surfaced at Mrs. Popitz's side. "The young lady was on her way out. Mr. Popitz won't be meeting with her today."

Mrs. Popitz ignored him completely and held out her hand to Rebecca, returning her smile: "I'm Susie Popitz. Listen, want to have a drink?"

"I'd love to."

"Good, the restaurant's over this way…"

James interjected, "But the bar is closed this early."

"Oh, bug off, James," Susie said angrily, "I'm sure I'll manage."

11:05 a.m.

Susie led Rebecca to a cozy, richly upholstered sitting room on the ground floor of the hotel that functioned as a cafe. Women in suits sat in large armchairs, sipping tea from translucent china cups and eyeing Susie pointedly as she sauntered past, but she ignored the stares.

"Here, let's sit here," she ordered Rebecca, and called out, "Michael, could I have my favorite?"

Several seconds later a waiter who looked like a younger version of James appeared with a glass of Drambuie. "I love Drambuie," Susie said, "it's so sweet, it's like dessert. When you have enough Drambuies you really don't need food. What will you have?"

Rebecca didn't want a drink, certainly not this early in the day. But she realized she had no choice now, that the only way to get something out of Susie Popitz was to drink with her. She settled on the drink that made her the least drunk, though she didn't much care for it. "Gin and tonic," she said, and to be on the safe side, she also asked for a muffin to buffer the alcohol.

Susie Popitz proceeded to vent: "The bastard told me we were going to look at apartments today. I've seen some great places on Park Avenue, but anytime I really want something, he finds a flaw, some excuse to kill the deal. Old goat's just playing with me. He'll never move out of here, I should've known better. He's lived here with his last two wives. Always outlasts them. I can't furnish anything, nothing is mine. I hate it here, but to him living in a hotel…it's like he can pretend he's a free bachelor, wives be damned.

"Sometimes I wonder if that's the only way he's pretending. Son of a bitch came home smelling of perfume last week. I recognized the scent. Stench of

Stephanie. You know his 'executive assistant'?"

Rebecca nodded.

"I'd like to know just how she assists him. Little slut."

Rebecca sipped her drink and tried to look sympathetic. She was afraid of saying anything that might stem the flood of Susie's words.

"Did you know that the company pays for this place in the Carlyle for him? The bastard lives it up on the shareholders' money. Typical. He screws everybody. You should see the prenup he made me sign. I have to stay with him at least five years or I'm totally screwed, but he could dump me anytime. Sooner the better, for him. And now he's going to screw these bankers he's talking with about restructuring his debt. He needs them now, so he'll turn on the charm, just like he did with me. But once he has what he wants from them, he'll change completely. Like Jekyll and Hyde. He's like a supervillain in a comic book, you know. He always makes a killing for himself, leaves everybody else with their bare ass hanging out the window. After he's screwed 'em good. And he gets away with it over and over again."

Susie Popitz took a long swallow of Drambuie and focused on Rebecca, as if she were seeing her for the first time.

"And what do you want from the bastard?"

"I'm doing a story about your husband."

"A story about my husband? I could tell you a few stories about my husband. I should. It's like I'm living in this golden cage. Like that song, 'White Bird,' you know it? 'White bird in a golden cage...' When I was just a little girl, that was my favorite song. Guess that's ironic, huh?

"I actually work, you know. I'm into art. For the last two years I studied art—Ron figured it would help us shop wisely at auctions—and then I got a job working for the Met. But now I hate it. They have me cataloging, it's so frigging boring. I should be there now, but I decided to stay in bed. I should really just call in and quit. I mean, that's the reason I gave up being an accountant, because I was bored outta my skull. Fuck it, you know?

"But that's how I met Ron, I was keeping the books, he was getting divorced, and he asked me out.

"During our first date, he told me how his father had died when he was a boy, and how he had to go work for a funeral home in Bay Ridge when he was just nine. Straight out of Horatio Alger. Couldn't help feeling some sympathy for that poor little boy.

"Heard the rest of the story after we got engaged. His job was to open the doors of black limos for the family arriving for the funeral, carry wreaths around, and then to steal jewelry from the casket. Wedding rings and stuff. Or any other valuables that the family might have put in there. Can you believe it?"

Susie leaned close. "By the way, that's a gorgeous necklace you're wearing."

Rebecca glanced down reflexively, startled and pleased but afraid Susie was veering off track. The piece was simple, a jade disk with an inlaid silver spiral. "Thanks, a family heirloom. Belonged to my mother."

"Well, it's lovely. Anyway, after the funeral was over, Ron was supposed to hand over the loot to the owner of the funeral parlor, but not before then. So if the family noticed that something was missing, the owner would act all indignant and search his employees and 'find out' that it was Ron who stole it. He would pull on Ron's ears until they turned all red, yell at him terribly and fire Ron on the spot. Then he would apologize to the family and return the stolen goods.

"So on occasions when the stunt didn't work, Ron got stuck with red ears and public humiliation. When it worked, and the stolen goods pleased the owner, he gave Ron a quarter. Those are the man's roots. So I guess it's no wonder he screws everybody.

"What are you writing about him anyway?"

Rebecca hesitated, took a deep breath and dove in. She felt like an Olympic diver stepping off the platform into a triple backflip with a twist. What she said to Susie steered a murky course between what she had said to Popitz's assistant, Stephanie, and the truth. She spun a tentative web of suspicion, insinuation and rumor, half guesswork, the rest implied. A story that might remain forever elusive without insider knowledge. Or inside documents. Memos, email.

She was careful not to step over any lines. Never came out and suggested anything. Simply waited for Susie to take the bait. Praying she had judged her correctly. Paused and held her breath until she realized that she'd stopped breathing, and black splotches suddenly peppered her visual field.

Susie Popitz frowned thoughtfully for several long seconds, then jerked up straight in her chair with a grin, spilling the remainder of her Drambuie across her lap. "Oh great, now I have dessert all over you know what…that's what I call a really sweet pussy." She giggled.

Michael the waiter scurried over with club soda. Susie allowed him to dab at her thighs and crotch for a minute, then shooed him off to fetch another Drambuie.

She leaned close to Rebecca and spoke in a whisper. "I'll give you the dirt on that bastard, my dear, we'll fuck him over good. You can't imagine the satisfaction this will give me. He brings all sorts of company documents home, and I could copy all kinds of stuff for you. And I can read a balance sheet, you know, know a top line from a bottom line. You probably want internal financial stuff, huh? Or early clinical trial results? Just give me your number and I'll call you."

"Sure, thanks, that would be great, that's fantastic." Rebecca dug out a business card and scribbled her cell phone number on the back. "The thing is, I really need the information soon. This week."

Susie narrowed her eyes. "Deadline, huh? I'll see what I can do."

"Thanks, I really appreciate this. Also…we should probably be careful about any future meetings. Being seen together."

Susie raised her eyebrows. "Paranoid too? Think he's having you watched?"

"No," Rebecca shook her head. "Not me. But maybe you."

Susie grinned, started to laugh, stopped. Paused. Knocked back her fresh Drambuie.

She stood up a bit unsteadily and stuffed Rebecca's card into a sticky pocket. "I have to go now…have to run..." She drew herself up straight. "Don't worry, I'll call you for sure. I'm gonna give you the story of your career, honey." She began to step away gingerly, as if picking her way through a minefield.

Then Susie stopped, turned, looked back at Rebecca: "You know what? Ron's father? The one who died when Ron was nine? Actually, he died two years ago. Turned out it was Ron's father who owned that funeral parlor.…You see, once you tear a hole in the tissue of lies…you're staring down a fucking rabbit hole."

Rebecca sat frozen, unseeing, her mind racing through permutations, already shaping tentative sentences. She had no story yet, but unless she was radically mistaken, Susie Popitz had just given her a killer lead.

5 p.m.

She hadn't eaten since the muffin that morning. Her stomach wasn't even churning anymore, but she decided to go to the greengrocer around the corner. For the moment there was nothing else she could do to move the story along. She had made maybe fifty phone calls that afternoon, most of which led nowhere, though she had managed to set up a lunch meeting with a potential source for the next day. What was disturbing, and ominous, was the growing silence. Her phone had stopped ringing. Her impression was that as the day wore on, more and more sources were tied up in meetings, and fewer and fewer were calling her back. The handful she had actually spoken with had seemed nervous, evasive.

Had Popitz somehow put out the word? Don't cooperate: Squelch this story or I'll squish you all like bugs? Probably she was just paranoid. She thought about Susie, wondered again whether she would really deliver. Waiting was the only part of reporting she hated, besides answering the phone, and this was the worst kind of wait: the anticipation of an imminent breakthrough. Nothing to do but hope. She stood and ventured out to the greengrocer because she couldn't bear to sit at her silent desk any longer.

Moving on autopilot, she bellied up to the salad bar and loaded her plastic container with rapidly aging tuna salad.

6:45 p.m.

Rebecca decided to burn off some stress in the company gym, which occupied the basement of the building. She headed straight for the treadmill and, without pausing to warm up, attacked it savagely, setting it on the highest speed. In front of her was a mirrored wall and a small television set. She kept switching channels, from CNBC to CNNfn and back again.

In the mirror she saw Helen stroll into the gym, sipping a bottle of water, and start into a set of stretching exercises. Sometimes Helen amazed her. How could she be so cool, methodically following her daily routine as if her muscle tone mattered today, as if nothing had happened, as if their professional life—which to Rebecca *was* life—didn't depend on that one story each of them had to produce? Helen liked to keep what she called the right balance in her life. Rebecca didn't know how. Not that she would want to. As far as she was concerned, balance was the enemy of success.

Rebecca had been a bit surprised when Roberts had included Helen in the competition for the top job. Clearly, he didn't realize that Rebecca had helped Helen with her best stories, talked them through with her, sharpened the angle, read the drafts, edited. The top job rightfully belonged to the master, not the protégé.

Helen saw that Rebecca had noticed her, and smiled warmly. Done with her stretching, she took the treadmill next to Rebecca. She set it on a moderate speed, half that of Rebecca's.

"Can we check if *Keeping Up Appearances* is on?" Helen asked.

Rebecca made a face. She always watched financial news while running.

"Okay, okay, sorry," Helen said. They had been through this same drill dozens of times, and Helen should know it was pointless. Rebecca never backed down.

Helen focused on the screen, suddenly interested in the news. "Oh, they're talking about Madsen…your dad's company.…You know, my story for Roberts is about Tom Richardson, he just took over the family investment firm from his father…and he took a big position in Madsen.…Did you know that?"

Rebecca nodded. "Will you be able to interview Richardson?" she asked.

"Yes." Helen beamed. "I was lucky. I've had that interview set up for a while. Great timing."

Rebecca smiled. Luck was fine, but only losers counted on it. "What exactly is your angle?" she asked.

"I guess what Richardson's going to do, how he's going to be different from his dad, what his investors can expect…the usual," Helen said. Yes, the usual, Rebecca thought. Your typical "new kid on the block" profile. Safe.

Her hair, damp with sweat, stuck to her forehead. She wiped her face with the bottom of her T-shirt and brushed her hair back with her fingers.

She was afraid that Helen would ask what she thought about the

Richardson story, and was thankful when she didn't. Rebecca didn't have time to help Helen. Not this time. And she didn't want to tell Helen that she didn't think much of the story. She didn't want to hurt her.

"What are you writing about?" Helen asked.

Rebecca started fiddling with the speed setting on her treadmill, pretending not to hear.

"Oh, come on, Rebecca, it's me, you know you can trust me, for goodness' sake."

Rebecca did know that and felt silly for a moment. But she took a look around to make sure that no one else from editorial was within earshot, especially Bruce or Preston. All she saw were a couple of clueless young blondes from the sales department in tight workout shorts, gossiping in the corner. They were no threat.

"Popitz," she said.

"That pharma jerk? He's really secretive, right?"

Rebecca thought that she saw a glimmer of admiration in Helen's eyes. Writing investigative pieces about unwilling subjects was the toughest part of the job, and something Helen was not naturally predisposed to do. She felt bad about trashing people. Rebecca had had to convince her that it was okay, that some people deserved a little roughing up. "Think about all the harm they do to their investors," she'd urged Helen, "all those little old ladies who could lose their life savings."

Rebecca never wasted her time on puff pieces. She did reporting, not typing.

The endorphins released by the exercise were rushing through her head. She suddenly felt an urge to get back to her office, to work on the story. She jumped off the treadmill, muttered a distracted goodbye to Helen and scrambled to the locker room. Too pumped up to bother with showering or changing, she just grabbed her gym bag and trotted up the stairs from the basement.

The story would happen. It had to. It would all fall into place at the eleventh hour, as it usually did. She would make Roberts happy. She would get the promotion, she would be editor in chief. She was going to make her father so proud.

7:23 p.m.

Rebecca's phone rang as she walked into her office. The inevitable moment of hesitation. Ringing phones had scared her ever since she was six years old, and her mother's cancer had come back. Every time her mother spent a couple days in the hospital for chemotherapy or some other procedure—many years passed before Rebecca realized just how aggressive that course of chemo was, how little hope the doctors held out—Rebecca was afraid someone would call to say that her mother had died. Whenever she heard the phone ring, she ran and hid behind the curtain in the living room, then pressed both hands hard on her ears. She did this even before her father—or her grandmother, who often looked after her during that time—could answer the phone, so she never knew who was calling, and even the most innocuous calls filled her with dread.

One night when her mother was in the hospital, Rebecca dreamt that her mother died, very quietly and simply. Just like that. She was dead and Rebecca was wide awake. She looked at the clock beside her bed: 4:17 in the morning. She turned on the light and read a chapter from *Peter Rabbit,* then went back to sleep.

The ringing phone woke her. For the first time she could remember, it didn't frighten her at all. She thought that nothing could be worse than the dream, which still seemed real, even though she was now awake. She heard her grandmother pick up the phone. She couldn't make out the brief, murmured conversation, but somehow she was sure her father was on the other end of the line. He must be calling from the hospital.

A short while later, her father came home, came to her room. His face told her everything, but she refused to read it. Then he said, "Mom died this morning. A few minutes after four." He held her for a long time. All her short life she had seen her mother's illness through a child's eyes, as a threat to the pillars of her existence. Now, along with her father's warmth and his smell, she sensed the sharpness of his pain, a physical sensation that reminded her of that day at the beach when she was stung by a jellyfish.

That was the only time she ever saw him cry.

7:23 p.m.

Rebecca picked up the phone. "Hello."

"Hi, it's Susie."

Hope and adrenaline surged through Rebecca. "Hi."

"Listen, I'm sorry about blathering on like that this morning. My life is not really that bad, you know. Actually, it's pretty good. It's just that seeing you reminded me how I met Ron in the first place, who I used to be…but it's different now, I am somebody else now. I'm with him now…and I would never do anything to hurt him.…Oh God, he's coming back, I have to go. Bye."

Click.

Silence.

Blankness.

Slowly, heavily, Rebecca set the phone back on its cradle.

She was still wearing her gym clothes. In a sort of trance, she turned and ran down the stairwell and out of the building. She turned right at the corner, heading west toward the Hudson River, her usually observant brain barely registering the parade of random evening strollers she zipped by: NYU coeds flashing freshly pierced navels, a drag queen showing off a new pair of stiletto-heel Manolos, a tight knot of Japanese tourists brandishing Minoltas. About half the people she zipped past spoke animatedly into thin air, most clutching cell phones, a few just crazy. In this after-work dog-walking hour, the sidewalks were a tangle of leashes: She almost tripped over one that connected a yapping Maltese to a prim, gray-haired lady who unleashed a string of salty epithets. She soon lost track of which street she was crossing, forgot to even glance at the traffic lights. A taxi screeched to a halt, its bumper a bare foot from her knee. The furious driver leaned out the window: "Got a death wish, bitch?" She didn't break stride.

She ran all the way to the Hudson, turned downtown toward Battery Park and lost herself in the mobile throng of runners, roller-skaters and cyclists. Here, it seemed the whole city was in restless motion, the only islands of stillness in the human river a few scattered couples immersed in public displays of affection.

She had run through the twilight for an hour when the cramps set in. She hobbled to the river's edge, gripped the cool metal railing and vomited into the black water.

TUESDAY, JUNE 17, 1997

12:30 p.m.

Rebecca stepped into an Upper East Side restaurant called Legalloue, an elegant eatery for ladies who lunch. Not the sort of place she would have chosen, but it was convenient for her source. She had a lunch date with the CEO of a small but promising biotech firm, a man who had once worked for Popitz.

The hostess eyed Rebecca—in her gray Banana Republic suit, simple black blouse and Timex watch—with ill-concealed disapproval, then studied the reservations book. "He's not here yet," she announced. Pursing her lips, she led Rebecca to a small table in the rear, near the entrance to the kitchen, and abandoned her there. Rebecca studied her surroundings.

Perched around the tables were mostly women, and they all seemed to be slight variations of the same basic model. Most of them had very blonde hair, and all of them wore too much makeup. Their suits were mostly light blue and yellow. Some wore peach-colored sweaters with matching lipstick and tan slacks. The light colors were accentuated by breezy cascades of diamonds—diamond-studded watches, diamond bracelets, diamond pendants. They were all nibbling on their fruit, humming ever so politely. Had they inhabited an impressionist painting, she thought, letting her vision slip slightly out of focus, they would be a field of pastel petals and, in the foreground, a basket of peaches glistening with drops of dew.

But when she snapped back into hard focus and looked closer, beyond the blurred impression, she couldn't help notice something creepy about this moneyed meadow. The women didn't look quite human, the same way that daisies dyed blue don't look like real flowers. Mothers didn't look any older than their daughters, only less realistic. Cosmetic surgery had rendered these women abstract. They belonged not in an impressionist painting, but in something harder-edged, a bit disturbing—a cubist Picasso.

She looked up to see the hostess bearing down on her again, but smiling warmly this time, the handsome biotech CEO in tow. Rebecca made sure to smile even more warmly than the hostess.

"Oh, hi, thanks so much for meeting me here."

"Sure, no problem, how you doing?" He scanned the room quickly as he sat down. "Place is really packed. It's not easy to get a table here," he said proudly.

"No, it's certainly not," Rebecca agreed.

She recognized the syndrome right away. He was still reveling in his primacy, in being number one. After years of toil, and probably humiliation, in Popitz's shadow, at last he was the alpha male in his own little kingdom.

So she spent the next several minutes managing his condition, alternating between softball questions that allowed him to brag a bit and outright flattery. When he had drunk a little white wine and she deemed him sufficiently relaxed, she gently steered the conversation around to Popitz.

No go. He deflected her question with a few dismissive syllables and brought the focus back around to himself. Rebecca gave him a few minutes, then tried again. And again got nowhere. This conversational dance continued as Rebecca grew increasingly desperate. He was a former employee, former high-ranking executive, of Alpha/Omega, and he was still in the business. Surely he could give her some insight. And just as surely, Popitz was the last thing he wanted to talk about.

By the time he got around to his pitch, half an hour into the lunch, she was expecting it: Why didn't she do a story about him and his feisty little biotech instead? On the cutting edge of research. Far more interesting than Popitz and his bloated conglomerate. Although she had braced herself for this, the pit of her stomach clenched with the certainty that he'd never intended to talk to her about Popitz at all.

Still, she refused to give up. Keeping her reaction to his story pitch as polite and noncommittal as she could, she tried to leverage his own proposition to her advantage in a sort of journalistic judo. Gently hinting without promising. Cooperation on Popitz now. Maybe a story about a dashing young biotech CEO later.

Her concentration was broken by an exclamation from a painfully thin woman at the next table. "Look at this!" She pointed at the fruit salad the waiter had brought her for lunch. "I could never eat so many grapes in my life! My God. Let's not waste all this food, could you take it back and bring me a more human portion?"

Looking not at all surprised, the waiter politely vanished with her plate.

Rebecca wasn't hungry either. She very much wanted to flee. But she tried again.

"What do you think about the new management at Madsen? They've got deep pockets, good cash flow. Can they threaten Popitz?"

He shook his head. "I doubt it. Oh, he might have a rough quarter, or even a down year, but…I wouldn't bet against Ronnie. You shouldn't either. You'll be wrong."

Rebecca looked away and took a sip of wine, swallowing her irritation. Who the hell was he to tell her she was wrong? What did he know? Popitz was a crook, a coffin robber. And Alpha/Omega's accounting was so convoluted—he had to be hiding something in that tangled mess. Sure, she knew that sometimes she could rush to judgment. But this time she felt certain she was right. She had to be. There was no time for any turnarounds.

"You know," he added, "this town's full of sharks, but Ronnie, he's a great white. Goddamn *Jaws*." He smiled. "Heard he's put on a few pounds lately, so maybe he's a great white whale." A flicker of fear crossed his eyes. "That was off the record. Deep background."

Rebecca didn't bother to nod in agreement, or smile.

"Speaking of Madsen," he said, "why don't you write about what Richardson's doing over there? If you ask me, I'd say he's gonna screw the place up, at least in the long run. He's cutting too much of the R&D budget."

Rebecca thought about Helen's story. Any other time, this might spark her interest. But not now. She had no time for anything other than Popitz. She desperately wanted to cut the conversation short.

"I can't write about Madsen. My father works there," she said, "it would be a conflict of interest."

That shut him up, as she expected it would.

This lunch was a waste, an hour and a half down the toilet.

She felt like throwing up again.

3:15 p.m.

A little green light.

Someone had called while she was in the restroom. Rebecca retrieved the message from her voice mail. It was her father. "Hi, baby, it's Dad, call me when you get a chance."

She shook her head. Had he forgotten her email? She didn't have time for chit-chat this week. Still, she supposed, her father's chattiness was a small flaw. She thought back over all the years of conversations they had shared.

All the way back to that one world-changing conversation when she was seven years old. He hadn't been chatty at all that time.

He was dropping her off at school in Brooklyn Heights. He helped her take off her jacket and hang it and her backpack on a little hook. The hooks were set close to one another, and the kids' winter jackets and backpacks were so bulky that she always had trouble trying to squeeze in her pack. It just kept falling on the floor.

"Oh, finally," she said, once he managed to force her backpack in. "I'll be late. I think everybody else is in the classroom already." She offered him her cheek to kiss her goodbye. He bent down and kissed her, but he didn't leave. He was still standing there.

"Dad?"

He just stood there, giving her an oddly serious look. Why was he still here? She really had to go to class.

"Dad?"

And then he knelt down so he could look her in the eye and started talking.

He was saying that Mom was not doing so well, that the doctors were worried and were telling him they had done all they could, that Mom was getting weaker and weaker, that Mom might not get better after all...

"Dad???"

She understood.

He was telling her that her mother was going to die soon. He had been trying to protect her from this hard reality. Now he was trying to warn her.

"Is Mom gonna die? When, today?"

His face twisted in a grimace. "Not today, honey. Not tomorrow. But it could happen in the next couple months. I can't lie to you, you need to know."

"Dad, does that mean I'll get a stepmother? I don't want a stepmother, stepmothers are wicked." She turned and ran into the classroom.

He listened to her. He took her at her word.

And a few weeks later, when her mother died, she realized she was grateful for the warning.

Afterward, they settled into a comfortable routine. Day after day he came home from work promptly at five-thirty, and he rarely went out in the evenings. He cooked dinner while she sat on the kitchen counter and told him all about school.

When she was eleven and nervous about being invited to her first mixed birthday party—one that included boys—he told her that when he was eleven, a thirteen-year-old girl kissed him playing spin the bottle, and he never ever played it again. She realized that boys were afraid too, and that helped a little.

When she was gripped with fear that she would die young, just like her mom did, they talked about genes and mammograms for hours, and she felt calmer afterward.

He taught her how to make waffles and omelettes, and she would wake up before he did on Sunday and make breakfast for both of them.

They had a perfect life together, just the two of them. They quarreled about stupid little things like an old couple, they went shopping together, they listened to music on vinyl LPs, jazz and blues and sixties rock. He taught her to love John Coltrane and Bob Dylan. She didn't feel any imperative need to date boys, and most of the time not much of an urge to do so, especially when she looked around at the local specimens.

It wasn't until her college graduation ceremony that she had suddenly realized how much he had sacrificed for her. She looked around and saw all of these women in their late forties. They had tiny crow's feet at the corners of their eyes, but some had pretty good bodies and nice hair, and they all wore some makeup and jewelry. They were lively and laughing. They seemed attractive. She could imagine men wanting to kiss them and sleep with them. And these men did. These women were her friends' mothers. But her father was alone. Because of her.

3:18 p.m.

Rebecca's phone rang. She glanced at the caller ID: some cell phone she didn't recognize. She swallowed and picked up. "Rebecca Morgan."

Words tumbled out of the phone in a rush. "Hi, it's Susie. Sorry if I scared you before. I have some stuff for you. I made that last call from home to throw him off, in case he's bugging our phone. You got me all paranoid now, I think he's having me followed, so I really have to be careful. I'll call you as soon as I can arrange a meeting. But please, please don't call me, okay?"

"Okay, I promise. But if I'm not at my desk, try my cell phone, any hour, day or night. You've got the number, right?"

"Yeah, got it. Call you soon."

5:21 p.m.

Rebecca looked up. It was hard to concentrate while waiting for Susie to call, but she had forced herself to focus on the arcane financial footnotes Alpha/Omega seemed to specialize in, taking swigs of diet soda all the while.

Now she had to go pee. The urge was sudden and insistent. But, of course, she knew with certainty that this was the moment her phone would ring. She stood and scooped her cell phone from her handbag, reflexively glanced at it—and froze. The battery was almost dead. Shit. She'd forgotten to charge it overnight. But she really didn't want to chance missing Susie. She couldn't. Rebecca fought down panic.

She kept a spare charger in the office. She plugged it in and snapped in the cell phone. She'd just have to wait until she had a partial charge.

She gave it half an hour. By then her bladder was a hot, painful balloon. She snatched up her cell and stood shakily. She wanted to run to the bathroom, but she was afraid any jarring movement would cause her to pee all over the floor. So she approached the ladies' room carefully, in a sort of slow-motion waddle, tears pooling in the corners of her eyes.

WEDNESDAY, JUNE 18, 1997

12:40 p.m.

The phone rang. For once, it was a relief: Susie. The Metropolitan Museum of Art at three. The Egyptian exhibit.

This part of reporting—secret meetings, deep-throat sources—was all too rare. Rebecca loved it. She felt like a spy.

2:45 p.m.

Rebecca dashed eagerly up the stairs to the Met's main entrance, turned right in the Great Hall and paid her admission, stepping through into the Egyptian section. She stopped short. Moving deeper into the wing, beyond the first large room, meant stepping through a doorway. That bottleneck was packed solid with giggling kids, dozens of them. The crowd looked like an entire grade school on a field trip. God, it was June already. Why was school still in session? The mass of children moved slowly through the opening ahead of her. Very slowly. My God, were they children or two-legged snails? Didn't children usually run and scamper? She couldn't see what was holding them up…

There had to be another way in. She struggled to recall the museum's floor plan. Of course, the Temple of Dendur. If she circled around through Medieval Art, she was pretty sure she could approach through the temple and come into Egyptian Art the back way. Rebecca hesitated, calculating, trying to decide on the lesser evil. The long way around would mean a detour of a quarter-mile or so. She was afraid Susie would lose her nerve and flee if she had to wait.

A boy at the back of the pack peered at her over his shoulder. Third-grader maybe, she guessed. The frames of his glasses were broken and had been patched together with duct tape. "Hi, what are you gonna see?" he asked excitedly.

"Sorry, what?"

"What are you gonna see?"

"Oh, I don't know, an exhibition," she answered absent-mindedly, peering ahead. Shouldn't the teachers be playing traffic cops?

"But of what?"

"Oh, something Egyptian, I think..." She tried to squeeze through the crowd, but it looked hopeless.

"Cool. We're gonna see the mummies too. Is it true that mummies can wake up?"

"Sorry, what?"

"Luke told me that mummies wake up and they just start moving. They start doing whatever they were doing when they died. So if a mummy guy died in a battle, he might suddenly wake up and try to stab you with something. What if the mummy wakes up when I'm standing in front of him?"

"Right, well, maybe..."

Come on. Faster, faster.

"So it's true? Have you heard about it too?"

"What?" She wished the kid would shut up.

"You know, this thing Luke told me about mummies."

At last, she was nearing the door to the Egyptian wing. She briefly considered diving into the crowd of children as if the entranceway were a mosh pit.

"Sure, whatever," she muttered, distracted.

The boy stopped, frozen where he stood. She noticed his face starting to crumple as she squeezed past him.

Behind her, the boy let out a piercing wail and started crying: "I'm scared. It's true what Luke said. This grownup says mummies can wake up. I don't want to go to the Egyptians..."

From the entranceway, someone who must have been a teacher peered back with concern. Just ahead of Rebecca, several children stopped and half-turned to see what the commotion was about. Sensing an opening, Rebecca pushed, wriggled and elbowed her way to the entrance and squeezed through.

2:55 p.m.

Susie stood in a corner behind a glass enclosure that indeed displayed a mummy.

Hmm, thought Rebecca as she stepped around the display case, mummy under glass. How appetizing.

Susie seemed nervous, twitchy, her eyes continually scanning the room. She wore a jogging outfit of deep blue—about as casual a choice as she could've made, but even her running clothes looked expensive. One arm was wrapped tightly around a plastic Barnes & Noble bag. As she approached,

Rebecca caught the scent of alcohol.

Susie handed her the plastic bag. Rebecca could see it was stuffed with manila envelopes.

"Here," whispered Susie. "Hide it somewhere for God's sake, he may have his people watching me. I've decided to trust you. Don't fuck me over." She paused, looked Rebecca in the eye. "I looked through the emails on his laptop. Found a love note from Stephanie the slut. So don't disappoint me. Nail the bastard."

She scanned the room one more time. "I need a drink," she muttered. Stepping quickly through a doorway, she disappeared.

3:00 p.m.

Rebecca slipped the Barnes & Noble bag under her linen jacket, holding it in place with one hand. If somebody had been following Susie, the bag would be easy to spot. She wandered off as casually as she could manage and turned left into the Temple of Dendur, in what she hoped was the general direction of the ladies' room. But the package was heavy and awkward. She envisioned it slipping from her grasp, manila envelopes cascading across the floor.

She noticed a man watching her, aware of the way his eyes scanned her body and glanced away discreetly. Okay, he was looking, but was he…watching? Following? She sensed his presence behind her as she moved down the hallway, and it required a major application of willpower to not glance back over her shoulder. Her palms were sweating, and the plastic bag grew slippery…

3:06 p.m.

Emerging into the American Wing, Rebecca ducked into a restroom, sat down in a stall and put the package on her lap. Luckily, she was carrying a fairly large shoulder bag. She removed a few items, stuffed them into her jacket pockets, slid the envelopes out of the bookstore bag and jammed them into her purse. Then she peeled off her jacket and draped it over the top of her purse to hide the contents. On her way out, she tossed the Barnes & Noble bag into the trash.

When she stepped out into the hallway, the same man was still there, lurking. Her pulse raced as she pretended not to notice and wondered how she could lose him.

"Finally," he said with a touch of exasperation.

For a disorienting half-second, Rebecca thought he was speaking to her. Her brain struggled to process this and floundered for a response. Should she apologize? She hadn't taken very long…

Then she saw the young woman who had stepped out of the restroom just behind her. The man took her arm and the two strolled off, debating

33

which exhibit to see next.

3:10 p.m.

"There she is!"

Rebecca looked up sharply. The third-grader with the broken glasses stood at the end of the corridor, pointing at her accusingly.

"My teacher says it's not true. Mummies can't wake up. And you're a bad grownup, scaring little kids like that…"

Several faces glared at her in outrage, children and a couple of teachers.

Without a word, Rebecca turned and walked away as quickly as she could.

3:46 p.m.

Rebecca didn't begin to relax, even a little, until she walked into her own office and locked the door. She took out the envelopes, stacked them on her desk and just stared at them for a minute.

Then she noticed the green light on her phone. She checked her message.

"Hi, hon, it's Dad. Call me when you can, okay?"

She sighed and smiled to herself. There was no urgency in his voice, no indication that anything was wrong. No, he just wasn't taking her email seriously. She felt a hint of irritation. The man just wanted to chat.

Still, hearing his voice pumped up her adrenaline even more. She would do him proud. He deserved that.

He used to keep a photograph on his desk, of him and the three other guys who had started in Madsen's R&D department in 1966. The gang of four, as they called themselves, used to hang out together, and the families invited each other over for weekend barbecues. She was friendly with the other men's children until they were ten or so. They had continued to see one another for a few years after Mom had died, but then the friendships had just gradually faded away. None of the other three guys called Larry Morgan anymore.

One of them became the head of the R&D department, and then an executive vice president, and he must have felt it would be uncomfortable to hang out with a former friend who had been left behind. The other two had quit Madsen in the 1970s. One went on to become president of a smaller competitor of Madsen. The other started his own company and eventually sold it for millions. Larry Morgan, meanwhile, did his research job extremely well, but it was more or less the same job he had in 1966.

He never complained—in fact, she was sure that if asked, he would claim to be far happier in his lab than in a corner office—but she realized that he hadn't really had a choice, that if it hadn't been for her he could have done as well as the other three guys. He could have moved up into management or started his own company, could have worked late hours and taken business trips and entertained clients.

She contemplated the stack of manila envelopes on her desk and smiled.

Her father wouldn't have to swallow the implicit humiliation much longer. She would become editor in chief, she would wield real power in the business world, and his former friends would take note. They would realize he had done something worthwhile with his life, that he had been by far the best father of the bunch, and they would regret having burned those bridges—or just letting them rot away.

3:54 p.m.

She couldn't bring herself to open the envelopes yet, to end the suspense. Part of what held her back was sheer terror—of disappointment. She had no clue what Susie had really gotten hold of, or how useful it might be. If it added up to zero, she had no story. And the other part was sublime anticipation. If Susie had truly delivered, she might be onto the story of her career.

She hid the envelopes in a desk drawer, locked it and ran out to the greengrocer on the corner. She couldn't remember when she had last eaten. Probably lunch among the Stepford ladies the day before. She packed tuna salad and cottage cheese into a plastic container and bought a couple of liter bottles of caffeinated Diet Pepsi. She wanted to make sure that she would be up for as long as she needed.

10:04 p.m.

A soft knock on her office door.

"Come in."

Helen poked her perfectly coiffed blonde head in. As always, she seemed annoyingly well put together, but her eyes looked tired, Rebecca noticed. Even Helen was starting to show the strain.

"How's it going?"

Rebecca shrugged, waved at the papers that covered her desk, the piles of documents on the floor. "I'm immersed in this stuff. Lot to wade through. And you?"

"A lot of stuff to go through as well. I know essentially what I'm going to say, so the toughest part is over. I still need to fill some gaps, double-check some numbers...pick the right quotes from the Richardson interview. He was great, by the way, so now I have too much....It's the mechanics of actually writing it." Helen covered a yawn.

Rebecca understood Helen only too well. In some ways, what Helen described really was the toughest part. Once you knew what you were going to say, the main challenge, the gut-wrenching question "what's my story?" was solved, and the adrenaline level subsided—but you still had to write the story.

"How late you staying?" Helen asked.

"Oh, I don't know, a while yet."

"Why don't you take a break, we could go out for some coffee and talk…"

Briefly, Rebecca wondered if she should tell Helen about the negative slant that the biotech CEO had taken on Richardson's handling of Madsen. She decided against it. It would be rather mean to put Helen through that now, all because of one guy's opinion. She herself hated being presented with new information late in the game, especially if the information contradicted her angle. You had to check it out, call sources, agonize for days deciding whether it killed your angle, if it should be included. In the end, Roberts would take it out anyway. He hated balanced stories. "We are not *The Wall Street Journal*," he always said. "We don't pee on both sides of our pants." So it would all be a royal waste of time and energy for Helen.

Rebecca declined Helen's invitation for coffee. "No, no thanks, don't have time now. I have enough Diet Pepsi to keep me up." She turned back toward her papers, and when she looked up a few seconds later, Helen was gone.

Such an odd one, she thought. Quite warm once you got past that cool exterior. So self-possessed, yet, around Rebecca, she sometimes seemed like…well, like some kind of puppy dog. A touch of mentor worship, she supposed. Helen was an only child, and Rebecca had long suspected Helen saw her almost as a big sister. Well, it was natural enough. Rebecca was a couple years older, and she had taken Helen in hand when she started as a very green reporter.

She sighed, wondering if she should have agreed to coffee. Sometimes she was hard on the girl. She was lucky to have a friend like Helen.

10:27 p.m.

She was still reading.

All too often, a journalist finds that every document, every interview, every tip leads to nothing. Researching a story is usually one disappointment after another. People have nothing to say, numbers are not revealing, tips turn out not to be true. Most stories are simply not there.

But not this time.

Susie Popitz had handed Rebecca scores of pages. She had printed out emails from Ron Popitz's laptop, months of internal memos. And she had bolstered that with copies of some revealing internal reports. Delays in the drug development pipeline. Disappointing clinical trials. Negative data that was not intended for outside perusal—data that pharmas were not required to reveal—was in her hands.

Most intriguing of all, there were signs of possible problems with Placidam, the popular anti-anxiety drug. Placidam had been on the market only three years, but it already accounted for a quarter of Alpha/Omega's sales. Now there were rumblings within the firm about side effects more severe than anticipated. Strokes. Liver failure. A few lawsuits had been filed. More alarming, a couple of HMOs had just removed Placidam from their list of approved drugs. And the Placidam troubles seemed to be linked to the company's rising inventory. Somewhere, mused Rebecca, warehouses were filling up with unsold pills.

10:53 p.m.
She looked up from her reading.
She had now studied the juiciest bits and at least skimmed the rest. Much that had been cryptic was now clear. Mysteries stood revealed.
For the first time in three days, she felt hunger. Once the fear that she had no story melted away, her body refused to sustain itself on pure adrenaline and demanded food. She quickly scarfed down the tuna salad and cottage cheese that had been sitting on her desk for hours. The food left a nasty, metallic aftertaste that she washed away with tepid Diet Pepsi. The taste reassured her that she was on a virtuous path, the path to success.

THURSDAY, JUNE 19, 1997

2:15 a.m.

She had to change gears.

She had inhaled a couple hundred pages of mostly numbers, jargon and bureaucratese. Now came the time to step away, decide what it all meant, select which numbers and facts she would use. It was time for cold analysis, but she was still possessed by the thrill of having gotten her hands on this stuff. The magnitude of what she had was still sinking in. The mother lode. Everything she needed, if she used it wisely.

There was definitely trouble in River City. With a capital T, and that rhymes with P, and that stands for...Popitz. What was that from? Oh, yeah, *The Music Man*. She remembered seeing the movie on TV as a kid. God, she was tired. Her brain was babbling.

Difficult to step back and calm down. She knew she should probably snatch a few hours' sleep and attack it fresh, but she was way too wired. Sleep was a couple hours away, minimum. In fact, her neck was so stiff she could barely turn her head to the left. Her lower back was sore. And her right calf was starting to cramp up. Once again, she scolded herself, she had wound up perched on the edge of her chair, bent over her desk, one foot tapping the carpet with excess energy while her legs twined into a pretzel.

She needed to relax and start her breathing exercises...

7:06 a.m.

She woke to the morning sunlight filtering through her office window and carefully uncurled from a fetal position on the carpet. She was sore, tired and grungy, but still excited.

She stumbled to her desk and fished out her emergency toothbrush, then dug through another drawer where she kept a change of underwear and a clean T-shirt.

12:36 p.m.

Rebecca stepped hurriedly into the restroom and almost bumped into Helen.

She was peering into the mirror, scrutinizing her lipstick. She glanced around and grinned. "Rebecca, come on, let's have lunch."

Rebecca shook her head. "Helen, I'd love to, but I just can't…"

"You have to eat. Tell you what. Let's run around the corner and I'll buy you a gyro wrap to go. You can eat at your desk. Take five minutes."

"Well…okay. Let me stop by my office and get my bag."

Back in her office, Rebecca noticed the little green light. She hesitated, looked up at Helen. "Sorry, better check my messages."

She punched buttons as Helen watched from the doorway, sighed as she heard the familiar voice. "Hi, it's Dad. Know you're busy, but call me at home tonight. Love you."

Helen arched her eyebrows.

"Just my dad," said Rebecca. "You know how he loves to talk."

"Yeah. Still, you should call him back."

Rebecca narrowed her eyes and smiled. "You're just trying to sabotage me, aren't you? You know it'll cost me an hour I can't afford."

Helen smiled back and shrugged. "He's your dad."

2:24 p.m.

Rebecca's phone rang. She looked up from her legal pad, which by now was almost full of scrawls and diagrams, notes that were evolving into a rough outline of a powerful story. Not immediately recognizing the number that popped up on her caller ID, she hesitated as usual for a few rings, then picked up the receiver.

"Hello."

"Who is this?" The woman on the phone sounded irritated.

"It's Rebecca Morgan," she answered, taken aback at the caller's rudeness.

"Stay on the line," the woman commanded. "I'll have Ron Popitz on the line for you shortly." Rebecca found herself on hold before she could respond.

She thought that she had long since drained her adrenaline reserves. Now she felt another jolt shoot through her.

She quickly rummaged through her desk for a fresh notebook and a tape recorder she could hook up to the phone.

2:41 p.m.

The woman came back on the line briefly. "Hi, are you still there?"

"Yes, I'm here."

"He'll be with you in a minute."

2:50 p.m.

"Hello?"

"Hello," Rebecca said.

"It's still me," said the woman. "I'm afraid he's too busy. He doesn't have time to talk to you today after all. But he does have time for dinner with you tomorrow, Friday. Le Cirque, seven o'clock." She hung up before Rebecca could respond.

FRIDAY, JUNE 20, 1997

3:02 a.m.

She looked up from her keyboard, yawned, saved the file and printed out a hard copy. She had a very rough first draft, full of blanks to be filled in later—not least of them, whatever Ron Popitz had to say. She knew some parts would have to be reworked. But the bones of the story were there.

She decided to go home and sleep in her own bed.

8:13 a.m.

Back in the office, first one there by far. Some old take-out food containers lay on her desk, starting to stink. She swept them into her wastebasket, then carried it across the floor and swapped it for the wastebasket in an unused cubicle.

She returned to her desk, opened her window and planned her calls for the day, scheduling them east to west by time zone. Time to talk once again to industry analysts, as well as Alpha/Omega's competitors, distributors and major customers. All people she had interviewed earlier, but now she knew exactly what questions to ask. It was surprising what people would admit to, sometimes even on the record, when they believed you already knew the answer to your question.

5:30 p.m.

Rebecca turned her attention to preparations for the evening. She had decided to wear gray, a gray suit and gray blouse. She was aiming for the most neutral effect possible. She would have preferred invisibility. If she could disappear in Ron Popitz's eyes, perhaps he would relax his guard and talk as if she weren't there.

First, she would toss him some softballs, get his thoughts on how his business was going. Then she would bring up a few key facts and numbers she had carefully selected from the internal memos and reports. She would phrase her questions with finesse, so he wouldn't be able to know for sure where she had gotten her info, where the leak was. But he would feel sure he had a leak, and that should be enough to enrage him. She hoped he might let something slip.

She wondered how he would handle it. Could she have misread the significance of all those facts and figures? Would he brush them off with a simple, devastating explanation? She didn't see how. She had certainly managed to unsettle a couple of analysts that afternoon—they, too, sensed trouble brewing. And the documents had to be authentic. Susie didn't have the necessary skills to forge such a variety of business documents so convincingly.

No, the most reasonable conclusion was that the facts and figures were accurate, and that they meant what she thought they meant. They would strike a nerve.

6:55 p.m.

Rebecca was a minimalist. She always felt most at ease in the simplest clothes and the most austere of interiors, and she always found the aesthetic of Le Cirque 2000 troubling. The restaurant was situated in an opulent 19th-century building done in neo-Italian Renaissance style. The elegant interior, with its marble staircase and intricately carved wood paneling, was incongruously filled with modern sculptures, neon lights, and high-backed red and yellow chairs. A hallucinatory palazzo.

A waiter led Rebecca to a large round table for six, still empty, smack in the center of the floor. Six? What kind of ambush had Popitz prepared? She glanced around, saw the eyes of other patrons on her, eyes full of curious envy. No doubt wondering what entitled her to the best table in the house.

7:00 p.m.

Rebecca practiced her breathing exercises. She had to keep a clear head and brace herself. She had thought that she would be dining with Popitz alone, but now it looked like he was bringing four other people. Probably lawyers and public relations crisis specialists, who would try to intimidate her. Worst case, he was treating this as a quasi-social occasion, and bringing Susie along. Rebecca could cope with four vicious men, but Susie... It was too easy to imagine a meltdown. Susie would surely drink too much and likely crumble under pressure or simply blurt out something she shouldn't.

7:15 p.m.

Four banker-looking types walked in, and a waiter started leading the men in Rebecca's direction.

Why wasn't Popitz with them? What kind of stunt was he trying to pull?

The waiter led the four men past Rebecca's table and into another room.

7:31 p.m.

Ron Popitz walked in alone, followed a waiter over to the table. He sauntered across the room as if he hadn't a care in the world. Certainly he seemed oblivious to the fact that he was half an hour late.

"Hi, there." He grinned and sat down next to her.

"Hi," she said. "I didn't know we were having company tonight."

"We aren't." Popitz smiled slyly, as if he were sharing a delicious secret with her.

The waiter brought water, and asked, "Would you like to see the menus, or would you like to wait for the other guests to arrive?"

"No, let's not wait, we'll order right away." Popitz turned to Rebecca. "I'm going to order the best wine you've ever had. I can afford it, but I can't pronounce it." He grabbed the wine list and stabbed a finger at the page. Rebecca peered over his shoulder. He was pointing at a Bordeaux almost as old as she was. "Waiter, bring us a bottle of this right away, and we'll have this Chateau d'Yquem with dessert." He smiled at her. "You'll love it. Oh, listen to me, I'm acting as if we were on a date," he laughed. "I'm just not used to reporters as lovely as you are, it's distracting. Let's see, I'll have…waiter, bring us two specials of the day, and they better be really special. This lady here is pretty demanding."

The waiter nodded and vanished. Popitz edged his chair a bit closer to Rebecca and leaned toward her: "Trust my choice, you'll really like it. They have the best food here, and my friends deserve the best. I hope I can call you a friend, right?"

He didn't wait for a response. "I hear you ran into my wife the other day at the Carlyle. I should warn you, Rebecca. I can call you Rebecca, right? Watch yourself around that woman, she'll only bring you trouble. She's brought me nothing but trouble, that's for sure. You know, they say every marriage goes through a few rough patches. This one has had just a few smooth patches instead." He chuckled at his own joke. Rebecca felt sure it was well-worn. "Oh, it's not dead yet, I guess," he continued, "but it's definitely on life support. She hates my children. Now they hate me for marrying her. I've been living in the Carlyle for almost twenty years, never had any problems with the staff, but Susie drinks like a fish and yells at everybody. Never happy with anything. If she continues this way, I think we might be kicked out of the hotel."

The waiter brought their appetizers, scoops of tuna tartar the size of M&Ms. "Do you expect the other guests will be arriving soon?" he asked politely.

"Oh, no, in fact, I don't think they'll be able to make it tonight. You can take their plates away," Popitz answered.

The waiter's face paled. He visibly struggled to control himself and couldn't help glancing at the smaller table nearby where a party of six huddled awkwardly. In that instant, Rebecca understood that Popitz had never invited any other dinner guests. He had told his secretary to reserve a table for six so he could sit at the best table—half empty—in the middle of the floor. Obviously, the waiter realized this too. Something told Rebecca that Popitz had used this tactic before. She made a mental note to talk to the maître d' later.

The waiter took a deep breath, managed a level voice. "But of course, I'll just remove these then." He began clearing the extra plates.

"So," Popitz turned to Rebecca, "you're doing a story about us? Or big pharma in general? How's it going?"

"Mostly about Alpha/Omega. And it's going better than I expected actually."

"You're going to say good things about us?" It sounded more like an order than a question.

"I'm not sure yet. Partly, it depends on what you tell me tonight."

"Really? Lot of responsibility. Listen, doesn't your father work at Madsen?"

She frowned. "Yeah, that's right. What does…"

"A man like that, his talent and experience…bet he's underappreciated over there. Underpaid. Way underpaid. You should tell your dad to give me a call. I could use a man like that."

Sure, she thought, and all the trade secrets in his head. This talk of her father unsettled her. Angered her. Popitz was trying to rattle her, and she couldn't let that happen.

She eyed him as coolly as she could. "You really think you can buy me off, Mr. Popitz?"

He smiled like a crocodile. "I think you care about your dad."

She felt a chill. Was that an implicit threat? To balance the proffered bribe?

She changed the subject: "Well, let me ask you, do you see Madsen emerging from your shadow?"

"You must be kidding me. You really think a money management firm can just take over an ailing drug company and turn it into a market leader? You have to know the business. We have years of experience. Oh, I think Richardson's firm will make money on their investment. The money men will cut costs, stop the bleeding, patch Madsen up and sell their stake. But Tom Richardson won't beat me, not at my own game."

"Suppose he buys Meditrina, too?" she asked.

Popitz looked at her sharply. "I heard that rumor. Anything to it?"

She shrugged innocently. "I imagine I heard the same things you did. Makes strategic sense, though. Besides, Richardson has very deep pockets.

And, I hear, a lot of promising drugs in the pipeline."

"So do I, lady." He took a sip of wine.

Rebecca had been waiting for this moment. She quietly mentioned a couple of disappointing clinical trials and smiled. "Side effects may include sudden death, stroke and liver failure."

He sputtered, almost spilled his wine. "What? Who told you that?"

Matter-of-factly, she began to cite numbers. Declining cash flow. Rising accounts receivable. She could almost feel the heat of the fury building inside him, but at the same time she sensed that half his attention was elsewhere. He flushed, his hands twitching on the table. As she spoke, he looked up at the ceiling, eyes unfocused, as if he were trying to remember something or solve a puzzle.

He didn't even try to evade or deny, just sat there turning redder and redder. When she mentioned Placidam, he lost control, standing so abruptly that he knocked his chair over backwards. Heads swiveled.

He leaned over her, right in her face, and spoke in a stage whisper. "Just write it and you are finished. I'll sue your little ass off. The whole fucking magazine will be finished, I'll wipe my ass with that goddamn rag before I'm through."

He turned away and stalked out of the restaurant.

The waiter came over as if nothing had happened, righted Popitz's chair and served her the first course—scaloppini with asparagus. As he set the plate in front of her, he smiled and whispered, "Don't worry, the maître d' will see that this goes on Mr. Popitz's tab."

She was hungry, and she realized that, for once, she didn't need to eat lousy take-out food to confirm her success. Certainly she was on the right track, and what better way to celebrate than sitting by herself at the biggest, baddest table in Le Cirque? Still, she had much work to do, so she ate quickly, trying to ignore the sidelong glances and outright glares from the tables around her. The special turned out to be medallion of wild boar glazed with plum wine sauce and an airy, spiraling confection whipped from potato. Fancy comfort food, she thought approvingly, a high-end version of the pork chops and mashed potatoes her father sometimes cooked.

And she had to admit the wine was excellent.

11:12 p.m.

Back in her office.

She noticed the green light. Another voice mail message from her father.

Almost done with this story, Dad, then I can talk to you. I'll see you Sunday, and I'll tell you all about it, and we'll laugh at the funny parts. But right now I'm dealing with a real world-class asshole.

She wondered fleetingly if he would actually sue, then put the thought out of her head. He could sue till he was blue in the face for all she cared. She

knew she had him cold.
  She started typing.

SATURDAY, JUNE 21, 1997

4:45 a.m.

A story's lead is critical: With the right lead in place, the rest of the story flows from there and the hooked reader follows along helplessly.

Susie had handed her one of the great leads of all time, gift-wrapped. It was almost a found object, like Marcel Duchamp's urinal mounted on a museum wall.

"Ron Popitz, the notoriously tyrannical CEO of Alpha/Omega, has terrorized so many people that a folk saying has arisen in business circles: Even the dead are afraid of him. They have reason to fear him, and to recoil from his sticky fingers."

She called him a coffin-robber.

She sculpted the anecdote into half a dozen finely chiseled sentences.

Then shifted smoothly to the present and the gist of the story. Internal documents from Alpha/Omega. Grave concerns about the company's financial straits. Negative results in clinical trials of major drugs. Perhaps most alarming, possible problems with Placidam. And reinvigorated competition.

By the time dawn broke through her office window, she had a solid draft. She looked up and blinked at the sunrise, yawned.

Time to go home.

10:13 a.m.

In the office again, feeling refreshed after four hours' sleep and some breakfast. Even if she hadn't set her alarm clock, her body would not have allowed her to sleep much longer when she still had work to do. That was something she knew she could rely on, no matter how many sleepless nights she had racked up. And she still had plenty of work ahead.

Had to double-check facts and figures, fill in the blanks, polish the prose.

Had to get this one just right.

SUNDAY, JUNE 22, 1997

1 a.m.

These finishing touches always took much longer than she expected. For the thousandth time, Rebecca marveled at the way writing could swallow up huge chunks of time.

She was finally done. There was nothing else she could do. She knew every word and number by heart. She moved the story onto the server and checked to make sure that it appeared in Roberts's folder.

Unable to help herself, she reread it several times, just admiring her baby.

2:17 a.m.

Home. Pausing just long enough to strip off her clothes and brush her teeth, she tumbled into bed.

12:47 p.m.

And woke into a nightmare.

This wasn't obvious to her, not at first. She became aware of something ringing, rolled over and almost fell out of bed. Several seconds passed before she connected the ringing with her doorbell.

Someone at the door? Who the hell? She sat up, groggy and disoriented, glanced at her alarm clock. God, she'd slept ten hours.

The ringing refused to stop. She stood, slipped into a bathrobe and stumbled to the door.

Opened it to see two men, one white and fortyish, one black and thirtyish, both neatly dressed in coat and tie. They flashed badges, introduced themselves. NYPD.

Baffled by the police on her doorstep, she apologized for her appearance. "I'm afraid you woke me up. Haven't gotten much sleep this week."

The older man spoke. "May we come in, ma'am?"

"Of course." She shut the door behind them. "How can I help you?"

"Please, sit down, ma'am."

She sat. "What's this about?"

"It concerns your father."

"My father?" Instantly awake. "Is he all right?"

The detective's face told her he wasn't.

"I'm afraid not. He died early this morning. An apparent suicide. I'm sorry."

"Suicide? Why would…How could he…" She felt nauseous.

"Can I get you anything? Glass of water?"

She nodded.

He brought a glass from the kitchen. "When did you last see him?"

"Thanks." She took a sip. "Couple of weeks ago."

"And how did he seem?"

She thought back to their last dinner together. "Fine, fine, just…normal…he was…maybe a little subdued, now that you mention it. Quiet, but…only for my dad. But not depressed or…oh, God…this can't… Of course, he…he always tried to shield me from things…ever since my mom died…I was only seven. He never got over that habit."

The morning was warm, but she gave a little shiver. God help her, she hadn't called him back. All those messages…

She had to know. "How? How did he…?"

"Well, somehow he got into the Madsen Labs building over the weekend…"

"Somehow? What do you mean? It's not that unusual these days for him to pop by the lab on a weekend." She hadn't switched to using the past tense yet.

The detective's brow furrowed. "You didn't know? Madsen laid him off on Monday. Corporate cost-cutting thing. So supposedly the security guard shouldn't have let him in the building, but it looks like the weekend shift didn't get the message. Your father jumped from the roof."

Vertigo spun her around. Surprising everyone, not least herself, she leaned forward and threw up on the nice detective's polished black shoes.

***

9:34 p.m.

Much later in the fractured course of that day—she couldn't say why, she was moving on autopilot—Rebecca checked her email and found her father's last message.

She stared, hesitated, afraid to click on it and read the note, unable to resist. Out of character for him to email instead of call. Maybe he didn't trust himself to speak. She noted that he'd sent it at 4:17 a.m. and caught her breath. The same time her mother had been pronounced dead. She'd seen a copy of the death certificate once among some of her father's old papers and memorized the details. Did he know that she knew that?

She imagined him sitting up all night.

She clicked on the message. "Rebecca, wanted to talk to you, but I know you're crazy busy. Something's come up, long story, work-related. Afraid I have to cancel our Sunday barbecue.

"Talk to you later.

"I love you, hon. Always remember how much I love you, and how much your mother loved you.

"Dad."

How like her father. Definitely a goodbye, yet not a goodbye. And thoughtful. He wouldn't want her to show up for their barbecue and find no one home.

THURSDAY, JUNE 26, 1997

2:31 p.m.

The funeral was small, simple and, for Rebecca, surreal. Afterwards, a very solicitous Helen insisted on seeing her home.

Helen sat with her, awkwardly, for a while, pouring them both cups of tea.

Eventually, she asked Rebecca how much time she thought she might take off from work.

Rebecca looked up sharply. "No, this week was plenty. I'll be in Monday."

Helen looked uncomfortable. "In that case, there's something you should know. I'm sure this is the last thing on your mind, but…Preston's gonna be the new editor. Roberts announced it yesterday."

Rebecca shrugged, indifferent.

"The thing is," Helen continued, "your story was the best of the bunch. Hands down. Hell, even my story was better than Preston's. And a few other things…well, I'm sure the fix was in. From the beginning. Llewellyn had already decided to pick Preston, and Roberts just wanted some good stories. Decided to motivate his writers."

Rebecca stared. She could see that Helen believed it, could see it in her eyes. She was riveted by their color, a smoky slate gray. The North Atlantic in winter.

PART TWO

The dust of rumors

TUESDAY, MARCH 17, 1998

Preston Gifford, editor in chief, perched on the leather chair behind his massive mahogany desk and poked furiously at the keyboard. It was Tuesday night, the final night of the biweekly closing cycle, when the last, most time-sensitive articles for that issue had to be transmitted to the printing plant. A bit late for reediting, but these stories would be so much better with just a little tweaking. They cried out for his inimitable touch. They needed to be Prestonized.

His fingers paused as he bent forward and peered at the screen.

"Stop that."

"Hmm?" He glanced up at Cindy, his wife. She was sprawled across the couch on the opposite side of the spacious corner office, idly flipping through *Vogue*.

"You're tapping your foot again."

"Oh. Sorry." He forced himself to stop tapping. Nervous habit. Made Cindy crazy, and he liked to pick his battles. Right now he needed to concentrate.

"Aren't you done yet? I'm bored, it's almost ten." ·

"Is it?" He studied his watch. "Okay, just a second, hon."

His fingers blurred in another keyboard flurry. He knew he had to call a halt soon. When she had phoned and said her book group was ending early, would he like to share a car service home, he had agreed. Couldn't very well hold her hostage in the office now, but he had another half hour's work to do. Best to feed the beast some sort of distraction, lest she grow cranky.

He looked up. "Don't forget we've got that dinner thing next week. Why don't you make some reservations while I finish up?"

"Oh. Okay."

He sent another redone edit to the copy desk and took quiet satisfaction in the frenzy of activity he knew he'd just unleashed. Reporters and copy editors would have to start working on these stories practically from scratch. The new facts Preston had inserted—most of them off the top of his head—had to be checked, new changes had to be applied to the text at the copy desk… In at least one case, he was sure, the art department would have to make a new layout. He was also sure they were all cursing him, but that didn't bother him at all. He had improved those stories, and even a marginal improvement was worth the trouble. More important, he had reaffirmed a fundamental principle: As editor in chief, he could do what he liked, when he liked.

He glanced at his wife and noted that his ploy had worked. Cindy sat on the glass table in the middle of the room, swinging her legs, working the phone. They were having dinner with a prominent venture capitalist the next week—a dinner that had been scheduled without much notice—and Cindy wanted to score reservations someplace fashionable. The Gifford name wasn't exactly working magic.

Preston closed his office door, opened a window—one of the advantages of an office building a few decades old, the windows actually opened—and lit a cigarette. He was breaking the no-smoking rules, but it was late at night. He started poking at his keyboard again, trying to ignore his wife's desperate grab for restaurant status, but Cindy kept updating him, each bulletin more petulant than the last. Nobu didn't even accept reservations after 5 p.m., and Preston wondered why she'd bothered to call. She had to know Nobu was impossible. Asia de Cuba offered them seats in three weeks, at 10:45 p.m., on a Tuesday. And that meant eating at a long communal table, family-style. Preston hated family-style. The maître d' at Daniel hemmed and hawed, suggested they check at the last minute for cancellations. Right.

Preston sighed. It was perverse really. Here he was in his dream job at last, at the top of his profession, the Big Kahuna. Yet the world of the financial press seemed like a small pond. New York was funny that way. Always another arena for degradation, and nothing was more competitive than reservations at a hot spot. If he were a movie star, or Cindy a supermodel…

"The Gotham?" he suggested. "It's five-star."

Cindy glared at him. The Gotham was just not fashionable enough. It was where the editorial staff met with presidents of midsize companies.

"You know, Preston, the least you could do is become a regular somewhere. Besides the Gotham. Just pick a chic place and eat there a few times a week. Reservations wouldn't be a problem. We'd have a fallback."

He turned away without bothering to respond, stubbed out his cigarette, lit another. She made more calls. He started to open up and reedit stories that had already closed, and to re-reedit those that hadn't. He tried to remember why he had married the woman. Okay, she was pretty, and she had a really nice ass, but was that enough? What the hell did she want anyway? Bill Gates?

Bill Clinton? Why were they all named Bill?

Another thought. This time he spoke up. "Try the Sutton Club. The owner was here for breakfast with the Llewellyns a few weeks ago. Make sure they know I'm the editor here and we'll always get a table there."

She gave him what he'd come to think of as her long-suffering look. "Oh, thanks for telling me, after watching me get humiliated for the last half hour."

Preston banged the keyboard feverishly, redoing yet another story. By now, he was aware that he was doing it out of pure, misdirected spite. But what good was power if you couldn't abuse it?

By the time they left for home, Preston was almost relieved, for once, that they were no longer speaking.

WEDNESDAY, MARCH 18, 1998

"Fuck." Preston hurled the issue of *Wealth* across his office, a look of disgust on his face. *Wealth* was *The Magazine*'s main competitor. Rebecca had defected there after her father's death. Helen was just stepping through the doorway for the biweekly editors meeting—they met the morning after they'd closed each issue to plan the next one—when the flying magazine smacked against her shins. Startled, she stumbled and nearly fell. Damn, she thought, this meeting's off to a good start. Helen was tired. It had been a tough close.

Much of the work done by the copy editors, art department and reporters the day before had been rendered moot by Preston's late-evening editing. Having already put in a hard twelve hours of work that day, they'd had to start again. They'd worked past three in the morning to patch up the damage and get the pages out. A few production people had been stuck until almost dawn.

This morning, reporters were still scrambling to catch errors that might have crept in with the rash of changes, little things people missed in a fog of fatigue, big things that were uncheckable in the middle of the night. Helen was sure the day would bring a lot of makeovers—changes made after a story had been transmitted to the printing plant but before the pages had rolled off the presses. Makeovers were expensive, and they made Helen nervous. There was always a risk of introducing new errors while fixing old ones, and it would be too late to catch these fresh mistakes. But who would dare tell Preston that all his frantic reediting was just pointless doodling, creating hours of senseless work for dozens of people?

Preston glared at the issue of *Wealth* now lying at Helen's feet. She followed his line of sight. The magazine had fallen open to the editor's letter. A photo of Rebecca graced the page, her brown eyes staring up at Helen. Apparently, the editor had decided to highlight her article in the current issue. Probably her recent promotion, too, she thought. Helen had been too busy with the close to even scan the newest issue of *Wealth*.

Preston looked as if he wanted to grind his heel into Rebecca's face. (He wore boots with slightly exaggerated heels to nudge his five-foot-ten frame closer to a respectable six feet.) Instead he whirled around and brought his wrath to bear on Helen: "How the fuck could you have been taken in like that?"

Helen scooped up the copy of *Wealth* and scurried to an empty seat. She flipped to Rebecca's story but was too agitated to read it properly. Her eyes flickered across the page, skipping randomly among the words. She focused on the title: "The Naked Emperor." Helen forced herself to slow down and read, but could only skim the story. Each sentence pierced her like a needle. She felt like a voodoo doll.

The emperor *sans* clothes was John Stryker, the founder of BuyLow.com. In her story Rebecca tweaked Stryker for patenting a business practice—essentially, competitive bidding—as old as the Middle Ages. She also had great fun at the expense of the U.S. Patent Office and the overworked, underpaid patent regulators who were clearly swamped and stymied by the flood of Web-related patent applications. How could they have approved such a thing? She predicted that BuyLow would lose various pending lawsuits questioning its right to own such basic business transactions, and that BuyLow's inflated stock would fall to earth.

Several issues ago, Helen had also written a piece about Stryker. Helen took a positive slant, but what was so wrong with that? She had bridled when she overheard Bruce snidely refer to it as a real blowjob. Okay, it had been titled "Gutenberg Redux," and compared Stryker to no other than the famous inventor of the printing press. The two men, Helen had argued, were comparable because they had revolutionized fundamental human activities: Gutenberg transformed reading and writing, and Stryker, buying and selling. Helen's story likened the invention of movable type to the invention of the "reverse auction," a basic business model in which sellers bid against one another to win a buyer's business. Stryker had built BuyLow on this model; it was what allowed him to sell airline tickets and hotel rooms based on what the customer was willing to pay.

"Johannes Gutenberg, what the hell were you thinking?" Preston's face slowly reddened as he turned on Helen, working his way into a serious rant, voice rising. "You want to hype this dot-com schmuck into a legend? On the basis of fucking patents? Fucking numbers of patents?"

His voice suddenly turned soft. Silky. Menacing. "Didn't look too deeply into the quality of those patents, did you? Not like Rebecca did. Didn't really think it through?"

Helen didn't point out that, after all, Preston was editor, he'd signed off on that story. He'd even written the headline. More than that, Preston had pushed her to find a positive Internet story. At first, Helen had been hesitant.

She and Rebecca had always talked about how the Internet was a bubble, and the two of them were determined not to follow the herd and puff it up even more like the rest of the press. But Rebecca had stuck to her guns, while Helen had eventually caved to Preston's pressure. He had been relentless, even though they already had more dot-com advertising coming in than they could really handle.

Helen flinched as he bore down upon her and snatched the copy of *Wealth* from her hands. Preston spun on his heel, crossed the room again, grabbed the Gutenberg issue off the table. He flipped to Helen's story, flipped to Rebecca's, shoved both magazines under Helen's nose.

Preston's jaw clenched. Unclenched. His voice was low. "You tell me, Helen. Which of these two stories is better researched? More insightful? Which of these is fucking better written? Which of these is more convincing?

"What's a reader to think, Helen? Do we look stupid? Or just lazy?"

The room was silent.

Helen swallowed. Preston couldn't make her feel much worse than she already did. She'd screwed up, and she knew it was her own fault. If only she still had Rebecca as a sounding board. That's how she and Rebecca had always worked—they had read each other's drafts and critiqued them, no holds barred.

Helen had seen Rebecca only once since the day of the funeral. Despite her promise to be back at work that Monday morning, Rebecca never did return to *The Magazine.* Helen had called her several times, but Rebecca had spoken in monosyllables and insisted she needed some time to be alone. The human resources department eventually sent a couple of maintenance guys to pack up her belongings. They carried out the boxes and locked Rebecca's office. After Rebecca landed a job at *Wealth,* she had called Helen and asked her when she was going to quit *The Magazine.* There was an awkward pause before Helen replied that she had decided to stay for a while. Rebecca grew silent. She stopped calling Helen after that conversation. Helen left Rebecca several voice mails, but her calls went unreturned. Finally, one time Rebecca picked up and agreed to meet her for coffee.

Café Loup was empty but for a bored waitress. Helen and Rebecca sat at a table covered with a white tablecloth.

There was so much catching up they had to do. Helen started to ask questions. About work first, a safe subject, Helen thought. But Rebecca deflected every question with a muttered monosyllable. Then she started to throw Helen's questions back at her. How are you, and how are you, what's new, and what's new with you, I'm so happy to see you. Then Rebecca stopped talking. The silence didn't seem to bother her, but it bothered Helen. She became very aware of the waitress leaning lazily against the bar, yawning.

Helen felt the moment's awkwardness grow between them like a tumor, until it mutated into anger. She was more than uncomfortable. She was fed up. She understood why Rebecca resented *The Magazine* and those who ran it. The manipulative bastards had treated her shabbily. Helen, too, for that matter. They were indisputable assholes, but they hadn't killed Rebecca's father. Was it reasonable to expect your former colleagues to quit in sympathy? Helen didn't think so. She decided to give up on Rebecca.

Now Helen reached for the issue of *Wealth* Preston held in his hand. Taken by surprise, he surrendered it to her, then extended his hand as if to snatch the issue back. But he looked up at Helen's face and paused, then retreated a couple of paces.

Helen folded *Wealth* in her hand, turning the page with Rebecca's face to the inside. She clutched the magazine so hard that her nails cut into the glossy paper.

She stared at Preston. "I won't let her beat me again."

***

Rebecca drew the black curtains in her Upper West Side apartment and sat cross-legged on the cool ceramic tiles of her kitchen floor. Slowly she unwrapped the bandages from her wrists and hands, unveiling the tattered flesh beneath with all the patience of ritual.

John Coltrane's liquid notes gently pelted her like warm blue rain, blowing in the open archway from the living room, where her father's vinyl copy of *Blue Train* spun on his old Thorens turntable. "I'm Old Fashioned," one of her favorite tracks.

She opened a well-worn Swiss Army knife. Starting near the tip of her index finger, she sliced carefully into the skin until it formed a small flap she could grasp. Moaning softly to herself, she then peeled back the skin, tearing it off in ragged strips with her free hand. She worked her way through her fingers methodically, one by one by one. The strips of skin formed a little pile on the cool tile floor, like pink carrot peelings.

EASTER SUNDAY, APRIL 12, 1998

Easter is the most important holiday in the Russian Orthodox Church. Every April as far back as Helen could remember the Tyrkova family gathered for an Easter party given by her grandmother, Tatiana Tyrkova.

Helen, called Elena by the Russian side of her family, sat on the purple sofa in Tatiana's parlor on East 93rd Street, under an icon that Tatiana's mother had snatched off the wall above her bed in 1917.

Helen had heard the story a hundred times. The butlers running down the stairs with the last suitcases and Tatiana's father yelling for everyone to hurry to the carriage—they had to get to the railway station in time to catch the train that would speed them away from the cresting wave of revolution.

Tatiana, who had been only three years old at the time, claimed to remember "running away from those Bolsheviks" quite vividly, and credited the Madonna on the icon with their safe escape to New York. Ever since, the Madonna on the icon had been the patron of the Tyrkova family.

Next to Helen, bent over a small coffee table, her cousin Andrei was tasting the Moskovskaya vodka that some real Russians had just brought from the motherland. Helen's cousins often invited visiting Russian artists and politicians to their black-tie Easter cocktail party. These new Russians showed up in jeans and leather jackets and chain-smoked. Andrei kept muttering, "*My ne kurim zdes,*" but everyone ignored him.

The cousins often fell into discussions on whether they should answer the historic call of their blood and return to Russia to take care of their people. Invariably, the cousins opted for organizing the Russian ball seasons at the Plaza and formed charities to help poor Russian children.

Helen was all too aware of her Russian cousins' disdain for the vulgar American ways of money grubbing. They held jobs in the curatorial departments of museums, ate bliny and socialized with European royalty. They looked down on Helen for getting an MBA and attending barbecues with bankers.

Her Russian family attributed Helen's workaholic tendencies to her British father, George, a municipal bond analyst. She didn't disagree.

"Great vodka, Elena, really you should try it," Andrei was saying.

"Thank you, Andrei, I have my white wine."

George Caswell was a white wine drinker and Helen decided to stick to her father's favorite that evening. She knew that small validation of her father's choice was just the sort of detail that would annoy her mother, Alexandra. Helen scanned the crowd and spotted Alexandra near the opposite wall, transfixed by something at the center of the room. Helen followed her mother's gaze. It was focused on a man who stood near the French doors, talking with Tatiana.

In this unexpected context, it took Helen a few seconds to place him. Of course. Tom Richardson. She had interviewed him for two hours over lunch once. She was curious as to how he'd ended up at the Easter party, but all sorts of people turned up at Tatiana's events. Helen was never clear on how her grandmother wielded the social clout to attract those she referred to as "interesting people," but over the years Helen had met everyone from Baryshnikov to Ed Koch. She wondered how her mother had recognized Richardson. Maybe Alexandra had seen him at some charity event. Or maybe she simply followed her natural radar. Her mother sensed rich and powerful men with the unfulfilled lust of a woman frustrated that she hadn't married one.

Richardson was listening attentively to Helen's grandmother. When Tatiana pontificated, everybody had to listen. Helen had almost forgotten how handsome he was. The original fortunate son. She tried to remember his age—fortysomething, she was sure, but he looked younger. Reminding herself not to stare, she wondered what Tatiana was up to.

"Elena, Elena, *Warum hast du keine Kinder*," Tatiana often scolded Helen in German. The old lady had a soft spot for German high culture. "And why do you work so much, as if you had to work like some servant? Where is your prince? A husband should take care of you. A butler, a maid, they are only so good. You need a husband by your side. Why not, Elena, you are so beautiful…"

Tatiana wore a simple dark brown dress and a regal air that Easter evening. Her hair, half brown and half gray, was meticulously coiffed, as always, and she was smoking a cigarette in her favorite cigarette holder, a lovely pre-Revolutionary piece of carved onyx, on which, when you looked very, very closely, you could see the faces of the Romanovs inlaid in silver. She was explaining something to Richardson. No, Helen decided, not explaining, she was describing something. She focused on her grandmother's hands. Helen had inherited her grandmother's gestures, so she could easily read the meaning behind Tatiana's hands. It was simple—the cigarette holder amplified and accentuated every movement, like a conductor's baton.

Helen started playing a game with herself, reading Tatiana's hands. The hands moved through the air more slowly than usual, defining long, elegant objects in space. Helen thought: "You are talking about an object, a work of art…" The icon. They were talking about the icon. The Modigliani features of the fifteenth-century Madonna on the icon would account for Tatiana's deliberate gestures.

Helen glanced back at her mother and caught a familiar expression on her face. She found her mother's face even easier to read than her grandmother's hands. The purposeful eyes, pursed lips, head held high. Alexandra was ready to make her move.

Helen knew what would happen next. She had seen Alexandra play her party game ever since Helen could remember. Alexandra would approach a powerful man, in this case Richardson, and then drag Helen's father over. The ostensible aim was to create a networking opportunity for George that would finally catapult him into the big leagues. Not that George wasn't comfortably prosperous, but Alexandra wanted to see her husband's name attached to the big deals of the city, written about on the business pages. Helen's father simply didn't see the point. He was more comfortable with balance sheets and numbers than with people. He often said that numbers spoke to him. Every time Alexandra dragged him over in front of an important dealmaker, George sputtered and mumbled, visibly uncomfortable, then retreated at the first opportunity.

In the earlier years of their marriage, every such encounter was followed by a fight at home. Alexandra would work herself up into a rant: "One more missed opportunity… what else do you expect me to do for you?…I deserve better, I can't stand mediocrity.…If you were a character in a Chekhov story, you would be one of those losers with ink-stained fingers and elbow protectors who worked their abacuses till midnight, counting other peoples' money."

George would hide from his wife. At night he would read to Helen before she went to sleep. Sometimes when she fell asleep and woke up later, she felt safe because she'd open her eyes to her father still sitting on the edge of her bed, reading a newspaper or dozing off. Sometimes Alexandra opened the door to Helen's bedroom to whisk him out. But Helen would always come instantly awake and beg her father to read aloud some more, and her mother would go away.

After forty years of marriage, Alexandra played her party game for the sake of playing. It had long since devolved into sadistic ritual. Afterwards at home, she didn't even bother to waste her breath ranting about one more missed opportunity.

Helen looked back at Tatiana and Richardson, trying to gauge whether she could reach them before her mother did, and began weaving her way through the crowd, determined to spare her father another humiliation. Tatiana saw her approaching and grinned broadly, waving her over with her cigarette baton.

Alexandra set out for Richardson simultaneously from the opposite end of the room.

Helen ducked around a knot of chattering people, closing the gap that separated her from Richardson and Tatiana. Tuxedos and black cocktail dresses blurred into dark smudges in her visual field. The party chatter faded into a distant buzzing, like voices on the beach muffled by the surf. Helen tried to hurry the pace, moving in a rapid shuffle, while not knocking over anybody's drink.

Ahead and to her right, she saw Alexandra stop to chat with Helen's cousin Stephen, a curator at the Met. He was a distraction, but Alexandra couldn't afford to ignore Stephen. He got her into all the right openings and classes at the Met, the ones that were also attended by the wives of the men at the top of the city. Even if her husband wasn't part of the right crowd, Alexandra made sure that she was. Helen passed close enough to overhear snatches of their conversation. "Nobody here thinks they are worth much," Stephen was saying to her mother, "because Russians have flooded the market....If you like icons, it's a good time to buy..."

Helen was now just a couple of moves away from Richardson and Tatiana. Alexandra stepped away from Stephen and narrowed Helen's lead. Then cousin Andrei materialized in front of Helen with a plate of bliny, cutting her off. Alexandra took another a step forward. "Let's have some of the bliny with the vodka, exquisite, exquisite vodka," cousin Andrei said to Helen. His cheeks were red from all the vodka he'd already downed.

Andrei saw that Helen was watching Tatiana and Richardson. "I bet Grammy Tatiana is bending his ear about the family estate. She's read somewhere that Russians will sell agricultural land soon, you know their government-run farms, the kolhozy, and she will be able to buy back the family estate. Will she ever stop? I'm sure that the barbarian nouveau riche will tear the old house down and build one of their McMansiovskis. But she's been obsessed about that estate. She wants it back in the family, says that it's ours forever, as if anything is forever in this world...."

Helen grabbed a glass of vodka and gulped it down. Then she pushed Andrei aside. She knew he was too tipsy to notice, much less remember. As Andrei fought to regain his balance, Helen took a sharp step forward. She stood face to face with Richardson, sensing her mother right behind her. The scent of sandalwood and roses, Chanel No. 19: Alexandra's perfume since Helen was a child.

"Mr. Richardson."

He smiled warmly. "Why, Ms....Caswell, isn't it?"

She smiled back. "You remember."

SATURDAY, JUNE 6, 1998

Rebecca wriggled forward a few more inches through the thorny green tangle at the base of the hedge, earning several fresh scratches on her forearms as she went. Savoring the pain.

She propped herself on her elbows and focused her binoculars on the woman. A skinny blonde, she was riding a white mare at a gallop, bareback and mostly bare herself. She was a good rider. Backlit on the patio of his East Hampton estate, Tom Richardson gazed into the dusk, openly admiring her form.

Rebecca burrowed still deeper into the bottom of the hedge that bordered Richardson's estate, adjusted her camouflage netting and checked her night-vision gear. She'd been in position nearly two hours already, and her muscles were starting to stiffen. She paused to reach back and massage an incipient cramp in her calf. These nights in the Hamptons could be chilly and wet, even in summer. She'd taken her usual approach route, wandering down the beach and over the dunes as if she were just another sunbather, but lugging a beach bag full of surveillance gear and warm clothes, then slipped into her usual vantage point when no one was in sight. Surprisingly easy, since the big curving dunes completely shielded her from view from the path that led to the beach.

Rebecca's gaze swept the length of the estate. The lawn was vast, with a small apple orchard and stables at the far end. The estate had been in Richardson's mother's family for generations, and the old Victorian house was charmingly ramshackle for a billionaire's Hamptons retreat. She could hear muted surf from beyond the dunes.

She turned back to study the rider. When her body pulled up, swinging her long hair away from her breasts, she could see a black bikini top. Each time the mare's white head moved down, she glimpsed the black bottom. The black geometric forms, twin triangles above, a lone triangle below, vanished and reappeared against the whiteness of the mare and the woman in a steady rhythm, on off, on off, like some inscrutable semaphore.

The rider slowed to a trot, then eased the horse up to the edge of the swimming pool. Pausing only to pull back her hair with a black hair band she'd wrapped around her wrist, she swung herself off the horse's back, dropping right into the water. The well-trained mare wandered off toward the stables as the woman started swimming laps.

Rebecca zoomed in. The woman's swimsuit was satiny yet austere. Black against pale skin, an inverse nun.

Done with her laps, the woman stood in the pool's shallow end, up to her hips in water. Rebecca watched Tom watch her, rapt, as she reached up to free her hair and shake it loose. She focused on the woman. Her hair half covered her face, draped itself across her shoulders. Her nipples stood hard and clear against the wet black satin. Then the swimmer looked up, gazing at the evening's first few stars. Her hair fell away, and Rebecca got her first good look at her face.

Helen.

Helen fucking Caswell.

TUESDAY, DECEMBER 1, 1998

Tom Richardson always relished the midmorning lull. The early whirl of phone calls, emails and meetings had subsided, and he could relax for a few minutes with a fresh cup of coffee and *The New York Times*, sheltered by the huge teak desk that stood in the building's northeast corner like a fortress, a stronghold commanding the vast carpeted plain of his airy office. Of course, he had scanned the headlines much earlier that day, and had thoroughly perused *The Wall Street Journal* and *Financial Times*. But he liked to pause and gather his thoughts while reading the columns on the op-ed page.

He sipped the coffee his assistant had just brought in, a mug of delicious Tanzanian peaberry, and suddenly remembered the résumé. Brooks had handed it to him over drinks last night. What was it he had said? A talented young lady Tom should meet. Had expressed interest in his firm. Too good to be languishing at Morgan Stanley. Tom smiled to himself. Brooks was an old friend, but he was not incapable of bullshit, and "too good for Morgan" certainly fell into that category. It wasn't like Brooks to usher Morgan's finest talents to the exit out of altruism. Still, Tom knew he'd give the woman an interview on Brooks' word alone. He made it a point to personally interview anyone who came recommended by someone he trusted, so he'd slipped the résumé into his briefcase without even a glance.

Now he wheeled his desk chair over a few feet to a side table and opened his briefcase, a sleek and supple thing the color of honey he'd picked up in a small artisan's shop in Milan. The soft, familiar leather was soothing under his hands. Ah, there it was. He fished out the sheet of heavy paper, unfolded it. Stared blankly.

Blinked. Stared some more as he struggled to regain his breath.

Kimberly Davis. Dartmouth, Wharton. Morgan Stanley.

Tom felt an almost physical lurch as the parameters of his carefully constructed world shifted beneath him. This was an unacceptable intrusion.

The walls that marked a compartmented life couldn't just burst open, could they? What was she thinking? But even through his shock, some part of his mind tried to grapple with this twist of fate, to sift the possibilities. Perhaps she simply thought she had proved herself worthy. Was this really a calamity? Or perhaps an unexpected blessing?

He turned and gazed absently through the floor-to-ceiling plate glass that framed the looming Waldorf-Astoria cattycorner across Park Avenue. But the Art Deco towers were invisible to him. In his mind, he was staring at a woman.

A warm September evening. New Haven, 1972. He was twenty, just starting his junior year at Yale. The whole world, it seemed, was rebelling and experimenting—or else already burned out from experimenting too much. Radical campus politics had pretty much wound down by then, but for those of a certain bent, college life was still defined by the quest for one peak experience after another. It was an ethos Tom—imbued by his father with a healthy respect for caution and calculation—had found eye-opening, then exhilarating.

He had cut quite a figure on campus, with his sandy hair pulled back into a ponytail, his dangling gold earring in the shape of a jodhpur, his fast, evil-looking motorcycle—a BMW, all black and chrome. It seemed funny now, but it had been the earring, above all, that had given his father fits.

His life then was an odd mix of tradition and transgression. Earlier that September Saturday, he had attended a Skull and Bones meeting, and then split a tab of acid with his friend Toby. He figured half a hit wouldn't fry him to the point that he lost all desire to socialize, and there were a lot of promising parties scheduled for that night. In fact, he was intrigued by the challenge of mingling and chit-chatting through a personally altered reality. It was a sort of game he played with himself, just to keep things interesting.

About four hours later, comfortably past the disorienting peak, their feet metaphysically planted on the long, gradual downslope of the psychedelic wave, he and Toby emerged from the Saybrook residence hall and wandered toward the first of the parties. This was an outdoor keg bash that had started in the afternoon, and the sun still washed the evening in liquid gold.

They'd just rounded the corner of the library when he first saw Margo, sitting cross-legged on the grass like a quiet revelation. A striking black woman, her smooth, flawless skin the color of mahogany. Curvier than the sort of girl he usually dated, she looked both earthy and intellectual, intent on the book in her lap. Thick-rimmed glasses camouflaged a pretty face, framed those eyes. Defiant eyes, maybe a bit crazy. Wild black curls pulled into a ponytail that threatened to come apart, held together by a simple rubber band.

Tom broke stride, hesitated, came to a full stop about twenty feet from her. Toby looked back over his shoulder with a puzzled frown.

"Why don't you go on, man?" said Tom. "I'll catch up with you later."

Toby glanced at the girl on the grass, peered at Tom, smiled and shrugged. "Okay, sure. See ya."

Tom stood perfectly still for what seemed to him a long time, staring at her through his sunglasses. She glanced up and looked right through him, as if he weren't even there.

He decided to step through the looking glass.

He walked right up to her, close enough that, even with her nose in a book, his blue suede Pumas had to be within her peripheral vision, and waited. When she looked up, he flashed a charming, slightly crooked grin.

"I feel like the Cheshire cat. But surely you can see my grin."

Warily, she looked him up and down. "Feeling invisible? Yeah, I bet a guy like you isn't used to that."

"No, not really. I'm Tom. Okay if I sit?"

She hesitated. "Guess so. I'm Margo."

As he sat down, she stared at his ear and snickered. "Is that a jodhpur?"

He smiled. "Yeah, kind of an inside joke."

She nodded. "Bet daddy finds that amusing."

He laughed. "You've got that right. What you reading?"

"Machiavelli, collected works. Hard-nosed mother. Saw things clearly." She shrugged. "I'm poli sci. You?"

"History major. European."

She nodded. "Can be useful."

"Yeah, it can put things in perspective."

The sun sank languidly behind a building as they talked, leaving them in deep green dusk. Tom removed his shades.

She frowned, looked hard into his eyes, then suddenly flashed the outspread fingers of her left hand across his field of vision. "Happy trails?"

He smiled sheepishly. His pupils must be huge. "That obvious?"

She laughed and shook her head. "So you're some kind of rich hippie?"

"No need to reduce me to a stereotype, is there?"

This made her laugh harder. "A psychedelic Wasp. That explains why you're chatting me up. You're in a purple haze."

He looked serious. "I beg to differ. I never see things more clearly than when tripping. Like the world is etched in glass. Besides, I'm not that twisted, only did half a hit. Not like my mind has left my body or anything. Was actually meaning to party-hop tonight, but I think I've lost interest in that."

She cocked her head to one side, studied him a minute, then seemed to come to a decision. She stood, smiling, and he noticed she was a bit short. "Come with me, Waspy boy."

Margo led him across campus to her dorm room in Pierson and opened a bottle of cheap red Spanish wine. She put some Hendrix on the stereo, his quieter, bluesier stuff. They talked. She was a senior, a year older than Tom, and brilliant enough to have won a full scholarship. She'd been born in Ohio but had grown up all over the place, a military brat: Germany, Turkey, Korea, Florida, D.C. and California, where her parents lived now. Her father was an Air Force colonel on the verge of retirement. He'd commanded a squadron of F-4 Phantoms in Vietnam. Her mother taught sixth grade.

Their conversation meandered without goal or destination, touching the personal and the political, the trivial and the transcendent. Years later, when he had long since forgotten the details, he still recalled vividly the sensation of their talk looping around and in on itself, lines of thought entangling and intersecting in startling ways. At one point he got wound up trying to explain why Janis Joplin was important, not just some paleface pretender to the blues. Margo finally allowed that he might be onto something. Her laugh was musical, generous, a warm invitation.

When they finished the wine, she scrounged in a small cabinet, came up with a bottle of sherry that was three-quarters full, then rolled a joint. They talked some more. Midnight slipped past unnoticed.

Tom blinked in surprise when he glanced down at his watch and saw that it was past two. They had talked themselves almost hoarse and listened to a tall stack of records. Margo was at the stereo again, lowering the needle onto some Miles Davis.

She turned and sauntered over to him slowly, a curious look in her eyes. She slipped off her glasses and leaned over him as he sat in her desk chair. She smelled of lemony shampoo and jasmine, of sherry, musk and a faint, sharp tang of sweat. She kissed him full on the lips—strongly but with no urgency, no desperation—and he surrendered to the delicate flick of her tongue.

She stood up straight, gazing down at him as she unfastened her ponytail, slipped off her shirt, let her bra flutter to the floor. He reached up and carefully cupped her full, dark breasts in his hands, brushed his thumbs across her nipples. She smiled and stepped back a pace, leaving his hands clutching air. Eyes locked on his, she unfastened her jeans, tugged them slowly down around her ankles, stepped out of them. She wore no panties underneath.

This simple revelation unhinged him. He stood, shedding his own clothes almost instantly. They tumbled onto her bed and into a fractured nightlong reverie of lust, tenderness and tangled limbs. The acid kept him awake till morning. She dozed between bouts. He watched her breathe, gently stroked his fingers along her curves. He let his thoughts run free, but they kept circling back to the odalisque beside him.

Early sunlight slid across the bed, dappling her legs and belly. When her eyes opened and she reached for him again, he knew that he was lost.

He remained lost, lost in an undergraduate idyll for months, Odysseus to her Circe. They each explored the other's world and body.

He was enraptured with her blackness, both physical and cultural, and was slightly annoyed to realize that Margo was just as fascinated by his whiteness. It irritated him when she forced him to try to explicate the mindset of a repressed Yankee Wasp. Of all the ethnic backgrounds to be saddled with, what could be more deadly dull?

He wondered how things had come to this. Surely his distant Anglo-Saxon ancestors of a thousand years ago hadn't been as uptight as his immediate ancestors. Not likely, given their barbarian penchant for pillaging and such.

For the moment, he gave himself up to happily pillaging Margo. But it was clear to him and, he believed, to her—even in their mutual enchantment—that this was a self-limiting love affair. Something more permanent, to fully incorporate her into his world…Well, he was honest enough to admit to himself that he might not have the strength or courage that would require.

The spell broke in the spring, when despite rigorous precautions, she got pregnant. Margo was furious. Mad at Tom, mad at her family, mad at the universe for subverting her plans. He realized that she'd wanted to walk away from him on her own terms, and that with her graduation looming, she'd probably been bracing herself to do just that.

He never really understood why she refused to have an abortion. Eventually, he would conclude it was out of sheer perversity, an angry refusal to let anyone off the hook, not Tom, not her family, not even herself.

Of course, Tom had provided financial support for the child. His father had arranged everything. It was all handled discreetly by the family lawyers. But after her graduation, Margo had severed all direct contact. She felt it was better that way, better for everyone.

So Tom had never met his daughter. A trust fund paid for her schooling, so he'd followed her progress at a remove: Dartmouth, Wharton. He'd heard she was working on Wall Street. But after a while, she'd come to seem slightly unreal to him, like one of those Third World children you could "adopt" through a charity for just pennies a day.

Now she wanted to meet. To work for him.

THURSDAY, DECEMBER 3, 1998

Barricaded behind his desk, Tom gulped his coffee, then silently cursed it for making him even more jittery. He surely didn't need anything jangling his nerves further, but he was desperately bleary-eyed. Anticipation of this meeting had made sleep impossible for him.

At least he'd had the sense to otherwise clear his morning, and to schedule the interview early: He'd be unable to focus on anything else until he got it over with. In fact, he'd cleared his whole day.

But he had no idea what to expect. Helplessly, he tried to damp down his wilder thoughts. He'd nursed dynastic fantasies all night. Clearly, his daughter was smart and ambitious. They would forge a father-daughter bond. He'd teach her everything he knew, until she became his trusted right hand...Whoa, there. He knew he was getting way ahead of himself.

She waltzed slowly into his office, preceded by a shy, warm smile. She was slim, lithe, of medium height. A black alpaca overcoat swung open to reveal a black Armani suit. And that face...mocha skin dusted with freckles. Those eyes. He stood uncertainly, started around his desk.

She paused in the middle of the room and looked him up and down. "Hi, I'm Kimmie. It's good to meet you at last."

He strode toward her, halted a couple of paces away and openly stared. "My God...you're even more beautiful than your mother, you know that? You have her hair. But those eyes...those are Aunt Cassie's eyes. Cassandra, my mother's sister. Such a pure shade of green."

She grinned. "Really? I always wondered. I bet these freckles come from your side of the family too."

Suddenly aware that he hadn't finished properly greeting Kimmie, Tom was paralyzed by awkwardness, and relieved when Kimmie rescued him by taking a step forward and opening her arms. Gratefully, he returned the hug.

"Well, well. I was stunned when I saw your name...that it was you. But happy. Come on, have a seat. Coffee?"

"No, no, thanks."

"How's your mother?"

"She's fine, the same, you know. She's changeless, like a force of nature."

He smiled. "I think I know what you mean. Does she know you came to see me?"

Kimmie shook her head. "Didn't think to mention it. I'm all grown up, you know, so this is just between us. Though she may go postal when she finds out."

His smile widened. "Indeed. I'd rather expect that."

She twirled and untwirled her fingers in her hair and smiled back just a bit too seductively. Tom was suddenly uneasy. Had he imagined it?

He cleared his throat. "So, um, Kimmie…is this…just curiosity? Or…I mean…this is an odd situation for a first meeting, isn't it? A job interview?"

She shrugged gracefully. "I suppose. But still, weirdly appropriate for people like us."

Like us?

She looked serious. "I do mean business. Thought I might get to know my father by working for him."

"I see." He fixed her in a pensive gaze. She twirled her hair and stared back unflinching, her eyes as green and defiant as the England of his Anglo-Saxon forefathers.

"And why would you want to do that?"

"Besides curiosity, you're the best. Your firm is the best. Wall Street may be full of pirates, but you're Captain Kidd."

He chuckled. "So, what did they really have you doing over at Morgan?"

Soon they were talking finance, and he could see that she was sharp. He also guessed she would make a slippery negotiator. Something about her unsettled him. Nothing he could pinpoint, but he had the feeling she was operating on several levels at once, working angles even he couldn't see. For Tom, that was a rare sensation.

He tossed out a routine question. "What do you see yourself doing three years from now? Five years from now?"

"Running a hedge fund for you. Or maybe a special situations sort of thing, finding potential turnarounds. And five years?" Kimmie flashed a sly smile. "Making partner—why not?"

Tom raised an eyebrow. Ambitious, certainly, even cocky. But was it more than that? During a first meeting that was also a job interview? It seemed presumptuous.

Finally, he told her that he'd have to think it over. They promised to keep in touch no matter what he decided, now that Kimmie had breached the wall. He asked her to have lunch with him and she pointed out that it was still midmorning. They settled on coffee.

He stretched things out by vetoing Starbucks and walking her all the way around the Waldorf to the Lexington Avenue side, where he steered her into Oscar's and ordered cappuccinos. They sipped the hot liquid slowly, lingering under the Art Deco ceiling, drinking each other in.

She intrigued him with her saucy charm. She stirred memories of Margo. She alarmed him.

Back at his desk, he stared out the enormous window, lost in thought. Why had she set off such warning bells in his head? Tom prided himself on his intuition, and he had learned to give it its due. Every once in a while—not often—he had a strong gut reaction to someone on first meeting. And ignoring that was hazardous. Kimmie set off danger signals like no one he had ever met.

He reached for the phone, punched a number on speed dial. "Yes, hi, I need you to run a background check on someone. And it needs to be especially discreet."

He stared out the window a long while. Captain Kidd, huh?

***

Rebecca tapped her foot impatiently beneath the tiny table for two, scanning the sidewalk through the bistro's plate-glass window. People scurried by, hunched deep into their coats, squinting into the wind. She allowed herself another small sip of Chianti. The girl was half an hour late, but Rebecca had learned to expect that.

Then she spotted her darting across the street, heedless of the traffic, in a navy peacoat and jeans. Clearly, she must have stopped by her apartment and changed. Rebecca had come straight from work, and now she felt overdressed in her tweed skirt and jacket.

The door swung open, and Kimmie peered around the dim room. Rebecca waved. Kimmie grinned and strode over, air-kissed and sat down across the table, their knees bumping.

Rebecca poured her a generous glass of wine. They moved through the initial pleasantries and ordered some food.

Kimmie gestured at Rebecca's gloved hands. "You keeping those on through dinner?"

Rebecca shrugged. "Probably. More elegant and mysterious than bandages, don't you think? The carpal tunnel has been acting up again, I need to keep them wrapped."

Kimmie nodded. "Right." Rebecca could see Kimmie didn't believe her.

Then Kimmie asked, "So, what's up? You just feel like dinner? I'm not working any big deals right now, you know, kind of a lull. No good gossip either."

Rebecca cocked her head, seizing her chance to look skeptical in turn.

"Really? You sure?"

"What do you mean?"

Rebecca smiled and refilled both their glasses, even though her own glass was still two-thirds full. "You know, Kimmie, you've been a big help to me. One of my most valuable sources over the past few months. And a reporter takes care of her sources." She paused, looked straight into those deep green eyes. "But I've come to think of you as more than a source. As a friend. And I take even better care of my friends.

"A reporter feeds on gossip and rumor, you know. I've heard things....Like you might be leaving Morgan soon."

Kimmie smiled. "Oh. That." She took a swig of wine. "Worried about losing your source? Don't be. Sure, I'm a little restless. A girl needs to explore her options."

"Kimmie. Don't bullshit me. Maybe I can help....That's not all I heard."

"Oh. That." Kimmie flushed through her mocha skin and took a bigger swig. "Stupid, huh? Should've known that would get out. But really, don't worry. I'll land on my feet."

"You think so?"

"I'm sure of it." She grinned. "And this time I'll stay off my knees."

Rebecca groaned, then chuckled, then topped off their glasses. "Okay. Why so confident?"

"Well...just between us..." Kimmie leaned across the table. "I had an interview this morning. Went well. At Hillburn."

Rebecca almost spilled her wine, fought to mask the shock she was sure had flickered over her face. "Hillburn? That's certainly high-powered."

Kimmie nodded, giggling. "Wouldn't you like to have a source there?"

"Wouldn't I? That would be..." Rebecca tried to will her pulse to slow as her thoughts careened wildly. So many possibilities... All these months of cultivating Kimmie, looking for a way to use her properly, she'd never dreamed... She took slow, even breaths. Had to stay in the moment, keep cool, sort this all out later.

"But still," Rebecca managed. "That has to be a long shot?"

"Maybe not so long."

For the first time that evening, Rebecca allowed herself a long, deep gulp of her wine, bracing herself for what might come next. A turning point. Had to play this right. She tried to look idly curious. "Really? Why?"

The waiter chose that moment to arrive with dinner. Rebecca wanted to stab him with her fork.

At last, the waiter disappeared. Rebecca prodded. "So?"

"Well, the interview...it was with Tom Richardson himself."

Rebecca didn't have to act. She blinked. Her mouth opened, closed. "Richardson?" Deep breath, more wine. "How'd that happen?"

"Well, actually, sometimes he does that, first interviews, if you come in connected. Brooks Thayer put in a word for me. But there's more." She giggled. "In terms of connected."

Rebecca was afraid to breathe.

Kimmie leaned forward and lowered her voice. "Just between us...very few people know this but...I told you about my mom, right?"

"Sure, the lawyer. Raised you alone, like my dad raised me in the end."

"Well...my father is Tom Richardson."

Rebecca tried to channel her exhilaration into looking surprised. It must have worked, because Kimmie grinned and looked mildly concerned all at once.

"You all right?" she asked.

"Yes, of course," Rebecca nodded, "I'm just...that's quite a revelation."

"Yeah, I suppose it is. Happened when my mom was at Yale. But you know, I'd never met him until today."

"What? Really?" Rebecca upended the last of the wine into Kimmie's glass. "Okay, I want to hear everything, all about your father, about today. We may need another bottle."

For most of that second bottle, Kimmie confided while Rebecca listened intently, empathetically, her grasp of Kimmie's every nuance uncanny.

Once, Kimmie remarked on it. "It's almost as if you already know what I'm going to say."

Sometimes that was true.

When the tide of confidences began to ebb, Rebecca judged the moment ripe and began to talk about her own parents, completing the exchange of intimacies. The declaration of trust.

Once again, no need to act. She let buried emotions surface on her face for the first time in a long while, using them in a righteous cause. Letting the old sorrow flow felt good. When she talked about her mother's death, Kimmie reached across the table and clasped her hand. Rebecca squeezed back. She mentioned her father's suicide to Kimmie for the first time, without getting into the circumstances.

By the end of that second bottle, Rebecca felt a warm glow, but not from the wine. Her relationship with Kimmie had transformed, jumping several levels of closeness in a single evening. The future was ablaze with possibility.

She studied Kimmie's eyes for a long second, sensing further possibility there. An openness. Rebecca knew her intuition was pretty accurate. How many more levels could she take this?

She was casting about for a way to naturally extend the evening when Kimmie did it for her.

"Look, it's only nine o'clock. My place is a few blocks away, and I've got a nice bottle of pinot just waiting to be opened."

TUESDAY, DECEMBER 8, 1998

Tom slumped in his desk chair, cradling the phone in one hand and a mug of coffee in the other. The sun was just clearing the skyscrapers, suffusing the cherry bookshelves of his study with a saffron glow.

Walter Richardson was not happy. Tom instantly sensed anger, impatience, incredulity in his father's brusque voice. Tom resigned himself. No escape.

"What exactly are you thinking? You ordered a background check? Are you actually contemplating hiring the girl?" He paused. "Did you think I wouldn't know? I may have retired as CEO, but I'm not dead. I have my sources. Certain red flags get my attention, and that girl is high on the list."

"Dad, she's a grown woman and very smart. Impressed me. Maybe I owe her a shot."

"You don't owe her a damn thing you haven't paid. She's trouble, and you know it. Did you even read the background report? I have a copy here in my hand."

Tom sighed. He should have anticipated that. Indeed, the report was bad.

Kimmie had been quietly asked to leave Morgan Stanley. She was considered…well, loose cannon didn't really do her justice. More like a loose nuke. Brilliant but not worth the trouble. Apparently, she had turned Morgan inside out in a matter of months. And there were rumors, persistent rumors, about the final straw. Whispered water-cooler stories of a sort particularly distasteful to a father, even one as remote, as theoretical, as Tom.

The scuttlebutt was that a Morgan partner had wandered into the firm's library late one evening, only to stumble upon another partner—and Kimmie—in a very compromising position. The senior partners just wanted the whole incident to vanish with as few ripples as possible. Kimmie, of course, had to go, had to be disappeared, but the firm was fearful of a sexual harassment lawsuit, or even bad publicity. So when Kimmie had mentioned an interest in working for Tom, Brooks—ignorant of the family connection—had been enlisted to smooth Kimmie's way. Morgan would smooth her way anywhere, as long as the way led out. As for her partner in crime…well, the rules were different for partners. The old goat would probably be sent to some sort of corporate reeducation camp and subjected to days on end of sensitivity and diversity training. Enough to break anyone's spirit, not that the bastard didn't deserve it.

Tom floundered for an argument, a line of attack, and realized all he had was guilt and sentiment. Neither would go far with his father.

"Dad, I know it looks bad…"

"Give it up, Tom. Don't even think about it. She's crazy trouble, just like her mother, and you know I'm right. You keep her away from my firm. I'm still the largest shareholder, and I'll fight you on this if I have to. For your own good. Call her and give her the brush-off."

"Okay, Dad, okay. I'll do what's necessary."

WEDNESDAY, DECEMBER 9, 1998

He called her in for another chat. Kimmie arrived full of smiles and bounce, clearly convinced Tom was about to offer her a job.

He studied his meticulously polished shoes until the pause became unsustainable, then looked up and cleared his throat. "Kimmie, I hope…I hope I didn't give you the wrong impression asking you back, but I felt we should speak face to face. I've thought about this a lot over the past few days, and I've decided that it's probably not a good idea for you to come work for me. Too many complications. But I'd be happy to put in a word for you anywhere else on The Street you like. Between me and Brooks, I'm sure…"

"Complications? Because I'm your daughter?"

"Well, yes, partly…"

"You hypocrite. You work in your daddy's firm." Her green eyes flashed. "How's that different?"

"Well, uh…"

"And what's so complicated about the fact I'm your daughter? What could be simpler than that? Father, daughter, father, daughter. Simple. Fucking simple."

Tom stared, thrown off balance by the anger in her face, the menace in her voice, and most of all, by the sudden mood shift. The room had slipped from sunny to volcanic in a heartbeat. He had encountered this before. Decades ago, and not since. Margo. Kimmie had Margo's craziness, only crazier.

Kimmie was just picking up steam. "Maybe it's so fucking complicated because I'm black. Would it be embarrassing to introduce your black daughter to your white-shoe golf buddies? God, so my father's a racist."

Tom sputtered. "What? How can you…"

Kimmie nodded. "Yeah, I see it clearly now. My racist daddy is ashamed of me. Kept me hidden away all this time."

"That's absurd…"

"Is it?"

"It was never about hiding you. Your mother…"

Her gaze pinned him to his chair. "Maybe I should call Page Six, *Vanity Fair*, the *Social Register*. Tell them you have a black love child you've never properly acknowledged. Maybe I could get on one of those morning talk shows, Maury or Montel or whoever."

Tom shook his head. "Kimmie, please, I know you're upset, but you're not thinking clearly. I wouldn't do that."

"Oh, really?"

"Kimmie…I know about what happened at Morgan. You get those media vultures poking around, that's bound to come out."

She stared at the floor several seconds, while her face flushed a darker coffee shade. But when she raised her eyes, they were defiant. "Good. Then they'll know you have a cocksucking black love child."

"Really, Kimmie, that wouldn't hurt me. Who would care? But you could damage yourself. If you want to work on Wall Street…"

"Fuck Wall Street, too."

He narrowed his eyes, wondering just how ugly this encounter would get. It pained him to admit his father had been right. His old guilt wrestled with the urge to call security and have her tossed out on her insolent little ass. After all, she was the employee gone wild.

Still, she was his daughter.…She did have some sort of claim on him.

"Kimmie…"

She stood and scowled down at him. "Don't worry, Daddy. I know when I'm not wanted. But one day, you'll regret this."

She turned and stalked out of his office.

He stared at her invisible wake, surprised at the emptiness she left behind.

***

Kimmie suddenly stopped sniffling and lifted her head from Rebecca's shoulder.

Rebecca straightened on Kimmie's couch and braced herself for another mood shift. As Rebecca reached for the bottle of red on the coffee table, Kimmie launched into a furious tirade about her racist daddy.

Rebecca let Kimmie's rant wash over her like angry surf while she sorted through her own emotions. This was a setback, a huge setback. Yet she knew it felt that way because she'd let herself get carried away by Kimmie's optimism. She'd let herself entertain the hope that things would fall magically into place. That never really happened. You had to wrestle them into place.

Lemons into lemonade. Her mother used to say that, it was one of the few things she recalled about her vividly. Her father would quote her teasingly, imitating her high-pitched voice whenever any little thing went wrong: "Lemons into lemonade." Rebecca was sure she would think of something. And on the upside, some things were going very well.

She was thrilled that Kimmie had called her in her hour of distress. Rebecca had become the confidante, the source of comfort. It was what she'd been working toward. They had spent hours on the phone this past week, talking every day. They had spent most of the weekend together. This was the payoff: Kimmie was hers.

When Kimmie paused for breath, Rebecca decided to jump in, before the anger mutated into some other emotion. Time to cement one more bond.

"You know, I haven't told you, but…I hate him too."

"What?"

"Your father. I have reason to hate him. He bought the company my father worked for, Madsen Labs. My father spent his career there, decades. A hard worker, loyal. Richardson laid him off, and my father jumped off the Madsen building. Richardson may as well have pushed him off that roof."

"Oh my God, Rebecca…" Kimmie looked stricken. "That's horrible. And…and you didn't…"

Rebecca shook her head. "You were so excited about reconnecting with your father…how could I…I wasn't going to tell you…"

"Oh, Rebecca. That bastard. You poor thing…"

Kimmie reached for her. As they kissed, Rebecca lost track of who was comforting whom, then realized that it no longer mattered.

THURSDAY, DECEMBER 31, 1998

Helen woke up in a shameless sprawl, still intoxicated by a night abandoned to delicious sin. She felt like a rosy-cheeked chambermaid in her master's bedroom, fulfilled, ready to serve again...

Very, very faintly, she could hear a distant, rhythmic rumbling. Or did she just imagine it? Could she really hear the surf from halfway up this mountainside? It was only then that she remembered where she was. Guadeloupe, on holiday in Tom's villa. She opened her eyes. Sunlight slipped between the wooden slats of the window blinds, painting warm stripes on her bare skin. She studied the pattern on her body, alternating bands of tan and butter yellow. A naked tigress. She smiled and turned her head.

She was alone in the bed, an indentation on the pillow next to her. A rumpled towel lay on the floor in front of the bathroom.

She peered at the clock on the night table: only 6:30. She was surprised that she herself was awake so early. The birds must have woken me, she thought. They were being so noisy. She wasn't used to so much nature. In Manhattan she serenely slept through the soothing hum of the traffic far below. Better than a white noise machine.

Her hair was tangled, and she automatically reached for a brush only to realize once again that she wasn't at home by her own bedside table. No brush. She worried for a moment that he might come in and find her disheveled. Where had she left it? Her handbag? Downstairs? She couldn't remember. Probably in the bathroom. She contemplated climbing out of bed to pee and hunt for a brush, but the prospect of such a major effort was too daunting for the moment. She settled for propping herself on one elbow and scanning the room.

Her white satin robe lay on the floor next to the bed. She considered reaching for it but dismissed the thought, kicked her legs free of the covers and stretched, luxuriating in her nakedness. She had the slightest of headaches. Not really painful, not really a hangover. More as if her sensations were echoing within her skull. Or maybe it was just the trade winds whistling in the eaves, maybe it wasn't in her head at all. She closed her eyes.

When she opened them again, Tom was standing by the bed, in his khaki shorts and golden tan. They matched his sandy hair so perfectly that he looked as if he were cast in bronze. He bent over the bed and kissed her.

"I'm a mess," she said.

"You look beautiful. Let's go looking for treasure."

She noticed that he was holding a metal detector, his latest toy.

"But I've already found my treasure," she teased him, hoping he was joking. She wasn't ready to go anywhere so early. She would much rather coax him back to bed.

"Come on, sleeping beauty. I've already been outside. It's a spectacular day."

"But why don't you come back to bed with me? It's so early. Could we go treasure hunting a bit later?"

"The greatest treasures have all been found early in the morning," he smiled.

She couldn't tell whether he was kidding. Perhaps it was true about treasures being found in the mornings. Her brain felt far too fuzzy to think it through, so she reluctantly decided to play along.

"All right. Let me dig my shorts out of my bag. Just give me a couple of minutes to get ready." She sat up slowly and swung her legs over the side of the bed.

"Why don't you come like this? No one's around. The security guys are down by the gate, and the stable hand is, well, all the way down at the stables. Mrs. Forster will be coming back to fix lunch around noon, but till then we're alone," he said.

She stood up with a delicate yawn, ran her fingers through her hair, and realized it wasn't as knotty as she had imagined. She bent down and reached for the satin robe.

"No, no," he said, "why don't you come like this?"

Chill on her skin. She was surprised by the coolness of the morning air up here on the mountain, defying the tropical latitude. It felt as if someone had taken a can of Coke out of the fridge and rolled it slowly along her body. The first moment of self-consciousness, when she stood on the porch naked but for a pair of flip-flops, faded as she realized that they were alone and unobserved. Well, she thought, I'm certainly awake now.

She followed Tom, who strode briskly down the rolling slope toward the woods. Gradually, her nakedness was beginning to feel natural. It occurred to her that it was a much more proper way to walk among the trees and bushes than dressed in linen or khakis. This was a paradise, after all. It was only appropriate to be naked. She smiled at the thought.

"So, Tom, what was that you said last night? Your family won this estate in a card game?"

He grinned. "Indeed. Used to belong to a French sugar cane planter who ended up drinking and gambling, and losing badly, on a trip to Jamaica. My great-great-grandfather—one on my father's side—was English. Had a rum distillery in Kingston. Also, clearly, was quite the gambler, and won that card game. He was in Boston later on business when he met my great-great-grandmother and decided to settle up there. Sold the distillery, but I'm glad he kept this land."

"Me too. But whatever became of the sugar cane planter?"

"Don't worry, he wasn't reduced to poverty. This was only one of several parcels of land he owned, including a good chunk of St. Barts. His descendants did all right.

"Let's start around here," Tom said, stopping suddenly. They were standing near a grove of allspice trees, overlooking the ocean below. The beach was still obscured by the shadow of the mountains. He handed her the metal detector. She half-expected him to continue with one of his full-blown history lectures. His mother's side of the family had settled in Amagansett, on eastern Long Island, in the 1600s. His father's people had deep roots in New Hampshire, in the area around Squam Lake. He loved everything about the past, especially about his family's past. He could be a downright bore if you got him started on genealogy. The metal detector was just the latest manifestation of this fascination with old things.

"I would say, start scanning there," he said.

"If you say so, Tom. But don't put too much pressure on me. I probably won't find anything."

"Well, this seems like a fine place to bury some doubloons or pieces of eight. You just have to think like a pirate." He winked.

She was beginning to feel chilly and thought that some energetic digging might warm her up, so she started sweeping the metal detector across the grass. It beeped within seconds.

"Tom, that's impossible. Why is it beeping?"

"I'd suggest you start digging and find out," he said calmly.

"But what if it's something fragile and I break it? What would someone have possibly buried here?"

"Probably just some old bottle top," he said handing her a little shovel, "but you never know, really. Could be gold coins, anything. I've heard that some of my ancestors had pretty strange habits."

She started digging, oblivious to his steady gaze and her own nakedness. About three inches below the surface, she felt something small and hard. A pebble? The ground here wasn't rocky. In the excitement of her first discovery, she tossed aside both the shovel and concern about her fingernails and pawed through the rich, loose soil.

When she uncovered the ring, she could immediately see the brightness and enormity of the diamond, even though it was covered in dirt. She gasped, picked it up, looked up at Tom in stunned confusion. Realized he was watching her face, not the ring.

SATURDAY, FEBRUARY 20, 1999

Alexandra Caswell was doing what she loved best: presiding over a victorious social event. And what could be more triumphal than a party to celebrate her daughter's engagement to Tom Richardson?

Half an hour into the party, everything seemed to be going perfectly. The couple stood in the huge banquet room of the Knickerbocker Club, on the corner of Fifth Avenue and 62nd Street, just across from Central Park.

Alexandra watched her daughter approvingly. Helen stood in the middle of the room, so elegant in her gray dress and pearls, greeting newcomers, devoting just the right amount of time to each new guest, graciously accepting their good wishes, and introducing them to the Richardson or the Caswell clan, and to her own people, of course, the Tyrkovas.

Alexandra couldn't help but notice that some guests walked in and headed directly for the bar, ignoring the couple of honor. Must be those journalists, she thought, still a bit miffed that Helen had insisted on inviting so many of them.

Alexandra could certainly understand inviting Robert Llewellyn. The top management of *The Magazine* was fine with her too. Preston, after all, had graduated from Yale together with Tom Richardson. Alexandra tolerated his presence even though she could not stand Preston's well-toned Brooklyn wife, who seemed to think that her recent nonworking status automatically transformed her into a socialite.

But Helen had insisted on inviting thirty people from *The Magazine*. "Thirty people," Alexandra had prodded her. "Who are these people anyway?"

"My colleagues," Helen had said, letting a hint of exasperation creep into her voice.

"Oh, colleagues, huh? You mean corporate comrades?"

So here they all were, her colleagues, at her party. Some of the male colleagues came without ties. During a lull in the stream of new arrivals, Alexandra took Helen aside and mentioned this.

"They're from the art department," Helen explained.

"Oh, well, then, in that case anything goes. License for anarchy, I suppose."

Reminding herself of the virtues of self-control, Alexandra struggled, swallowed hard, refrained from voicing the observation that Helen's colleagues were all drinking too much, eating too much and mingling a tad too forcefully with the other guests, as if they were interviewing them rather than making conversation. The colleagues were throwing off her appetizer count. Alexandra had opted for the tiniest of appetizers—nothing baked, greasy or involving potatoes. And while she had ordered vast amounts of alcohol, the appetizers were limited to four pieces per person. That should please the Richardsons, who, being true Wasps, always underfed their guests. But the colleagues were wolfing down appetizers as if they were dinner.

"When is the food coming?"

Alexandra recognized her mother's voice and pivoted abruptly.

Tatiana was pointedly balancing a tiny salmon crostini in the same hand that held her cigarette holder.

"This is the food, Mother," Alexandra answered, "we are not feeding an army of Russian peasants, though some of these magazine people that Helen insisted on inviting certainly eat like peasants."

For a moment, Alexandra relived her own engagement party forty years ago in Tatiana's Upper East Side apartment. Tatiana's Russian servants had served bliny with big splashes of rich sour cream and chives, and plenty of Russian vodka. She remembered several old army officers in their dress uniforms, adorned with rows of elaborate, shiny medals, and their spectacular gray moustaches. "Delicious, delicious," they had complimented Tatiana, smacking their lips with sour-cream-lined moustaches, reaching for more bliny. Alexandra remembered standing in the middle of the room, painfully aware of the differences between the two families, afraid that the more restrained Caswells would consider the Tyrkovas more ethnic than charming.

"Your guests are hungry, my darling," Tatiana insisted. "And what about music? Is there going to be any music? The youth would like to dance, I am sure…"

"This is an engagement cocktail party," Alexandra sighed, "not a ball in the Winter Palace."

"You are unfortunately right, my darling, this little gathering of yours is nothing like a ball in the Winter Palace."

Tatiana walked away and, in effect, planted her flag in one corner of the room, next to the grand piano. She started gathering her Russian contingent and scanning the room for anyone who might add character to her impromptu soiree.

She cajoled Princess Natalia's niece. "Play, my darling, play some Chopin mazurkas, let's add some mirth to this event." When the young woman demurred, Tatiana embraced her tightly and steered her toward the piano. The royal niece had no choice but to walk or be dragged along. "Play, my darling, play."

"Andrei," she gesticulated at her nephew, "come here, my boy." When Andrei obediently edged closer, she commanded, "There is nothing to drink for us here. Please, remedy this situation."

Andrei snatched a bottle of Johnnie Walker from the bar and brought it to the piano.

"And Andrei," Tatiana asked, "who is that handsome young man with the adorable brown curls standing by the bar? Have you met him?"

"Oh, him. I think his name is Jack? Jake? He's one of the magazine crowd," Andrei answered. "Seems to be drinking a lot."

"I would love to have him over here," said Tatiana. She didn't mind the magazine crowd at all. She thought they added a deliciously disreputable flavor to the otherwise dull event. If anything, it was a shame they weren't a more bohemian bunch. Poets rather than journalists.

Jake, hmm, that sounded familiar. Tatiana realized she had seen this young man—upon a second look, she decided, he wasn't so young after all, more like early forties than early thirties—with Helen at some cocktail party several years ago. Ah, yes, it was all coming back to her now. She remembered this Jake drinking heavily and openly sizing up every woman in the room, while poor Helen had pretended not to notice. She was glad Helen had done so much better for herself. The girl didn't need that much heartache. But men like Jake had their uses.

What a pleasure it would be to have this rascal by the piano, with all the young Russian beauties. Tatiana winked at Jake and beckoned him over. He hesitated, looked around in confusion as if he thought she must be signaling someone else. Tatiana smiled, nodded at him, waved again until he tentatively approached. Once he reached the piano, Jake clearly realized within seconds that this corner was shaping up as the party's center of fun. He was soon sharing the bottle of scotch with Andrei and happily peering down at the royal cleavage while the princess's niece switched from Chopin to old American standards. What was the name of that song she was playing? Ah, yes, "Falling in Love Again." Tatiana had always liked that one.

She smiled, savoring the vibrant, reckless energy of youth around her, and the promise of romance, and all kinds of improprieties....She felt almost as if she were nineteen again herself, surrounded by army officers and not too unwilling to let them shame her. She longed for a midnight escape in a horse carriage through the dark streets of St. Petersburg.

Eager for more action, Tatiana swept the room with her eyes. She spotted a man she'd been introduced to earlier but whose name she couldn't recall. Some uncle of Tom Richardson's on his mother's side, on his way back from the bar. Quite the distinguished silver fox. Tatiana waved him down. Henry, that was his name. A good, strong name, she thought. Tatiana proceeded to flirt outrageously.

Henry reminded her of her father. Tatiana had always thought of herself as her father's daughter, had grown up on the many tales about his adventures, his romances and acts of heroism, a life she had tried to emulate. Young people these days, these rappers and hippers and hoppers, they acted like they'd invented honor and respect—dissing, that was the word they used. What did they know of respect?

Her father had once kicked his servant in the face with a steel-toed riding boot, after noticing that the boot had not been polished properly. Then he insisted that the man finish polishing the shoes before picking up his teeth from the floor.

Tatiana whirled around as Helen wandered past.

"Helen! Come here. I'm so happy for you. You look so beautiful. You must know Henry here?"

Helen nodded. "Yes, we actually just met today…"

"A most charming man, Helen, most charming. I was just telling him what a wonderful boy his nephew is, but that despite that, Tom's still extremely lucky to get you."

Helen laughed. "Tatiana…that's very sweet…"

"No, really, I mean it. And not even you fully realize what a dear wonderful boy your Tom is."

"I don't?"

"No, Helen, my dream is coming true, thanks to him. One day you will inherit the family estate."

"The…which estate?"

"*The* estate. The one in Russia, near Novgorod. Tom's going to buy it for me, as a sort of wedding present. He told me. And I leave it to you."

"Why…oh my God, that's so sweet of him. But wedding present?" Helen chuckled. "Sounds more like a bride price. I didn't realize I was worth that much."

"It has made me so happy, Helen."

"And I'm happy for you, Tatiana."

Helen stepped forward and gave her a hug.

Tatiana, without breaking the embrace, reached out with her left hand and clutched Henry's sleeve. It would be criminally careless to let him slip away now.

She beamed at Helen. "This all worked out better than I could have dreamed."

Helen frowned. "What do you mean?"

"Oh, when I read your article about Tom…"

"You read that?"

"Of course, I read all your articles, my dear. Unlike your mother. And I thought, Holy Mary, Mother of God, the man's single, a billionaire, and handsome too. Not many of those in the world. And my granddaughter's already met him! So I invited him to my Easter party."

Helen blanched. "You mean…that was all a setup?" She started to laugh. "Oh, God, Tatiana, you're too much. I guess it worked, didn't it?"

Tatiana grinned. "Indeed, it did, and I'm quite proud of myself for that."

"My God, I suppose I should thank you. So, thanks. I think I have to go find Tom."

Tatiana sighed and turned back to Henry. Young people. What did they know of romance?

THURSDAY, MARCH 11, 1999

Kimmie Davis showed up for the job interview dressed like a teenage whore.

Still, it was the contrast that most disoriented Helen, the tension between outerwear and innerwear. Kimmie's overcoat was an elegant Calvin Klein in black alpaca, the sort of thing Helen might have worn herself. But as the elevator doors slid open to reveal this hopeful interviewee, so did the coat. A short, tight black leather skirt was slung so low that Helen caught herself wondering if the young lady was scrupulous about bikini waxing in winter. Then she was struck by the denial of seasonal reality. After all, it was still pretty chilly outside. A black T-shirt worn braless ended well above her diamond-studded navel, revealing a depressingly flat expanse of light brown skin. All Helen could focus on was that diamond—she felt it was winking at her.

Pretty gutsy, even for New York. After all, this wasn't an advertising agency or a hip new restaurant or the theater. It was the most influential financial magazine in the city.

The would-be reporter stepped off the elevator and grinned. "Hi. Ms. Caswell? Everybody calls me Kimmie."

Helen recovered smoothly, smiled, shook her hand. "Call me Helen," she replied. She was determined to reserve judgment until she had a sense of this young woman's qualifications. Such a brazen disregard of convention could signal audacious confidence or self-destructive craziness. Helen had to decipher that signal. Whatever it meant, Helen allowed herself to hope this interview would not be tedious.

A couple of veteran editors—old-fashioned types, the sort of guys who defiantly lit up cigars in the office despite the new smoking rules, who stormed down the hallways cursing furiously at least once a week—huddled by the coffee pot in the corner. They leered openly at Kimmie as Helen steered her past.

Helen quietly closed her office door.

"What made you think about applying to our magazine?"

She had a couple of questions for starters, so that she could launch the interview on autopilot and float a little while. Few people ever said anything that caught her attention, especially during the first few minutes. Many started into what seemed like a canned spiel.

"Are you kidding?" Kimmie stared at her, wide-eyed. "I would absolutely love to work for *The Magazine*. It would be a dream job, and if you give me a chance, I promise, I'll never let you down." Her voice was both solemn and seductive.

Helen felt the flicker of a smile play upon her face, suppressed it. So earnest. A provocative trait for such a siren. Helen found it hard not to feel a bit superior toward compulsive rebels, especially showy ones, and Kimmie's lack of propriety just reinforced Helen's sense of control. Helen was proud of her own unflappable composure, but she had learned not to expect it in others.

"I appreciate your enthusiasm, Kimmie. But why do you think we should hire you? What are you offering us?"

"Well, as you can see, I do have some journalistic background, as editor of "The D," the Dartmouth paper. And I know Wall Street. I'm aggressive, tenacious, not easily intimidated. Besides, *Wealth* magazine has been raiding your staff lately. Maybe you could use some new talent." She smiled sweetly.

Helen raised her eyebrows, wondering where Kimmie had heard that.

Kimmie answered her question without being asked. "I've been doing my homework, reading that newsletter, the one full of gossip about the financial press."

Helen found Kimmie's boldness charming. But Helen would not be hurried, and she would hire strictly according to her own judgment, as always. Out of courtesy, she occasionally saw people who sent résumés to the owner of *The Magazine*—Duncan Robert Llewellyn III, universally known as Bob. Usually the nieces and nephews of golfing buddies and such. But she had never hired one.

She had two openings and had interviewed about fifteen people to fill them. Most left her without any impression at all. She looked at their résumés and couldn't remember their faces or voices or words. It was surprising how many people were completely forgettable. Those faceless gray applicants never got hired.

Kimmie had a beautiful face: an oval framed by a long, wild mane of wavy black hair, with a delicate nose and almond-shaped green eyes. Eyes that were quite striking against her cafe au lait complexion. A few endearing freckles highlighted her cheekbones. This woman should be sashaying down a Paris runway in an evening gown, thought Helen, not jockeying for a reporting job. She idly wondered what mix of ethnicities had created such a head-turner.

Kimmie reminded her of a woman she'd once met at the U.N.—the wife of a Haitian diplomat—who was a ravishing blend of French and African blood. With an effort, Helen forced her attention back to the interview and tossed another innocuous question in Kimmie's direction.

Helen was used to young people who came in thinking they were hot stuff. She was always searching through fool's gold for the real thing, with a special eye for the brilliant eccentrics. She needed them because she was deeply convinced that *The Magazine* and its staff stood apart. They had defined a niche of their own. Of course, they measured themselves against other business magazines, but no one else had quite the same approach.

They wore what they wanted. They said what they wanted. Few really cared to go home to their families at 7 p.m., even on those evenings when they could—those who had actually managed to create families and hang on to them. Instead, they would rather write, or talk about writing. They called each other at midnight. They slept with each other.

They wielded power: The richest people in the country returned their calls, fearful of what they might write.

And they were passionate about their stories. Senior editor Meg Greenbaum had once attacked a desk with a steak knife when a mere reporter had the nerve to imply that her story had been prefigured elsewhere.

"What the fuck do you mean you read it somewhere else?" Meg had screamed, stabbing the desk. The blade had quivered in the wood, dangerously close to the reporter's hands.

"I just meant that…"

"Nobody had this story, nobody." Meg had yanked the knife free and slashed the air for emphasis, heedlessly drawing a fine line of blood on the terrified reporter's upraised forearm. "I'm the first to get a story on those bastards."

That little incident had entered the realm of *Magazine* legend.

Wealth could poach her staff and steal their ideas, but it would never be more than an imitation.

"But, of course, nobody can be quite like you…" said Kimmie.

Funny how she's saying exactly what I think, thought Helen.

Kimmie's right hand played obsessively with a lock of her hair, twirling and untwirling it around her fingers. Her legs kept crossing and uncrossing. Helen thought even Kimmie's toes must be in motion.

Her résumé was full for her twenty-seven years. A raft of summer internships, starting when she was seventeen. Managing editor of a school newspaper. Dartmouth, Wharton. A brief stint at an Internet startup, couple years at Morgan Stanley.

Kimmie Davis was willing to give up a lot of money for the $40,000 *The Magazine* paid rookie reporters. Helen had seen this sort of thing before—bankers, lawyers, analysts who got it into their heads they wanted to be journalists. Lucky for Helen. What was rarer these days was someone who wanted to work in print, rather than on the Web. Even luckier. She decided not to query Kimmie too closely on this last point. She was tired of losing reporters to Web sites run by kids who handed out stock options like candy. And it would be nice to add to the staff's diversity—the financial press was still way too white.

Kimmie came off as arrogant, but Helen didn't mind. She could see that Kimmie was no schemer. No stab in the back, just a fist in your face. Helen actually liked the in-your-face types, much better than the ass-kissers. Many people would have harbored doubts about Kimmie Davis—understandably. She may as well have worn a neon sign around her neck that flashed "trouble." Helen found that quality attractive. With a little work, that brash daring could be molded into some fine reporting.

***

The subject line: "!!! SHE TOOK THE BAIT"

Rebecca Morgan swore softly but with feeling as she opened the email. Blank, no message beyond the one in the subject line. Sent from one of those new BlackBerry things. That was the way Kimmie usually wrote her emails. She had no patience for typing longer messages in the main field. Rebecca had spent only a few minutes in the restroom. No doubt Kimmie had tried and failed to reach her cell phone during that stretch. So she had fired off a message, unable to restrain herself.

Rebecca deleted the message immediately. How many times did she have to warn that girl? E-mail left an electronic trail. She knew that Kimmie shrugged off this cloak-and-dagger stuff as paranoia.

Back when Kimmie had fed her confidential information from Morgan Stanley, the only risk to Rebecca had been losing a good source. Now Kimmie was integral.

Rebecca picked up her cell phone and dialed Kimmie's cell, almost instantly heard Kimmie's cheerful "hello." Kimmie always said hello in a way that made you feel she was waiting to hear from you. Part of her dangerous charm.

"I swear, if you email me again…"

"Okay, okay…"

"Where are you?"

"I'm at a coffee place around the corner from *The Magazine*."

"Be careful what you say, don't speak too loud, that place is always lousy with *Magazine* people....How'd it go?"

"Peachy," Kimmie whispered theatrically. "Helen loved me, she wants me, who wouldn't?"

"Don't be too sure of yourself. What did you wear?"

"That black coat, the alpaca. Don't worry, mama, I made an impression. Gotta go, talk to you later." Kimmie hung up.

WEDNESDAY, MARCH 17, 1999

At the end of the meeting Helen told them about her new hires.

"Kimmie Davis." She recited the highlights from Kimmie's résumé.

"You said her name was Kimmie Davis?" Bruce Buccino asked. He was the only one who took the hiring of junior reporters seriously. Preston trusted her, and no one else cared.

Bruce cared about everything in *The Magazine*, whether it was any of his business or not. He would regularly open the current issue in front of Helen, place his finger on the masthead and go down, name by name, commenting on every person. He usually went: stupid, stupid, stupid. Sometimes he would say: This person is even more stupid than everybody else you hired. On rare occasions: not stupid.

He started grilling Helen now: "Why do we need another Ivy League princess? Why isn't she going to the Web site like the rest of them? Isn't she drawn by the smell of stock options? Are you getting us another rich kid?"

Years ago, when they were young reporters, Helen and Bruce had attended a business lunch at the Four Seasons with the chairman of a powerful company. The chairman had ordered tuna. Bruce had said he'd have the same thing. The waiter set Bruce's plate down first, and Bruce protested: He must have brought him the wrong dish.

"This is your tuna," the waiter had insisted.

"Are you sure? It should be pink and flaky."

Meanwhile, the waiter half turned and set the chairman's plate in front of him. It bore the same grilled slab as Bruce's plate. The chairman looked puzzled and uncomfortable. The waiter realized what was going on and gave Bruce a patronizing look mixed with pity. Then Bruce knew. Everyone at the table knew... Bruce had never seen grilled tuna. The only tuna he had ever eaten had come from a can.

"Maybe it's too overdone," Helen said, trying to help Bruce out.

"Should've ordered it rare." But Bruce didn't appreciate the gesture.

"Let's just eat. It's fine," he muttered.

After that lunch Bruce had written an angry story about the chairman's mismanagement of the company.

Now he wouldn't let go of Kimmie. "Kimmie Davis, Kimmie Davis," he kept repeating, as if trying to remember something.

"Is she this leggy young thing with a navel ring I saw you with by the elevator the other day?" Preston interjected. "That getup sure could work for us when she's interviewing the dot-commers, but I hope she won't dress like that for the Old Economy types."

Jake Rosenberg perked up, suddenly alert. He reminded Helen of a hunting dog who'd just caught a whiff of rabbit.

Bruce looked at Jake with disdain. He frowned, muttering, "Kimmie Davis, Kimmie Davis…" Finally, he shrugged and shook his head. "Let's just hope she's not stupid."

***

As Bruce ducked through the library entrance, Linda looked up from her desk, her eyes narrowing. He leaned over and whispered: "Have one of your librarians do a search for me."

Linda grimaced. Nobody was supposed to call them librarians anymore. These days they were information specialists, presiding over screens filled with precious data, dispensing information only they knew how to access, and striking deals with database and Internet companies. Bruce had no patience for their pretentious insecurity, and he enjoyed needling Linda.

"What should we be looking for?" she asked coldly.

"Search in the law magazines, *American Lawyer, ABA Journal,* anything like that. I'm interested in any mention of a young female lawyer named Davis."

Linda snickered. "That doesn't narrow it down much."

Bruce refused to rise to the bait. "Not just a passing mention, some sort of profile or bio, maybe with a photo. Oh, and she's probably black."

Linda raised her eyebrows. "Probably?"

"It's…" Bruce shook his head. "It's complicated, I can't be sure, but yes, probably. That might make it easier to find. Young black woman, possibly something of a pioneer in the legal world at the time. If it mentions that she has a daughter named Kimberly, that's definitely her. Start with 1975 through 1990. And don't tell anybody what you're doing."

By five minutes after four, Bruce stood in front of Linda's desk again, perusing one of the first issues of *American Lawyer,* from the early 1980s. This was it, what he'd remembered—he'd read this issue when it was new. It featured a roundup of a few dozen young Turks, leading lawyers for the next generation. One of them was Margo Davis. Yale. Harvard Law. *Law Review.* And by virtue of being a black woman, a bit of a trailblazer. Not only that, but a single mother. With a nine-year-old daughter named Kimberly.

Bingo.

He wondered idly how the hell she'd gotten through law school as a single mom. Hmm. Margo Davis had specialized in constitutional law. By 1982 she was already arguing important cases for the ACLU. Certainly an overachiever. But not the income-maximizing, white-shoe kind.

Bruce did the arithmetic. When Margo Davis's daughter was conceived, she would have been…

He looked up, his eyes wide with inspiration.

"Yearbooks. Linda, don't we have some college yearbooks in the stacks?"

"Well, yes, but only Ivy League. It's one of the quirkier aspects of our collection."

"Yale?"

"Sure, back to 1946."

"Fantastic. I just need to see the early '70s."

"Okay, let me show you where we keep those."

Twenty minutes later, alone in the mustiest, most obscure corner of the library, Bruce found it. More than he'd dared hope for. He had to fight to keep himself from letting out a yell of triumph.

The 1973 Yale *Banner.* A black-and-white candid shot, bare trees and scattered patches of snow forming a backdrop for the happy couple. A young but unmistakable Margo Davis in a navy pea coat, laughing as a young white man grabbed her from behind and nuzzled her ear. Bruce stared in disbelief. He was very young, sporting a ponytail and an earring, but recognizable. My God. Tom Richardson.

His mind spun wildly, sorting through implications. This proved nothing, of course, but it was more than suggestive. So much made sense. It could explain why Margo Davis felt no need to chase big bucks. And Helen…yes. It all fit.

He came charging out of the stacks, clutching the old yearbook like a trophy.

"Linda! Linda, I could kiss you."

She leaned away from him. "Please, that…that won't be necessary."

"Copies, I must copy something."

She pointed toward the copy machine, eyeing him warily.

Bruce hummed tunelessly along with the machine. He could almost feel the power accumulating within him, like an electric charge.

FRIDAY, MARCH 19, 1999

11:25 p.m.

Kimmie stood behind an ancient oak near the edge of Central Park, shadowed from the glow of the streetlamps. Rebecca faced her, their noses six inches apart, sharing the tree's shadow. Quietly fussing like a mother hen, Rebecca ran through the plan for the hundredth time, then made Kimmie repeat the story they'd concocted once more. Kimmie's stomach fluttered, then sank into nausea. She flashed on the school play in seventh grade, when she'd played Cleopatra. Her first of many acting roles in school. Waiting to step onstage, she'd been sure she would throw up. When the curtain rose, the nausea vanished. It was always like that.

Crouching, her back against the tree, she pulled a half-pint of vodka from her purse, took one last swig and handed the bottle to Rebecca. Kimmie hiked up her skirt and tore her pantyhose to shreds. She stood and assessed her work. Rebecca reached down and ripped a long tear in Kimmie's skirt, then turned it around so the zipper was in front. Kimmie untucked her blouse and ripped it open—all the buttons popped. As Kimmie mussed up her hair, Rebecca stepped back and surveyed her critically, then nodded.

"Costume's ready," she said. "Now for the special effects."

Kimmie shivered, zipped up her jacket, turned to face the tree, took a deep breath. "Make it good the first time."

Rebecca grabbed her by the hair and smashed her right cheek hard against the oak, not head-on but at an angle. Kimmie swore under her breath, startled at the sharpness of the pain, gently touched her face, brushed off a few bits of bark.

She paused, waiting for the pain to dull a bit before she absorbed any more. Then she stepped away from the tree and nodded. Rebecca's gloved fist smacked into her mouth. It hurt but, she knew right away, not enough. No blood, though she could feel her lower lip start to swell a little.

Rebecca inspected her. "Okay, Kimmie, one more time, I'm being too careful. I don't want to knock out any teeth, but we want blood."

This time Rebecca hit her so hard Kimmie stumbled backward. The pain left her dizzy. She sat on the grass and leaned shakily against the tree. But the thin, warm stream of blood that flowed down her chin and dripped onto her clothes gave her a sense of accomplishment. She smeared some blood across her face.

She had thought that the tears would be the tough part, but she proved herself wrong. Between the pain and her stage fright, she was already on the verge. So she slapped her lacerated cheek and poked at her lip a few times, and the tears began to flow.

Rebecca cradled her own hand, flexed it a few times, then grinned. She zipped up her leather jacket, lifted a backpack off the grass and slung it over one shoulder. "Now or never, Kimmie girl. Break a leg."

Kimmie got up. Rebecca sent her off with a gentle slap on the ass.

She ran two blocks as fast as her boots allowed—she wanted to be out of breath—then dashed across Fifth Avenue and through the entrance to an apartment building, almost bouncing off the uniformed doorman. He was short, wiry, dark, sported a mustache. Gotta be the guy Rebecca meant. Then she saw his name tag: Michael. Yes! She almost smiled in relief, then caught herself. As far as she could see, there was no one else in the lobby, but from her angle she couldn't be certain. Careful to stay in character, she launched into her spiel.

"Please…please help me…"

"My God." The doorman stepped back, wide-eyed. "What happened to you? I mean—never mind. You must be Rebecca's friend. Relax, place is deserted. Really, you okay?"

"Yeah, I'm fine."

"Ready to go?"

She nodded.

"Okay. Stand over here, so he can see you over my shoulder." He took her arm and led her gently to a panel of buttons set in the wall, surmounted by the lens of a video camera. Kimmie unzipped her jacket and held the front of her blood-stained blouse together with one hand, ignoring the doorman as he sneaked a peek.

He buzzed the penthouse. Tom Richardson's voice, sounding slightly annoyed, came over the tinny speaker. "Yes?"

"Mr. Richardson, I'm sorry to bother you, but this young lady says she's…"

"Kimmie?" Tom must have looked up at his security video. "Kimmie, is that you? My God, are you all right?"

Kimmie sobbed incoherently.

"Well, send her up, Michael, send her up right away."

He was waiting by the elevator, his eyes wary. She sobbed again, and this time—it was getting easier—the tears flowed freely. She slumped against his chest, staining his white shirt with blood. Reflexively, he caught her in his arms and made reassuring noises as he led her inside. "There, there. You're okay now. You'll be fine."

She caught a quick, jumbled impression of the apartment as he led her to a sofa. Spectacular views across the park. Well-worn Oriental rugs scattered on polished oak floors. Mahogany shelves sagging with books. Eclectic furniture—she noted a pair of French club chairs in burgundy leather, a few touches of Victoriana and a wooden Shaker table. Stuff that looked as if it had been in the family for decades. Probably had.

He sat her down, stepped back and studied her a moment. "My, you're quite a mess. You need a doctor? I have a friend, very discreet. He'll even make a house call."

She shook her head. "Thanks, but no. Not necessary." She could see the questions in his face, but for the moment he refrained from asking them. She admired his restraint.

He disappeared for a second and returned with a T-shirt. "Here, why don't you wash up and put this on. Bathroom's over there. I'll get some ice for that lip. And a brandy."

"Brandy," she repeated dully. "Yeah, thanks."

It was only when they were both seated on the sofa, brandies in hand, that he finally asked. "Okay, Kimmie. One, what the hell happened to you tonight? And two, what are you doing here?"

She could see his guard was up. Well, of course it would be. She had to make this good. "Listen, uh…first, I want to apologize. For what I said last time…last time I saw you. I didn't mean it, I was angry…angry and hurt and I…I have this temper. Like Mom."

She sighed. "Sometimes it gets the better of me. I say things I don't mean…and I didn't, any of it, I was just pissed off. I'm sorry."

He nodded cautiously. "Okay. Apology accepted. Forget it, never happened. Behind us. Now, what happened to you?"

She shrugged. "I went out on a date. Hazards of the single life, I guess."

His eyes narrowed. "Some date."

"Yeah. Guy was a jerk. Our first date, and I'd just decided it would be our last. He's a bond trader, good-looking but full of himself, you know? By the end of dinner, I was bored silly but trying to be polite. He insisted on cruising around in this absurd limo he'd rented for the evening, some kind of stretch SUV. Wanted to go clubbing, he said. Then…

"I didn't encourage him or anything. I mean, I don't pretend to be the Virgin Mary, but it was our first date and…and I like to be seduced. Unless I'm doing the seducing. This asshole couldn't be bothered, I guess. Next thing I know his hand's up my skirt. When I tried to push it away, he just went nuts. Berserk. Scary. Then we were wrestling in the backseat, slapping, hitting. He called me things…"

She blinked back tears that now welled up almost of their own accord.

Tom's jaw muscle twitched. "Where was the driver through all this?"

"Well, the partition was up, of course, and it's pretty soundproof back there. Anyway, we stopped at a light, I kneed him in the balls, got out the door and ran like hell."

She sipped her brandy, flinched as it stung her lip. "I've got to start going out with artists or something. These Wall Street guys are all assholes." Pause. "Sorry, I didn't mean…"

Tom waved off her apology, signaling her to go on.

"I ran, just blindly for a while. Stopped at the park. Realized I was only a couple blocks from your place. I knew you lived here—did my homework before I looked you up. So…I…I don't know. I didn't know what to do. Didn't want anyone to see me like this, didn't want to be alone, didn't want to go home…

"I know I'm imposing. I'll just finish my drink and be on my way."

"No, no, not at all, you should stay here tonight. It's late, and you've had a very rough evening. You'll stay over in the guest room. We can talk some more in the morning."

SATURDAY, MARCH 20, 1999

2:30 a.m.

Michael Andros slumped behind the desk in the lobby and stared at the television he had tuned to ESPN, the sound muted. It was showing highlights from the "World's Strongest Man" contest: Mutants on steroids were flipping cars down a course, carrying boulders around, pulling a line of three tractor-trailer cabs along a road.

He yawned—from the boredom, not fatigue. He was used to the graveyard shift. As the building's youngest doorman, he got stuck with it a lot. Luckily, he didn't mind much. Sometimes he even volunteered for it. The shift had its advantages. The TV was one perk—the doormen weren't supposed to turn it on during the day. The quiet was another. Few people bugged him, and minimal contact with the residents was a definite plus.

Restless, he glanced at his watch, pushed his visored cap higher up on his forehead and opened the *New York Post* to the sports section, where he'd squirreled away a porn magazine. He began to flip through the pages, idly contemplating the lewd images and acrobatic positions, his thoughts tinged with anticipation. She'd promised to come tonight.

She was the only exciting thing in his life, the only thing that made him feel young. Hell, he was barely into his thirties, and his life wasn't so bad in many ways. He had a secure job, union wages, benefits, fat tips at Christmastime. Yet he was already starting to feel middle-aged, to sense the possibilities of life closing down around him. He could almost imagine himself turning into one of the old guys on the building staff, and he shuddered at the thought. Maybe it was just the fact that he had two school-age kids now. Or the cramped apartment in Brooklyn, only blocks from his parents' house in Windsor Place. Or the vision of life unreeling before him as an endless series of family get-togethers with his Italian cousins on his mother's side. Or the high school sweetheart who'd turned into a slightly plump wife. He felt a faint twinge of guilt at that last thought. He genuinely liked his wife, even still loved her in his way. But what the hell—a man needs a little spice in his life. The guilt passed like the shadow of a scudding cloud.

Rebecca had grown up a couple miles away, in ritzier Brooklyn Heights, then moved to Park Slope, a dozen blocks and a world away from him, when she was fifteen. Her family was on the leading edge of the wave of gentrification that swept the neighborhood in the 1980s.

Rebecca had descended on St. Saviour High School like a dark conquering angel, a raven among owlish nuns, triggering hoots of flustered disapproval. All the more devastating for being only dimly aware of her power, she had flustered the boys even more—and according to rumor, some of the girls as well. She had never been one of the "popular" girls in a mainstream sense. Too intense and heedless of high school hierarchy for that, she had blazed a path across disparate worlds, at ease in them all. She had quickly come to dominate the literary magazine, the school newspaper, the yearbook and the bohemian crowd that staffed those publications. That same crowd had snickered when she joined the computer club, then the chess club, becoming the face that launched a thousand geeky fantasies. Rebecca had shrugged the snickers off, uncaring. That was the source of her power and freedom: She didn't care. Many envied her for that, and some worshipped her.

Michael had worked on the yearbook and had worshipped her for years— well, junior and senior years—at a safe distance, his eyes tracing her smoldering path down the school's endless hallways. And she had known it, had grown comfortable with her own magnetic field over time. He could see the knowledge in her eyes. Sometimes, in the cafeteria or chemistry lab, he had stood close enough to inhale a lungful of her scent. Orange blossoms and musk.

All too often, people you knew in high school were such a disappointment when encountered decades later. Grown flabby and dull. Not Rebecca.

He stood, stretched, glanced at his watch yet again. Maybe he'd step outside for a smoke.

She walked through the door.

Tight jeans and a jacket of butter-soft leather wrapped around her small, slim frame. A backpack that seemed too heavy for her. Black kid-leather gloves, even softer than the jacket. That mass of dark curls. That lopsided grin. "Hi, Mikey."

No one else called him that. If anyone else had tried, he would've stopped it cold. He didn't mind it from her. "Hi. I was starting to wonder if you'd show."

"You know I always keep my promises. How'd it go tonight?"

He shrugged. "Smooth as silk."

Her crooked grin grew wider. "You've done great, Mikey. Let's get out of sight. I brought you a treat."

Eagerly, he led the way back to the huge freight elevator. Once they'd stepped in and he'd closed the doors behind them, she reached into her pack for a compact. "Time to powder our noses," she said as she carefully tapped lines of white powder from a small vial onto the mirror.

"Good stuff?" he asked.

"Of course, real Peruvian flake. You know me, only the best. After you." She handed him a small plastic straw.

He inhaled two lines and savored the tingling numbness in the back of his throat. His senses sharpened, his thoughts raced. As she finished snorting her lines and bent over to put away her compact, he ran his fingertips gently along the curve of her hip.

She swatted his hand, stood and smiled. "Now, now. Business before pleasure. But here." She tossed him the half-full vial. "Have a wild weekend."

"Thanks. I will."

"Let's go up."

"Okay." He pulled the lever and the elevator climbed slowly toward the seventeenth floor, just below the penthouse.

"And the security tape?" she asked.

"No sweat. Like I told you, they reuse the same tape every seven days anyway. But just in case, I'll replace tonight's tape with a blank one before I go off shift."

The doors opened to reveal a dim hallway carpeted in gray.

He led her to the end of the hall, just past the garbage chute, and opened a small access panel in the wall. Behind the panel was a shaft full of wiring, phone lines and coaxial cables.

"Fuckin' A, Mikey," she whispered. "This is perfect."

She fumbled with her pack, extracted an electronic device the size of a hardcover book. "You say his security guys swept last week?"

"Yeah. Should be another few months if they keep to the pattern."

She placed the device in the shaft, secured it with duct tape, extended an antenna, plugged something in, flipped a switch. "There, done." She closed the panel.

"So," he asked, "you bugging this guy or what?"

She gave him a look.

He nodded. "Yeah, okay, I get you." What did he care? He knew she was some sort of reporter digging up some kind of dirt on the billionaire, and he figured that was exactly what the press should be doing. Anybody as rich as Richardson had to be a son of a bitch. Deserved whatever he got.

Descending in the freight elevator, she turned to him, her voice husky. "Time for your reward."

He gave a little shiver and stopped between floors.

They kissed as he unbuttoned her shirt.

She pushed him back into a corner, reached down and unbuckled his belt.

Unzipped him.

He slid into the smooth leather of her glove.

Later, as he stood out on the sidewalk, finally savoring a cigarette, he checked his watch and realized with a start that her entire visit hadn't lasted more than forty minutes. Fingering the vial in his pocket, he contemplated the weekend ahead. He felt good, up, ready for more. Alive.

***

2:45 a.m.

Ensconced in the guest room, Kimmie sat silently in bed, gazing idly out the window at the hulking mass of the Metropolitan Museum of Art. She figured she was done with the hardest part—though not the risky part—but the waiting was proving surprisingly difficult. Sitting quietly in the dark, doing nothing, did not come naturally. And the relief she had felt at finding herself alone in this room, combined with the effects of the brandy, conspired to produce a deep, seductive sleepiness. Sleep, of course, was out of the question.

Carefully, she reached over to the night table, found her purse and fished out a small inhaler. Clicking it open, she took a quick snort of cocaine, then tapped out a little extra and rubbed it on her tender lip.

She listened to the stillness for more than an hour after the last sounds of Tom's puttering around the apartment had died away. She checked her watch: 2:45. Zero hour, Kimmie girl. Tense as she was, the call to action came as an immense release.

Wrapped in the terry-cloth robe Tom had provided, she opened the guest room door, giving thanks that the hinges were well-oiled and that the master bedroom was on the opposite side of the sprawling penthouse. She moved slowly, her bare feet testing for creaky floorboards. Move like a cat, Kimmie girl. Like a cat. And remember to breathe.

She found the study easily enough—it was gently illuminated by the flickering light of a screensaver on Tom's PC. She exhaled a silent prayer of thanks that he hadn't bothered to turn the computer off. The damn things always beeped like bleating sheep when booting up.

She pulled a floppy disk from the pocket of her robe and slipped it into the proper slot. The disk drive whirred softly, and a disk icon popped onto the screen. Two double-clicks of the mouse, a five-second wait, and the Trojan horse program had installed itself in the utilities folder under an innocuous name. Rebecca was a bit of a geek, surprisingly comfortable with computers, although she didn't look the part. She had downloaded the basic program from a hacker Web site, then tweaked it to suit their purposes. Kimmie ejected the disk and returned it to her pocket. So easy.

Now. Step two. From her other pocket she extracted what appeared to be an ordinary electrical multiplug adapter. Cautiously, she knelt and peered behind Tom's desk, searching for an electrical outlet. Ah. Perfect. She unplugged two lamps, plugged the adapter into the outlet, then plugged the lamps back in through the adapter. She smiled to herself, marveling at the gadgets one could buy these days. The thing actually functioned just fine as an adapter, and the tiny bug inside worked off the juice from the outlet. No batteries required. Hidden in plain sight. She had to admire its elegance. Its transmission range was limited, so the signal would need a boost from a larger transceiver within the building. But that was Rebecca's job.

Back in the guest room, mission accomplished, she slipped into her tattered skirt, the T-shirt Tom had given her and her jacket. She would carry her boots as far as the elevator. Better not to face him in the morning. Tom might accept her actions on this night as an aberration on her part, in the stress of the moment—a complete change of character would be pushing it. But she'd have to leave a note.

Pen in hand, she paused, hung up on the salutation. Should she call him Tom? None of the possibilities seemed right. Finally, she plunged ahead.

Dad,
Thanks for everything, you were great. I don't
mean to be rude, I just can't sleep and I want
to get home. Don't worry, I'm fine. Thanks again.
Kimmie

She stole silently out the front door and paused to exhale. She felt the slightest hint of a twist in her gut, but she put it down to nerves and the cold pizza she'd eaten for dinner. In the elevator, she pulled on her boots as she descended. The lobby was completely deserted—no sign even of the doorman. Fine with her.

Out the door and she was free, basking in the anonymity of the streets. She'd pulled it off. Exhilaration hit her, and she decided to walk some of it off before flagging a cab. A crescent moon was setting behind the Met. What a fine crisp night.

***

The radiator in Rebecca's apartment hissed and gurgled. Kimmie sighed, sat up on the couch and pulled off her sweater. Already too damn hot in here. Typical overheated prewar apartment building. She stood, walked over to the radiator and opened the window above it to the chilly gray sky.

Rebecca sat in a corner of the room at her battered old oak desk, headphones on her ears, twiddling the dials on a piece of electronic equipment with all the intensity of a safecracker. Oblivious to Kimmie's restlessness. She'd been futzing with the fucking thing all morning.

Kimmie was just as anxious as Rebecca was to find out if their scheme would really work, at least this part of it. Here on Columbus Avenue, in the West 70s, they were almost directly across Central Park from Tom Richardson's apartment. They should be well within transmission range, without a lot of buildings in the way. But this was boredom squared.

Kimmie stepped into the tiny kitchen and started to pour herself yet another cup of coffee even though she was really too warm to drink hot coffee. Sudden movement in her peripheral vision made her stop in mid-pour. She glanced out through the archway to the living room. Rebecca was sitting ramrod straight, her face rapt, one hand cupping an earphone. The other hand was pushing the record button on the microcassette machine.

Then Kimmie was at her elbow, coffee and boredom forgotten. "It's working? It's fucking working? Put it on speaker, I want to hear."

Rebecca tapped a button and Richardson's voice echoed from a tinny speaker. "No, I agree with you on this one, Dad, I don't see how we can back down…"

Oh, this was perfect, he was on the phone with his father.

They listened intently and quickly caught the gist of the conversation. Some dispute about compensation with a group of venture capital guys.

"Huh," Rebecca said. "Richardson just hired that bunch a few months ago. Trying to buy some Internet investment savvy. Everybody needs some these days. But those VC types are real cowboys. Seems dumb to quibble over pay. Can't end well.

"But it works." She grinned at Kimmie. "Works great. Now we hope they talk investments. This just isn't relevant. Stupid move, though. Too bad we can't use it."

"Yeah," Kimmie muttered. "Too bad."

MONDAY, APRIL 5, 1999

Tom handed her a mug of steaming coffee, then disappeared into his walk-in closet.

"Thanks, dear. Mmm." Helen took a sip, set the coffee down and tried to focus on her eye shadow. No matter how carefully she planned and prepared, there was something disorienting about starting the workweek from Tom's place. She always seemed to forget some little thing. And there were small annoyances…like the light. The light in his bedroom was never quite right for applying her makeup. Especially eye shadow. If she weren't careful, she could show up at work looking like Vampirella.

The mahogany armoire was open, and the TV that Tom kept tucked inside it was tuned to CNBC. Maria Bartiromo was bantering with whatshisname and whosit about the prospects of a company Helen had never heard of before. Microfreak? Could it really be called that? Apparently, its stock had tripled in six months.

Tom emerged from the closet, now fussing with his necktie. "Microfreak, huh? I don't know, seems a little shaky to me."

"Microfreak? Why do they call it that?"

"Huh? Oh. It's spelled F-R-E-Q, like frequency. Microfreq. They make little gizmos for fiber-optic networks. Specialized market, very few suppliers, which is why the stock's hot. But also few customers. Almost all their revenue comes from Nortel, and I hear Nortel's flirting with another supplier. If they ever lose that contract, well…"

He flashed Helen his mischievous grin. "…then Microfreq is Microfucked."

TUESDAY, APRIL 6, 1999

Helen often prowled the cubicles in the late morning, chatting up the reporters. She found it a surprisingly effective way to take the staff's pulse.

Now she stopped by Maureen's cube. The redhead was half-buried by stacks of SEC filings and analyst reports on the telecom sector. Microfreq's annual report was open on her lap.

"Microfreq, huh?"

"Yeah, I'm just doing a short piece. Front-of-the-book thing. Still, it takes all this…" She waved her hand at the piles of paper. "Everybody loves this stock."

"Really?" Helen raised one eyebrow. "I'd be careful. Can't hurt to be a skeptic. Take a good look at that Nortel contract."

Maureen smiled. "Okay, I'm impressed. You know something?"

Helen shrugged. "Heard a rumor that relationship could be shaky."

Maureen nodded. "All right, sure. I'll do that. Thanks."

SATURDAY, APRIL 10, 1999

Rebecca sat alone in her panties and T-shirt, hunched over a small notebook, scribbling even though the cassette machine was recording. The radiator clanked and hissed loudly. She turned up the volume on the receiver and tucked some stray curls under her headphone strap.

Tom Richardson was on the phone with his father. "...Yes, Dad, we finished unwinding that position last week. Made 38 percent on that one....I agree, a lot of froth out there...Oh, yes, in fact, we're shorting Microfreq, as of last Monday. Definitely overhyped....No, it's a modest position, it's covered. And I don't think we'll have to hold it too long....Okay, I'll let you go then, have fun. I'll see you tomorrow."

Rebecca sipped from her fourth cup of coffee that morning. So Richardson was betting that Microfreq's stock price would fall. She wished she could use that, but she couldn't see how. It sounded as if he'd already placed the bet, not like a big position that he might build slowly, over weeks or months. No point in planting a story now unless she could travel back in time.

Too bad.

She stood and stretched, decided a fifth cup was unwise. She started to empty the dishwasher, then paused to turn on some music. Dylan's most recent comeback. An old man, sick of love, muttering darkly at a strange world. It soothed her as she puttered about the apartment.

Once she had put things in acceptable order, she pulled on shorts and sneakers and went out for a quick run in the park. By two o'clock, she had showered, eaten a light lunch and read the *Times* thoroughly.

Finally, the buzzer, only half an hour late. Kimmie.

A minute later, she was sprawled across Rebecca's couch, yawning and twirling her hair around her finger. "God, I'm tired. Up half the night."

"Some tea?"

"Sure, that'd be great."

Rebecca put the water on to boil. "So, how're things with Jake?"

"Peachy. Spent last night at his place. Seeing him tonight, too."

"Monopolizing his time already? That was quick. Be careful not to peak too soon."

"Don't worry, mama. Got him eating out of my hand. Among other places." She giggled lewdly.

"Nice."

"Speaking of appetites, you got anything I can use yet?" Kimmie asked. "Need to start feeding him stories."

Rebecca sighed. "Maybe, but...not just yet."

"What does that mean? We've been listening for weeks..."

"We?"

"Well...um...you..."

"That's right. And it's not like we bugged his office. We don't know every move he makes, just bits and pieces. The timing has to be incriminating, you know that. We have to catch him building up a large position so we have time to plant a story."

"Yeah, yeah, I know. Sorry, I'm just itchy for some action."

"Patience. Not your strong suit, I know. But I told you this would take a few months. We'll get our man. By the end of summer, we should be ready to move."

"End of summer?"

"That's my prediction." Rebecca poured hot water into two mugs. "I've got a hint of something. Forsooth, the software company? Richardson's slowly selling off a big position there. And he hinted that he might short the stock once he's unloaded it. Not sure why though, he was kind of cryptic. Gonna do some reporting, see what I can find."

Kimmie sat up, eager. "That sounds good."

"Possibly." Rebecca looked up. "Relax. Believe me, as soon as we've got something we can use, you'll be the first to know."

"Yes, mama."

MONDAY, MAY 3, 1999

Helen sat up groggily, pulled on a robe and stumbled toward the smell of coffee. As usual on a weekday, Tom was up first, already showered, shaved and dressed, hunched over *The Wall Street Journal*. The small TV in the corner of the kitchen was tuned to CNBC. She didn't even really need to be awake yet—the magazine world got going so much later than the financial world— but the fresh-brewed coffee had lured her into consciousness.

He looked up. "Morning, dear."

She patted his shoulder absently as she eased past his chair and poured herself an oversized mug. "If you say so."

He grinned. "I do say so. Here, top this off for me, would you?" He extended an arm, mug in hand. "Thanks."

He glanced back at the TV and snorted. The anchor was starting to interview a CEO. "God, not Jonathan Almond. Look at this clown fawning over him, you'd think he was Einstein."

Helen peered at the screen. The graphics at the bottom showed the company's name, Cluster Node, and the stock's recent climb. More than doubled since October, and unlike so many companies these days, this one had actual revenues. "I gather you think he's no genius."

"He was in a couple of classes with me at Yale. Solid gentleman's C's. Otherwise, struck me as a nonentity."

"Hmpf. Still, it's certainly a hot stock. I thought it was supposed to be a conservative way to play the Internet. Real assets, all those server farms."

"That's the problem, it's too hot. And they've taken on a lot of debt to build those server farms. Would've been a good idea a year ago, but now..."

He looked thoughtful. "You know, you hear people joke about using this show as a counterindicator, shorting every stock they hype. But it might actually work."

Helen smiled and downed her coffee. "I'm off to shower. Maybe you should spend the day backtesting that strategy."

Tom chuckled. "You know, I just might."

MONDAY, MAY 10

Helen was in the ladies' room, touching up her lipstick and taking a two-minute break from a runaway day. A couple of young reporters were talking. Andrea, the dark-haired one, mentioned she was writing up Cluster Node. A short, positive piece for the front of the book.

Helen frowned. Should she warn her? Why not? She wasn't conveying any information, much less the source of it. She didn't have any real information to convey. She was merely urging some contrarian skepticism, always a good quality in a reporter.

"You know, Andrea, I'd take a careful look at that company. They've piled on a lot of debt."

"Well, yes, that's true, but the stock..."

"Exactly. How hot is too hot? All I'm saying is, take a good, hard look before you leap."

"Okay." Andrea nodded thoughtfully. "I'll do that. Thanks, Helen."

Helen took one last critical look in the mirror, drew a deep breath and plunged back out the door into the day's chaos. Three reporters were out sick with a nasty springtime bug that was sweeping the office. A fourth was in Chicago for a family funeral, and a fifth was on vacation in Greece. Twenty percent of her reporters out. She was juggling frantically, trying to even out the extra load everyone had to take on and still deploy people efficiently. She wanted all her reporters playing to their strengths. This was no day to broaden horizons by pulling someone out of a familiar beat.

Kimmie dashed around a corner, almost colliding with Helen. She dodged and twirled past, stopped and grinned. "Sorry. Oh, Helen, I'm helping Jake with a little front-of-the-book piece, so I was thinking I might as well check it too, okay? See ya."

She spun away and darted off before Helen could respond.

What the hell, it made sense. Kimmie already knew the story, and Jake's stuff was easy. Not worth a second thought.

MONDAY, MAY 17, 1999

Sitting at her desk, Helen finished scribbling, looked up and studied the words on the writing pad with a growing satisfaction. Good, the phrasing seemed fine to her. Now she just had to run it past her mother and Tom before placing an order for the wedding invitations. Feeling slightly guilty about focusing on her wedding rather than work for the past hour, she turned to her computer screen and started reading stories she was about to assign to fact-checkers.

Every fact in every story they published was checked by a reporter. The reporter called back sources, listened to taped interviews, studied the annual reports again, made sure the names were spelled correctly and that no biased sources were used. Or at least that any biases were clear.

In *The Magazine*, reporters toiled at the bottom of the editorial pyramid, doing much of the grunt work and catching most of the shit. Most of them saw fact-checking as paying dues before being promoted to writers or editors. They tried to check stories as quickly as possible, so they would have more time left for their own writing.

Kimmie Davis, for one, had turned into one of the fastest fact-checkers on earth, and some of her exploits had become instant legends. She got through to one source on a cell phone while he was attending a funeral. Tables that required the checking of dozens of numbers were done in an hour. Some writers and editors suspected that she cut corners, but nobody could prove anything, and so far they had no reason to complain. In her two months at *The Magazine,* she had made no mistakes.

A story by Jake caught Helen's eye. The file was slugged HILLBURN, the name of Tom's money management firm. Strange. What could Jake be writing about her fiancé's firm? Hillburn was famously tight-lipped with the press, and Jake wasn't very enterprising these days. Jake's stuff was usually fine for checking by the least experienced reporters because his stories hadn't been sensitive or controversial for years. He based most of his articles on the analyst reports that floated on Wall Street. It was no wonder Preston hated Jake's stuff. Most of the editors prided themselves on being skeptical about Wall Street analysts. They considered analysts to be Pollyannas at best, and crooked at worst, because they invariably issued positive reports about companies that their banks underwrote. Jake bought the analysts' PR bullshit.

All a reporter had to do was make sure that Jake summarized the report right. So Helen gave Jake's stories to the junior reporters, usually without even looking them over.

Helen opened the file and started reading.

PENNYWISE, POUND FOOLISH
Tom Richardson's first blunder?

BY JAKE ROSENBERG

The Magazine has learned that the top five venture capitalists at money management firm Hillburn Richshire, disgruntled over their new compensation package, are about to quit and form their own venture firm. This would leave CEO Tom Richardson essentially stripped of his Internet investment arm for now, and in this arena of the "first-mover advantage," that could prove a serious handicap.

Tom Richardson has made a brave effort to fill the enormous shoes left empty by his father, Walter Richardson, the legendary money manager who retired from his firm a year ago. But now it seems that the younger Richardson is trying to follow too closely in the footsteps of his father's Old Economy style....

Helen scanned the rest of the story, took in its pattern at a glance: a little history and background, a couple paragraphs of snarky speculation, a quote from a rival.

She picked up the phone and started dialing Tom's number. Time for some damage control. Then she put down the receiver abruptly, startled at her own carelessness. She closed the door to her office, and started dialing again, stopped. No. Maybe tonight.

Or not. Was it a breach of ethics to warn Tom? Did she care? Maybe she could find a way to soften the story, or even kill it, but she knew she had to tread lightly.

She took a deep breath. Where had Jake gotten this stuff?

***

By the time Jake sauntered into Preston's office, Bruce, Meg the Knife and Billy the Bully had already gathered. Everyone had read the story. Word traveled fast when there was a hot story in the system, and everybody took a look.

Preston began: "Let's keep this meeting confidential. For obvious reasons I didn't invite Helen. But we have to be delicate about checking this thing. So, how solid are we here?"

Meg spoke up. "Where the hell did you get this, Jake?"

"Anonymous source mailed me a tape," Jake said. Wouldn't do to let on that Kimmie supplied the tape. God only knew how she'd really gotten hold of it, but it would raise too many questions for a story like this to come from a new reporter. And Jake desperately needed a scoop if he wanted to revive his career. "It's definitely Richardson, that's clearly his voice, and he mentions Hillburn. He's talking to his father on the phone. We only hear one side of the conversation. But he talks about the compensation package, and the resistance to it. How he won't back down."

Bruce: "Why you, do you think? Why would this anonymous source send you the tape?"

Jake played it cool, skated past the subtext he knew was there: Why a washed-up hack like you and not me? "Dunno. But I heard a rumor couple weeks ago about some discontent at Hillburn, so I chatted up a few sources, asked around. Didn't lead to anything, but I guess word got back to someone that I was interested."

Meg: "And what sort of agenda does that source have?"

Jake: "Dunno. Hell, I wouldn't be surprised if one of the VC guys made the tape somehow. Doesn't make the story untrue."

Preston said, "Even if the tape was made illegally—and we have no reason to think so—now that it's in our hands, we have the right to publish. Remember the Pentagon Papers."

He continued: "Could the tape have been tampered with, spliced or anything?"

Jake shrugged. "I've listened to it many times, very carefully. Hey, I'm not the FBI, but if that thing was edited, it's not obvious. Had to be a real professional job. So somebody would have to be going to a lot of trouble to embarrass Richardson. Seems a bit far-fetched to me."

Preston: "And the part about the VC guys walking?"

Jake: "That's the only iffy part. Couldn't get it on the record. But one of Kimmie's old colleagues at Morgan Stanley is now an assistant to one of the VC guys."

Bruce raised his eyebrows. "So it's scuttlebutt from a rookie reporter?"

Jake ignored the jibe, even as he detected something in Bruce's tone besides the usual disdain. Amusement? "The assistant overheard these guys. We know it's true, we just can't attribute it."

Billy chimed in. "I have good contacts at Hillburn. Friendly with some of those assistants myself. Let me make a few calls. Bet I can run this thing down for you."

Preston rolled his eyes. "Or tip our hand."

Jake couldn't help notice the open disdain in Bruce's face. Billy was always showing off, insisting he knew everybody, everywhere.

Preston: "This is how we play it. Hold off till tomorrow to make checking calls, then do just the minimum. Call the VC guys first, then Richardson, just to give them all a chance to comment. Or probably not comment. And hedge the wording a little. Don't say the VC guys will definitely quit unless we know that for sure, just probably or they're thinking about it. We'll run the wording past the lawyer."

TUESDAY EVENING, MAY 25, 1999

For once, Rebecca failed to notice the ancient elevator's ingrained reek of tomcat and disinfectant as the rickety brass-and-steel cage creaked slowly to the fourth floor. She failed to marvel that this half-dilapidated former factory in SoHo contained sleek, airy apartments, with exorbitant rents. She stared unseeing as she rose, focused completely on restraining her own fury and dealing with the management problem at hand.

She stepped briskly off the elevator, a tightly rolled copy of the new issue of *The Magazine* clutched in her right hand, marched down the hall and rapped on Kimmie's door. It swung open, and Kimmie danced away in her underwear, smiling sheepishly. Like a little girl who knows she's been naughty.

"Rebecca, hi, come in. Glass of wine?"

Rebecca stepped inside, closed the door and stood silent, facing Kimmie.

Kimmie twirled a strand of hair around her finger and chewed on her lower lip. "Are you mad? You are, aren't you?"

"Are you insane? Do you expect me to believe you're not responsible for this Hillburn story?" Rebecca strode toward Kimmie and waved the magazine in her face.

Kimmie studied her own toes. "Well…"

"I ought to toss you out that window right now, you crazy bitch. What do you think you're doing? You just jeopardized everything right when it's all finally in place. And it's starting to work. We're gonna pull this off if you don't fuck it up."

"But Rebecca…"

"But nothing. Who's running this show anyway?"

"I'm sorry…"

"You're sorry."

"I know I should have cleared it with you. I'm sorry, I really am. But look

121

at it this way: Jake is hooked now. I've revived his career, and he knows it. I've got something on him, and as I feed him more stories, I'll have even more. Besides, the brighter his star shines, the more useful he'll be. And…and…I just couldn't resist taking a slap at Richardson."

"You idiot, that slap could ruin everything. We can't risk anyone suspecting you and Jake are out to get Richardson. Your daddy will pay for his sins soon enough. But if you want to see him really sweat, we need some leverage first."

Kimmie bit her lower lip. "You're right, I was stupid."

"You bet I'm right. I mean, goddammit… How the hell can I trust you with anything?"

WEDNESDAY, MAY 26, 1999

West Fourteenth Street: cheap dresses on sidewalk racks, bins full of $5 shoes, heavy gold chains displayed behind plate glass. Dark, hawk-eyed men stood guard over rhinestone-studded jeans and velvet paintings, smoking and leering at the endless parade of decadent American sluts. Helen could almost feel their broad, suggestive smiles brush against her body like eels. This was the only part of town where men whistled at her. She felt naked.

On the Upper East Side, where Helen lived, men draped their sexuality in expensive suits. Helen found that erotic, trying to imagine what lay beneath the fabric. Up there, even the air was discreet, a suggestion of taxi fumes and the ghosts of perfumed women. Down here, sweet incense smoke cloyed at her nostrils. It hung like a curtain in the still, warm evening, vying for attention with well-spiced mystery meat spit-roasting on a sidewalk cart and the black plastic bags full of overripe trash piled on the curb for pickup.

She turned north on Sixth Avenue, heading toward Jake's apartment. Her plan was to take him out to dinner and ply him with alcohol. She intended to find out how Jake had gotten the Hillburn story.

Jake wasn't bohemian enough to live in the East Village, and he couldn't afford a decent-size place in Greenwich Village proper, but he was too hip to dwell among the sterile Upper East Siders. So he compromised with a floor-through apartment in a brownstone in Chelsea—on the edge of fringe art and sex and far away enough from people who prized discretion and respectability.

There had been a time some years back when she had often walked to his Chelsea apartment. Jake would whisper to her in French. Naked, he would play the piano, and, sipping champagne, sing her songs from Brecht's *Threepenny Opera*. She had been drawn to his boyish face and thick brown hair, and his childish belief that everything in life should come to him easy. At times it seemed a self-fulfilling belief. After all, Helen had come to him.

Thrown herself at him, in fact. She flushed, remembering.

She regularly stumbled upon stray earrings between the sofa cushions. Once, she found a pair in the refrigerator. Another time, red lace panties on the floor of his closet. His bathroom was full of nail polish, from pink through mauve to bloody red, and boxes of tampons. He tried to convince her that these were all old things that belonged to his ex-live-in girlfriend.

Like any woman in the middle of an affair, Helen was delusional. But she wasn't stupid. She could see new stuff appearing all the time. There was always a new color of nail polish on the bathroom shelf.

He would argue, his blue eyes brimming with incredulity, "Now, now, Helen, what do you mean you haven't seen that nail polish here before, you must have had too much to drink last time...." All the while steering her toward the bed.

She offered silent thanks that she was over him, and had been for several years. To her surprise, they had become good friends.

She rang his doorbell. He buzzed her into the building and waited on the third-floor landing, leaning against the doorjamb, his trademark grin in place.

"A drink?"

She had to use the bathroom first. Feeling a twinge beneath her temples, a thundercloud of pain to come building in her head, Helen opened the medicine cabinet in search of painkillers. It was immaculate and orderly, displaying an array of fashionably retro shaving implements and other grooming devices. No pills.

She called out through the closed bathroom door. "Jake? Got any Tylenol in here?"

"Yeah, try the drawer."

She pulled open the drawer beneath the sink. Ah, yes, a generous selection of painkillers, including her favored Tylenol. And other things. Birth control pills in one of those ring-shaped dispensers, still a few pills left. A diaphragm case and tube of jelly. And in a back corner of the drawer, a lone condom. She'd expected a whole box, at least. Hell, she half-suspected Jake ordered the things wholesale.

As she emerged from the bathroom, he stood by the bar, pouring martinis. Helen couldn't resist a comment. "Looks like you're having a Trojan crisis, Jake. Time to stock up."

He shook his head. "Not using those now. I have to say, it's liberating."

She frowned. "What do you mean you're not using them?"

He shrugged. "We've been tested. Not necessary."

Her frown deepened in confusion as he walked over and handed her a drink. "We? But...how could..."

Jake smiled. "Easy. There's just one."

"One? One woman?"

He nodded.

She laughed. "Okay, very funny. You almost had me."

"I'm serious."

"Don't try to snow me, Jake. You've got both pills and a diaphragm in there, that's at least two."

"Yeah, that's a funny thing about her. In most ways, she likes to live dangerously. Takes chances, gets off on it. But in this one area...she's a belt-and-suspenders girl. She uses both."

Helen opened her mouth, closed it, opened it again. "I think I need to sit down."

She was beginning to believe him. Struggling to adjust. It was impossible, absurd, as if the pope had suddenly declared himself a pagan, or a lion announced he was turning vegetarian.

Helen hadn't been good enough to be the one. No way around that. While they were together, she'd convinced herself that it was a character flaw in him, nothing to do with her. Women were one of his addictions. He kept relapsing, but she was the one who mattered.

Late one Saturday night, she was up, restlessly rummaging through his fridge while he slept deeply, knocked insensible by sex and too much wine. The phone rang. Helen walked into the living room and hovered curiously over the answering machine. Jake and many of his friends kept late hours, but who would call at quarter to three? A wrong number? Some sort of emergency? A woman spoke, her voice low and smoky: "Jake? It's Melinda. You home? You alone? I am, and I'm hot and restless and awake. So if you listen to this before dawn, call me. I've got a bottle of that cognac you like so much, and things you like to eat... God, I want you to speak French to me and do that twirly thing with your tongue....I even got my piano tuned. We can have breakfast in the afternoon and you can play me some Brecht. Hope I hear from you. Bye."

Helen stared at the answering machine for a full minute, her breathing shallow. She stole into the bedroom, gathered her clothes, dressed quickly and fled. In the street and in the cab uptown, she sobbed uncontrollably. At home, she called Rebecca. There wasn't much Rebecca could say other than to curse Jake as an unworthy dog. She couldn't even pretend surprise. But she listened, till dawn.

Now Jake sat on the sofa, his eyes fixed on Helen. She sensed he was ready, even eager, to confess something...but what?

"Come on, Jake, just one woman? Doesn't sound like the Jake I know at all."

"It's true." He gulped down his martini too quickly and stood up. "I need a refill. You want another too?"

"No, thanks. Why just one? Is there a sudden shortage of women in New

York? Or have you gotten lazy about snake-charming them?"

He shrugged. "I'm crazy about her."

"Really? And who should we thank for this metamorphosis?"

He eyed her over the rim of his martini glass. "Kimmie Davis."

Jake and Kimmie, Kimmie and Jake, Jake and Kimmie, Kimmie and Jake...

"Oh."

Jake and Kimmie, Kimmie and Jake... Why did she find the thought so unsettling?

"How long has it been going on?" she asked, just to say something.

"A few weeks. Six, seven. I really love her...."

Love?

Jake had never told Helen he loved her.

Now that he had confided in Helen, he was eager to talk about Kimmie some more. Helen realized that Jake assumed that as a former lover and good friend, she was happy to listen. She wasn't, not at all. But she knew she had to humor him. She wanted his source on Hillburn Richshire. He wouldn't tell before first unloading on her about his new love.

She had never warned Tom about the story. Now she wanted to redeem herself if she could, perhaps help protect him, by warning him about the source.

So she was doomed to hear Jake out, even if it made her squirm.

"Before Kimmie, I could never be with just one person, I was compulsive, like with smoking....Like if you could smoke two or three cigarettes at the same time, that would be great....The same with women...I had to have several, one by one, I had the same craving for women that I have for nicotine....Being with one woman was torture, like being allowed to smoke just one cigarette a day."

Helen allowed herself to smoke only rarely. Now she reached over to the marble side table where Jake had left his pack of Camels, shook one out and lit it.

Jake plunged on, oblivious. "With Kimmie I don't crave anybody else. It feels so fucking good. It's like being able to have one cigarette a day, but I feel as if I smoked the whole pack.

"Usually, when you're with someone, you know what she's gonna say, how she's gonna react....Fuck, you know it too well, you hear too much of it. This last chick I had before Kimmie was totally compulsive, afraid of fire, and she would ask me every time I put out a cigarette, 'Jake, are you sure you put it out right? You're not gonna start a fire, right?' Imagine, I heard it thirty times a day, and even at night sometimes, I'd wake up and step into the kitchen for a smoke and hear her calling from the bedroom, 'Jake, are you sure you put it out right? Are you sure you're not gonna start a fire?'...Chinese torture, drip, drip, drip. I hope that bitch is fucking a fireman these days....

"With Kimmie, I never know who I'm dealing with. It keeps me interested, but it's scary sometimes, the way her mood shifts. Hot, cold, angry, happy, sad...in a flash. Like last night, she was fine during dinner, maybe a little wired, then, no reason, she got all quiet and withdrawn. I hate that. Shut me out. I couldn't break through.

"And then some friend of hers called, and Kimmie retreated into the bedroom and talked for like an hour. When she came out, it was like magic. She was so serene, like—I don't know, I can't make her relax like that even when she finally comes, which sometimes takes forever, you know..."

Enough, that was enough.

Helen decided she couldn't wait to ease into her own chosen topic. She had to change the subject now. "So, tell me something, Jake. Who was your source for the Hillburn story?"

He hesitated. "Helen, you know normally I would...I'm just not sure...I don't think I should tell you this time."

What? He wouldn't tell her? He had told her too much already.

"Jake, how many times in the past few years have I saved your butt? Have you kept count? Don't I always watch your back?"

Unable to meet her gaze, he studied the floor.

He sighed and mumbled, "Kimmie."

Was he not done talking about her?

"Kimmie what, Jake?"

"Kimmie got part of it, about the VC guys being ready to quit. Part of it came to me anonymously. But we had hard evidence, Helen, that's all I can tell you. That's how it got past the lawyer. That's why I felt I had to run with it." He looked up. "Please, don't let on that you know about Kimmie's role in this, she made me swear not to tell you."

Helen took a deep breath and stubbed out her cigarette.

Hard evidence—that probably meant documents. Most likely leaked by the disgruntled venture capital guys. They had the motive, they hadn't been with Tom's firm long enough to develop the expected level of loyalty. And now they had one foot out the door anyway.

Hiring that ungrateful little bitch had come back to bite her. She had bet that Kimmie's audacity would work well for *The Magazine*. Hell, she was proud of herself for that, saw herself as a taker of calculated risks.

She'd miscalculated this one.

THURSDAY, MAY 27, 1999

Helen looked up at the lurking figure in her office doorway: Bruce. She wondered what he wanted, and how much of a pain it would be for her.

"Uh, Helen." He stepped through the door. "I've got a story that's gonna be ready for checking soon, it's the one about hedge funds and derivatives. Complicated. So could I get a checker who's not an idiot? How about Paul?"

Helen sighed. She hated humoring Bruce, but it made life much easier. Besides, he was half right: Not every checker would be good for this story.

"Paul's tied up on that big project with Meg. Tell you what, how about Nikki?"

Bruce grunted. "Okay, I guess Nikki will do."

Helen grew puzzled as Bruce lingered, as if hesitating. Normally, he would turn on his heel and vanish.

When he sat down across the desk from her, she knew something was up. She gripped her mug of coffee and took a cautious sip.

"So, Helen, I admit I'm curious. I assumed you were doing your boyfriend a favor, but it doesn't look that way now."

Helen frowned. "Bruce, what are you talking about?"

"Hiring Kimmie."

"Kimmie?" Confused, Helen stared blankly. "What does Kimmie have to do with Tom?"

Bruce smirked. "Besides being his daughter?"

Helen spilled coffee across her desk. Bruce jumped up, cursing, to avoid a lapful of hot liquid, almost knocking over his chair. Helen reached into the drawer where she kept a stash of paper napkins and began mopping up the puddle on her desk. She paused to move stacks of paper out of harm's way, then reached into her drawer for more napkins, working systematically from the edges of the spill toward the center, dabbing and wiping even after the surface was desert dry, her eyes obsessed with the swirling grain of the wood.

She used her tone of command, her voice cold: "Shut the door."

The door closed with a soft thunk.

Only then did she straighten and look up at Bruce. "What?...Tell me what you know."

He leaned against the door, studying her. "Surely, you know more than I..."

"Don't fuck with me, Bruce. Tell me everything."

He looked wary. "Don't really know much. Happened at Yale. Mother's a lawyer, Margo Davis. Seems Richardson supported the girl, but kind of an arm's-length thing. Kept it quiet."

Yes, she thought. Real quiet. "My God...I..."

"Wait a minute." Bruce perked up. "You didn't know?"

"Well...I..." She floundered for a way to minimize her humiliation. "I knew...of course...he had a daughter, but... It was something from his past he didn't talk about. I...Kimmie? I never saw a picture, never knew her last name..."

Bruce grinned, and she loathed him for it.

"My, my," he said. "The plot does thicken."

She took a breath and gave him her iciest glare. "Bruce. Obviously, I have a...delicate situation to navigate. You won't spread this around?"

He shook his head. "Knowledge isn't power if you give it away. Why should I share the joy?"

***

Helen turned the corner onto Park Avenue, darted up some concrete steps and entered the skyscraper's subdued lobby. The dark wood paneling and marble floor whispered of money. She nodded to the lone security guard and signed in at the desk, then rode a short escalator to the main lobby level and the bank of elevators. Tom's money management firm occupied the building's top five floors.

Helen stepped out onto the twenty-ninth floor, the last floor reachable by elevator. The floors above were exclusive, accessible only by a set of stairs. The receptionist, an elegant woman in her fifties with just a wisp or two of gray in her black hair, had been working for the Richardsons for decades.

"He's waiting for you upstairs," she told Helen.

Tom's office occupied the northeast corner of the thirty-first floor—a quietly plush expanse of some 3,000 square feet, with a high ceiling and glass walls. Helen usually felt on top of the world there, on eye level with the twin spires of the Waldorf. Now she wanted to reach across the street and break one of those spires off. Use it as a club. She would have enjoyed that, playing Godzilla to the city. Helen took a deep breath. Had to maintain her composure. She wanted to broach this on her own terms.

"Hello, hon." His embrace was gentle, respectful of her uncreased tan Armani suit. His kiss was gentle too, so as not to smear her lipstick. She responded absent-mindedly.

He led her into a separate dining area, where he often lunched with chairmen of companies and heads of state. There was a fresh bouquet of flowers on every table. Bernard, the office waiter, started serving them lunch.

Helen sipped her Perrier, conscious of her own weird calm.

"Champagne?"

"Yes, I could use a drink today."

Tom poured the champagne.

Only hours ago, she had felt guilty that she hadn't warned Tom about the Hillburn story. Not that she could've done anything about it. In fact, had she tried to intervene with Preston, he might well have reacted by making the tone of the story even harsher.

She was glad now she hadn't warned Tom about it, and not for reasons of journalistic ethics.

They clinked glasses. She fixed a blast-chilled smile on her face and summoned up her most matter-of-fact tone.

"You know, Tom, if you'd mentioned that you had a daughter, I might have been able to avoid hiring her. And then she might not have planted that story about the venture capital guys at Hillburn. Did you know Kimmie was a prime source for that? I just found out recently myself. Just before I found out who she was."

Tom's expression changed. He, too, kept his feelings quarantined until he was sure they were safe, and it startled Helen to see an emotion that hadn't been precisely calibrated flicker across his face. It was as if an invisible force hit him, as if his features were responding to a burst of acceleration or a gust of wind.

"I need to tell you some things," he said softly.

"I should say so."

"Well, I would have, I meant to, I just…" He stared down at his hands. "It was wrong of me, I should've told you before now….Partly, it just didn't seem relevant, not really part of my life. But also…I guess some part of me has always felt a little guilty about the whole thing. I was afraid you'd somehow think less of me for it."

"You should have told me, Tom."

"I know."

So he did. He told her about Yale and about Margo, how things were then and how things had ended.

She sensed he was a touch overanxious to justify the self-limiting nature of that relationship. He prattled on about parallel universes.

"You can step through the looking glass for a while," he said, "it was an adventure for both of us—but…I was hooked, for the time being.

"You know what I mean, Helen.…Imagine the Petrushka ball at the Plaza. Princess Natalia would never say anything if I arrived with a black woman. Nobody would, even back in the Seventies. Everybody is too cultured for that.…But it would put the princess in a position of discomfort, and me, and Margo…especially Margo.…Everybody understood that, her family, my family, and they were right…you can't blame it on us only, her family also understood how things were… sometimes I felt that they thought of me as some foreign tourist they needed to educate about black culture."

Helen shifted in her seat, suddenly uneasy. She certainly understood the dynamics of self-limiting affairs, having experienced more than her share. But it unsettled her that Tom was trying so hard to rationalize this. She knew she was a bit of an idealist in her way. She truly believed in meritocracy, in individuals, not group labels. Was Tom now using other people's prejudices to justify his own? Or was he simply a ruthless pragmatist? It took her only a moment's reflection to decide upon the latter. A side of Tom she'd never fully recognized before, but it fit. Well, the pragmatism complemented her idealism. And the ruthlessness—with a disturbing little thrill, she realized she found the ruthlessness attractive.

Tom continued. "We were always careful. Somehow she got pregnant anyway. Margo was furious. She decided against an abortion. Honestly, I think that was an act of defiance of some sort. Against her family, against me…

"She graduated that year, and I haven't seen her since then. I never saw my daughter. Margo insisted on that, on keeping me away. I've been supporting her financially, of course, but it's all handled discreetly by the family lawyers. Paid for her schooling, so I've followed her progress somewhat at a distance. Dartmouth, Wharton. Heard she went to work on Wall Street. But never, not once, had I laid eyes on my daughter."

He told her about the résumé, the interview. The background check. Kimmie's fury, and her threats. How she stalked out.

Helen sat back in her chair and studied her fingernails, absently scanning them for tiny flaws. "So she did get you—with the story. God, do you think she got herself hired just to do that?"

"I don't know. Maybe she just seized the opportunity, as long as she was at *The Magazine*. A more pressing question: Is she done? Was that it, her vengeance? Or is she still a threat to me? Or even to you?"

"My God, Tom. You really should have told me."

"Yeah, I know, I wish I had." He paused, thoughtful. "I don't suppose you could have her fired?"

Helen shook her head and glared. "Goddamn it, Tom, you've left me with quite a mess to clean up. And this one won't be easy. We're talking about a promising young black woman with an Ivy education. Besides, at the moment, she's got Preston wrapped around her finger. She's a good reporter. And she's dangerous, especially to you."

She frowned. "Have to come up with the right approach. Something that'll make HR want to get rid of her."

Tom leaned across the table and reached for her hand. "I'm sure you'll think of something. In the meantime, you'll just have to watch her."

Helen pulled her hand away.

TUESDAY, JUNE 1, 1999

Rebecca clutched a subway pole and swayed to the rhythm of the Number 1 train, frowning in concentration. She was listening to a tape the voice-activated machine had recorded earlier that morning, probably while she showered. Richardson on the phone to his father.

"Yes, there's already some short interest on this one…Believe me, Dad, I understand the need for discretion, but I'm sure we can confirm the rumors quietly.…Yes, the rumors are consistent, and if they're accurate, then Unfettered represents a huge opportunity…Of course, Dad, speed and stealth. Always."

They were discussing Unfettered, a teen apparel company, and rumors of a potential scandal. A romance between a vice president and a fabric supplier, some padded contracts steered the boyfriend's way. If it was true, it would come out, and Unfettered's stock would tank.

Rebecca tingled with excitement. This was perfect. Luckily for her, Richardson managed his investments with few restrictions. He ran private investment pools, some of them organized as hedge funds, so he regularly sold stocks short, placing very large bets that certain stocks would fall. He could profit from negative news.

And Rebecca loved to do negative stories.

She rushed from the subway stop to her office and closed the door behind her. Let them all think she's working on that damn Greenspan profile.

She went online and scanned a few stock market chat sites, printed out a couple of analyst reports and started working the phone. She spent the morning chatting up short-sellers, who always had an interest in spreading rumors and bad news. One thing led to another, until she was fleshing out gossip about a romantic weekend getaway. She spent the afternoon calling hotels in Bermuda.

***

Tom looked up from his desk as the man from Vandenberg Associates walked into his office. Though "walked" was too crude, too clumsy a term to capture the motion. He glided in, weightless as Fred Astaire, moving with such subtle grace that the soles of his polished wingtips seemed suspended a half-inch above the carpet.

"Dennis Flaherty. An honor to meet you, sir."

Tom rose and extended his hand. "Tom Richardson. It's a pleasure."

Flaherty looked trim and fit, but no gym rat. Medium height, average build, sandy thinning hair, pale blue eyes. Try as he might, Tom couldn't peg his age any closer than thirty to fifty. His face was pleasant enough, but there was nothing distinctive about it whatsoever. Instantly forgettable. Anonymous.

He was immaculately dressed in a charcoal pinstripe suit. Beautiful lining of pearl gray silk. Real buttonholes. Definitely bespoke. And there was something about the drape of the fabric, the cut of the lapels...

"Nice suit," Tom ventured. "That wouldn't happen to be a Henry Poole?"

Flaherty smiled. "You have an excellent eye, Mr. Richardson."

"Well, I've worn a few of those myself. Family tradition, my father ordered his suits there."

Tom paused—of course, the man had dressed for this meeting. Had he actually researched the tailor?

"Have a seat, Mr. Flaherty. When I told Frank Vandenberg I needed some discreet surveillance done, he said you were the best."

Flaherty molded himself to the chair, merging with the furniture. "I suppose I have a knack for it. Even in high school, I was known as 'The Invisible Man.' Sometimes I think I'm the only person left who doesn't want to be famous."

Tom smiled. "And you were once FBI?"

"Yes, like many at the firm, I used to be with the bureau. Counterterrorism unit."

"Indeed. That sounds hard-core."

Flaherty shrugged. "It's all surveillance. Of course, some of those targets inspired extra caution. But it's always about watching without being noticed."

"Well," said Tom, "you should find this job a piece of cake.

"I want you to keep an eye on this young lady, Kimmie Davis. I'm afraid this photo's a few years old, but here's her address. I want to know where she goes, who she sees, especially if she makes contact with anyone at my firm—generally what she's up to. She's a reporter at *The Magazine*."

Flaherty looked thoughtful. "*The Magazine*? Doesn't your fiancée work there?"

Tom leaned back in his chair. "Yes, as a matter of fact, Helen is her boss.

Oh, one other thing that might be useful. I understand Kimmie is, uh, going out with one of the writers there, Jake Rosenberg. Here's his address. That should be enough to get you started."

"Oh, yes, more than enough. You're making this easy for me, Mr. Richardson. But…if I may be so bold…"

"Yes?"

"What am I looking for? Why am I watching this woman? What's your relationship to her? It would help me do my job to know these things."

"Yes." Tom frowned. "Yes, of course. I see. Well, it's a long story…but in a nutshell…between us…"

"That goes without saying, Mr. Richardson."

"Of course. Kimmie Davis is my daughter. The product of an affair in my college days. And she seems to hold a grudge against me. Recently, she got herself hired at *The Magazine*—Helen didn't know, of course, though she does now—and in short order planted a story that was rather damaging to me. At least, I believe she planted it. Now, that may well be the extent of it—she may have gotten this out of her system…"

"But?"

"But I'm not sure of that. She's smart and, I'm afraid, a bit…volatile. I don't want to be blindsided again."

"I see. And you believe you have a leak here…"

"Almost certainly."

"You've had your own people check the office phone logs, email?"

"Of course. Turned up nothing."

Flaherty nodded. "Would surprise me if they had. Presumably this source would be careful enough not to use the office phone to call a reporter. So I'll keep close tabs on this young lady personally."

"Good. But discreetly, Mr. Flaherty."

"Discretion is my watchword."

"Nothing too intrusive, nothing illegal. And…don't take this the wrong way…"

"Yes?"

"No need to be too…voyeuristic. She is my daughter, after all."

"Of course not, Mr. Richardson."

***

Her 11 a.m. meeting with Karen filled Helen with dread. But it had been her own idea, and it was the right thing to do. Helen had just about convinced herself of that. This wasn't her usual style, conniving behind someone's back in meetings outside the editorial department. But she had no choice.

At ten to eleven Helen touched up her hair and makeup in the restroom. "I'm sorry, but I made a mistake," she mouthed as she studied her expression in the mirror. She had rehearsed the same lines at home the night before, in front of her bathroom mirror. She wanted her voice and her face to convey selflessness and responsibility. She hoped that Karen would be disarmed. So few people admitted mistakes, after all.

She stepped off the elevator on the tenth floor and took a moment to orient herself. She seldom ventured up here to the summit of the building, where most people were senior vice presidents of something. The corporate types, or as reporters called them, the Corps. The Corps were, figuratively and literally, above everybody else at *The Magazine*. Reporters sat right in the belly of the building, on the fifth floor. The Corps referred to reporters as "talent," and to *The Magazine* as a "product." Reporters thought that the Corps were uncreative, and considered their jobs menial at best, counterproductive at worst. The two groups came in contact only on the ground floor, in front of the elevators. Reporters wore flip-flops and khakis and sulked in silence. The Corps wore suits, smiled constantly and exchanged chirpy, upbeat greetings.

Helen walked down a long, bright hallway, glancing inside some of the offices as she passed. Unlike reporters, who drowned under stacks of files and newspapers, the Corps kept their desks organized and neat. They used their inboxes and outboxes, and filed documents instead of throwing them on the floor. It was eerily quiet. No one was shouting, slamming the doors or hanging out by the cubicles, chatting. In fact, nobody passed her in the hall. Helen assumed that they were too efficient to simply walk and talk, and instead communicated via email and memos. Compared with the fifth floor, the walls looked lighter and cleaner. The air conditioning seemed to be cranked up to a cooler setting than in the rest of the building. The tenth floor was chilled, blank and antiseptic, like an operating room. Helen half-expected someone to ask her to change into one of those backless hospital gowns.

Karen, the senior vice president for human resources, was a perfect fit for the floor. Her desk was clean, her gray pantsuit unwrinkled. Helen couldn't remember seeing Karen in anything else but that pantsuit, even though she knew that was impossible. Karen motioned Helen to a chair in front of her desk. On the wall behind Karen was Charles Ebbets' famous photo depicting the construction of Rockefeller Center. Construction workers lunched on a beam suspended hundreds of feet above the streets. That print was a New York perennial. Helen had seen it on postcards and displayed in the windows of picture-framing galleries. She wondered idly if it had come with the office.

Helen focused on Karen's face. Blank, yet calculating.

"I'm sorry, but I made a hiring mistake," Helen said. She paused. "We need to terminate a new reporter, Kimmie Davis." Helen paused again. She was pleased with her voice. She sounded the same as when she had rehearsed it in her bathroom.

Karen remained expressionless. Helen had no idea what impression her words had made. Whenever they talked, Karen made her feel as if Helen didn't understand some basic truth about the world, as if she were missing a glaring clue cosmically obvious to everyone else.

"Why?" Karen asked. Instantly, Helen felt stupid for pausing before explaining why.

She started reciting the reasons, hoping her voice stayed even and self-assured. First, she explained Kimmie's breach of journalistic ethics: She had checked the Hillburn story even though she should have recused herself because she was related to the subject of the story. Helen used the world *ethics* as many times as she could. An *ethics* breach could lead to a lawsuit. A reporter without *ethics* had no right to be at *The Magazine*. Helen could overlook many things, but not the lack of *ethics*.

Helen felt this was sure to work. If Karen didn't agree with her, it would mean that she didn't care about *ethics*.

Helen had chosen her ammunition carefully, considering other reasons for getting Kimmie fired. She couldn't blame Kimmie for sleeping with Jake. That would only get Jake fired. After all, he was a senior male, and Kimmie was a junior female. But she did bring up Kimmie's attendance. In her first two months of work, Kimmie had missed eight days, or almost all the vacation time she got the first year, and she often wandered into the office around noon. At night, during closings, the copy desk could never find her.

As she spoke, Helen struggled to tamp down her rising irritation, tried to purge it from her consciousness. She shouldn't have to be doing this. Karen didn't know zip about editorial. She was a Corp, not a writer. Helen should just be able to fire Kimmie herself.

That's the way it had worked once, under Roberts. He hadn't let the Corps push them around. They had hired and fired at will, and the Corps had been too afraid of Roberts to meddle. But Preston kowtowed to the Corps. With Preston came the era of managers' manuals, written warning letters, forms for performance reviews and documented conversations. It was the age of the official paper trail. You could still do anything to anybody as long as you had a proper paper trail, and of course, the Corps were the only ones who knew how to create one. Helen hated the new process. She believed in speaking plainly, face to face. But she couldn't get rid of Kimmie without the paper trail. And for that she needed Karen.

Karen brought something up on her computer screen and studied it for a while. Helen assumed it was Kimmie's file, though she couldn't see Karen's screen from where she sat. Then Karen started asking questions. About the story. About Kimmie's fact-checking record. About Kimmie's background before coming to *The Magazine*. Helen answered, then was careful to mention her own connection to Tom Richardson. She wanted to seem forthright. Karen didn't react. Helen wondered if Karen already knew about Helen's relationship to Tom. She had to know, Helen decided. It was no secret. She probably read the gossip columns along with everybody else.

Helen asked Karen if she should draft a warning letter to Kimmie.

"I'll get back to you on that," Karen said. "Have a nice day."

SATURDAY, JUNE 5, 1999

Rebecca clattered around Kimmie's kitchen impatiently, trying to make more noise. She thought she heard a faint moan coming from the bedroom. It was almost nine, and the time factor was critical.

She had seen this coming, and so had insisted on staying over at Kimmie's even though it had meant babysitting her while Kimmie worked her way through two bottles of wine, turning more sullen by the hour. All while Rebecca transcribed her own tapes and organized her notes for Kimmie. For God's sake, she had done all the real work—all Kimmie had to do was show up and type it in. Now even that seemed like a problem.

She paused, smiled to herself. Of course. Kimmie had a coffee grinder. And whole beans. She loaded the grinder, started it up and laughed out loud. The noise would wake the dead. And the aroma was fantastic. She'd shove a fresh cup under Kimmie's nose like smelling salts.

Rebecca poured extra beans into the grinder and grinned as she turned the dial once more. Had to make sure she had enough for a full pot and then some.

The grinder's deafening whine died away a second time. Rebecca heard a scuffling sound and turned. She had to admit that Kimmie retained a disarming seductiveness even when she looked like one of the living dead.

Now the zombie nymph pawed spastically at the kitchen counter. "Have…you…lost…your mind?"

Rebecca smiled sweetly. "It's nine o'clock, dear, and time is not on our side. You need to go into the office and type my notes into the system. And be sure to save a copy on the network server."

Kimmie's face quivered. She whispered hoarsely. "Why are you punishing me?"

"Don't be silly. Coffee will be ready soon, and then you'll feel better. The sooner you do this, the better, you know. Richardson's going to realize those rumors about Unfettered are true, and my guess is he'll confirm them this weekend. And short the stock Monday morning. So we need those notes on the server today."

Kimmie slumped against the counter. "When, Rebecca? When did you develop a taste for torture? God, my head…"

"Here, take these with some water."

"You can't deny this is cruel… and unusual …and… un… unconstitutional…"

"Whatever. Here, coffee's done, let me pour…"

"Oh, yes, please. Please, God, coffee…"

MONDAY-THURSDAY, JUNE 7-10, 1999

Lunchtime, but Jake wasn't hungry. He was reaching into his desk drawer for some more aspirin to chase away the dregs of his hangover when Kimmie popped in and shut the door.

He eyed her warily, suddenly gripped by an irrational fear that she might pin him to the floor and pour more booze down his throat. He recognized the look in her eyes. The look of a cat ready to pounce. How in God's name could she be so awake? Was she doing more cocaine already?

She spoke in a rush. "Jake, I've got a hot one. You know Unfettered, the teen apparel company? I was talking to some short-sellers. The buzz is that one of the company's vice presidents is fucking a fabric supplier—literally," she giggled. "And she's ordering crap fabric from her lover boy at way inflated prices."

"Slow down, Kimmie." He raised one eyebrow. "You know you have to be careful about short-sellers spreading dirt…"

"I know, I know, so I've been following up, and so far it checks out. I know they went to Bermuda together for the Memorial Day weekend."

He shook his head and smiled, amused despite his headache. "And how do you know that?"

"Checked out a short-seller tip. All I had was Bermuda and Memorial Day, so I called all the best hotels in Bermuda pretending to be Ms. Vice President. Asked if they'd found some prescription sunglasses I lost. Of course, I didn't remember the room number I stayed in, so they had to check their reservation records, and when they came up blank on her name, I asked them to check under Mr. Fabric Supplier. The first three places were totally befuddled, but the desk clerk at the fourth place actually remembered me— uh, her. I got the impression she's a big tipper."

"Good for her." Jake had to laugh. "Then what?"

"Then I called Mr. Fabric Supplier, pretending to be the hotel. Talked to his secretary, asked if he'd left behind some sunglasses. She put me on hold to relay the question, came back with, 'No, he has his sunglasses with him, must be someone else's.' Not 'What are you talking about, he was never in Bermuda.' What do you think? If we don't run with this, the shorts will feed it to someone else."

Jake nodded. "Okay, okay, you've hooked me. You really are something else, babe." He paused, thinking. "Unfettered…didn't they have some layoffs recently? Maybe we could find some ex-employees willing to dish on the veep."

Kimmie grinned. "That's my boy. And you can bet all the rival fabric suppliers who got screwed out of deals will talk." She gazed up at the ceiling, suddenly thoughtful. "I wonder. Is she just a smitten idiot? Or is this a lovers' scam with kickbacks? I'm betting she's greedy rather than stupid."

"All right, let's go for it." Jake felt the last of his hangover evaporate in the excitement of the chase.

Over the next couple of days they settled into a rhythm, with Kimmie camped out in Jake's office. She seemed to be right about Unfettered, and all the spurned fabric suppliers happily served up dirt. By Wednesday they decided they had enough ammunition to start calling the company. The executives refused to talk, but Jake and Kimmie plowed ahead anyway, gleefully firing off questions by email, fax and voice mail to Unfettered's chief financial officer in case he ever decided to return their calls.

Jake fielded a brief call on Thursday afternoon, then turned to Kimmie, who was sitting on the floor, surrounded by stacks of paper. "Guess what? That was security downstairs. The Unfettered flack is here, and he's brought along a lawyer." He grinned. "They must be really sweating. Trying to catch us off-guard with an unscheduled pop-in. That's a sign of desperation."

Kimmie grinned. "Let's have some fun with them."

The four of them sat around a long mahogany table. The Unfettered spokesman and lawyer on one side, Jake and Kimmie on the other. Something was awry with the air conditioning that day, which had turned oppressively hot, and the conference room was warm and airless, a sharp departure from the building's usual summer chill.

The flack was thin, nervous, twitchy. Jake focused on him, started firing questions: "Is it true that Unfettered is buying more-expensive fabric from…"

"The company considers every bit of information about its contracts confidential, and will not release…" the lawyer interjected. He was fat and bald, a wheeze in his voice.

What a pair, thought Jake, they sent us Laurel and Hardy.

Jake shot back: "Okay, okay, let me tell you what we have so far…"

An old trick. If you ran whatever you had by the company, that made it legitimate. Some PR people would actually lie and deny, but some were afraid—if they knew the information was true, denying it might be illegal. A simple "no comment" meant you had the story right. Jake tossed out fact after fact. Copies of the previous year's contracts—furnished by spurned suppliers—none of them renewed. An item in the retail trade press quoting Mr. Fabric Supplier: He was bragging about the big new contract he'd landed with Unfettered. Later items in the trade press sniping at Unfettered for the decline in the quality of its materials. "By the way," Jake added, "your customers are starting to notice too. Kimmie here spent a recent afternoon in a New Jersey mall talking to teenage girls. Lot of complaints about crappy fabric, quality not what it used to be."

No outright denials.

"The company considers all our contract information confidential, any mention of that without our confirmation would be negligent…" the lawyer interrupted again. The flack's eyes darted left, right, his mouth opened and closed. He was a useless appendage.

Kimmie, dressed for the heat in a skimpy tank top, leaned across the table and stage-whispered to the lawyer in a husky voice: "You are not going to tell us anything, are you?" Her tone and expression would have fit seamlessly into a porn flick—they were discomfiting in the conference room. Jake knew that was exactly the effect Kimmie intended. The pin-striped lawyer broke into a profuse, angry sweat. He seemed riveted despite himself by the vision of Kimmie breathing freely—the curves of her breasts rose and fell, sharply defined under the thin cotton.

Jake chose that moment to toss a pair a black-and-white photos onto the table.

The lawyer frowned. "What's this?"

"The house is in Westchester, belongs to your vice president. The first shot shows her and your principal fabric supplier entering the house last Tuesday evening at 9:34. The second one shows your supplier leaving the house Wednesday morning at 7:22. Long business meeting."

The flack paled. For a second Jake worried he might faint. The lawyer sputtered, tiny flecks of foam collecting at the corners of his mouth. "Wh…what…where…"

Jake shrugged. "Had to confirm the relationship, so we had photographers stake out their homes. Nothing illegal about that."

The lawyer tried mightily to rally and sound menacing. "You little bottom-feeder. Any article citing irresponsible information that you just quoted, the company would have to consider a malicious attack, and undertake appropriate steps…"

Kimmie leaned over him further, showing him more of her easy breathing. "You wouldn't be threatening us with a lawsuit, would you?" she whispered.

"You'd just…just…better be careful, young lady."

Jake grinned, enjoying the spectacle tremendously. He was excited by Kimmie's performance, and growing impatient for the meeting to end. He caught the lawyer's eyes and was sure he realized it too: He knew Jake and Kimmie were engaged in foreplay, and all he had to anticipate was a sweaty cab ride and the wrath of his CEO.

MONDAY, JUNE 14, 1999

Dennis Flaherty settled down for his evening's vigil in SoHo. Following Kimmie Davis home from her office was no sweat—she certainly wasn't trained to detect surveillance, and once she entered the subway station for the southbound F train, he could safely assume she was heading home. He didn't even have to ride in the same subway car.

Then, just after she'd entered her building and started up to her fourth-floor loft, Flaherty strolled matter-of-factly to the dark commercial building directly across the street, opened the door with a key, slipped inside and punched the proper code into a keypad, deactivating the burglar alarm. That was the really sweet part about his billionaire client, the unlimited expense account. The owner of the small, struggling art gallery on the fifth floor—once he had established Flaherty's bona fides with Vandenberg—had been unable to resist the offer of $10,000 cash per month, just to allow Flaherty to use the place after hours. He even let Flaherty keep some of his equipment in the storeroom.

Now Flaherty opened the windows opposite Kimmie's building and then set up that equipment, methodically checking and positioning each item. The Nikon with telephoto lens on a tripod. The Leica 8x30 Swiss Army binoculars. The 5.5x56 Nighthawk night vision binoculars, originally developed for the Russian military. The Toshiba CCD low-light camera. The laser listening device, which looked like a videocamera but actually bounced an infrared beam off Kimmie's window. It detected vibrations in the glass and translated them into sound, allowing Flaherty to listen in on her apartment. Not that he anticipated anything of particular interest this evening. But if she made any phone calls, at least he could monitor her side of the conversation.

He wheeled a padded leather desk chair to his chosen spot, sat down and spoke softly into a small tape recorder. "9:06 p.m. Subject returned straight home after work, alone. No unusual activity." Then he poured himself some coffee from a large thermos and waited.

This was the high life. He'd paid his dues. In the course of his career, he'd spent hundreds of hours watching from rooftops and from vans parked in the street. Too often, from rooftops pelted with cold rain or vans baked in the summer sun. And if necessary for this job, he'd do it again. He was a professional, after all. But sitting in a comfortable chair in a dark art gallery was infinitely preferable. The only drawback he could think of was that he didn't care for the art—mostly paintings of stylized fleshy nudes in poses that managed to be lewd without being sexy—but in the dark they were just dim, bulbous shapes anyway. And there was a big advantage to watching from one of a row of commercial buildings that were usually empty at night: The subject tended to be rather careless about closing her blinds.

What made Flaherty especially thankful for this carelessness—aside from professional considerations—was the subject's penchant for wandering around her loft stark naked. There she was, coming out of the bathroom, tossing the last few shreds of her clothing onto a ragged pile in the corner. He reached for the Leica binoculars and focused as she padded over to the fridge and poured herself a glass of wine. He studied her curves as she tuned the TV to some old black-and-white movie and sank onto the sofa. He meditated on the parabolas defined by her swaying breasts as she sat up and leaned over the coffee table to roll herself a joint. My God, what a dream assignment this was.

He remembered his conversation with Richardson, and for a fraction of a second he felt a microspasm of guilt. What the hell. Clients never understood. Surveillance wasn't just another line of work. To Flaherty, it was a calling. And the prurient interest wasn't even the main thing—that was just a bonus. No, there was something about watching people when they believed themselves unobserved, when they were supremely unself-conscious. There was transcendence in it, the purity of truth. He wasn't just some hack observer. He was an artist of surveillance. And to fully practice his art, he had to peer inside his subject, to take notes on her soul. To understand her. He always came to identify with his subjects in the end, rather in the way biographers identified with theirs, he supposed. Unrequited intimacy. Sometimes he thought it was the closest that he'd ever come to genuine love. Sometimes he thought that it must be better than love.

He was pouring a second cup of coffee when she lay back and began to masturbate, idly at first, then with gathering force. He sat up straight, peering through the Leica, noting how her fingers moved, studying the expression on her face. He stood and moved to the Nikon, focused the big lens, began snapping photos. No one else would see these, of course. He'd develop them at home, for his private files. Suddenly aware that he wanted sound, he looked up long enough to flick on the laser and put the headphones on. Small moans, quick, shallow breaths. Click, whirr, click, whirr. Slow down now. He forced himself to conserve film, not wanting to miss anything while changing rolls. It seemed to take a long time, but when she finally came, it was loud and violent, her whole body spasming. Click, whirr, click, whirr. Flaherty focused on the change in her face, from yearning to utter abandonment.

Click. Rewind.

She kept going, heading for another peak.

He sat down and reached for the Leica.

TUESDAY, JUNE 15, 1999

No one has mapped the way to the end of the earth, that place of numb, eternal twilight reached by only the most intrepid and foolhardy travelers. But if *The Magazine* were the whole world—and indeed, for some it might as well have been the universe—the end of the earth would have been photocomp.

For the last twenty-five years John Squinzano had spent most of his evenings there. It was a small, windowless room on the fourth floor, tucked behind the copy desk, hidden away in the very heart of the building. Hunched over his keyboard, bathed in the unnatural fluorescence of the overheads and the phosphorescence of his computer screens, he typed in last-minute changes to the copy, tweaked the arcane specs that fit the text to the layouts and printed out hard copy to be approved by the copy desk and art department. Finally—usually in those bleak hours between midnight and dawn when women give birth, when those leaning against death's door stumble through at last—with a small sigh of relief, he pushed the button that unleashed a burst of electrons over the phone lines, transmitting that night's last completed page to the printing plant in the Midwest, in one of those states starting with an I, Indiana or maybe Iowa. On press days, John was the last one to leave the building.

On this night, as the movement of pages between departments picked up its pace, John propped open the door between photocomp and the copy desk to expedite the flow, as he often did. He enjoyed watching through the half-open door as the comedy developed in the wee hours of the morning.

Shortly before midnight Preston stopped by the copy desk to say good night. John knew the copy editors struggled to hide their irritation at staying behind to clean up the verbal mess he had created while editing and reediting the stories.

"I'll be at home if you need me…"

"Sure, sure." Naomi, the copy chief, didn't bother to disguise her tone of cynical resignation. No one in her right mind would willingly wake Preston at three in the morning. John smiled at the sight of Naomi's narrowing eyes and the withering look she focused on Preston's retreating back.

Preston didn't bother to bid good night to John. He never did.

Helen stopped by the copy desk about fifteen minutes later, her usual drill. She was careful about not leaving the building before Preston did, which was prudent, considering the chaos he often left in his wake. John suspected her protectiveness toward her reporters was another factor. Her attitude verged on the maternal, and Preston was known for subjecting random reporters to sudden, unpredictable rants.

The copy desk after midnight was a rumpled scene. Plastic containers with the remains of takeout meals and half-eaten sandwiches were strewn about like body parts on a battlefield. Some reporters dispensed with their shoes. Women put their disheveled hair up and fastened it any old way, their original hairstyles long since blown apart.

But Helen seemed to have stepped out of a midday time warp, her jacket on, her makeup perfect, every strand of blonde hair in place.

She chatted with Naomi a minute and scanned the list of stories that were still not ready to go. "Good night, please don't hesitate to call me at home…"

Sometimes they did call her, and she never seemed to mind.

Helen leaned through the half-open door to photocomp. "Good night, John. Try not to stay till dawn."

He smiled shyly. "Do my best."

Some twenty minutes later, Meg the Knife loomed out of the fluorescent night, bearing down on the copy desk like a battleship, technically in violation of the rules. Although story editors were consulted on major problems, at this point in the game, fact-checkers and copy editors were supposed to polish the stories without interference from the writers. Writers supplied the necessary raw material, but too many of them were divas about their prose. Especially Meg the Knife, who argued over the grammar and precise wording of each sentence and every tiny factual detail, and was usually wrong.

An exasperated Naomi waved her away: "Listen, let us do our jobs, you'll see everything on a transmitted page tomorrow."

"Yeah, yeah, fuck you," Meg seethed, cursing through clenched teeth. When she finally retreated, some of the copy editors chuckled with relief, muttering, "Psycho bitch" and other terms of endearment.

A few minutes later, John was startled by the creak of a door hinge. He whirled. The Knife stood there, blade in hand. She had found the back door to photocomp—the door few people even knew existed—and slipped in. John opened his mouth to shoo her out, but before he could make a sound, Meg strode up to him, moving with impressive speed for a woman of her bulk. She held the knife to his windpipe and put a finger on her lips, motioning him to keep silent. Madness. John thought he detected foam at the corner of her mouth. He nodded okay.

The Knife positioned herself behind the half-open door to the copy desk and listened to the reporter dictating changes on her story, her face contorting in ugly grimaces. "They're butchering my copy," she whispered.

John sat frozen, his brain registering the scene with eerie clarity. He was amazed to see a tear roll down Meg's cheek when she heard that the word *probably* was being inserted into the most inflammatory sentence in the story.

They put in those *probably*s just to be on the safe side, just to make sure that the company they were trashing wouldn't win a libel suit. But to Meg, *probably* was a weasel word, contemptuous—it reeked of the garrote in the dark. She always yearned for the banzai charge, the bullet between the eyes. A matter of honor.

Apparently having heard enough, Meg just nodded to John and slipped out the back way as suddenly as she had arrived. John felt himself dissolve in a puddle of relief, assuming that was the end of it.

But as soon as John had transmitted the last page and the last weary copy editor had stumbled out of the building, Meg reappeared, blade glinting, like a bad acid flashback.

"Okay, John. There's one page you're going to resend."

John sputtered protests, but he knew from the start they were in vain. And he wasn't about to try to wrestle the knife away from her. In the end, he used all his technical expertise to cover his electronic tracks as best he could while he tinkered with the text and retransmitted the page. Meg was shrewd enough to limit her changes: She merely deleted the despised *probably* and a couple of other qualifying words.

John wondered whether to undo what he'd just done as soon as she was gone, then report the lunatic to Preston. But as she left that night, she looked John in the eye. "Thanks. And if you ever breathe a word of this—to anyone—I'll hunt you down and gut you like a fish."

WEDNESDAY, JUNE 16, 1999

Jake sat at his desk, reading Preston's congratulatory email for the twentieth time. Phrases jumped out at him. "Intrepid reporting." "This magazine needs more stories like that." Best of all, Preston had sent the message to the entire staff.

The print version of the story wouldn't hit the newsstands for a few days, but rumors about the article had started circulating on Wall Street earlier that week. Afraid that *The Wall Street Journal* or some other daily might beat them to print with it, Preston had taken the unusual step of posting the story on *The Magazine*'s Web site. Jake went online to check Unfettered's stock price: down 25 percent that morning. As he stared at the screen, an item popped up on the business wire services: Unfettered VP Resigns, Board Promises Full Investigation.

He read Preston's email for the twenty-first time, basking in glory.

***

Rebecca felt a surge of adrenaline as she clicked on the bookmark for *The Magazine*'s Web site and the page opened on her screen.

God, there it was. By Jake Rosenberg. She suppressed a snort.

And look at Unfettered. The stock was already in a nosedive. The business wires were all aflutter with the story.

Curious as to how the article had turned out, she began to read. Usually, she maintained as tight a control over her own prose as she could, and it felt odd to have handed in raw notes, to be this removed from the final product. She knew Jake could shape a story well, though he sometimes overdid the literary flourishes. But what would Preston do to it? The man couldn't edit his way out of a paper bag.

For a full minute, Rebecca couldn't get past the lead. A tangled mess. Oh, it delivered the requisite hook, at least, promising corporate scandal with plenty of greed and sex. But it piled up the metaphors and mangled them irretrievably, as if figures of speech had been put through a mental Cuisinart.

My God. That was certainly Preston trampling the paragraph to death.

She shuddered and forced herself to read on.

The article quickly improved after that unfortunate opening, as the story itself took hold, because the story itself was so good. Rebecca felt every inelegant phrase—and there were plenty—as an almost physical pain, yet halfway through the piece she had to admit that it was a classic of its kind.

They had copies of the contract with the fabric supplier. Textile experts quoted on the fabric's decline in quality. Bitching from the suppliers who were cut out.

Time-stamped photos of the fabric supplier spending the night at the VP's house.

Smokescreens and corporate obfuscation from the flacks. Lots of harrumphing.

Rebecca laughed out loud when she got to the bit about Bermuda. There was a photo of the hotel where the couple had stayed Memorial Day weekend. Kimmie had flown out, talked to the staff, tipped generously, found the maid who had cleaned up their room. Like all longtime hotel maids, she was jaded about guests. She probably wouldn't have remembered the discarded bottle of Kama Sutra love oil in the wastebasket if she hadn't found a pair of fur-lined handcuffs under the bed.

She wondered what the headline writers at the *New York Post* would do with this, snickering at the possibilities. Unfettered Bondage. Or maybe, Kama Sutra Leaves Exec in Awkward Position.

Damn Jake. He'd get a book contract for this, if not a Loeb Prize. Probably a made-for-TV movie on some cable channel before it was over.

She finished reading and nodded in quiet satisfaction.

She'd done good work.

***

Helen stared at the photograph of construction workers on a crossbeam. Flecks of sun glinted off the glass in the frame, creating the illusion that the beam was moving. Karen's assistant had told Helen that Karen was running late, but Helen wanted to wait. She was afraid that if she left, she wouldn't be able to make herself come back.

Helen had read and reread Karen's email: "Please come and see me today after lunch, okay? Around 2." She tried to read between the lines. At first, Helen thought that the tone was harsh. But the more she read it, the less ominous the message sounded. It was merely efficient, that was it, that's the way the Corps communicated, she decided. By two o'clock, Helen had almost convinced herself that Karen would tell her that it was okay to fire Kimmie. Still, the waiting was hard.

Karen materialized without warning. She was holding a white plastic bag that looked like it might be from the corner grocery. Her gray pantsuit was crisp, as if it had just been ironed. Karen said hello and unpacked her plastic bag. It contained three blemish-free tangerines and a bottle of water. Karen placed the tangerines and the water on her desk in a neat line. Helen wasn't surprised that Karen was a healthy eater, another difference between the Corps and reporters. Outside their building was a stand with fresh fruit, and Helen for years had promised herself that she would one day forgo a soup or snack from the deli and buy fruit from the stand. She never did. Still, she could have been so much worse. She thought of Rebecca. Helen had often chided her about the smell of old tuna salad that lingered in her office.

Karen picked up a tangerine and held it in her hand. "Imagine that this is Kimmie," she said. She seemed perfectly serious.

"These tangerines are your employees, Helen," Karen continued. "That's how you should look at them, devoid of emotion. They are all the same."

Juicy, orange and round, thought Helen. She didn't say it out loud. She didn't say anything. She felt talked down to, like a third-grader who was being taught about sex, the tangerines, the birds and the bees.

"You aren't going to go through an emotional process to decide which of the tangerines you're going to eat," Karen said. "You should approach work in a similar way. We're all equal."

She really was being serious, Helen realized.

"I talked to Kimmie. After our conversation, I believe that you're basing your decision to fire her on your own connection to her father."

Karen handed the tangerine to Helen. "This is Kimmie. She is just like everybody else. That's the way I want you to think about her."

Helen found herself standing in the empty hallway, numb with disbelief, holding the tangerine, which was warmer than she expected. Later, she remembered it as a startling drop of color and heat in that antiseptic realm of the tenth floor. By the time she sat down at her desk, the tangerine was gone, but she couldn't remember disposing of it.

The numbness slowly dissipated, leaving behind a cool, disturbing, unfamiliar rage.

***

It was evening before Helen allowed the stress of her day to really hit her, and then it hit hard. She was weary down to her marrow. She stood at the door to her apartment, one hand clutching the plastic bag that contained her dinner of takeout sushi, the other hand fumbling with her keys. Still, when she heard the ritual meow of greeting through the door, she couldn't help but smile.

Once inside, she bolted the door behind her, locking the outside world outside where it belonged. At last she could drop the mask, the iron control. In here, it was just her and Rasputin, and he never passed judgment on her. He was above that.

He was an elegant, affectionate black Bombay, and at the moment he was rubbing against her ankles and purring loudly. She bent down to scratch behind his ears. "Hi, Razz, how's my little boy? Did you miss me? I missed you too, honey."

She scooped up the cat, who perched happily on her shoulder, kicked off her shoes, tossed her dinner onto the kitchen counter and headed for the bedroom. As she passed the bathroom, she wrinkled her nose. "God, what did you do in there, Razz?" She sighed. "I've really got to change that litter. Later. Time to get comfortable. You don't know how lucky you are, Razz, not worrying about clothes."

Rasputin purred.

He sat on the bed and watched attentively as she stripped down to her panties and threw on a baggy T-shirt. "There, that's better. Sometimes I think I'll scream if I ever have to put on a suit again. Of course, that would be tomorrow. Well, let's have dinner."

Settled on the living room couch with a glass of wine and her plastic tray, she reached for the remote and turned on the news, then frowned in annoyance. CNN was recycling the same idiotic feature story she'd seen the other day. Wasn't anything happening in the world? She flipped to the *BBC World News*—political scandals in Argentina, mudslides in Turkey. At least it was real news. Sometimes cable was a wonderful thing.

She shared her sushi with Rasputin, then sprawled back on the couch and let him curl up in her lap. Maybe she'd have a long, hot soak in the tub tonight, with Rasputin supervising, as usual. After she dealt with the litter. After she finished her drink.

"God, what a day I had, Razz. I'm sure you just snoozed all day. You wouldn't believe the conversation I had with HR."

Rasputin made himself comfortable and listened patiently.

THURSDAY, JUNE 17, 1999

The too-late end of another long and irritating day. Helen, tired and hungry, stepped from the office building's polar air-conditioning into a swampy dusk. The street was sultry, too steamy for June, the air a wet slap in the face.

She'd barely recovered from that tropical shock when she almost tripped over Jake and Kimmie as they stumbled, drunk and giggling, out the door of the Gotham. No doubt they'd just finished a fine dinner, courtesy of Jake's expense account.

Jake, leaning on Kimmie for support, drew himself as erect as he could manage and tried his best Cary Grant smile, innocent and insolent at once. Helen knew that look all too well. "Helen. How you doing tonight?"

"I'm fine, Jake. How are you?"

"Me? I'm ex…excel…lent…"

"You're plastered, Jake." She turned to Kimmie. "He needs someone to take care of him when he's like this. You should take him home."

Kimmie bridled. "I take very good care of him, don't I, Jake?"

"That's right, Helen. Very good care."

"You bet." Kimmie leered.

Helen almost gagged. Instead, she said to Jake, "Don't you see how she's using you? All to get back at her father? How can you let her do this?"

Jake looked confused. "Her father?"

Kimmie's eyes narrowed. "Shut up, Helen."

Helen paused for a heartbeat, blinked. "She didn't tell you? You really don't know? I thought I was the last to find out. Tom Richardson is her father."

Jake half-staggered. He looked stupid with his mouth open.

Kimmie shrugged Jake's arm off her shoulders, stepped close to Helen and slapped her, hard. "Mind your own business, bitch."

Slapped her again, with her other hand.

Helen snapped out of her shock and slapped Kimmie backhanded, as hard as she could.

Kimmie reeled back, gathered herself and leaped.

Helen felt her breath knocked out of her twice, once as Kimmie tackled her, a shoulder smacking into her solar plexus, then again like an echo as they slammed onto the cement sidewalk. The two of them lay stunned for a second, then Kimmie straddled Helen, her arms flailing.

Instinctively, Helen grabbed Kimmie's wrists, trying to keep her fingernails away from her face. Kimmie yelped and pulled back, grabbing at her own dark curls as someone hauled her up by her hair, yanked her off Helen, then helped her to her feet. Jake. He reached down and pulled Helen up.

"Ladies, please…that's enough."

Helen stumbled, caught herself, looked down and kicked off her shoes. Broken heel.

Jesus. Helen glanced down, assessing the damage. The lining of her jacket was ripped. At least Kimmie looked worse for wear. Her cheek would bruise nicely.

Kimmie glared at Helen, her breath quick and shallow.

Helen stood silent, mortified.

An empty taxi cruised by. Helen scooped up her shoes, flagged down the cab and scrambled in without looking back.

PART THREE

You know something is happening here

WEDNESDAY, JULY, 1999

The close had run especially late, keeping the last copy editors at their posts till almost 5 a.m. John Squinzano had stayed even later. Now he emerged briefly into the dawn, then trudged down the subway stairs to catch the F train to Astoria, in Queens. A winner at last, he rode the ultimate reverse commute on a half-empty train. He was going to bed, to sleep, while these poor schmucks who surrounded him were going to work. As the train passed through midtown and headed for Queens, he knew, it would empty out even more, but this only made the ride better. He could always get a good seat. Sometimes he even sprawled across several and put his feet up.

The fallout from the Meg incident had subsided over the past few weeks. By the time the story editor realized that something had gone awry, it was too late. The page had run through the presses, the issue was bound and shipped to subscribers. Preston launched an investigation, but John was appointed to look into the technical side of the process. He eventually concluded that a rare combination of factors had triggered an obscure glitch in the software, causing the page to revert to an earlier version as it was transmitted. John instituted a new failsafe procedure to double-check page versions and ensure this wouldn't happen again.

The company Meg had targeted made noises about a libel suit, but then filed for bankruptcy.

And whenever Meg passed John in the hallway, she gave him a knowing smile. Every time, his stomach clenched, anticipating the slice of cold steel.

Now John scanned the other people in the subway car. Most were peering at the world with half-open eyes. Some yawned or sipped takeout coffee. A woman sitting across from him was putting on makeup. "Shit," she said each time the train jerked unexpectedly, almost driving the eye pencil into her cornea.

John opened his backpack and reached inside, hunting for a paperback to while away the ride home. The feel of slinky plastic. Damn, the Saks Fifth Avenue bag, the one Daisy had packed his lunch in. She was taunting him.

During the good times, John had often found a little reward waiting for him at the end of the ride. A morning quickie with Daisy. Sometimes he would crawl into bed and wake her. Sometimes she would be barely up when he got home, drinking her first cup of coffee, drying her hair or maybe putting rollers into it.

He would drag her back into the bedroom. The rollers had a forbidden air about them, as if he had sneaked a peek while she was still primping for him. He fantasized that she was a prostitute in a brothel, preparing for a client by smearing lipstick on her mouth and spraying perfume between her breasts. In fact, Daisy was grooming for her job as a receptionist in a doctor's office.

But the rollers unrolled his imagination. As he mounted Daisy, he would close his eyes and move his head closer to her and feel the rollers on his cheek, and imagine that he was doing it with a black woman. He associated black women with hair rollers—they were the only women he ever saw walking around in the street with rollers in their hair.

This morning, Daisy was still blow-drying her hair when he came in. She greeted him with a scowl and leveled the nozzle of the blow-drier in his direction, like the muzzle of an oversized revolver. The nozzle roared at him, ready to attack if he dared come any closer. He slunk away to the living room, poured himself a double shot of cheap bourbon and turned on CNN.

They hadn't made love in months. First, she was running late, and had to scramble to get to work. Then it was, leave me alone, is that the only thing you have on your mind when you come home? And then the rejections had turned into accusations: So you think that's how you prove your manhood? Maybe you should concentrate on getting what makes men attractive to women. These days, they were down to silence and the angry blow-drier.

It was all because of that damn Russki. The Russki had recently married Daisy's younger sister, Rose. He didn't even speak English well. In fact, he had asked John to fill out all of his official papers for the immigration service. John had, and he and Daisy had exchanged looks, and after the Russki left they had asked each other if this country needed any more citizens, especially ones who couldn't write proper English.

Rose kept telling them about some degree from some polytechnic school in some unpronounceable town in Russia that the Russki apparently held. But who could ever check on that? And what's some Russian degree worth anyway? And what job was he going to get without an American degree? How was he going to support Rose?

So Daisy and John had looked askance on Rose's marriage and suspected that the Russki married her only to get a green card. But before long that feeling of superiority had turned to envy. And the most vicious type of envy, because the object of Daisy's pity could now pity her.

The damn Russki turned out to be a much more successful provider than John had ever been. In the first six months of the marriage he made so much money day-trading stocks that he bought Rose an apartment in Manhattan, and she quit her job as a receptionist—a job that Daisy had found for her several years before.

John knew that day-trading brokerages required a large initial stake—traders had to put up $50,000 or $100,000. The Russki was always suspiciously vague when asked where he had gotten his stake. When he was pressed on the subject, his English, which had been improving, would suddenly desert him. And rumor had it that the small brokerage where the Russki placed his trades was financed by the Russian mafia in Brooklyn. The conclusion was obvious to John: The man had done something dangerous and almost certainly illegal for his stake. He had probably borrowed from loan sharks, gambled in the market and gotten very, very lucky. He had taken a wild, reckless chance and pulled it off. No doubt he had long since paid off the debt and was free of the sharks. But it could easily have gone the other way. He could have lost his kneecaps, or his life.

The thought just made John bristle all the more. What the hell did Daisy want him to do, start taking insane chances like that? Would she like making love to a man with no knees? He might as well become a cocaine smuggler.

The Russki's overnight wealth was too much too soon, and he would have zilch in the end. That was John's belief and fervent hope. The damn Russki was bound to make a stupid bet that would erase all his gains. Perhaps a crazed fellow trader would shoot him. Or the market would finally crash. It had to slide sometime. Something would happen and the Russki would lose everything. But John no longer even bothered to assert this to Daisy. He just prayed for sweet justice.

Meanwhile, his home had turned into one of the outer circles of hell. He tried to think exactly which circle. John's father had instilled in him a love of Dante, but it had been many years since he last read the *Inferno*. Probably the fourth circle, he decided, the one for the greedy. Rose had taken to shopping at Saks, then detouring by their Astoria apartment just to show off the loot to Daisy. And when the Russki accompanied her, he yapped about positions and stocks and his trades—it all sounded Greek to the women, so they admired him even more.

Having worked at a financial magazine for twenty-five years, John understood investing much better than the Russki. But whenever he launched into a discourse about financial analysis and the dangers of momentum trading, the damn Russki gave him a rich man's condescending look. And Daisy eyed him with contempt.

These visits always inspired Daisy to sprinkle the conversation with barbed comments. She'd say, "I know of men who start making real money in their first year on the job," or "it would be so nice to stay at home and not have to work."

Last weekend Rose had shaken salt onto his wounds when, in addition to the usual Saks bags, she brought over some travel brochures and asked John sweetly where she and the Russki should go on vacation. Daisy scanned the brochures and pronounced, "But the Bahamas, of course, you should go to the Bahamas," as if John and Daisy regularly vacationed there rather than on the Jersey shore.

Briefly, John was gripped by a vision: The damn fair-haired Russki would indeed travel to the Bahamas, and, too macho to use any sunscreen—John had heard him say that men who slathered on sunscreen must be gay—he would burn, sizzle, peel and squirm, in exquisite pain.

Daisy emerged from the bedroom, finally ready for her day, and flitted out the door with a perfunctory goodbye. John grunted in acknowledgment.

He got up off the couch and poured some more bourbon.

WEDNESDAY EVENING, AUGUST 4, 1999

Dennis Flaherty eased through the door to the gallery and glanced across the street to Kimmie's loft. Oh shit, that Rebecca woman was already there. He ran to the closet where he kept his gear and launched into a flurry of precise motions as he set up, starting with the laser mike. He started the tape recorder, adjusted his headphones, checked the cameras.

Kimmie was talking as she opened a bottle of wine. "…don't know how long I can keep up this front."

"What do you mean?"

"Well, it's…maybe I'm just getting bored. It's Jake, he's…he's so weak. So easy to manipulate. Not enough challenge there. When I'm not engaged enough, I tend to drift off. Lately, I've even wondered if he's not picking up on something. I'm afraid I'm just phoning it in."

"Well, then, focus, girl, focus. Just a few more weeks, but you need to keep him happy till then. Better that you stay a step removed from the stories. Besides, it's a suspiciously good string of stories for a rookie reporter."

Kimmie poured the wine.

Rebecca took a sip. "I like your hair up like that." Kimmie had gathered it into a loose chignon. "Reminds me of when we first met, back in your Morgan Stanley days. You were always a good source. Hot, too—and how many Wall Street types can you say that about?" She stood behind the couch and began to rub Kimmie's neck and shoulders.

Kimmie closed her eyes. "Mmmm, that feels good. And you were always a good friend. Especially after that…um…research library incident. Most people treated me like I had leprosy."

Rebecca giggled. "Ah, yes, the research library incident, that's a good term for it. But you're far too lovely to be a leper."

"Thanks…I think. Or is that faint praise?"

"No, not at…you know better than that, my beauty. And what, exactly, did you learn from your research?"

Kimmie frowned as if pondering deeply. "Well, Mr. Braithwaite has a birthmark shaped just like a teapot on his..."

Rebecca leaned over and shut her up with a kiss. "I think I know too much already."

THURSDAY, AUGUST 5, 1999

Flaherty stood in the shade, across the street from the offices of *The Magazine*, smoking a cigarette. He glanced at his watch impatiently, a long-practiced gesture designed to give the impression that he was there to meet someone. Actually, having just followed Kimmie to work, he was deciding how to structure the rest of his day. Knock off until evening and pick Kimmie up again when she left? Or hang around in case she ran out and, say, met someone for lunch?

There were multiple factors to consider. This day would be uncomfortably warm and humid. And it would be difficult, even for someone as bland as Flaherty, to loiter in the area all day without being noticed. Of course, given that he was running up a billionaire's tab, he could always call in reinforcements from the agency, but he was reluctant to resort to that unless absolutely necessary. He preferred to work alone. He could always disguise himself as a crazy, homeless street person, but Flaherty didn't enjoy that much, and there were other drawbacks. It was often an excellent tactic for static surveillance—no one was surprised to see you sitting on the sidewalk all day—but not so good once you were on the move. People became too aware of your presence, in order to give you a wide berth.

Before Flaherty could settle on a plan, Jake Rosenberg emerged from *The Magazine* and stood blinking on the sunny side of the street. And with him, wasn't that Richardson's fiancée? Yes. Interesting. Problem solved.

The two strolled off, heading downtown. Flaherty stubbed out his cigarette, crossed the street and fell into step about half a block behind.

Helen had been surprised when Jake asked her out for coffee—they hadn't spoken much for weeks—and even more surprised when he suggested their old cafe. Once upon a time, they had gone there almost every morning after making love to have their "naughty cappuccino" before work. Jake had always laughed when Helen glanced around furtively, afraid that someone from *The Magazine* might walk in and see them together. "So what, who cares, we could just be talking about work," he would say, as if anybody might actually believe that.

Now, as they sauntered through the West Village, Jake complained about the heat. Helen just shrugged. It was barely midmorning, and she could already smell alcohol on his breath.

They hadn't walked far before she found the suspense unbearable. "Okay, Jake, talk to me. What's up?"

He sighed. "Jesus, Helen, I think I'm gonna go crazy."

"What are you talking about?"

"It's Kimmie. I'm sorry, I know there's no love lost between you two, but this is for my sake. All of a sudden, she's like a different person."

Helen raised her eyebrows. "I thought that was part of her appeal."

"No, no, this is different. Working together, that's still good, still…productive. But outside work, sometimes I think she's avoiding me. And even when we're together, she's…distant. Keeps me at arm's length. At least most of the time. Every once in a while, the old Kimmie resurfaces, just as if nothing had changed. Then—bam—ice queen again. That almost makes it worse. It's like that experiment where they made cats neurotic by giving them random rewards and punishments. I can't figure out the pattern, so I'm going nuts."

"Why are you telling me all this? You want relationship advice from me? About Kimmie?"

"Yeah, maybe it's not fair, or sensible, but…Helen, I know a lot of women, but not many of them as friends. And you've always been good for a woman's perspective…"

Helen chuckled. "Does that mean you think this is a hormone surge?"

"No, not really. I think it's something else. But I guess…I thought you might know something. After all, you and her father…"

"Please, don't refer to Tom that way," Helen said. "It just irritates me."

"But has she been seeing a lot of her father? I mean Tom. Lately? I mean, where is she all the time? She keeps calling someone, and she doesn't want me to hear their conversations…"

"Tom hasn't mentioned anything to me, and I'm sure he would have said something." Helen looked up and realized they had reached the cafe.

"So what's happening? Does she have some other guy?"

Helen shook her head. Poor sap. She felt a sense of superiority and a profound relief that silly infatuations were behind her now that she had found Tom. "Let's go inside, Jake. It's air-conditioned."

She was grateful for the piercing soprano wailing on the cafe's stereo system, muffling Jake's pathetic nonsense.

Flaherty lingered in front of a nearby shop window, peering intently at a magnificent array of silk Italian ties, as they entered the cafe. He let the second hand on his watch sweep out a full minute before he moved on, his eyes and ears recording every detail as he strolled past the cafe's entrance. Damn. They were sitting at a small round table near the middle of the room. It would be hard to get close. He caught a cool air-conditioned gust as a young lady with pierced everything pushed open the door and walked out. And a high-decibel blast. It was one of those old-style Italian cafes with a tin roof and tile walls. Chatter ricocheted off those hard surfaces like rubber bullets. And some soprano was belting out a despairing aria over the stereo.

He continued on, then paused at another store. This one sold nothing but leather clothing. Flaherty thought hard. The terrain was not good, especially the audio terrain. He'd never get close enough to overhear them. But every snoop instinct in his body told him to listen in. One factor was in his favor: The cafe had a takeout counter.

He pulled two sticks of gum from his pocket, stuffed them in his mouth and chewed furiously.

Flaherty ordered an iced cappuccino and waited at the counter, his left hand in his pocket, toying with an object roughly the size and shape of a large button. It was a disposable bug—a mike and transmitter, hundred-foot range, two-hour battery life. As he picked up his cappuccino and turned away from the counter, he coughed into his left hand, discreetly spitting out the gum.

He was passing Jake and Helen's table when he tripped and stumbled. His thigh bumped the table's edge, almost—but not quite—spilling their coffee before he caught his balance with his left hand. Then he was gone in a cloud of muttered apologies.

Outside, Flaherty sipped his drink, studied the leather clothing some more and adjusted what appeared to be a Walkman.

…hiss…static…hiss…clatter…

static…the soprano: "aaiyiiiieeee…"

…hiss…Helen: "…you want out of this?"

Jake: "No, I think…Kimmie…" static… "she wants…"

…hiss… "two lattes, skinny…"

Jake: "…afraid of what she'll do…"

Helen: "…your shoes…wouldn't trust her…"

Soprano: "…ooooooooooooooooooooo…"

Jake: "…whatever happens, whatever Kimmie…" …hiss… "you'll always stand by me, won't you, Helen? You'll always be there."

Helen: "Of course…" …hiss… "…know I will…"

…static…

Flaherty frowned. What the hell was this all about? And why was Richardson's fiancée so chummy with Kimmie's boyfriend? Were they plotting against Kimmie? Or with her? Did Richardson know? It wouldn't be the first time a client had failed to share all relevant knowledge. That was more the rule than the exception. Still, Flaherty hated feeling out of the loop. And suppose Richardson was clueless about whatever this was?

He decided to keep a close eye on Helen Caswell for a while.

***

Helen turned off the shower and reached for a towel. First time in hours she'd felt clean. She hated this sultry weather.

She opened the bathroom's frosted glass window to let the steam escape. Thank God, it was beginning to cool down outside. New front moving through this evening. Distant thunder.

Open or closed, the window had never concerned her. It looked out on the high-rise's setback roof, and the only other windows with a line of sight were distant enough that a voyeur would need a telescope. Anyone going to that much trouble, she figured, deserved an eyeful.

Nor did it concern her when Rasputin jumped into the still-wet tub with her. The cat was a little eccentric and liked to play in puddles. But it did concern her, very much, when her wet black cat streaked past her face on his way to the window—and out.

"No! Rasputin! Come back here!" She wrapped herself in the towel and reached through the narrow window, hoping for a handful of feline. She came up empty.

Wriggling further through the window, she scanned the roof. "Razz! Come here, you stupid cat." It was tough to spot him at night against the black tar. She got her shoulders out the window and the towel came loose. She tried to pull it up but couldn't work her arm back through the window far enough to grab it. Finally, she let it fall. It was just in the way, and there was nobody out here but Razz. Somewhere.

She was halfway out the window, out almost to her waist, when she saw the cat, just a few yards away. "Rasputin! Come back here right now!" He leveled a cool, insolent gaze at her, sat and yawned. She glanced down and noticed the sooty smudges that covered her body. The windowsill was filthy. She'd have to shower again. "Razz, I swear, I'll have you made into a hat."

Lightning flashed. She froze. In that split second of false day, she found herself looking at a man on a nearby roof, maybe fifty yards away. She couldn't see his face because he was watching her through binoculars. Before she could react, lightning flashed a second time, catching him as he lowered the binoculars. His face was pale, mild, forgettable. But familiar somehow.

She had twisted herself most of the way back inside the window when the thunder hammered out its double crack. A wet, black, terrified cat hurled itself in after her. Rasputin hated thunder. She slammed the window shut and locked it, then slumped against the cool tile, trying to digest what had just happened.

Must be some neighborhood pervert. Probably a harmless peeper. Maybe that was why he looked familiar, she'd probably seen him in the corner deli or at the dry cleaners. Still, it was creepy. She had more than one reason to shower again.

She stood, tossed the cat out of the tub and turned the shower on hot.

FRIDAY, AUGUST 6, 1999

The next morning, still half asleep, she pulled on a robe, padded barefoot across the living room and reached, as usual, to open the blinds. Something made her hesitate. Then she remembered, and came fully awake. This is silly, she thought. Still, she peered through the slats and scanned the street. This is just paranoid, just...

She saw him. He was standing at the bus shelter across the street with eight or nine other people. Reading the paper. Slowly, carefully, she moved away from the window. Took a deep breath. It was probably nothing. If he lived in the neighborhood, he was most likely just waiting for the bus.

She walked to the kitchen, poured herself a shot of orange juice, made a pot of coffee. Poured a cup. Sidled back up to the living room window. He was still there, but now there was only one other person waiting. So a bus had come—and gone. But not him.

It was then that he glanced up, fleetingly, in her direction. And then she knew.

The cafe. That's where she had seen him. He had bumped into their table.

She felt herself spinning into vertigo. What was going on? Was he some kind of stalker?

A sudden impulse to document the situation surfaced in her head. Yes. She would turn the tables. She rushed for her Minolta, snapped on the telephoto lens, checked to make sure it was loaded with film. Back to the window. Ease one slat open. Now. Yes, that's right, you move out of the way. Click. Now, look up. Up. That's it. Click. Click. Now away, a profile. Click. Beautiful. Got you.

Helen slumped on her couch and wondered whether she should call the police. No, something told her not to, not yet. Not until she had a clearer idea what was going on. But she couldn't go out there, not while he was watching. She would call the office, say that she was coming in late. She would outwait him.

Helen walked into *The Magazine*'s offices at 11:30, a couple hours after the apparent stalker had given up and vanished. She had just dropped off her film at a one-hour photo-developing shop around the corner.

She spent about twenty minutes trying to catch up on her day, answering phone calls and email, but found it impossible to concentrate. At last she shut her office door and opened her window. There were several half-stale cigarettes left in a pack she had stashed in her desk. She didn't smoke often, but this day struck her as an excellent day to indulge. For the next forty minutes, she puffed and paced back and forth, her steps tracing and retracing a semicircle around one side of her desk. Exactly one hour after her arrival, she dashed back out to the photo shop.

A few minutes later she strode back in, pictures in hand, and headed straight for Jake's office. She almost collided with him as he stepped out the door.

"Helen, whoa. Love to chat, but I'm late for lunch with…Helen, are you all right?"

"Not really."

"Hmm, must be serious. Tell you what, I'll hurry back from lunch and we can…"

"Jake." She looked him in the eye. "I have to show you something. Now. It's important."

He paused. "Okay. Come into my parlor…"

They retreated into his office, and Helen closed the door. She selected two photos of a pale, sandy-haired man and shoved them under Jake's nose. "You recognize this guy?"

Jake held the photos by their edges and studied them a long moment. "You know, he does look familiar. Damned if I can place him, though." He looked up at Helen quizzically. "Can you give me some context?"

"Yesterday, in the cafe. Some guy bumped into our table, remember? That's him."

"Really?" Jake squinted at the pictures again, then shrugged. "If you say so. I'm sorry, Helen, I barely glanced up. Didn't get a good look at his face. But why do you have photos of this guy?"

"Because he was watching me, watching my apartment. I spotted him last night, then again this morning. When I realized it was the guy from the cafe, I…I guess I freaked out a little. I don't know if he's stalking me or what."

"Yeah, well, I can see how that might freak you out. But are you sure it's the same guy? I mean…"

Jake stopped, stared hard at the photos. Something in his eyes clicked into sharp focus. "Wait a minute, I have seen this guy. And not at the cafe. Yeah…I'm sure of it. Near Kimmie's place, hanging around her block, a few times. I figured he lived in the neighborhood. That's weird."

He raised one eyebrow. "He couldn't be stalking both of you, could he?"

Helen shook her head. "I doubt it. Aren't stalkers supposed to be obsessed with one stalkee at a time?"

"Yeah, I guess so. Damn weird, though."

"Look, Jake, it's probably nothing. Wild coincidence or something. Go to your lunch and we'll talk later."

"Okay, sure. But I'll keep an eye out for this character."

"Thanks."

Jake left. Helen stood in his office, staring at the wall. The fear that had gripped her all morning dissipated, only to be replaced by a feeling just as disturbing. Something was beginning to crystallize in her mind, something she wasn't ready to examine closely. What had Jake said? "He couldn't be stalking both of you…" But if the man was not a stalker, what was he? And if she was being watched…and Kimmie was being watched . . .She broke out of her trance and walked quickly toward her office. She still had two cigarettes left, and she would need them both.

MONDAY, AUGUST 9, 1999

Flaherty slouched in the soft leather chair across the teak desk from Tom Richardson and studied the billionaire's artificially perfect tan with more than a hint of awe. His own lightly freckled skin allowed for no tan at all, much less something so eerily even.

So far, he'd been reporting to Richardson mostly by phone, but some things were best done in person. There were times when, to make further progress, you just had to go back to the client. Flaherty wanted to study Richardson's face.

"So that's it as far as Kimmie's movements and contacts, sir.…Sometimes she sleeps with this Jake, sometimes with this woman, this Rebecca…"

"Any significance to that?"

Flaherty shrugged. "Other than personal, probably not. Seems to be just another financial journalist."

"But, sir, if I may…You're engaged to marry a certain Helen Caswell I believe?"

"Yes. How is that relevant?"

"Well, in keeping an eye on Kimmie's associates, Kimmie led to Jake, and Jake led to Helen Caswell. I realize that they're colleagues, of course, but…Well, what can you tell me about their relationship?"

"They're friendly." Richardson straightened in his chair and glared down at Flaherty. "Look, I gather that once upon a time they had a thing, a brief affair. Don't really know the details except that it didn't amount to much and they remained friends. This Jake is something of a skirt-chaser, I hear. That's it. I didn't hire you to spy on my fiancée."

"No, sir, of course not. But I couldn't help notice Jake and Helen speaking intently the other day. Followed them to a cafe, did a bit of eavesdropping. What do you make of this?"

Flaherty produced a pocket tape recorder and hit play.

… hiss…Helen: "…you want out of this?"

Jake: "No, I think…Kimmie…" static… "she wants…"

…hiss… "two lattes, skinny…"

Jake: "…afraid of what she'll do…"

Helen: "…your shoes…wouldn't trust her…"

Soprano: "…ooooooooooooooooooooo…"

Jake: "…whatever happens, whatever Kimmie…" …hiss… "you'll always stand by me, won't you, Helen? You'll always be there."

Helen: "Of course…" …hiss… "…know I will…"

…static…

Flaherty kept his eyes riveted on Richardson's face, and thus learned two things. The man was baffled, utterly clueless as to whatever might be really going on here. And somewhere deep inside, beneath that perfect tan, he was shaken.

FRIDAY, AUGUST 13, 1999

Traffic was already congealing on Route 27, but Luis, the driver, remained serene as always. In the backseat, Tom and Helen sat in silence on the slow cruise to Bridgehampton. Helen punctuated the emptiness by quizzing Luis about his kids, and Luis happily filled her in on Ramon's baseball scores and little Lorraine's ballet classes.

Helen was puzzled by the tense distance Tom was maintaining. Was it work? Whatever the reason, she thought she had the cure. The surprise she had in mind for the evening should break this sullen spell. There should be no silence after the surprise. Not exactly words, maybe, but no silence either.

She always enjoyed visits with her grandmother. Tatiana's house didn't feel at all like a Hamptons beach mansion. It wasn't close to the ocean, modern in style or trimmed in white marble. Tatiana's father—Helen's grandfather—had bought the house in the 1940s because of his fear that the Germans would bomb New York. He had planned to move his family to the shore, and the house he selected had belonged to a wealthy farmer who used to live there year-round. Its wide-plank hardwood floors were now graced with Persian rugs threadbare enough to have been in the family for generations. The Tyrkovas had furnished the place in simple rustic style, with a piano and several icons in the living room. Bedrooms were austere. Each featured a bed, a little commode and a cross above the door. The place had a monastic feel, the kind of severe simplicity that wouldn't dream of competing with the beauty of the ocean and the dunes, or of creating vulgar Jacuzzi luxuries next to God's real surf.

The paint was peeling on the veranda railing, and the unruly hedges were overgrown enough to block too much of the sunlight. Inside, pine bookshelves sagged along the walls of the library, bent by the burden of too many thoughts encoded in hundreds of books, most in Russian, French or

German. If she were observing her usual routine that afternoon, Tatiana would be curled into an overstuffed easy chair, book in hand. She'd mentioned to Helen that she was reading the love letters of a Russian countess, Madame Hanska, to Honore Balzac, by whom she was pregnant at the time. It was the sort of reading, Tatiana felt, that lent historical perspective to the discussions of her household.

For the latest court gossip of this unfortunate modern age flowed through Tatiana's house as pedigreed Frenchmen and Italians dropped by to give her updates on Princess Natalia's niece's stormy love affairs in Paris, and the displeasure of the house of Windsor at the marriage of the king of Greece to a nouveau riche American, the daughter of some tycoon who owned a string of duty-free shops or something equally awful.

Tatiana never went out to socialize in Bridgehampton, never attended barbecues given by bankers or celebrity weddings. Whenever she needed a walk, she ventured to the nearby grocery store. That was as far as she would extend herself to mingle. Helen had once accompanied her on one of these excursions.

Wearing a simple floor-length brown cotton dress, her shoulders covered by a shawl—her arms were slim and in good shape for her age, but showing off one's arms was vulgar—and carrying an orange sun parasol, Tatiana swept into the nearby grocery with all the gravitas of a head of state. Once there, she stood by the cashier's, list in hand, waiting to be served, not bothering to wander the aisles herself, even though it was a self-service store. Helen, uncomfortable, tried to explain in a quiet voice how this was usually done, but Tatiana waved away her objections, noting that she was not "most people."

Most of the store clerks regarded her with skittish awe and addressed her with such respect that Helen found it comical. When one insolent clerk—a new hire—balked at fetching Tatiana's stuff from the shelves, the store's owner flew into an apoplectic fit, followed by fulsome apologies to the great lady. Tatiana Tyrkova was the closest that the town had to royalty.

Tatiana was still reading when Marusha, her Russian maid, ushered in Tom and Helen.

"Oh, how wonderful to see you two. You'll want to freshen up, then come down to the parlor. Marusha, bring out the bliny…"

Tatiana got up, straightened her long dress and stole a glance in the mirror, checking that her bun, in which swirls of brown and gray hair spiraled toward the center, was in perfect order.

"Helen, darling," she said warmly as the two of them embraced and kissed, "you won't believe the bliny tonight…"

"Oh, they are so fattening, and not too healthy…" Helen started to say.

"Oh, Helen, please stop that nonsense right away. You sound like an

American!"

Marusha reappeared. The bliny, Russian pancakes served with caviar and sour cream, materialized like a dream come true.

Tom usually enjoyed ganging up with Tatiana to tease Helen. But tonight he stood in the hallway, distracted. Remote.

Cousin Arkadii, an old bachelor who devoted himself to caring for Tatiana, started playing the piano. Having eaten one blina, Helen leaned back in the armchair fighting the desire to have another one. Like any good Russian, she loved bliny, and wanted to eat and eat and eat them. That's why she hated being around them so much. Invariably, her discipline won, and she emerged from the evening a winner over bliny and vodka.

The Chopin joyful mazurka—the incorrigible Arkadii chose Chopin over Russian composers—muffled the uneasy silence between Tom and Helen. Thank God for Chopin. Helen was so grateful that she didn't make any cracks to Arkadii about playing Mussorgsky, Helen's favorite composer.

Across from her, Tom balanced his plate on his knee, with the blina still lying on it, uneaten, the sour cream beginning to melt. Strange, he adored bliny, and just to spite Helen used to scarf down several of them, all the while exchanging looks with Tatiana, mocking Helen. The two of them must have thought they had some secret pact, and Helen didn't bother to dispel their belief.

But today Tom wasn't eating or joking around with Tatiana. He was engrossed in the music. A deep line creased his forehead, the first time ever that Helen had noticed such a mark worn in the smoothness of his face. The line unsettled her. An alien thing, it didn't belong there. New and coded with unknown meanings, it left her disoriented.

While nobody was looking, Helen reached for a glass of vodka and downed it very quickly, all in one gulp. The surprise she had planned demanded not only finesse in execution, but some courage as well.

"Marusha, give Mr. Richardson some fresh bliny, can't you see this one is melting away," Tatiana commanded, "no, not just one, at least two…"

"Thank you, Mary," Tom said feebly, ignoring Tatiana's obvious displeasure at this anglicizing of her maid's name. "Actually, Mary, one would be plenty, thank you.…I think I'll go to bed early tonight."

Helen had one more quick shot before following him upstairs. A silent mantra echoed in her head as she climbed the steps, flushed from the vodka, ready to make love: "I will talk to you like a princess, I will fight you like a man, I will fuck you like a maid." She kept one hand tucked inside her loose cotton blouse, within which she was smuggling a dark red crystal wine glass on a long, thick stem that, Tatiana insisted, had once belonged to the Tolstoy household in Yasnaya Polyana.

With Tolstoy's glass, full to the brim with red muscatel, hidden under the bed, she waited for Tom to go to the bathroom. Once alone, she changed quickly, crossed herself while looking at Christ on the crucifix above the door, and started slowly pouring the wine down the front of her white linen nightgown. The gown had long sleeves and reached all the way down to the floor without revealing a square inch of skin.

On Helen's orders, Marusha had ironed the starched gown for over an hour, until it became so crisp that its edges could give one paper cuts. Only a naive virgin who didn't understand desire would wear a gown so intimidating, a virtual fortress guarding her chastity. Unless she understood that a man would see it as a dare, a sexual gauntlet thrown at his feet.

Muscatel formed a deep red stain starting at Helen's breasts, cutting her gown in two, dripping all the way to her bare feet. She sat on the edge of the bed, her lips pursed into a bow.

"Please come and help me," she stage-whispered as Tom came back to the bedroom. She summoned what she hoped was a virginal whimper: "I am so cold, I have never done it before." Then she stood, gulped the last of the wine, and, suddenly transformed into a seductress, kissed him hard, spilling some of the muscatel into his mouth. Underneath the virginal gown, Helen was wearing her surprise—austere black satin lingerie, as wet as her black bikini when she had climbed out of his pool in East Hampton.

"I love you, Tom," she whispered.

His voice was quiet and detached. "Your gown is wet. You'll catch cold if you don't take it off. Sorry, I'm very tired. I need to get some sleep."

TUESDAY, AUGUST 17, 1999

Helen walked briskly back from the well-stocked magazine store around the block, her copy of *Women's Wear Daily* tucked tightly under her arm, marched straight into her office and shut the door. Very deliberately, she sat at her desk and studied the cover photo of Naomi Campbell for a minute, hesitating.

Reluctantly, Helen turned to the last page. A celebrity photo essay included a shot of her and Tom at a Republican Party fundraiser. Seeing her picture in the daily made Helen uneasy in an uncharacteristically superstitious way. If she were already Tom's wife, that would be different. But she wasn't, and she was suddenly afraid that the photo might jinx their future.

She started reading the long caption beneath the photo and caught her breath. "Helen Caswell, senior editor at *The Magazine* and the luckiest woman in Manhattan, no doubt still wondering if she's dreaming or if she's really nailed down handsome billionaire fiancé Tom Richardson. After all, he's eluded some of the best. She'd better not count her chickens yet, or have any skeletons in her closet. We hear he's checking her out. Could his feet be getting chilly?"

God, what were they talking about? It's not true, oh my God.

She took a deep breath, told herself not to be an idiot. If anyone should know better than to take this seriously, she should. Journalists could be so vicious, so casual about disrupting lives…it still stunned her sometimes.

She felt the need to get out of the building and walk the streets for a while, wilting summer weather be damned. It would do her good, she'd sweat out her anger.

She stood, tossed her *WWD* into her wastebasket and strode out of her office. Across from the elevators, the back end of a row of cubicles formed a gray wall on which people posted interesting tidbits. She noticed a flyer about their new medical plan on which some wag had drawn a skull and crossbones. Then she stopped short.

In a central spot on the gray wall someone had pinned up the photo of Helen and Tom, carefully cut out of *Women's Wear Daily*—complete with caption.

***

Another night in photocomp. Around 10 p.m., John took a sandwich from yet another hated Saks bag. Well, soon he would be able to afford shopping at Saks, he thought, unwrapping the sandwich. Perhaps take a fancy vacation. He had a momentary vision, a flash of his wife lolling in the Caribbean sun, wearing nothing but coconut oil and a smile, and with curlers in her hair. He was going to show Daisy that, just like the damn Russki, he could be a conniving opportunist.

He was breaking all the rules. He felt a surge of exhilaration at the thought. Hell, he had already risked his job at Meg the Knife's prodding, and for what? Simple fear. He was more afraid of Meg than of Preston.

Now he was violating the most sacred rules of financial journalism, and he was doing it for fun and profit. No one on *The Magazine*'s staff was allowed to trade a stock that was the subject of a story until after publication, when the readers had a chance to act on the same information. Short-term trading was also forbidden, so any stock John bought, he was supposed to hold for at least six months. Until now, John had always played by the rules and had always felt like a loser. He would be a loser no more.

Usually, George Diller worked in photocomp during the day, but he had apparently come down with a nasty case of food poisoning, so John had come in early to work a double shift. Around lunchtime Bruce Buccino had sent a story through the computer network to Preston for its final edit, and John had sneaked a peek. It was an upbeat article about the prospects for Wyrdmetric Corp., a biotech firm that had developed a biochip that performed automatic gene analysis. John's mind had raced as it absorbed the possibilities Bruce sketched out. Within a few years every hospital, clinic and doctor's office would be using these chips to analyze every patient who walked through the door. In the meantime, all the biotechs and pharmaceuticals would order scads of these things to use in their research. And since the product wasn't a drug, it didn't face all the uncertainties of clinical trials.

John had hesitated only a few minutes before logging on to his TD Waterhouse account. His stock portfolio was small and dull, mainly safe blue chips like AT&T. Out of boredom and frustration, he had recently dumped his Procter & Gamble and bought some Enron. Now he sold his GE and Wells Fargo stock, which gave him about $10,000 to play with. He used it all to buy Wyrdmetric.

John was perfectly aware that Wyrdmetric was a volatile stock, sometimes gyrating wildly in the course of a single day, but he couldn't resist checking on it a few times during the afternoon. Every time he looked, the share price had dropped a little further. By the time the market closed that day, it had dropped almost 25 percent since John had bought in. He grew mildly annoyed. Could have gotten a better price if he had waited a few hours. Still, he shrugged this off. Shouldn't get too greedy. He was sure to make a killing on this one.

In a week the story would be on the newsstands and in the hands of subscribers. Bruce would do the TV rounds—probably CNBC in the predawn hours—to talk up his story, the stock would shoot for the sky, and John would sell it, thus violating the short-term trading rule. Hell, break one rule, why not two? John wondered how much profit he would make. With a stock like Wyrdmetric, it could be 50 percent, maybe more.

He was just finishing his sandwich when he noticed that Preston had sent the story on to the copy desk. A little more polishing and it would be on its way to the printing plant. He took another look to see how Preston had tweaked it.

He hadn't gotten beyond the second paragraph when the wave of nausea hit. He read on frantically, cursing as he scanned the text. "Motherfucker…how can…goddamn it, no, no…you fuck!"

Apparently, Preston was still insecure enough in his position to feel the need to slavishly emulate Roberts, his mentor, in certain ways. From an editorial point of view, the problem with this was simply that Preston wasn't as good at these things. Not as deft or economical in his prose, not as incisive in his insights. But the editorial point of view was not what concerned John at the moment.

The particular type of surgery Preston had just performed on Bruce's story had been perfected by Roberts. It was a classic example of what the writers called a reverse edit with a twist. Through editorial alchemy, Bruce's positive, optimistic story had become a negative one. Of course, as editor in chief, Preston assumed that he knew better than whoever actually reported the story, and he felt the need to establish that principle among the staff. An intimidation edit was fairly easy to get away with when it came to the more junior writers and reporters. Not so easy when it involved someone as senior as Bruce. That was the problem from a management point of view. Bruce would no doubt rant and sulk, perhaps demand that his byline be taken off the story. It hardly seemed worth it. But John had no empathy to spare for Bruce's problems, much less Preston's. The management perspective failed to engage him.

He could see things only from his own point of view, and right then it felt anchored to the bottom of a deep well. The essential facts in the story remained the same, but shifts in emphasis and tone had transformed it. There was concern about competitors in the U.S., in Europe, in Taiwan, rivals scrambling to market their own—possibly cheaper or more versatile—biochips. Much space was devoted to the risks of several patent lawsuits now moving through the courts. Questions were raised about how to value the stock, especially since Wyrdmetric wasn't earning any money yet. And the story raised doubts about the near-term prospects of the biotech sector as a whole—was it not due for one of its periodic drubbings at the hands of the market? The conclusion: Keep away for now. This stock might be worth another look after the share price craters.

John sat helpless, mouth half open, hands twitching, pinned to his swivel chair like an entomologist's prize specimen on display.

***

A truly thorough purge of an edit is the writer's equivalent of a rectal exam. And this one was not gentle. As Bruce read Preston's edit of his Wyrdmetric story, his face burned with humiliation over every sentence Preston had violated. And was there a word left he had not degraded? Preston's edit mode highlighted everything he had typed over in a glowing cobalt blue. The story looked radioactive. Everybody in the magazine could open up the story and see the cold blue marks that Preston's ungloved fingers had left on Bruce's work.

Bruce's eyes read on, unable to stop, as if they were watching a train wreck. Humiliation transmuted into rage. This was an insult. Preston was just throwing his weight around, too stupid to see what an idiot he was. He had made hash out of the story. Well, they weren't running that garbage, not under his byline. He'd storm right into that fuckhead's office and have it out...

No. Bruce took a deep breath. No, not this time. He wouldn't give Preston the satisfaction of a scene. Sometimes he thought the son of a bitch was just trying to get a rise out of him. This time he wouldn't yell or threaten. He wasn't about to beg Preston to change it back. He wouldn't stoop to engaging him in a debate, painstakingly pointing out the reasons Preston was a moron, as if the asshole had any real grounds for his opinions. No.

He fired off an email to Preston: "Your edit is an outrage. Not under my byline."

There. Preston would run it with no byline, and probably count himself lucky to have gotten off with an angry email. Or maybe Bruce's relative restraint would leave him edgy, wondering why Bruce hadn't exploded, waiting for the other shoe to drop. That was a delicious thought.

Bruce looked forward to the morning. Cool, calm and collected, he would walk in and quit. And despite everything, Preston the idiot would be surprised, he was sure of that. He would plead, he would cajole, but Bruce would be the ice man. This time Preston had gone too far. There were other magazines out there. This damn rag needed him more than he needed it, but Preston was such a self-important ass he couldn't see it.

Having resolved his course of action, Bruce felt slightly better. But only slightly. He peered out his office door toward the cubicles. How many people were reading the Wyrdmetric story even now, and snickering? He had to escape the office. Yes, best to get out now, just disappear. Eyes downcast, he slipped out his door and made a quick beeline for the fire stairs, not daring to risk a wait by the elevators. He didn't exhale until he had lost himself in the humid Fifth Avenue evening. Clean getaway. He definitely needed a drink.

TUESDAY-WEDNESDAY, AUGUST 17-18, 1999

John slumped in his chair, his mind reeling. There had to be something he could do to save his investment, to salvage his honor. Yes, he could add to his sins by transmitting an earlier, positive version of Bruce's Wyrdmetric story, just as he had done with Meg's article. It was tempting. He was tired of feeling like a nobody. Most of the editorial staff had only the vaguest idea of what he really did, and even less interest in it.

Except for that hot little number, Kimmie. Much to John's surprise, she had introduced herself to him in the elevator—arching her back in such a way that her breasts seemed to be introducing themselves to him as well—and had shown a lot of interest in his work, or "his role in the magazine," as she put it. "The production side is so fascinating," she had said, "I'll visit you down there sometime if you don't mind." "I'd be honored," he had stammered, trying not to hyperventilate.

Momentarily emboldened by this memory of their little sexual exchange (yes, Kimmie wants me, all women want me, the hell with Daisy, fuck Preston), for a few seconds John was prepared to go through with it, to mess with the copy again.

But he couldn't. Reason returned, deflating his courage. It would be stupid, way too risky. After all, he had assured Preston that he had dealt with the software problem he had concocted to explain the Meg incident, that that sort of glitch would never happen again. This time the spotlight would be focused on him, and given today's little stock trade... No, he'd lose his job.

He sighed. Really there was nothing for it but to cut his losses. He logged on to his brokerage account again and placed an order to sell his Wyrdmetric stock as soon as the market opened. He'd pissed away $2,500 in an afternoon. He decided he'd invest what was left in something more solid. Probably split it between WorldCom and Nortel.

He was never going to show up that damn Russki. Cursing softly, he reached into the file cabinet behind him for a bottle of red wine.

He still had several bottles from last year's Christmas party. Preston had given him the leftovers. They didn't make John feel like an appreciated employee—more like a poor man waiting for handouts.

By the time he'd finished the evening's shift, he'd also finished the bottle. Despite the alcohol buzz, he still felt lousy.

John wanted to feel good. He needed to feel good. He had the right to feel good, the same undeniable, goddamn God-given right to feel good as every other man in this magazine, as every other man on this earth. He knew of only one thing to do.

At night he escaped. Fortified by Preston's wine, he found fulfillment roaming the empty cubicles and offices. By now even the copy editors were gone, and John was free to surf the hard drives. The only real risk, a small one, was that a wandering security guard might stumble across him. In that case, John figured, he'd say something about the network flagging a problem with that particular machine, babble about nodes and routers until the eye-glaze set in—which rarely took more than a few seconds—then change the subject to the Yankees' pennant prospects. He was on pretty good terms with the security guys anyway, especially the night shift, which couldn't hurt.

The most intriguing information in the building—all the personal stuff—was buried in the individual computers, invisible to the office network unless you were Craig, the system administrator with godlike computer powers. Craig controlled software that let him poke through the hard drives remotely. But even if John had possessed such power, that kind of long-distance rummaging would have left an electronic trail. Far more discreet to simply wander from machine to machine.

John was perpetually amazed at how careless people were about guarding their privacy. At least half the computers were left on all night, so anyone who happened by could just sift through the data. The more paranoid writers and reporters switched off their machines. To boot one up again, you needed that person's password. For some years this had frustrated John, who had convinced himself that the juiciest tidbits must be hidden on the dark machines.

This was no longer a problem, thanks to the server incident a couple of years ago. A virus had slipped through the company firewall and taken down the network servers during a closing. Editors had been forced to scramble to recreate stories from the latest surviving versions on individual hard drives. One article proved to be a special headache. The only surviving edit was secreted on the writer's computer, but the writer was trekking in Nepal and utterly unreachable. Craig had access to everything and a list of all passwords, of course. But he was out celebrating his wife's birthday that evening, and his cell phone's battery had gone dead. (Or so he later claimed.) Precious hours had been lost before Craig was found and the story retrieved. To prevent a repetition of this fiasco, photocomp had been quietly granted access to the list of passwords for the editorial staff.

This was power John abused without hesitation. While most of the city slept, he sifted through other peoples' lives. When he looked at those people in the daylight, he felt like a man with X-ray vision.

He walked to the fifth floor and opened the door to Meg the Knife's office. As usual, she had forgotten to turn off the light and the computer. He sat at her desk, glancing nervously at the locked display case mounted on her wall that showed off choice specimens from her collection. This added luster to her legend and intimidated young reporters. The steely array of edged weapons was neatly labeled: Bowie knife, Ka-Bar, bayonet, knuckle duster. Serrated Air Force survival knife. An elegant British Fairbairn-Sykes commando knife. Two evil-looking curved blades: a Chilean *corvo* and a *kukri*, favored by Gurkha troops. He forced himself to look away, but as he turned toward Meg's monitor he found himself staring at a jumbled mound of white plastic on her desk, dozens of disposable forks and knives from the nearby greengrocer. Some sort of cosmic joke.

John briefly scanned Meg's private files. Her divorce was final at last. He tried to remember how many husbands she'd run through. Three, at least. Maybe it would dawn on her that marriage didn't suit her. Meg was also trying to convince her cranky widowed mother to move to an assisted-living home. She didn't seem to be having much luck with that. Her life looked even more depressing than his, John thought, and left her office.

Billy the Bully's office was next to Meg's. John turned on the light and sat in Billy's leather chair, as always wondering how Billy got to have a chair like this while everybody else sat on cheap fabric. Billy was also the only editor, apart from Preston, who kept a refrigerator in his office. It was usually stocked with good vodka, and John was tempted to take a swig. He opened the little fridge, drank some Belvedere straight from the bottle and then turned on the computer and typed in Billy's password—Monica. Billy had changed his password recently. John guessed this was in honor of Clinton's intern scandal, because he found no trace of a girlfriend named Monica in Billy's files, and Billy's wife was named Gretchen.

John read Billy's love letter to a woman named Marge: "I can no longer come without seeing your blue eyes looking up at me." From the rest of the letter it became clear that Marge was an executive assistant to a Wall Street financier. Billy was no doubt angling for access to her boss. Most of Billy's love affairs were with assistants of powerful men.

John kept moving from one dark office to another. He noted résumés and glanced at freelance pieces written for other magazines. He had an unspoken agreement with Preston to report any "irregularities" to him.

He wasn't looking for any irregularities now, or anything boring. What did he care about freelancing? Or tawdry divorces? He wanted something that would give him pleasure. Something every other man in the office wanted but couldn't get.

He went for the most mouth-watering piece of meat—he booted up Kimmie's machine. It was the second-best private activity he could indulge in with her.

Some sexy, hurtful revelations—the kind to make a decent person cringe—were what he needed now. Maybe some explicit messages from those goons in editorial who always ogled her. No, even better, he realized, would be her own thoughts about all of these wimps who propositioned her, who pined with their hands below their desks. Maybe she kept a diary, he hoped she did…Some snide remarks about these losers, descriptions of her turnoffs and their futile attempts would please John immensely. He would possess humiliating information about them that they didn't even realize existed. And if she actually had something on Preston, or Jake…that would be too delicious.

But a sinking feeling stole over John as he eyed the directory of Kimmie's files. Virtually every file was named after a company. Stroke after keystroke, each file that John opened turned out to be exactly, boringly, what the filename implied. The file called UNFETTERED was exactly that—notes about the company for a story about Unfettered that had already run in the magazine. He perked up at a file called VSECRET, but it was about a lingerie company's marketing tactics. And betweenthesheets.doc turned out to be a drink recipe.

John was surprised at the amount of work she seemed to have done. She had dozens of files, with transcripts from interviews, notes about the companies' financial statements, different drafts of the stories. Then it struck him: Several of these stories had run under Jake's byline, but clearly Kimmie had done most of the work. Why would she do that?

John kept scanning file after file, mesmerized by all that research, until an odd note caught his attention. It sat at the top of a file about Unfettered: "MUST RUN AFTER JULY 1."

He paused. Funny. He could think of any number of reasons why a reporter would want a story to run *before* a given date: fear of being scooped by the competition, fear that events would make the story irrelevant, even fear that the editor would change his mind about running it. But after? That seemed peculiar. Another file criticized Forsooth, a hot new software firm: The file was dated April 14, but a note read, "RUN AFTER JUNE 1." He opened up yet another file, one slugged GENESIS, full of pages and pages of notes: "As an infrastructure firm, Genesis is a more conservative play on the Internet boom than investing in e-tailers. This could become the essential company of the Information Age." At the top, a note: "HAS TO RUN IN AUG 31 ISSUE." But the file itself was dated July 16. Somehow that didn't sound like a writer's usual urge to see the story in print as soon as possible. Everybody knew that a story that didn't run right away got stale fast. And stale stories sat around for a couple of weeks, only to be discreetly moved to the holds queue, the equivalent of a story graveyard.

John thought hard. Something was off, but he wasn't sure exactly what. He opened up her email inbox. Hundreds of messages, most of them in-house, work-related and dull. Some from analysts and flacks. A flirtatious note from Jake that made John want to puke. Here was one from outside, five days old, from someone who styled herself emmapeal: "told you not to email me. DON'T BE STUPID, will talk later. Remember, read this & delete."

Well, well, well. That was certainly intriguing. Guess Kimmie got a little careless about deleting. But what was it all about?

Of course. If she was sloppy about deleting from her inbox, how about her outbox, full of messages she'd sent? John switched to it and scanned the list eagerly. Sure enough, a message to emmapeal. He clicked on it: "hi doll, know this is bad but just can't get u on phone, genesis date? & we on for tonite?"

Genesis date. John's brain raced: emmapeal, emmapeal…of course. Mrs. Peal, the character played by Diana Rigg in that old TV series. What was it called? Oh, yeah. *The Avengers.*

WEDNESDAY, AUGUST 18, 1999

Helen woke with a start and gasped with pain as she moved her stiff neck. She had dozed off at her desk. She peered at her watch: 1:24 a.m. The closing had been going smoothly when she last checked, and no one had bothered her since. Surely Preston was long gone. Probably most everyone.

She stood, stretched, found a brush to run through her hair. A quick stop at the restroom, she thought, then a cab home.

She was halfway across the floor when she heard the clicking sound. Like a keyboard. Could one of the reporters still be working? She turned right, down a row of cubicles.

The sound came from Kimmie's cube. She approached warily. But that wasn't Kimmie…

"John?"

He whirled around as if he'd just been tapped on the shoulder by one of the undead, face pale, eyes blinking rapidly. "Jesus! Helen, it's you, you scared the shit out of me. Thought I was alone up here."

"Yeah, me too. Dozed off for a while. I guess the pages all shipped?"

"Oh, yeah, we're all done, finished up an hour ago. *No problemo.*" He grinned and winked at her.

She studied his unfocused eyes. He reeked of alcohol.

"So, John. What are you doing on Kimmie's computer?"

"Huh? Oh, that. Don't worry, I'm authorized. By Preston. I do spot checks sometimes, for irreg…irregu…regulari titties."

Helen fought to keep a straight face. "Irregularities?"

"Thas right." He nodded happily. "I have the passwords."

"I see, that's very interesting, John. And did you find anything… irregular?"

"Well, maybe, not quite sure." He brushed his hair back with one hand. "Not the usual crap, and nothing entertaining. But weird shit. Definitely weird."

"I see," she said, though she didn't see at all. "But, John, you're drunk."

He sat up straighter. "I beg your pardon…"

"Stop it, John, you're obviously loaded. And you probably shouldn't be doing this…this checking…in this state. You should go home. And we'll keep this quiet, okay, just between us."

He nodded. "Okay, Helen, juss between us. You're right, I should go home." He stood unsteadily, muttered a good night, started off, then stopped and turned. "Helen," he said, "you're one classy lady." He saluted her sloppily and ambled off.

She stood by Kimmie's cube and watched until he disappeared down the stairwell. Then she stared at Kimmie's computer. The screen pulsed with a psychedelic screensaver. Weird shit, huh?

Helen sat down and reached for Kimmie's mouse.

***

Bruce stumbled out of the chill of Bar Six into the warm embrace of the small hours on Sixth Avenue, dizzied by the balmy air. He had consumed five scotch and sodas, two bowls of peanuts and three empty hours. He had wallowed in his humiliation, perversely courting further rejection, it seemed to him now, by rashly attempting to flirt with various glossy women. He wasn't good at small talk. Every one of them had brusquely put him in his place with a cool, polished cruelty that made Preston look like a piker. Time to go home.

Damn. He'd left his briefcase in the office. Was there anything vital in there? Oh, yeah. His cell phone. His house keys. Shit, he had to go back. He peered at his watch. Place should have cleared out by now.

The security guard behind the desk in the lobby barely looked up as Bruce walked in. He muttered a cursory greeting and refocused on some old movie on the TV screen. The guards were used to seeing Bruce come and go at all hours of the night.

He rode the elevator up, quickly retrieved the briefcase from his office, realized that he had to take a piss before heading out to Brooklyn, and strode toward the men's room. There was a new, handwritten sign taped to the door: Out of Order. Great.

Bruce scrambled down the stairway, emerged on the fourth floor and marched straight into the men's room there.

Two steps in, he halted in his tracks, startled by the sight of another human being, bent over a sink, splashing water on his face. The human straightened up unsteadily.

"Bruce. My man. How ya doing?"

"John." Recovering, Bruce moved over to the urinal. "What you still doing here this late?"

John shrugged. "You know how it is. Always the last to leave. Say, man, you want a drink? I got some decent red wine back in photocomp."

Bruce studied John in the mirror as he washed his hands. The man was bleary-eyed and swaying a bit. Bruce himself had a pretty good working buzz going, but John, he realized, was pixilated. "Thanks, but it's late, I should really…"

"Oh, come on, man, I bet you could use a drink after the way Preston fucked with your story tonight."

Bruce cringed. Jesus, this was just what he needed.

But John wouldn't stop. "Fucking Preston. Bastard fucked me over good too, you know. Fucked me real good."

"Yeah? How?"

"Well, you see, he…" John shut up. Some tattered shred of animal cunning surfaced in his eyes. "Never mind. Take it from me, he fucked me in the royal manner. You know, I really hate that smug, Waspy motherfucker. What kinda name is Preston anyway?"

"John, you're even drunker than I am. I think it's time for us both to go home."

"Come on, just one drink. One for the road." He leaned close for a stage whisper. "I'll let you in on Kimmie's secrets."

The words blew through Bruce's brain like a cold steady wind, clearing the alcohol haze. John had his complete attention.

"Okay, John. One for the road."

Back in photocomp, John poured from a half-empty bottle. Bruce noticed another one, empty, in the trash can.

"This is just between you and me," John began. "In theory, I should tell Preston, I guess, but fuck him. Fuck 'em all. But you…you're all right, Bruce. Maybe you can use this."

Bruce mustered his limited supply of patience. "Okay. Just between us. Use what?"

"You see, I was pissed off tonight, sort of like you. I wanted to have some fun, a man's type of fun, if you know what I mean. I went poking through Kimmie's computer, and she wasn't fun at all, that's for sure. I have her password, see. I have the master list. Frankly, I was hoping for something juicy, something personal. Found zip. But I also found out that she's been writing all these stories for Jake, or at least doing all the real work. Everything he's done the past few months. She has tons and tons of research notes. Funny, huh? I mean, why would she do all that work and then just hand him the stories? For what, some middle-aged hack Casanova? When she could fuck any guy in the building?"

"It does seem odd."

"But there's more, man. Someone—probably from the outside, someone using a Yahoo account—is telling her when these stories should run. Pretty fucking weird, huh?"

Bruce could almost feel his neurons firing, a web of tiny sparks tracing out the possibilities. All thoughts of quitting in a huff over that stupid Wyrdmetric story had vanished. "Yeah. Weird.

"Listen, John, don't say anything about this to anybody. Just go home and we'll talk in a day or two. I'll take a look through her files myself and tell you if it's really that important, okay? Right now, let's get you downstairs and into a cab."

"Sure, okay."

Grabbing John just above the elbow, Bruce steered him into the elevator and then hustled him past the guard downstairs and out into the street. This late at night, midweek, there was no competition for taxis, and Bruce flagged one down within seconds. He almost shoved John into the back, slammed the door, then leaned in through the cab's open window.

"John, I almost forgot. What's the password?"

"Oh, yeah." John spelled it out in a loud whisper. "L-U-V-C-H-I-L-D."

"Love child?"

"Yeah. I always did like that song."

"Go home and sleep it off, John."

Bruce stood on the curb, thinking. Should he do it now? No. Tomorrow night was soon enough. He was tired and half-drunk, and he couldn't afford to screw this up. Better to take his time and be careful.

The night held one last surprise. As John's cab barreled off toward Queens, Bruce discovered that John had a fine singing voice. He could hear his tenor from a block away, belting out, "Love child, never meant to be…Love child, scorned by so-ci-e-teee…"

THURSDAY, AUGUST 19, 1999

His office was dark, the door closed, but Bruce sat behind his desk, still as a stone. Long ago, he had briefly dated a California girl who was into all that Zen claptrap. She would go on and on, yapping about cultivating stillness until he'd wanted to throttle her. Well, that's what Bruce was cultivating now, stillness. He was being careful. He wanted to minimize the number of people who might recall that he had stayed in the office late that night. So he sat, dozing fitfully, as if he were trying to sleep on a plane.

He planned to emerge around 1 a.m. He had set the vibrating alarm on his wristwatch in case he fell asleep. Now that the magazine was not going to press, he should be all alone on the floor by then.

At 12:55, Bruce turned off his alarm. He didn't need it. He was too nervous to fall asleep.

He walked out of his office at exactly 1 a.m. The timing was arbitrary. He could have easily done it an hour earlier or an hour later, but doing things according to a schedule gave him a feeling of control.

He strode toward the middle of the fifth floor and ducked into Kimmie's cube. A Prada bag, annual reports, books, bottles of nail polish and perfume, pantyhose and tampons lay strewn across the desk, chair and floor. He couldn't imagine how anybody could concentrate in such a mess. He sat down in her chair and turned on her machine.

Concentrate. He angled the machine around slowly, so that the screen was now turned away from the cubicle's opening. If somebody ambushed him sitting in Kimmie's cube, at least it wouldn't be obvious what he was looking at.

He scanned Kimmie's directory. John was right—she seemed to have done tons of work on stories that were published under Jake's name. Bruce studied the names of the files, sweating profusely. There were scores of files, and he started opening them for a quick glance, then closing them again.

Various drafts of stories, notes on companies, transcripts of interviews. And yes, a few notes on when the stories should run.

He opened up her email and found the messages John had mentioned. Indeed, John had been right to suspect something odd. The outlines of the situation were becoming clear to Bruce. Someone outside *The Magazine* was feeding Kimmie stories, even offering editorial comments and advice, then instructing her on when the stories should run. She was using Jake to place them. Bruce couldn't yet be sure what the motives were, and he had no idea who this emmapeal might be. But whatever was going on, it smelled.

He was overwhelmed by the number of files. He couldn't possibly sit there and study them all. Besides, if she were up to something shady, he'd need evidence. He pulled several blank floppy disks from his pocket and started to hunt for the slot...

Oh shit. Kimmie had one of those new iMacs. The thing looked like a damn bubblegum machine. It had no floppy drive. And the CD-ROM drive on this model had no burner, so that wasn't an option either. Goddamn, he'd failed to consider this little complication. Stupid of him. But how about the moron of an engineer who'd decided this was an elegant design? Bruce briefly entertained the fantasy of tracking him down and shoving a motherboard down his throat.

He forced himself to calm down and think. He couldn't very well email them all to himself. That would leave electronic trails all over the place. Ditto for moving the files through the network server, but probably worse. Not just trails, but big electronic neon signs. Shit. No way around it. He'd have to print them all out.

The printer sat on the opposite side of the floor. He had a fleeting vision of Kimmie waiting by the printer as he approached to pick up the pages, waving a fistful of paper in his face.

Insane. He dismissed the thought and went back to studying her directory, but paranoia ate through his concentration like acid. The hairs on the nape of his neck stood at attention as another vision came to him: Kimmie standing behind him right now, standing in the opening to her cubicle, arching against the frame, twisting a wisp of her hair, preparing to coo, "Hi, Bruce, what are you doing? Need any help?"

He turned around. Nobody there. Just an empty hole in the wall of her gray cubicle looking out on the wall of another gray cubicle. He was alone. Just to be on the safe side, he moved his chair so that he faced the opening. It was not a comfortable position because he had to contort his body to read the screen. But at least he could see the screen and the hallway simultaneously.

Okay. Calm now. Methodical is the way to be. Systematic. First, he opened the handful of email messages to or from this emmapeal and printed them all. Then he worked his way through Kimmie's directory, trying to select the most interesting and relevant files at a glance, trying not to waste time printing multiple drafts of a story that differed only slightly, hitting the print button over and over.

Within a few minutes that seemed to stretch into infinity, he reached the end of her directory. Done. He stood a little shakily and walked over to the printer.

He stared in horror. Only half a dozen pages had printed. A small amber light blinked at him: paper jam. In a panic, he opened the front of the machine, then the back, and cleared the jam, cursing all the while. The machine resumed printing. Goddamn thing jammed all the time, he'd been complaining they needed a new one for months, to no avail. Cheap bastards. He'd have to stand here and watch the thing in case anything else went wrong.

He checked the paper trays, made sure they were fully loaded. He had a lot of pages to print, couple hundred probably. The machine had spit out the first fifty or so when it jammed a second time. He cleared it again, getting toner all over his hands, his curses growing ever more heartfelt and ornate.

A thought: Suppose someone came by, a security guard doing the rounds maybe. Did he really want to be standing there with scores of pages in his hands? What if the guard got curious about this massive printout and glanced at the pages as they emerged from the machine? Better to get his briefcase and slip the files in there as they printed.

Bruce dashed toward his office, the first fifty pages tucked under his arm, hurrying in case the machine jammed yet again. He had almost reached his corner of the half-darkened floor when his knee smacked hard into the edge of a metal file cabinet. He fell face first, scattering the pages across the industrial carpeting.

He bit his lip and blinked back tears, trying to keep quiet. He was almost out of curses anyway. God was punishing him for what he was doing, that had to be it. No, that was crazy. No way God was on Kimmie's side. This was no time to lose it. Just keep it together.

He gathered up the pages, their order now hopelessly scrambled, pulled himself to his feet, limped into his office, grabbed his briefcase and shoved the paper inside. Then he hobbled back to the printer as quickly as he could.

A new stack of freshly printed pages was waiting for him. He added those to the pile in his briefcase. Then the machine jammed again.

Bruce cleared two more paper jams before the last page rolled out of the printer. By then, beads of sweat were dripping off his forehead onto the paper. At last. It was all safely inside his briefcase.

He scurried back to Kimmie's cube and shut down her computer. Another thought struck him. Returning to the printer, he tore open a new ream of paper and refilled the trays. He was probably being overcautious, but he didn't want anyone to notice that someone had done a lot of printing overnight. He looked around, took a few deep breaths. That should be it, he'd covered his tracks…

Oh. How about the printer's memory? It had some sort of buffer, didn't it? Which no doubt still stored the last few pages it had printed. What if someone accidentally hit one of the many mysterious buttons on the printer and it started regurgitating Kimmie's files? Unlikely, but…the thought gave him a chill. Okay. How do you clear a buffer memory? Bruce thought it over and decided on the crude but effective approach. He unplugged the machine and counted off thirty seconds, then another thirty to be sure.

He plugged it back in. The printer automatically cycled into self-test mode and began beeping at him loudly.

Cursing furiously, Bruce fled the building.

SATURDAY, AUGUST 21, 1999

Helen slumped against the doorframe and leaned into Tom's study. "Honey? Sorry it got so late."

Tom looked up from his computer, blinked and yawned. "Hi, glad you're here." He stood up, walked over and kissed her. "It's almost one. You work too hard."

"Tell me about it."

"Well, it's the weekend now. You can sleep late, and tomorrow I'll cook that brunch I promised you. Listen, dear, I'm really sorry, but I was about to go to bed. I'm beat."

She smiled. "Don't worry about it. I'll just sit up a while and watch TV, maybe have a drink and unwind. You go on to bed, it's okay."

"All right, just don't stay up too late."

"No, I won't." She gestured at his PC. "Okay if I go online a minute? I should check my email."

"Sure, go ahead. You're too conscientious."

He shuffled into the bedroom as she sat at his desk. She clicked a key.

And found herself staring at lists of folders. Companies, analyst reports. Memos. She clicked one open, her cheeks flushed with shame. Quickly scanned the contents. Clicked on another. And another. Against her will, she thought she sensed a pattern in the volume of reports on certain companies. In the dates. Unfettered, Genesis, Forsooth.

Dread infiltrated her body like hypothermia, seeping to her core. Could Tom actually… No. No, she refused to even complete the thought. She felt dirty even half-thinking…

Her eyes scanned another list of files. Two company names jumped out at her. Names that had nothing to do with Kimmie, or any of Jake's stories.

Microfreq. Cluster Node.

Helen closed all the folders and stood up, her breathing shallow. Time for that drink.

***

Brooklyn, 1 a.m. Home at last. Bruce tossed his briefcase onto the couch, changed into a bathrobe and checked the fridge. Good, a few bottles of Optimator left. He popped open one of the dark German beers and sat down to study Kimmie's files, eager to get back to work on them. By 2 a.m. he'd worked out a diagram, connecting companies, stories and key dates.

He had more work to do, a lot more, just to make a good start on this, but he knew he should stop for now. His brain was fried. Better to try and unwind, get a few hours' sleep, then start again. He had the whole weekend ahead of him.

He turned on the TV. He downed two more beers and watched *Night of the Killer Klowns.*

By 11 a.m. he was guzzling coffee and surfing the Web. He searched the SEC's Edgar database for filings on the companies in Jake and Kimmie's stories. Form 4. Form 144. Unfortunately, there was a lag—as much as six months—between the time certain trades were made by insiders and the deadline for filing the forms. But Kimmie's earliest articles were several months old by now. Maybe he could find traces of a suspicious pattern.

He did. The name that kept coming up was Tom Richardson.

Mostly, Richardson ran private money in a hedge fund, and it was damn near impossible to get a clear picture of a private hedge fund's current holdings without a source on the inside. But Richardson often took big positions in companies, then threw his weight around. He'd take a seat on the board and influence strategy. If he bought more than 10 percent of a company's stock, he had to file Form 144. A board seat made him an insider, so he had to disclose any large stock trades. And in addition to the hedge fund, Richardson ran a couple of mutual funds that were open to the peasants. Bruce checked the mutual funds' top holdings for the last couple of quarters, to see what had changed from one quarter to the next.

Dinnertime. Bruce rubbed his eyes and popped some more aspirin. He'd had nothing but coffee and a slice of toast all day. He picked up the phone and ordered a pizza, then switched from coffee back to beer. He'd left the TV tuned to the History Channel with the sound muted: Allied paratroopers drifted silently down over Holland, all in shades of gray. Elvis Costello snarled from the stereo, claiming he wasn't angry. His living room floor was covered with stacks of paper, some Kimmie's files, some stuff he had downloaded and printed off the Web. His coffee table was festooned with several large sheets of paper he had taped together. They were decorated with scribbles, arrows, dates. A flow chart of corruption.

He had more work to do first, but he was sure he was on the right track. Kimmie had planted stories in *The Magazine*—stories touting the virtues of certain companies—just after her daddy had loaded up on their stock. Those stories had boosted the share prices. Richardson's funds had made a lot of money. A couple stories were negative in tone. They had appeared just after Richardson sold off his holdings in those companies. No doubt the hedge fund had also shorted the shares.

Helen was probably in on it too. She was the one who'd wanted to hire Kimmie, after all. For now the details remained obscure. Was Kimmie giving her daddy stock tips—that is, mentioning the companies she was writing about—or was dear old dad feeding her story ideas based on the stocks he was buying?

He had an intriguing circumstantial case. No smoking gun. Still, it was enough to take to the SEC. Definitely a suspicious pattern. With their subpoenas, they could nail the bastard. Of course, he had no intention of going to the SEC.

The last thing he wanted to do was alert the SEC and be reduced to reporting that it was launching an investigation that involved *The Magazine*. If he had to go public, the least he could do was skewer Richardson himself. Best of all would be to go straight to Bob Llewellyn, damning evidence in hand. With a little luck, they could handle it quietly and save *The Magazine* a scandal. Force a few resignations from people who would have to stay silent or risk jail. Bruce smiled. That would likely include Preston. This mess had happened on his watch, and he had clearly favored Kimmie. When Llewellyn looked around for a successor, Bruce, savior of *The Magazine,* would be standing there.

But he was getting ahead of himself. He needed one more nail to seal this coffin. He needed emmapeal.

SUNDAY, AUGUST 22, 1999

Helen poured herself another cup of coffee, cinched her robe more tightly around her waist and padded barefoot back into the master bedroom. She rummaged through her handbag and fished out a small reporter's notebook, nervously eyeing the bathroom door. When she heard Tom turn on the shower, she walked down the hall and into the study, coffee and notebook in hand.

She sat in front of his PC and scanned the same folders and files she'd seen late Friday night. This time she took notes, focusing mainly on dates. Timing was everything, after all.

She even timed herself as she did so, allowing herself five minutes. Tom would probably spend ten minutes in the shower, giving her a margin of error. The second her five minutes elapsed, she closed her notebook, put the PC to sleep and walked out of the study. She slipped the notebook back into her bag in the bedroom. Tom was still in the bathroom.

She walked back to the kitchen and drew a deep breath. Later. She would study her notes later.

MONDAY, AUGUST 23, 1999

As the gray light of an overcast morning filtered through the art gallery's tall windows, Dennis Flaherty woke with a start, then grimaced. Getting too old to sleep in a chair, he thought. He glanced at his watch and for a split second felt panic—then he remembered it was Monday. The gallery was closed on Mondays. No need to rush.

He reached for his binoculars and peered across the street just in time to see a naked, groggy Kimmie climb out of bed and stumble to the kitchen to start the coffee. On the other side of the bed, Jake Rosenberg dozed on. The two of them had been up quite late the night before, drinking and talking shop, then making energetic, almost frantic, love. Kimmie had seemed unduly excited about some story she was working on, a positive piece about a company that made Internet software. Flaherty wondered idly if he should log on to his brokerage account and buy a few shares. Why not? Could always use a little bonus.

Flaherty slipped on his headphones and flicked on the laser mike. Kimmie and Jake didn't seem to be saying anything of particular interest this morning, but Flaherty dutifully watched and listened while they showered and dressed, just in case. He watched as they finally left the building. Kimmie smiled and nodded at the superintendent, who was sweeping the sidewalk. The super— mid-fifties, paunchy, balding, Hispanic-looking—grinned and called out a greeting. He paused as the couple passed by, then leaned on his broom and stared at Kimmie as she walked away. Apparently deciding he had swept enough, he disappeared into the building.

Flaherty was removing the laser mike from its tripod when his peripheral vision registered motion across the street. Instinctively, he glanced up and out the window. The super stood in Kimmie's living room, pocketing a large key ring.

Flaherty paused. Probably meant nothing. Maybe Kimmie had a plumbing problem. Still, you never knew. He sat down and reached for the binoculars.

The super looked around furtively, then entered the bedroom and crouched in the corner where Kimmie tossed her dirty clothes. When he stood and turned so Flaherty could see his face, he held a pair of white panties to his nose. Looked like some sort of floral print. Flaherty zoomed in. Roses, the pattern was roses. He watched the super's chest rise and fall as he inhaled great lungfuls of Kimmie's scent.

The man walked over to the bed and inspected the rumpled sheets. Apparently satisfied, he dropped his pants and lay across the bed, stroking himself. Suddenly he sat up. Opening a drawer in Kimmie's nightstand, he extracted a vibrator. Why, you naughty boy, thought Flaherty. Not your first time, is it? You know where she keeps things.

Wearily, Flaherty lowered the binoculars, shaking his head. Degenerate son of a bitch.

***

Helen sat in her office, sipping coffee, and flipped the pages in her notebook back and forth. The dates Kimmie's files were created and the dates the stories ran. And Tom's dates: research reports, stock trades. Kimmie's dates, Tom's dates, Kimmie's dates, Tom's dates. Back and forth.

She had come in early so she'd have some quiet time to think. But she didn't know what to think. There was some sort of pattern there, a suspicious one. Pure coincidence seemed a stretch. But the pattern was suggestive, not conclusive. And the idea of Tom and Kimmie, conspiring... That seemed even more of a stretch.

Then there was Microfreq and Cluster Node. Kimmie had nothing to do with those. And Tom's actions there violated no law. Just casual conversation. Opinions. Talking down the stocks to her. She now suspected that he'd shorted those stocks. Had he meant to influence *The Magazine*'s coverage of those companies? Ethically, she supposed, that fell into a gray zone. Dirty gray, gray enough to piss her off. But perfectly legal.

Should she confront him? With what? Wild suspicions? Conspiracies? If she accused him of God knows what and she were wrong... She cringed inwardly at the damage that would do. And if she were right, that would be worse.

No. She needed more.

TUESDAY, AUGUST 24, 1999

Helen paced her office as she scanned the sheet of paper she'd printed out one last time. Nothing but a list of numbers and slashes: dates. Kimmie's dates. She'd decided to leave out Tom's side of the equation. Still, it should be enough to provoke a reaction.

Forcing herself to sit behind her desk, she focused her gaze out her open door, kept it leveled across the gray expanse of cubicles. Lunchtime. Kimmie should run up to the cafeteria soon, or maybe go out.

Fifteen minutes. Twenty. Last day of the close, so everyone was busy. Too busy to glance in her office and notice she was staring into space. But she couldn't stare forever, she had work to do too.

There, at last, Kimmie on the move. Her curls retreating toward the stairwell.

Helen stood, tucked the sheet of paper and a couple of random folders under her arm, and wandered through the maze of cubes. As she walked past Kimmie's cube, she tossed the sheet of paper onto her chair in a casual, fluid motion, without breaking stride. Over in the next row of cubes, she paused to check in with a couple of reporters, the way she always did. Asking about fact-checking problems, letting them grumble a little.

She wanted to linger and position herself to watch Kimmie's face when she returned, but the cubes were emptying out as more reporters went to lunch. She finally retreated to her office and watched the cubicles from there, impatient.

Then Kimmie returned, sat. Stood up suddenly, stared at something. Sat again. Stood up and dashed for the stairwell, cell phone in hand.

Helen got up and strode past Kimmie's cube again. A sandwich and soda sat on her desk, untouched. The sheet of paper was gone.

***

Rebecca stepped into the lee of a hot dog cart, letting the lunchtime current of hungry midtown workers swirl and eddy around her.

"The important thing is to stay calm," she said into her cell phone. "Someone's messing with you, trying to get you to make a mistake. It's a fishing expedition. If they really knew anything, you'd be fired or arrested by now."

Kimmie's voice: "Yeah, I guess you're right. But who?"

"You let me worry about that. Take a deep breath, smile and walk back into the office. Freaking out is the worst thing you could do right now, it would just let them know they're onto something."

"Okay, but...can't we hurry things up?"

"No, we can't get rattled, everything has to be in place. Don't worry, this'll all be wrapped up in a couple weeks. It'll be fine. Just bring that piece of paper home tonight, I'll be waiting at your place. I want to see it."

"Okay."

"Now go back inside and eat your lunch, all right?"

"Okay, here goes. See you tonight."

Rebecca snapped her phone shut. Fuck.

She was in a race to the finish now, and far more rattled than she'd let on to Kimmie. Who the hell? She'd have to trim all the loose ends to make this work.

Fuck, fuck, fuck.

WEDNESDAY, AUGUST 25, 1999

About one-thirty in the morning, as the evening's closing started winding down, Bruce ambled into photocomp with a couple of large, cold bottles of dark European beer. A particularly nice porter he'd recently discovered.

John accepted one gratefully and took a long swig. He nodded appreciatively. "Very creamy, smooth." Only then did he study the label: Baltika. A Russian brew. He had to struggle to hide his irritation. Damn Russki brother-in-law. There was no escaping him.

Bruce perched on the edge of a chair and leaned forward, speaking softly. "Listen, John, I gotta thank you for the tip about Kimmie. You've put me onto something major. I owe you one."

John shrugged. "Sure, man. No big deal."

"But it is, it's a very big deal. You wouldn't believe the shit I've dug up. Kimmie's running some kind of scam. I think she's tipping off her old man. Insider trades."

John's eyebrows rose. "So, you going to Preston with this?"

Bruce shook his head.

"Bob Llewellyn?"

"No, not yet. See, I need a little more. Gotta figure out exactly how this scam works. And I don't want this circumstantial.

"Truth is," Bruce went on, "Kimmie's become one of Preston's pets. His favorite rising star. Plus, there's the whole minority angle. So I've gotta be careful, back up any allegations so she can't weasel out."

John shifted in his seat, suddenly uncomfortable under Bruce's unwavering gaze. Insight dawned. "Hell," he said, "this involves me, doesn't it?"

"Well, you're pretty familiar with the computer network here, right? You're friendly with Craig Morton. I've seen you guys hanging out, talking tech gibberish."

"I don't know this stuff the way Craig does," John replied cautiously. "But yeah, I know how the network's set up."

"And you understand the phone system, right? Voice mail and all that? That's all controlled out of Craig's office too, right?"

"That's right."

Bruce lowered his voice even further. "I've been thinking about phone logs. A record of Kimmie's calls for the past few months could really help me piece this together. In theory, you could get hold of those, couldn't you?"

"Well, maybe, but…"

Bruce sat up straight. "Could we monitor her calls? Actually listen in?"

"No." Increasingly alarmed, John wanted to put a stop to this conversation. "No, there's no way to do that undetected. Unless you actually put a bug in her office. And what if she uses her cell phone for everything? She's always blabbing on it."

"Yeah, that could be a problem, but I can't assume she does. I'm looking for a break here. How about voice mail? I bet you could hack into that. That reporter did it for that Chiquita exposé."

"Yeah, and as I recall, that pretty much ended his career, didn't it?"

"You have a point. But it could be done? In theory?"

John squirmed. "Possibly. Possibly. But why in the name of God would I want to have anything to do with this? I don't even want to know about it."

Bruce took a long swallow of beer and leaned forward again, his dark eyes intense. "Don't you see, John? We'll save *The Magazine*. Cut out the cancer. Llewellyn might even figure a way to keep it quiet, avoid a scandal. No one will care that we bent a few rules. We'll be heroes."

"Fuck heroism. Remember what Patton said? Or George C. Scott, anyway: 'All glory is fleeting.' This could cost me my job."

Bruce leaned back, pensive, and took another swallow of Russian porter. "All right, fair enough. You're not in it for the glory. But I meant it when I said I owe you one. And if you did this one thing for me, I'd owe you a really big one. Maybe something more tangible would motivate you."

John's eyes narrowed. "Like what?"

"How about a vacation? You were moaning just the other day about not being able to afford your dream vacation. So picture this: You fly down to the Caribbean island of your choice and spend a week in one of those all-inclusive resorts. You don't spend a dime while you're there. I pay for the whole thing up front and no one's the wiser. You just sip rum and soak up the rays on a topless beach. Rekindle the romance with your wife. It would do your marriage good, wouldn't it?"

John felt himself slipping over the edge of a cliff. "Two weeks."

"What?"

"You're asking me to risk my job. Besides, it's off-season. I want two weeks in the Caribbean."

Bruce sighed, nodded. "Okay, John. Okay, I want this really bad too." He rose to leave. "Just do this one thing for me. Do it soon. Then it's piña colada time."

***

Three a.m. The bustle of closing had subsided into a hollow, comatose peace. John stood, stretched and emerged warily from the recesses of photocomp. Even the copy editors were gone. With any luck, there would be no one left in the whole building except John and a couple of bored security guards watching TV in the lobby downstairs.

Just to be safe, John walked the halls all the way around the perimeter of the floor, alert for signs of life. Nothing.

He found himself standing in front of Craig's office. The door was ajar, the office beyond, dark. He was sweating despite the air-conditioned chill. What the hell. He took a deep breath, slipped through the door and locked it behind him.

John left the lights off. The room was crammed with half a dozen computers, two of which were on. The flickering colors of their screensavers cast a ghostly light.

He sat down in front of one of the glowing screens. The PC hooked up to it controlled the server for the voice mail system. John was hoping that for once in his life, he'd get really lucky, and that Craig had been a bit careless. He scratched his chin. He licked his lips. He typed in a command. A dialogue box popped up on the screen and asked for a password.

Shit. John slumped back in the chair. He'd allowed Bruce to convince himself that he was some kind of whiz who could crack anything, figuring Bruce would feel better about bribing him if he thought he was paying for some esoteric expertise. In fact, John was technologically literate and familiar with *The Magazine*'s computer network, but he was certainly no hacker. He knew his only real edge lay in his being somewhat friendly with Craig. Sometimes John would stop by Craig's office to catch the latest gossip. A couple of times the two of them had downed a few beers after work. Craig liked to talk shop, and unlike most people, John could follow the technotalk well enough to get the gist of it.

So now he'd just have to guess. He was sure Craig wouldn't have left the program set to the manufacturer's default password, but he had to start somewhere. John typed in *password*. *Invalid,* the computer replied. He tried *guest. Invalid.*

This was stupid. Craig wasn't the sloppy type.

John knew that many of these password routines gave you three chances to type in the right code, then locked you out. He had two strikes. So he hit the key combination that would restart the machine.

It rebooted with a loud beep. John almost toppled from his chair. That beep sounded like an air-raid siren to him. In a near-panic, he scrambled to the door, cracked it open and peered down the hallway. No one in sight. No one to hear that deafening beep.

Still, this would never do. At this rate, he'd be rebooting a lot, and he didn't think his heart could stand all that beeping. He rummaged around on Craig's desk until, triumphant, he found a pair of headphones he could plug into the computer. That would keep the damn thing quiet.

John settled into the chair again. He had to think this through. As a technogeek, Craig would avoid the obvious: birth dates, his mother's maiden name. And besides computers, his only passion was…Dylan. Of course! Not one, but two Bob Dylan posters hung on Craig's office walls. He was a Dylan fanatic. Euphoria briefly gripped John. The more he considered it, the more certain he became that Craig's passwords would be Dylan-related. But as he mulled this over, his spirits sank. All those songs, those convoluted lyrics. The task was epic, the possibilities infinite. He thought it likely that Craig would use classic Dylan, from the mid-Sixties. Even so . . .

But he might as well give it a shot. He typed in *zimmerman*. Invalid. *Hibbing.* Invalid.

Reboot.

Too biographical. Stick to the man's work. The songs, the words.

Highway61. Invalid. *Napoleoninrags.* Invalid.

Reboot.

Gatesofeden. Invalid. *Thoughtdreams.* Invalid.

Reboot.

Maggiesfarm. Invalid. *Desolationrow.* Invalid.

Reboot.

Sad-eyedlady. Invalid. *Warehouseeyes.* Invalid.

Reboot.

Queenjane. Invalid. *Babyblue.* Invalid.

Reboot.

Tomthumb. Invalid. *Raininjuarez.* Invalid.

Reboot.

More and more desperately, John free-associated whatever Dylan he remembered. What if he were on the wrong track entirely? He glanced at his watch. Past four. And each time he rebooted, he had to wait at least a full minute for the damn machine to start up again. What if one of the security guards showed unusual initiative, realized John was the only employee who hadn't signed out of the building and came looking for him?

Sweetmelinda. Invalid. *Goddessofgloom.* Invalid.

Reboot.

Lot2laugh. Invalid. *Train2cry.* Invalid.

Reboot.

Nodirectionhome. Invalid. *Mrjones.*

And the voice mail program opened for him like an eager lover.

John just sat there, staring at the screen, for a long moment. Slowly, a huge grin took shape on his face. He'd done it. He was in.

Snapping suddenly back into focus, he realized he'd better do what he came for and get out. He started clicking the mouse, scrolling through screens, tapping keys. The phone logs were simple. He just copied Kimmie's records onto a blank floppy. Then he tinkered with the voice mail. It took him about five minutes to set things up the way he wanted. Kimmie's voice mail would continue to greet callers and record messages in the usual fashion. But a copy of each of those messages would be instantly and automatically forwarded to Bruce's voice mail.

John sat still for a few seconds, calming himself, inhaling deeply. He could almost smell it: salt air, suntan oil, creme of coconut.

FRIDAY, AUGUST 27, 1999

Helen propped her elbows on the edge of Maureen's cubicle and flipped through the reporter's well-thumbed copy of *People*. She was running low on idle chitchat and starting to despair. For three days now, she'd spent an inordinate amount of time hanging out among the cubes, waiting for her chance. She was afraid people were starting to notice.

Opportunity finally sauntered past in the form of Kimmie. Helen glanced quickly over her shoulder, saw her enter the ladies' room, then made a show of looking at her watch.

"Oh God, I lost track of time, have to make a call. Thanks, Maureen."

She tossed aside the magazine and strode off purposefully, choosing a path that led past Kimmie's cube. Yes. Kimmie's cell phone sat on the edge of the desk, alone, beckoning.

Helen palmed it smoothly as she walked past. She didn't breathe again until she stood in her own office, the door closed behind her.

Exhilaration. Dread. Deep breaths as she sat behind her desk. She flipped the phone open and clicked to the list of dialed calls. Each call with a date and time. Should be easy to narrow it down, Tuesday around 12:40. When Kimmie had found the list of dates on her chair and run outside.

Jesus, Kimmie made a lot of calls. At least fifteen just this morning. Helen's excitement evaporated as she scrolled down the list: Thursday, Thursday, Thursday, Wednesday... Damn. The phone remembered the fifty most recent calls, but the earliest one was Wednesday, 10:53 a.m.

Frustration. Relief. Did she really want to know? Yes, she had to.

She studied the numbers more closely. None seemed familiar or especially suspicious. She jotted down a few that Kimmie had dialed more than once, then repeated her scrutiny on the lists of received and missed calls. Nothing there either, at least, nothing obvious.

Finally, she turned to Kimmie's contacts. A few innocuous, expected ones. Jake, a handful of other people in the office. Helen herself. Mom. But most of her scores of contacts were listed by initials: AD, KS, EP... At least there was no TR, or Tom. Or worse, Dad.

But still... Dead end.

Helen slipped the phone into her purse, slung the bag over her shoulder and marched out to the restroom, keeping her eyes focused straight ahead, ignoring the commotion to her right as Kimmie frantically ransacked her own cube. Two other women in the restroom. Helen locked herself in a stall and waited, listening. As soon as she was sure she was alone, she stepped out of the stall, set Kimmie's phone down beside one of the sinks and walked back to her office.

SATURDAY, AUGUST 28, 1999

Helen rolled over in a tangle of sheets, reached for Tom, wrapped her arm around...more sheets. Her eyes snapped open. She heard him in the bathroom. The shower turned on and she sat up, fully awake.

His night table. Book, watch, cell phone.

She had to know. If Kimmie were conspiring with Tom, surely she wouldn't call his office phone.

She scooped up his cell phone, braced herself, checked the received calls. Luckily, Tom didn't take as many calls on his cell as Kimmie. Tuesday, nothing between noon and 1:30. Nothing at all from Kimmie.

Missed calls. Dialed calls. Contacts.

Nothing at all.

She put the phone down and lay back on the bed, limp with relief. She had made herself insane with suspicion, and for what? She felt ashamed.

Had to put this nonsense out of her head. Next weekend was Labor Day, they'd be out in East Hampton. A chance to relax and regain perspective. She needed that. After all, she was marrying the man in October. The wedding was basically planned by now, but there were endless last-minute details.

She had things to do.

TUESDAY, SEPTEMBER 7, 1999

Jake dashed to the printer, hoping to retrieve his expense report before anybody else noticed it. The dollar amount at the end of the "reimbursement from the company due" line was too high to be publicly flaunted—even Jake realized that. Six thousand bucks for business entertainment (meaning mostly eating out and drinking with Kimmie). Jake was hoping that Preston would pretend not to notice in light of Jake's recent string of hot stories.

The printer was deserted, thank God, but there were stacks of printed paper lying around, and someone's rather lengthy document was still being spit out by the machine. He'd have to sift through a lot of pages fast to grab the expense report.

"Jake, how's it going?" Unpleasantly surprised, Jake straightened and turned around. Bruce.

Strange. Jake wondered if the long document still printing was Bruce's. The probability of simply running into Bruce by the printer—or the fax or the soda machine or any casually public spot—struck him as low, the odds against Bruce engaging in small talk astronomical. Bruce didn't like to waste his time with empty chatter, and he was notoriously secretive. He didn't want to field questions about the angle of the story he was writing, its topic, his sources, his deadlines or his interviews. He never asked anybody to read his stuff before he shipped it off to an editor, or consulted his colleagues as he tinkered with a story's lead.

"Hi," Jake answered, planting himself firmly in front of the printer, blocking Bruce's access to his overblown expense report. Out of all the people in the office, Bruce was the most likely to be appalled by Jake's extravagances.

But Bruce didn't seem interested in the printer at all. Clearly, he wanted to talk.

"You won't believe what I'm working on," he said. "Remember that story on Alpha/Omega that Rebecca Morgan wrote around the time that Roberts was leaving? It was her last story for us, the one that she hoped would get her the corner office…"

Jake didn't remember. In fact, he'd never even read it. He'd been drinking too heavily around that time to read much in the magazine. But he decided to acknowledge the story with a nod.

"Well, believe it or not, she was wrong. Rebecca was wrong."

Bruce looked almost pained to say it. Rebecca was virtually the only peer he even acknowledged, and certainly the only one he admired.

He qualified: "Well, she was half wrong. She was absolutely accurate about what was happening then, Popitz had dug himself into a deep hole, and Madsen could have been a real threat. But she was wrong about how this would play out. Popitz's a wily bastard, and he's managed to somehow pay down a lot of debt and consolidate his position. And she bet that Tom Richardson knew what he was doing when he took over Madsen. But Richardson cut too much muscle from the company. Now Madsen's got no R&D, no product pipeline. Thing is, he just might have gotten away with it, at least long enough to rebuild, or to merge it again with another acquisition, or to sell Madsen for more than it's really worth. But there's more…"

Bruce leaned in uncomfortably close, lowered his voice. Clearly, he'd had onions with his lunch. Why the hell was he talking to him like this?

"I've been looking into this more deeply. Popitz has hired several former research guys from Madsen, some of the same people Richardson got rid of. It's pretty ironic…Rebecca's father was one of those research guys. If he hadn't killed himself… Anyway, Popitz has been picking their brains. And on that basis, he's getting ready to slap Madsen with a bunch of lawsuits challenging their most valuable patents. I have this from good sources. And you know what? Popitz just might win a couple of those suits eventually.

"In any case, the market hasn't factored this into the stock price yet, it's trading way high. But now I'm going to take it down. Tom Richardson is going to take a bath on this one."

Bruce's eyes gleamed, somewhat maniacally, Jake thought.

"I love stories like this," said Bruce. "Investors sitting on a hot tin roof but not yet smelling their burning asses."

Jake couldn't figure out what was really happening. Bruce's enthusiasm and blood lust certainly seemed genuine, but normally with a story like this, Bruce would worry obsessively that someone would beat him to it. If he saw the story, didn't everybody else? Wasn't it obvious? Better keep it quiet and write it as fast as he could. And yet Bruce went on talking:

"I'm gonna see Preston today and pitch this story. Would make a great cover, don't you think?"

"Yeah. Interesting," Jake mumbled, a bit desperate by now to escape. "Good luck with that."

He watched Bruce finally walk away, extracted his expense report from the pile of paper on the printer and retreated to his office, befuddled. Was that a calculated performance he had just witnessed? But then, what the hell was Bruce trying to provoke?

WEDNESDAY, SEPTEMBER 8, 1999

Kimmie kept looking up from her desk and glancing toward Helen's office. Helen had mentioned that she was going to lunch with someone today. When she left, that would be Kimmie's cue.

She shuffled some papers around her desk, pretending to concentrate on one of them. They were moving into the final phase now. The very thought made Kimmie tingle.

At last, there was Helen with her handbag, her makeup perfectly retouched, heading for the elevators. And gone. Time to move.

Kimmie grabbed a few random papers from her desk and strolled into Helen's office as if she were dropping something into her in-box. It took her no more than thirty seconds to slip into Helen's chair and fire off an email in Helen's name. And in truth, the risk level was virtually zero. Sending prank emails from other people's accounts had become a favorite pastime among the reporters. Even if Helen caught her red-handed and read the message, Kimmie could plausibly claim it was a prank. After all, it was addressed to Tom Richardson, and the subject line read, "I'm sitting here wearing nothing but pearls…"

The body of the message was blank, but that wouldn't matter. The next time Tom checked his email, the Trojan horse program she had planted in his PC would sense the presence of that subject line and obediently commit suicide, but in the manner of Samson in the temple. Before erasing itself, it would overwrite Tom's entire hard drive, reducing all those lovely ones and zeroes to…just zeroes. The big zilch.

This was sweet. Not only would they cover their tracks, it would look as though Tom had tried to destroy the evidence. But there was more than enough evidence backed up on *The Magazine*'s servers to finish him.

Kimmie giggled and almost skipped out of Helen's office.

***

She was leaning over the desk. With each thrust, her left breast swung a millimeter closer to the screen on Jake's computer.

The screen said IBM was down three-quarters of a point, "oh my god," Motorola was up two points, "oh my god, oh my god."

Just about anybody can have sex in the office if the door is locked. Jake had wanted to lock the door, the wimp, but that would have killed the whole kick. Kimmie had talked him out of it.

The editors' offices were all situated against the outer walls of the huge building, along with a couple that belonged to senior writers like Jake. They got the windows. In the middle of the floor were reporters' cubicles. It was midafternoon, and almost everybody was back from lunch, back to work. Kimmie could hear feverish typing coming from a cube just outside Jake's office. "Hey, listen to my lead," a reporter was begging. "Now, if that doesn't turn you on, nothing will."

Finally, her nipple bounced against the cool glass screen, once, twice, thrice….A surge of static electricity crackled through her breast.

She jerked her head back and moaned and hoped the rhythmic motion inside her would numb her brain into her favorite high. That's the ticket, Kimmie girl, turn off that old neocortex. Shut down all higher thought centers. Sometimes she thought she would have been happiest with just a brainstem. And whatever else you need for things like emotions and sex. Limbic system, hypo something. And definitely a pleasure center. Now there's a thought. Scrape out the frontal lobes—what was that song, "Teenage Lobotomy"?—to make room for a huge, mutant pleasure center. Perfect bliss.

But it just wouldn't happen. Her nipple was now starting to get a little sore. It had been smacking the computer screen every second or so for several minutes. At least the static charge had spent itself quickly. The edge of the desk was cutting a deep crease into the front of her thighs.

Novell up three-quarters, "oh my god, oh my god," Procter & Gamble down. Wonder why the stock is down, they're doing so well in their international operations, she thought, and then, Why the hell do I have to think all the time?

"Oh my god, oh my god, oh my god."

I cannot forget, I cannot, I cannot.

Her legs were stiffening up now. Her back was beginning to hurt. Her nipple was a bruised little berry. She considered a change of position but couldn't decide if it was worth it. She didn't want Jake to lose any of his momentum.

As she looked back over her shoulder, Jake saw her face in profile: blank, a study in ennui. Jake knew her boredom would lead quickly to restless impatience. Lately, she had even pronounced "pure sex"—as she disdainfully called it—tiresome. She preferred it flavored with an intriguing mix of drugs.

He needed her cooperation for a couple more minutes. Untiring as a machine, her body continued bouncing back to meet him, but the blankness in her face made Jake anxious that she might just call a halt before he was done. It was too early for him. He needed to distract her with something that didn't require a change of position.

"Guess what? Bruce is doing a story on Madsen," he blurted out. Kimmie always seemed interested in what other writers were up to. It might intrigue her that Bruce was working on something related to her father's business.

His tactic backfired.

"What?" she gasped. "Bruce? Madsen?"

Kimmie immediately forced herself up and away from the screen, grabbing the keyboard—and almost losing Jake, who had to adjust his angle of attack. She started searching the network, looking for some version of Bruce's story, notes, a memo, a draft.

"Here it is," she exclaimed, "now let's see what this bastard is up to." She started reading. Jake knew he needed another minute, maybe two.

He got about forty uninterrupted seconds while she skimmed Bruce's draft.

She squirmed beneath him. "Shit, I need to make a call." She turned to the left, almost losing Jake again, but he grabbed her hips and held her in place.

Another minute. Don't move. Give me another minute.

Kimmie arched her back and stretched out her left arm. Her Prada bag lay just out of reach on the corner of the desk, the strap inches from her fingertips. "I need to make a call. Now," she hissed. "I need my cell phone."

Jake ignored her. He couldn't let her go, not now. As his rhythm quickened, she lunged left again, snagged the strap, pulled the bag close, rummaged through it, flipped open her phone. Cursed the battery. "Motherfucker. It's goddamn dead. Can't believe…forgot to fucking charge it…"

"Yeah…oh, yeah…Kimmie…"

"Jake, hand me your cell phone."

"Huh? It's in my jacket." Which he had tossed on the couch. Across the office.

"Go get it."

"No…fucking…way.…Use my regular phone. It's in front of your nose."

She made a face. He knew she detested regular phones. So big. So clunky. So un-hip.

"Please, God," he moaned.

"Okay, okay." She picked up the receiver and punched in a number as the wave Jake was riding finally crested and broke. He was only vaguely conscious of her words. "Hi, it's me. Listen, Bruce is doing a story on Madsen, the bastard's up to something. Call me as soon as you get this. Oh, and call my office phone, my fucking cell is dead."

A minute later, Jake had to ask. "So, who'd you call?"

"Never mind, just a source." She quickly brushed her hair. "You know I like to always stay a step ahead of Bruce. I'm going out for a smoke."

***

At six in the afternoon Bruce sat in a bar nursing a beer, gazing through the plate-glass window across the street to the building that housed *Wealth* magazine. The people working in the tall glass buildings nearby were finishing their day and rushing out. A few wandered into the bar, but most headed straight for the subway.

Behind one of the windows across the street was Rebecca. Bruce was waiting for her, watching the revolving entrance door intently, though he didn't expect her to leave work that early. She had always worked late hours.

He had rushed over to *Wealth* immediately after listening to the message. He hadn't stopped to think it through, he'd just felt it was the right thing to do. Ever since John had rigged the voice mail to forward Kimmie's messages to him, he had been scrupulous about checking all messages every time the little green light on his phone went on, several times a day. He had listened to a lot of irrelevant nonsense. Then the message he'd been waiting for had come.

Bruce had hoped the message would be from Tom Richardson, about the Madsen story Bruce was writing. Then he would have had proof that Kimmie was feeding him advance information.

Instead Kimmie had gotten a call from a woman.

He hadn't recognized her voice at first. When she had worked at *The Magazine,* she had always spoken slowly and softly, and the woman leaving a message for Kimmie had barked out commands like a drill sergeant.

"Got your message. Don't do anything. It will all still work. Bruce is trying to make you react because it's your daddy's company. That sheet of numbers was Bruce too, for sure. He's clueless, just ignore it. Do nothing. We're almost there."

Sheet of numbers? What the hell? Bruce had replayed the message several times until he was certain it was Rebecca's voice.

Now he was waiting for her. When she emerged, he would cross the street and run into her, as if by accident. They hadn't spoken in almost two years. He'd invite her over to the bar to have a drink and catch up.

The bartender was a shapely twentysomething blonde with a bare midriff and a ring in her navel. She smiled at Bruce, but he ignored the invitation.

Couldn't afford the distraction. He was planning his conversation with Rebecca.

Of course, he couldn't tell her he knew about her phone call to Kimmie. But he needed to sound her out. What was she involved in? Richardson had to be the link, but Bruce couldn't quite make sense of it. Could Kimmie have drawn her into something? The little tart could be manipulative. Reputations and careers were at stake here, and appearances mattered. Kimmie could cause a lot of damage.

It was past seven when Rebecca stepped into the late-summer dusk. She was hidden from view by a cluster of people as she walked out the door, and Bruce almost missed her. When he spotted her, she was already heading for the subway stop on the corner. Definitely her. Who else wore long white lace gloves? They had become her summer trademark during those months right after her father died. Bruce had insisted on visiting her several times that summer. Her old carpal tunnel syndrome must still be a problem.

Bruce dashed out the door and across the street, dodging traffic to the rhythm of honking horns.

He sprinted down the shallow marble steps to the Sixth Avenue subway, shoving past commuters and almost knocking over a pregnant woman. He lost Rebecca in the crowd, remembered that she lived uptown, turned toward the uptown platform…and caught her in the corner of his eye. Whirled back the other way. Downtown. Okay. Maybe she wasn't going home.

He swiped his MetroCard and ran onto the platform as the F train pulled in. He lost her in the crush of people again, then glimpsed her struggling to board the next car up. He wedged himself into the train. At the next station, 42nd Street, he got out but stood close to the door of the subway, watching out for her. He didn't see her get off the train, so he hopped back on. He got off and back on at 34th Street, 23rd Street, 14th, West Fourth…Broadway Lafayette. Bruce stood close to the door as Rebecca ran by him, heading towards the stairs. She ran up, two stairs at a time. Bruce followed her up into the border zone between Chinatown and SoHo.

She turned down Broadway into SoHo, then right on Prince, then left again down a narrow cobblestone street. Nineteenth-century industrial architecture transformed by money and fashion. Overpriced galleries, cafes, restaurants. And above it all, overpriced loft apartments.

She stopped in front of a loft building across from an art gallery and let herself in with a key. Bruce stepped into the shadow of a store awning at the corner. Interesting. Unless she'd moved recently, this wasn't Rebecca's neighborhood. A boyfriend?

The building was mostly dark. Shortly after Rebecca had disappeared inside, lights flicked on in the fourth-floor apartment.

Bruce strolled down the block. A narrow alley opened next to the art gallery, and the building next to the gallery had a fire escape. Bruce hesitated, then darted into the alley. The building in question was dark. No one looking. There were even a couple of convenient metal trash cans in the alley. He was a reporter, after all. He should show some initiative.

He moved one of the trash cans directly underneath the fire escape, stepped up onto the lid as quietly as he could, reached up and swung himself onto the lowest landing. From there it was easy to climb up four stories to the roof. He clambered over the parapet, dusted himself off and approached the street side of the roof. He could see directly into the loft opposite.

And he could see Rebecca. He was pretty sure this wasn't some new apartment she'd moved into, that this wasn't her place. The decor just didn't have a Rebecca feel. Still, she clearly felt at home there, kicking off her shoes, turning on the TV, pouring herself some wine.

Ten, fifteen minutes passed. Bruce was starting to feel vaguely guilty. What was he doing there anyway? His plan to bump into her had fizzled. What did he care who her boyfriend was?

Another woman entered the building, but by the time Bruce noticed her, her back was to him. She was just a shape in the fast-deepening twilight. Then she entered the loft.

Kimmie.

Bruce froze. Oh God, it was Kimmie's place.

The women were talking, laughing. Rebecca handed Kimmie a glass of wine. Soon the women were kissing. Rebecca's blouse came off and floated to the floor. Her breasts were small but perfect, more glorious than Bruce had ever imagined. The long lace gloves stayed on, and Bruce fleetingly wondered why he found that so erotic.

He would have been incapable of moving, had it ever occurred to him to try.

Flaherty scrambled to set up his listening gear, but by the time he was ready, the women were beyond conversation.

Oh, well. Flaherty looked up and was reaching for his binoculars when something in his peripheral vision brought him up short. He swung to his left, stared. The gallery was on the fifth floor, and the building next door was only four stories high. He looked down at the neighboring roof. A man stood there, staring at Kimmie and Rebecca. Flaherty studied him through the binoculars. He was familiar. Yes, *The Magazine*. He had seen him entering and leaving the building a few times.

Flaherty pondered. An interesting development. But things were getting way too crowded. No elbow room. Had to protect his turf.

Inspiration struck, and Flaherty grinned to himself. He reached for his cell phone—it was a prepaid disposable phone, untraceable—and dialed 911.

"Hello, I'd like to report a prowler." He recited the address. "Yeah, some guy on the roof, could be a burglar, maybe a peeping Tom. You should send someone to check it out."

He sat back to wait. In the meantime, he focused on the action across the street. He kept one ear free to listen for the police, the other ear against the laser mike headphones. He peered through the Leicas. Kimmie buried her head between Rebecca's thighs.

He checked the roof to his left. Guy was still there, still staring. Checked his watch. Three, almost four minutes had passed. What if this clown got spooked and left? Time to goose the cops.

911 again, this time with his voice pitched higher. "Yeah, there's a guy on the roof of the building across the street, and I think he's attacking a woman. I heard her scream. Yeah, it's going on right now, hurry." He repeated the address.

The response restored his confidence in the NYPD. Less than a minute passed before he heard sirens in the distance. The sirens died as they got closer, and the flashing blue lights went dark as two police cruisers turned down the block. Must not want to scare the guy off. But the most gratifying touch of all was the unmistakable chugga-chugga-chugga of an approaching helicopter and the blinding white searchlight from the sky that pinned the startled interloper against the parapet. The voice of God thundered through a bullhorn: "Don't move. This is the police. Keep your hands in plain sight and slowly place them on top of your head."

By the time Flaherty stopped laughing, his ribs ached.

THURSDAY, SEPTEMBER 9, 1999

7:36 a.m.

"So, did you say you were going out with Jake tonight?" Rebecca stood in Kimmie's bathroom, brushing her hair. Through the half-open door she could hear Kimmie dressing in the bedroom.

"Yeah, we're gonna grab dinner somewhere and then hit the clubs around midnight."

"Oh, by the way, where's that G you ordered on the Internet? Weren't you getting us, like, a case of that stuff?"

"Not here yet. Seems it was back-ordered. Should be here by next week, though."

Kimmie looked disappointed.

Rebecca opened the medicine cabinet and picked up a 32-ounce plastic bottle that was one-third full of pink liquid—it looked like lemonade. "Well, you've still got some Jolt left."

Kimmie slumped against the doorframe and sighed. "Yeah, I guess that'll have to do for tonight. You know I prefer that GH Gold."

Rebecca shrugged. "Can't always get what you want."

"Yeah, yeah, yeah."

"Now get out of here, I need to pee." Rebecca gently shoved Kimmie out of the bathroom and closed the door.

Turning to face the handbag she'd set on the toilet lid, Rebecca tossed in her hairbrush and unzipped an inside compartment, extracting two small brown bottles labeled GH Gold. She opened one, then opened the bottle of Jolt and poured the colorless GH Gold inside. The active ingredient in both GH Gold and Jolt was the same—a molecule called GBL. Legally, it inhabited a sort of limbo: The FDA frowned on it, and you couldn't get it in health food stores anymore, but you could still buy it on the Web. Chemically, it was similar to GHB, sometimes known as liquid ecstasy or the date-rape

222

drug. In fact, the human body quickly metabolized GBL into GHB, so the effects were essentially identical. In one form or another, G had been popular among New York clubgoers for more than a decade.

But there was one key difference between Jolt and GH Gold. Jolt contained 3.6 grams of GBL per ounce, about 115 grams in a full 32-ounce bottle. You were supposed to do a couple tablespoonfuls of it. GH Gold came in a 2-ounce bottle, but it was 99.99 percent pure. Those 2 ounces contained 69 grams of GBL. You were supposed to put a couple drops in a glass of orange juice.

Rebecca ran through the math in her head. Bottle of Jolt a third full, that's 35 or 40 grams, plus 69. She had almost tripled the dose. Should be plenty. She hesitated, then shrugged. Better safe than sorry. She added the second bottle of GH Gold too, shook up the pink concoction, replaced the fortified Jolt in the medicine cabinet, checked her face in the mirror and flushed the toilet. She was supposed to be peeing, after all.

***

Jeff Norton, editor in chief of *Wealth,* set down the empty pipe he had been toying with and wondered if he'd ever get used to not smoking in the office. The pipe was a fine old bent billiard carved from Algerian briar—the sort of wood that country hadn't exported for decades—with a lovely bird's-eye grain. Too bad he didn't get more use out of it. He often fantasized about quitting and freelancing from home. He'd sit there in his pajamas, tapping away at his laptop, happily ensconced in billowing clouds of smoke. Just one problem: no escape from his wife.

Shrugging off the daydream, he picked up the phone and called *Wealth*'s lawyer. "Hi, me again, I'm just about to send Rebecca's story to production…yeah, the latest version should be coming over your fax now, so take a quick look and let me know if there's anything else you want to bring up.…You sure we have enough documentation to cover our asses? Of course the reporting's solid, it's brilliant, you know Rebecca.…Yeah, tomorrow we'll make the routine fact-checking calls to Richardson and *The Magazine*. I don't want to give them too much warning. Then, if nothing blows up on us, we go to press." The new issue would hit the newsstands by Tuesday. "Yeah, I'll check back with you tomorrow. Okay then."

He hung up and called the managing editor. "Let's go with it. Rebecca's story is the cover." Glancing up at the bulletin board on his wall, he contemplated the cover mockup tacked to the cork and wondered where this would all lead. One thing was certain: He was sure sticking it to Preston Gifford. He smiled in satisfaction and wracked his brain for a full thirty seconds, trying to think of some other son of a bitch who deserved it more. Came up blank. Yeah, sticking it to Preston made it all worthwhile.

By the time Rebecca stepped through the revolving glass doors of the *Wealth* building and onto the still-cooling sidewalk, it was pushing midnight. She let the warm, moist air caress her skin as she smiled the kind of satisfied smile that hadn't crossed her lips in years. She had done it. The final countdown had begun.

Just a few loose ends left.

***

11:24 p.m.

Later, much later, Kimmie would reflect on the ways her fate turned upon a bottle of good Chianti, upon laws of gravity and motion, upon politics and chemistry.

Jake was just emerging from the bathroom, bottle of Jolt in one hand, glass of wine in the other. "So where's that GH Gold you were gonna get? This Jolt is for wimps." He took a swig from the bottle.

"Soon, honey, soon," Kimmie called from the couch.

They had retreated to Kimmie's place for the Chianti after a late supper at a Village bistro. Now it was time for the G, then the club. Kimmie didn't like to take the stuff along with her. In these Giuliani days, you couldn't whip out eyedrops in a club without some security goon hustling you outside.

She took a sip of wine. Jake walked toward her, smiling. Perhaps in the end it was a mistake to wear the suede skirt on such a warm evening anyway. Still, she'd been in a suede mood. She noticed the small ripple in the rug just before Jake's toes encountered it, far too late to escape the consequences. He didn't notice it at all, being preoccupied with a second swig of Jolt. Jake tripped but recovered his balance in time to avoid falling on his face. Much of the wine in his glass, however, traced a parabola that ended with a splash on Kimmie's skirt.

The next few moments were a blur of unladylike curses and dabbing with paper towels, but Kimmie quickly segued from annoyance to focusing on finding a dry outfit. She half disappeared into her closet, only to be gripped by uncharacteristic indecision. Still, no more than a few minutes had passed before Jake started nagging her.

"Kimmie, come on already, let's go."

"Just one more minute," she promised.

He nodded and swallowed some more Jolt.

But when she emerged at last, Jake was nowhere in sight. "Jake?" she called uncertainly as she approached the couch.

When she got close enough to see over the back of the couch, she froze for a heartbeat or two. Jake was sprawled face down on the rug. The Jolt was forming a pale pink puddle on the hardwood floor.

She vaulted over the couch and crouched over him, called his name, slapped him. He wasn't breathing.

She scrambled for the phone.

FRIDAY, SEPTEMBER 10, 1999

12:07 a.m.

Michael Andros was just putting his cigarette out on the sidewalk when the cab pulled up. He adjusted his cap, then grinned when Rebecca emerged. She was wearing jeans, a tank top and long, white lace gloves, like Victorian ladies used to wear. Weird, but kinda sexy.

"Hey, babe, how you doin'?"

"Hi, Mikey." She smiled. "I'm good. How you been?"

"Good, good. I've missed you."

"Yeah? That's sweet. I've missed you, too. Well, soon I'll have more time to relax."

He felt a fluttering in his gut.

"Everything set?" she asked.

"Yeah, just like you wanted. I'm doing the evening shift Tuesday, 3 to 11. Soon as he comes home, I call you."

She beamed. "You're a prince, Mikey. Shall we go up?"

"Yeah, sure."

He held the lobby door open for her, then led her to the freight elevator. Soon they were at the access panel where she had left the transceiver. In less than two minutes she had disconnected it, stuffed it in her bag and replaced the panel on the wall. Wordlessly, they started back down in the elevator.

He stared down at the floor, shuffling his feet, realized she was studying him. He looked up.

She was smiling. "I've gotta run, Mikey. But I promise, when this is all over, I'll be back." Her voice dropped to a husky whisper. "We'll have some fun."

He found it hard to breathe, even as he wondered if she'd keep that promise.

***

Kimmie drained the dregs of her Diet Coke, rearranged her stiff limbs in the faux-leather chair and stared numbly at the small TV screen mounted above the hospital bed. It was afternoon, so a soap opera was on, but it made no sense to her. Her mind couldn't get a grip on the flow of events. She had hoped some of the surreal sense of things would fade along with the effects of the wine and the pot, but she couldn't shake it.

She turned her head and gazed at Jake, still and peaceful in his gown. The doctors didn't really know what would happen now. He could wake up tomorrow, or next week. Or never.

She hadn't slept at all since it happened. She supposed that didn't help with the sense of unreality.

That morning she had made some calls. Helen had been very upset and concerned, told her to stay with Jake, not to worry about work, that she'd stop by later.

And Rebecca. The words had been cool, calculating. "Absolutely, stay by Jake's side. You should probably camp out there this weekend, for the sake of appearances." But the tone…the tone of her voice had belied the words she used.

She had sounded genuinely shaken, even a bit shocked. Sometimes Rebecca could be endearingly human despite herself.

Kimmie reached over and changed the channel. Another soap. This one made no sense either.

***

"Hello, I'm trying to reach Helen Caswell." The voice at the other end of the line was young, male and nervous.

"This is she."

"Hi, I'm a reporter for *Wealth* magazine," the young man introduced himself.

Helen thought she understood why he sounded so anxious. He must have been calling about a job interview.

She tried to put the young man at ease. "You know, I'm pretty sure I never got your résumé, but I would definitely be interested in meeting with you. Why don't you re-send your résumé first?"

She smiled to herself, relishing the thrill of a small victory. *Wealth* had been stealing their best people for too long. Finally, someone from the other camp was trying to defect to their side.

"Oh no, no, I'm not calling about a job, I'm just calling to verify some facts…"

"What do you mean?" asked Helen, bemused. "You mean about our fact-checking system?"

Helen knew that *Wealth* had recently scaled back their own fact-checking, and checked only potentially libelous stories, while *The Magazine* still checked them all. She was afraid that *Wealth* might be sniffing around to see what they were up to, and she grew cautious.

"Can you tell me why exactly you're calling?"

"I just wanted to verify your name, and that you are engaged to Tom Richardson," the reporter said.

"My name is on the masthead, and I don't comment on my personal life," she replied. "And why are you asking me these questions anyway?"

"I'm just fact-checking a story. So it wouldn't be a mistake to say that you are engaged to Tom Richardson, after all it's public information, *The New York Times* had an announcement about your engagement. I am just trying to fact-check…"

"What story are you fact-checking?" Helen asked, even though she knew that he wasn't allowed to say.

"Well, I don't know, I haven't seen the story, I was just asked to check some basic facts," he said.

Bad sign. Helen knew he was lying. That was exactly what she advised her reporters to say when they were checking negative stories. Play dumb, Columbo-style. Get info without giving any away.

"And would you have access to Tom Richardson's personal computer?" he continued.

Tom's computer? What on earth was he talking about? This sounded serious. *Wealth* was doing a story involving her and Tom, and it was negative enough that they were checking it. She had to get off the phone right away.

"Why don't you just email me your questions?" she said and hung up.

She dialed Tom's number, got it wrong, started dialing again when her phone rang. The other line lit up with Preston's number. She sat there frozen, let it ring. Couldn't talk to him just yet. Had to compose herself. The ringing stopped, and the little green light that signaled voice mail lit up.

She stared blankly at the light, turned and stared blankly at her computer screen. A new email message came in from Preston, cc'd to Jake. The subject line was in red, tagged with an exclamation mark: READ THIS NOW.

She forced her hand to move, to click the message open: "Helen. Jake. *Wealth* is sniffing around, fact-checking some story, something to do with you guys and Tom Richardson. What the fuck is going on?????? Come to my office ASAP."

FRIDAY-SATURDAY, SEPTEMBER 10-11, 1999

Passport control at the Santo Domingo airport was a new experience for John Squinzano. It was the first time he could remember standing in an hourlong line and thinking, Not such a bad way to spend some time. A squad of airport employees was handing out free rum to welcome the tourists, no limits on refills. John took a long sip of the sweet, dark liquid. Clearly, these people knew how to mellow out.

On the flight down from New York, Daisy had held his hand, the first time in months that she had touched him that way. At least, he hoped it had been that way, and was a harbinger of what this trip would bring, not just a reflex triggered by her fear of flying. Now, as he started on his second rum, he draped his arm over Daisy's shoulders. She didn't shrug it off.

Thank God, it was working, he thought with relief. Two weeks in the Dominican Republic, an all-inclusive package in the three-star Juan Dolio resort, would do the trick. He would finally get a break.

By the time they approached the end of the passport line, John was working on his fourth plastic cup of rum on the rocks and contemplating his new life of crime. Who said it didn't pay? He felt no remorse, no anxiety. Just a pleasant tingle of excitement and a sense of satisfaction, of, yes, manliness at having pulled it off.

He hoped that Daisy had remembered to pack her Velcro rollers. She should, after all, be planning to set her hair when they went out for nice dinners.

Indeed, once they arrived at the hotel and started to unpack, he reassured himself that she hadn't forgotten the rollers. Before they went down to dinner that first day in Santo Domingo, he suggested going to the best restaurant and pointed out it had a dress code (no shorts or bare torsos), so she put rollers in her hair and started ironing her blouse, and then she didn't stop him when he came up from behind, nibbled on her neck and nudged her toward the bed.

Next day, midmorning, John sat on a poolside deck chair, eyeing the crowd around him. Reggae tunes blared from the pool bar, almost drowning out the excited shrieks of children splashing in the water. The smell of cigarettes hung heavy in the humid air. The bar counter ran along part of the pool's edge, and there was a row of concrete, underwater barstools, which made it easy to stay up to your waist in cool water, sunburn your back and get loaded simultaneously. If you could snag a seat, that is. As soon as the bar had opened, right after breakfast, all the stools had been swarmed by a group of pasty tattooed Brits. Now that it was almost 11 a.m., most of them were on at least their third piña colada. They were growing raucous, and a couple of them were already turning lobster red, but they showed no inclination to give up their spots at the bar anytime soon.

Clearly, not many Americans at this resort. Lots of Brits, some French, some Germans. John was starting to realize that a resort full of Europeans had its advantages—mainly, the predominant bathing fashions. Well, it probably wasn't so great for Daisy. Too many middle-aged, paunchy guys in tight Speedos. But it certainly was a treat for him.

He repositioned his chair slightly to improve his view of an attractive, topless brunette across the pool. She was in her late twenties, he guessed, and her perfect breasts stood alert, sentries guarding the plain of her flat stomach. Breasts tanned the color of milk chocolate—they reminded John of Hershey's Kisses. She was smoking a cigarette and talking in French to a group of male scuba divers, who were sitting on the edge of the pool and checking their gear. She sat up straight, took a sip of her drink, leaned forward to say something. She'd had her hair done in those beaded braids that were so popular down here, and now those beads brushed the shoulder of one of the divers.

John shifted in his seat. He imagined the quick, irregular flicks of the cool beads, falling like rain across his chest, teasing his belly, dribbling down…

He looked over to the far corner of the pool, where several local women had set up a hair-braiding station. The black women themselves all wore their hair in braids, and were busily braiding the hair of a couple of newly arrived tourists. He watched the quick, precise movements of the braiders' hands, their fingers curling around the wisps of hair, fluttering like dark birds. One braider finished up with a customer, a blonde, blue-eyed young German with a balding husband who called to her from the pool. She stood and stretched in her bikini, touching her new braids, playing with them, tossing her hair and grinning.

Suddenly John knew what he must do. He stood and walked straight over to the braider who'd just done the hausfrau, asked about price. She turned to face him, smiled and left him speechless with her beauty. Those high cheekbones. That wide mouth. Those eyes. Those beads.

He stammered out something about his wife, returned to his chair, reached over and tapped Daisy's shoulder. She opened one eye.

"Hon, you should get your hair done like those women are doing. You know, those beaded braids."

"Really? You think I'd look good like that?"

"Good? You'd look gorgeous. And you know what? You'd look really hot, too."

"You really think so? Well…it might be kind of a hoot…"

"You oughta go for it. Have a little fun. That woman over there is free right now, it's thirty bucks."

Daisy smiled. "Okay, tell you what. Bring me a piña colada and I'll do it."

"You got it, babe."

John fetched drinks, then settled back to wait and watch as those dark fingers flew. My God, the braider's face was stunning, her beads clicking softly against each other in the breeze. He let his eyes close, imagined a cascade of beads above him, touching his skin lightly, rhythmically as they swayed closer, then away, closer, away, as the woman moved on top of him, her breathtaking face ecstatic, her ebony breasts tracing arcs in the sultry air…

He sighed with pleasure, contemplating Daisy's transformation and the tropical days ahead. Indeed, this was paradise.

FRIDAY, SEPTEMBER 10, 1999

Helen sipped her cold white wine and watched the sun set languorously over Central Park. From up here on Tom's penthouse terrace, the tawdry concerns of the workaday world seemed remote.

Still, it made her uneasy to be on the receiving side of the press's attention. She and Tom had compared notes on the questions *Wealth* had asked them, tried to analyze them for clues as to what kind of story might be cooking. They had made little progress.

"I wonder why they asked about your PC, the one in your study?" mused Helen. "What do you keep on there, state secrets?"

"Not much of anything right now. Thing's suddenly on the fritz, won't start up. I think the hard drive may have died. Had to switch to my laptop for now."

Tom, thought Helen, looked even more worried than she felt. He seemed distracted as they let themselves drift into a conversational lull. Finally, she decided to break it.

"Tom, there's something I think you may be able to shed some light on." She sat up straight and rummaged through her purse. "So I have to ask. What do you know about this man?" She pulled out the photo she had snapped of the guy who'd been following her and shoved it under Tom's nose.

She watched his eyes as she did so. Clearly, she had surprised him. She could see him struggle to control his reaction, but the flash of recognition was unmistakable.

"So, Tom, you do know him."

"How…where'd you get that?"

"I took it myself while he was watching my apartment. Did you hire this guy?"

Tom slumped back in his chair. "Yeah, okay, I hired him. Private detective, specializes in surveillance."

"What? You had me watched?"

"No, no, not you, he was supposed to watch Kimmie. I was worried she might be up to something…not that it's done me a lot of good. I'm surprised you spotted him. Guess he's not as good as he claims to be."

"So why was he following me? Damn it, Tom, I thought he was some kind of psycho stalker. He scared me silly. And I do not appreciate being spied on by your…your lackey."

"Helen, I…I'm so sorry. Believe me, I never intended for him to follow you. This guy, he…maybe he's a little overzealous in his work. Mainly he was watching Kimmie, but from time to time he'd follow someone connected with her: Jake Rosenberg, you, this Rebecca Morgan…"

Helen sat up even straighter. "What? Wait a minute, hold on. Kimmie's connected with Rebecca?"

Tom nodded. He seemed suddenly weary, the few lines on his face deeper. Perhaps it was a trick of the light. "Yes, there's a connection. They're lovers."

"Oh, my God." Helen sat back and drained the rest of her wine, then poured herself another. Paranoia seized her like a malarial fever. Rebecca and Kimmie, Kimmie and Rebecca…

MONDAY, SEPTEMBER 13, 1999

Everyone was very solicitous of Kimmie when she showed up at work on Monday. They were concerned. They murmured vaguely encouraging things about Jake and were careful not to mention anything so crass as work or gossip. Some seemed afraid to approach her.

So it was midafternoon before she heard about the fact-checking calls.

She was in the restroom brushing her hair when Meg the Knife wandered in.

"Kimmie, hi, I heard about…How you holding up?"

"I'm okay, I guess."

"Jake?"

Kimmie shrugged. "Not much to say. He's in a coma. I think the doctors don't know much."

"Geez, that's just…just awful. I'm sorry."

"Yeah, thanks. You know, everybody's treating me like I'm made of porcelain today, and it's creeping me out. What's new around this place?"

"New? Well, there's a rumor floating around that Bruce got arrested the other day…" An odd expression came over Meg's face. "No, you wouldn't have heard, would you? Word is that *Wealth*'s gonna run a story, something to do with Helen and, uh, Tom Richardson. Supposedly they made some fact-checking calls here Friday. Nobody who really knows is talking, but Helen's not herself. Looks like a scared rabbit."

Kimmie tried to look blank, afraid she might grow dizzy or break into a cold sweat. There was a metallic taste in her mouth. "Gee, wonder what that's all about?"

"You got me."

"Well, thanks, Meg."

Kimmie almost lurched out of the restroom and stumbled to her cubicle. Something was horribly wrong. She dialed Rebecca's number at *Wealth*, but got her voice mail: "Rebecca, what the fuck is going on? Why is *Wealth* fact-checking some story about Helen and Tom? Call me back now."

She fired off an email to Rebecca with the same message, then thought to dial her cell phone. Voice mail again. She repeated the same message and settled down to wait. And wait. She checked her email. Waited. Checked again.

After fifteen minutes she could stand it no longer. She dialed both numbers again. Voice mail. Voice mail.

An idea came to her. She dialed the main number for *Wealth,* trying to sound calm and businesslike. "Hello, this is the office of Carly Fiorina at Hewlett-Packard. We had a phone interview scheduled with Rebecca Morgan, but we have to do it half an hour earlier. Ms. Fiorina is available now. I tried calling Ms. Morgan, but I'm getting her voice mail. Could you please help me find her?"

A call from Carly Fiorina, the most powerful woman in American business, should send the *Wealth* receptionist on a mad rush to find Rebecca.

"You want to talk to a Fiorina?" the receptionist said. "I don't see this name on the phone list. Could you spell it?"

Goddamn fucking moron temp.

"Could you please transfer me over to the editor in chief?" Kimmie said. The editor's assistant should know what to do when Carly Fiorina calls.

"Hello, I'm calling from Carly Fiorina's office. I have Ms. Fiorina on the phone for Rebecca Morgan, but she doesn't seem to be in her office. Can you help me find her?" Kimmie said.

"Oh my gosh, but of course, of course. I'll go try to find her," said the assistant, "can you please hold on?"

While the assistant was looking for Rebecca, Kimmie checked her email again. Nothing. She double-checked her cell phone. From the corner of her eye she glimpsed Helen heading toward Preston's office. What the fuck was going on?

The *Wealth* assistant returned: "Hello, I'm so sorry, I looked for Rebecca everywhere, I even checked the ladies' room, but nobody knows where she is right now....I am so sorry...I'll have her..."

Kimmie slammed down the phone.

***

3:45 p.m.

Rebecca Morgan held her breath as the ancient elevator creaked upward. Partly because of the tension—every muscle fiber in her body was strung tight as a trip-wire. But mostly against the smell, a weird distillation of rancid sweat, decaying linoleum, cat piss and ammonia. For the hundredth time she marveled at the stratospheric rent Kimmie paid to live in this fashionable dump. The loft interiors were civilized enough, but the hallways and stairwells looked as if they hadn't been renovated since World War II.

The elevator lurched to a halt and its doors grudgingly slid open. Rebecca stepped into the dim, high-ceilinged hall and exhaled at last. The building was quiet, the hallway deserted, just as she'd hoped it would be on a weekday afternoon. This was one day she couldn't afford to be seen entering or leaving. Quickly—and almost silently in her running shoes, trying to avoid the creakiest floorboards—she moved to Kimmie's door and let herself in with her key.

Once inside, she paused for a moment, leaning back against the door, savoring the apartment's air-conditioned chill, waiting for her heart rate to subside. She had to be calm, controlled, methodical.

Stepping away from the door, she turned and regarded it critically, studying the closeness of its fit in the door frame. The seal was far from airtight, of course, but it should do.

She moved deliberately through the loft, checking to make sure all the windows were shut tight, turning off the air conditioners, closing the bedroom and bathroom doors. She ended her tour in the kitchen area, which was marked off from the living room by a counter and a pair of bar stools. There she unplugged the toaster and the coffee maker, realizing as she did so that this was no doubt an irrational precaution, but not caring. She couldn't chance any premature sparks.

At last she faced the gas stove, giving silent thanks that Kimmie's idea of cooking was reheating takeout leftovers in the microwave. Otherwise she might have pressured the landlord to replace this relic. No electronic ignition here.

Carefully, Rebecca lifted the cover of the range top and snuffed out the pilot lights. Then she opened the oven, peered inside and extinguished the interior pilot light. Leaving the oven door open, she set the gas for the oven and all four burners on high.

Quickly she rummaged through a kitchen drawer, searching for an appropriate tool, settling on a screwdriver. She walked to the front door. On either side of the door was a wall sconce, both of them controlled by the light switch next to the door. Standing on tiptoe, Rebecca reached behind the shade of one sconce with the screwdriver and tapped the lightbulb carefully until its glass shattered, leaving the filament intact, then repeated the operation on the bulb in the other wall sconce.

She replaced the screwdriver in the drawer, then took a moment to survey her handiwork. It would be dusk at least by the time Kimmie got home. She'd open the door and reflexively, almost simultaneously, flip the switch. Probably before the smell of gas fully registered. Spark and boom. Mysterious gas explosion. Well, the oven was old.

Crude but effective. She had tried the discreet, surgical approach with the

GH Gold. No more pussyfooting. Time for the sledgehammer.

Dennis Flaherty was loitering in wait across the street as Rebecca stumbled out onto the sunbaked sidewalk. In his Bermuda shorts, aloha shirt and Minnesota baseball cap, he looked every inch the tourist from the heartland. The camera he was using was a fairly simple, lightweight point-and-click, but it did have a built-in zoom and automatic time-and-date stamp. Very handy for surveillance sometimes. He got a nice shot of Rebecca's profile as she stepped out the door.

***

Rebecca checked her cell phone as she walked back to the subway station. Damn, more messages, no doubt all of them from Kimmie. Time to feed that girl a soothing line of bullshit before she did something stupid. Something to calm her down for a few hours. A few hours was all she had left anyway.

She dialed Kimmie's cell, got an answer on the second ring. Kimmie sounded wound up and freaked out.

"Rebecca, where the hell have you been? What's going on?"

Rebecca tried to come across as simultaneously frazzled and matter-of-fact. "I've been underground, goddamn it. Had an interview downtown with a fund manager, then I got stuck in a broken-down F train. Was stranded between stations for an hour and a half, no air-conditioning, no cell phone signal. Thought I was gonna pass out. Now I'm all sweaty and gross."

"So where's the fire, why all the messages?"

"What's up with the fact-checking calls? *Wealth* is calling about Helen and Tom. What the hell??"

Rebecca laughed. "Oh, that. Relax, it's nothing."

"What do you mean nothing?"

"We're running some stupid piece about eligible rich people, and recently eligible ones. The timing is perfect with Richardson, we can write about the upcoming wedding."

"But if it's just some puff piece, why are they being cagey about the checking? Helen and Preston are all paranoid."

"Well, we are talking about billionaires here. Some of them are media savvy, and we might want to say something snarky. We'll surely estimate their net worth, and they can be touchy about that."

"Well…" Kimmie was winding down. "You could have warned me, you know."

"Sorry, but I just heard this morning that we were including Tom and Helen. Never occurred to me that the checker would call *The Magazine*."

"You know," she added, "this might actually work to our benefit if it's making Helen and Tom paranoid. A little reminder of what the wrong sort of media attention can be like."

"I guess, maybe." Kimmie sighed into the phone. "But clue me in next time. I've been freaking all afternoon. Thought maybe someone stumbled across, you know, the false trail we left…"

Rebecca cut her off. "Not on the phone. Look, we'll talk some more tonight. I'll meet you at your place after work, okay?"

***

Mildly bored, Flaherty sat at the dark mahogany bar of the Cedar Tavern, nursing a beer. Not that the boredom bothered him really. If you couldn't handle boredom, you had no business in surveillance.

He was waiting to pick up Kimmie's tail as she left work. It was just past six o'clock, but she rarely emerged from the office before seven at the earliest. In a few minutes he would saunter over to the steps at the entrance to the college near *The Magazine* and commence his stakeout, sitting and chain-smoking among the ever-shifting cast of students who clustered there. In his faded jeans and black work shirt, he could easily be mistaken for a professor, or perhaps an aging graduate student.

The Yankees game showing on the TV above the bar trailed off to a dispiriting conclusion, and the bartender started flipping through the channels, searching for more sports. As he flipped through the local news, Flaherty glanced up at the reporter's excited voice. "…massive explosion demolished the entire…" He froze. He'd caught just a glimpse of the street scene before the bartender clicked to the next channel. But he knew that block.

"Go back!" he snapped. "Back to the news!" His tone made the bartender comply.

"…police have sealed off the street, and the fire department is evacuating the adjacent buildings. Four people who were on the sidewalk nearby when the explosion occurred are being treated for minor injuries. The miracle here is that there weren't many more casualties. The tragedy, of course, is that we do have one confirmed fatality. We won't know for sure if there were any more until the rescue teams finish sorting through the rubble. That one fatality has been identified as Hector Salamanca, 53, the building superintendent. There's been speculation that he may have smelled a gas leak and gone to investigate. Again, there was a devastating explosion this afternoon…"

As the reporter recapped the breaking story, she mentioned the building's address. But by then Flaherty was already certain. That was Kimmie's building.

He sat perfectly still, staring intently into his beer, feeling the pieces click into place. That Rebecca woman stops by Kimmie's place today. Does what?

Then the super wanders in. Was it really the smell of gas that lured him? More likely a very different smell, thought Flaherty: He popped in to perv on her panties again. Boom. And the other night, Rebecca stays overnight at Kimmie's. That evening, Jake the boytoy OD's. Sure, you could call it circumstantial, but Flaherty made a point of not allowing for coincidences. Someone was either trying to kill Kimmie and missing the target, or was trying to scare her, to warn her off something. And Rebecca Morgan was in it up to her eyeballs.

He stood, threw a few bills on the bar and walked out. He should call Richardson, consult with his client. His hand was halfway to his cell phone when he hesitated. What was Richardson's game here, anyway? After all, he was having his daughter followed. Clearly he considered her some sort of threat. Maybe he was behind all this himself, and the right hand had no clue what the left was doing.

He lit a cigarette and turned the corner. No, he wouldn't call Richardson, not yet. Had to think first. He'd have to call, of course, and relay the bare-bones news once it was obvious that he had to know—once he had followed Kimmie home to a pile of rubble. But he didn't have to mention his suspicions. No, better to act on his own, find some way to alert her. Something anonymous yet convincing. As with many of his subjects, he admitted to himself, he had grown attached to Kimmie. He really didn't want to see her get hurt.

***

Kimmie wandered down the halls of St. Vincent's Hospital in a daze. She wasn't quite sure what she was doing there, and she certainly couldn't remember how she'd gotten there. Some peculiar impulse had pulled her to the hospital and into Jake's room. She felt so odd. She wasn't even annoyed to find Meg the Knife there.

"How's he doing?" she asked.

Meg looked up and shrugged. "Same, I guess. Just lying there." She frowned, looked harder at Kimmie. "Are you all right?"

Kimmie shook her head and slumped into a chair. "I... I just stopped by my place. It's not there anymore. Cops and firemen...they have it taped off, like a crime scene. Some kind of gas explosion this afternoon. Super was killed. Nothing but rubble left."

"Oh my God, Kimmie, that was your place? I just saw something on the news.... That's awful."

"Yeah. I guess it's lucky I didn't have much that's irreplaceable...you know, sentimental stuff. Everything's gone."

"Kimmie, if there's anything I can do..."

"No, no, I'm okay, thanks. I'll just...uh...you know, I've got the keys to

Jake's place. I'll probably just stay there."

"Well…you sure you'll be okay?"

"Yeah, yeah, I'll be fine. Guess I'll need to buy some clothes and stuff tomorrow." Kimmie flashed a crooked grin. "It's just turning out to be a hell of a week, huh? I'm kinda numb. Having trouble processing it all."

"Yeah, I'll bet. Listen, I was just leaving, but I could stay a little…"

"No, no, go on, I'm okay. I wouldn't mind sitting alone with Jake for a while."

"Well, all right. See you tomorrow, okay?"

"Sure. Thanks, Meg."

Kimmie's eyes settled on Jake. She watched his steady breathing and wondered idly if this was some karmic lesson in counting your blessings. After all, Jake still had an apartment, but what good did it do him? At least she was still conscious.

God, she'd almost forgotten. She was supposed to meet Rebecca. She should call and let her know…

She glanced up as some guy in a baseball cap entered the room, his face obscured by a spectacular bouquet of lilies and irises. How nice of someone, she thought. Damn, I should have brought some. But he's in a coma…what difference would it make?

Instead of setting the flowers down on a table or somewhere, the guy handed them to Kimmie. Reflexively, she accepted them. He nodded, turned on his heel and was gone.

She glanced down at the card. The envelope said, "Kimmie."

She frowned, trying to make sense of this. Weird. She set the bouquet on the bedside table, opened the card and stared. Stared a long time.

The card held a photo of Rebecca leaving Kimmie's building. It was stamped with date and time. This afternoon. There was a message in the card in neat block letters: "Watch your back. —A Friend"

TUESDAY, SEPTEMBER 14, 1999

Still dazed, Kimmie wandered into the office early—ridiculously early by her standards. It was barely 9. She felt as if she'd been beaten up and locked in a trunk all night. That mysterious flower delivery had left her paranoid and squirrelly. She hadn't called Rebecca. She had decided that she felt safer in a bustling hospital than alone in Jake's apartment. What little sleep she'd gotten she'd managed while curled up in the chair in Jake's hospital room. She was so stiff she could barely move her neck, and she was still wearing yesterday's clothes. A carelessly torn stocking was one thing, but she'd always hated the feel of dirty underwear. Maybe she'd just toss this pair into the trash and dispense with underwear entirely, at least while the warm weather lasted. Go commando.

She slumped at her desk, sipping a Styrofoam cup of lousy coffee and staring into space. She was vague about how much time had passed when the mailroom guy came by and tossed a stack of stuff on her desk. She glanced up and almost spilled the dregs of her coffee. From the cover of the new issue of *Wealth*, Tom Richardson's smug face taunted her.

Kimmie snapped into instant focus, frantically flipped to the table of contents, felt herself float into a sickening free fall. Rebecca's byline on the story. She turned the pages and began to read.

By the time she'd scanned the first two paragraphs the words had started to blur.

She forced herself to read on as Rebecca elaborated the backstory, the motivation. The pressure on Tom Richardson to prove himself after his legendary father retired. His initial missteps.

And then how the firm's performance had improved dramatically. How *The Magazine* had published several stories about companies soon after Hillburn Richshire made large bets on the direction those very stocks would move.

Then Rebecca laid it all out.

In every case Tom Richardson took these positions within a few weeks before the publication of the articles, at the very time those stories were in the works. *Wealth* has learned that repeatedly over the past several months, someone used a PC and the phone line in Richardson's Fifth Avenue apartment to log on to *The Magazine*'s computer network. That someone used a password that belongs to Helen Caswell, a senior editor at *The Magazine* and Tom Richardson's fiancée. That someone also downloaded copies of the stories in question. Almost simultaneously, Hillburn Richshire traded in the companies that were the subjects of those stories.

It was a solid case of insider trading. Rebecca had sprinkled the story with references to highly reliable sources. Kimmie knew those sources didn't exist. Rebecca mentioned undeniable evidence. Undeniable: Everyone knew that was code for tape recordings, documents—or computer records. This evidence did exist. Kimmie knew it did because she and Rebecca had gone to some trouble to create it.

Rebecca listed specific companies, incriminating dates. Unfettered. Genesis. Forsooth. Kimmie was afraid she might throw up all over the glossy magazine pages. More stocks and dates followed, but she already knew the relevant details.

She looked up, muttering a string of curses that would have reddened the cheeks of a drill sergeant. She grabbed her cell phone and started to dial, then stopped. No. Rebecca had caller ID at her office, and Kimmie had a feeling that Rebecca would be dodging her calls today. No. Better to surprise her.

She forced herself to take deep breaths and think. What did that stupid, double-crossing bitch think she was doing? Advancing her career? Kimmie couldn't fathom it. Rebecca had thrown it all away. This was supposed to be about the money. Simple blackmail. Create a false but highly incriminating trail of evidence, then go to Richardson and threaten to expose his "crimes." To besmirch his cherished reputation. He would have paid them off to protect that, to protect the family firm. They would have been set for life. Hell, the whole brilliant scheme had been Rebecca's idea.

She felt as if a blast of arctic air had blown the cobwebs from her brain. And the last shreds of doubt. Rebecca had tried to kill her. Whatever the hell she was up to, Kimmie was now a loose end. An impediment. Damn, Rebecca was probably responsible for Jake, too. Tried twice and missed. Sloppy of her.

She wouldn't get a third chance.

Kimmie stood up and scanned the floor, peering over the top of her cubicle. A few reporters were just starting to drift in, but the cubes were mostly empty. Meg's office was still dark, and it lay in the same general direction as the restrooms. Kimmie ducked back down, stuffed a roll of masking tape into her handbag, flung the bag over her shoulder and strode purposefully in that very direction. She glanced around quickly, edged into Meg's office and shut the door.

She approached the wall, sizing up the locked display case. As she whipped out her masking tape, Kimmie prayed silently that the glass wasn't bulletproof or anything. She applied strips of tape across the glass in the shape of a cross, then more strips in an x-shape. Selecting a particularly heavy economics tome from Meg's bookshelf, she tapped the glass gently, trying to keep quiet. Then harder. Relief flooded through her as it started to break. A few small pieces fell, but most of it stuck to the tape. Finally, Kimmie lowered a gently tinkling mass of glass and tape to the floor.

She straightened up, exhaled and studied the weapons a moment before settling on a Bowie knife with a nine-inch blade. She slipped it into her Prada bag.

***

Kimmie decided to walk through the warm morning all the way to *Wealth*'s midtown offices. It wouldn't do to arrive too early, in case Rebecca was running late today—she didn't want to risk an accidental encounter. No, she would choose the time and place. Besides, she needed to think, to work the stiffness out of her muscles and to burn off some immediate rage—it might be hours before she could confront the bitch. She just prayed Rebecca was in the office today. But the office had always been Rebecca's true home. Kimmie felt pretty sure Rebecca would spend this day in her lair, savoring the fact that she'd fucked everyone over.

By the time she reached her destination, it was almost 11. She entered the cool marble lobby, strode over to one of the wall phones and dialed Rebecca's extension. When Rebecca answered, Kimmie hung up. Good. Rebecca didn't know it, but she was trapped. Like vermin hiding behind the walls. Well, the exterminator would be waiting. When she came out on her lunch break, the hunt would begin.

Kimmie found a coffee shop across the street. She ordered a latte, settled into a spot near the window and pretended to read *The New York Times.*

Lunchtime came and went. By the time Rebecca emerged, Kimmie had moved from the coffee shop to a nearby bar and nursed her way through two light beers. It was well past five, and Kimmie counted herself lucky to have spotted Rebecca through the rush-hour hordes. She threw some money on the bar and scurried out the door.

Rebecca was walking north, toward Central Park. Kimmie dashed across the street and almost caught up with her. At first, in the midtown crowds, she followed as closely as she could, afraid of losing her. Rebecca skirted the edge of the park and continued north up Fifth Avenue. As the foot traffic thinned out, Kimmie dropped back, until she was following from a distance of a block or so.

Where was she heading on the Upper East Side? Her apartment was on the West Side. Kimmie tried to think like Rebecca. Where would she go on this day of her triumph, this day when she had screwed everyone in sight?

As they proceeded farther up Fifth Avenue, a sneaking suspicion congealed into certainty, then proved correct. Rebecca marched into Tom Richardson's apartment building. Kimmie stood watching from a block away, impressed by the woman's sheer effrontery, then darted around the corner and lit a cigarette. What the hell was the bitch up to now? She had to know. She'd loiter here for a couple minutes, then follow her all the way inside.

She thought for a while, stubbed out her cigarette and jogged the rest of the way to Tom's building, trying to arrive looking flustered. Michael Andros looked up from his desk.

"Oh, hi," she smiled. "Michael, right? Remember me?"

He smiled back uncertainly. "Yeah, sure. You know, you look pretty good when you're not all beat up."

"Thanks. Listen, has Rebecca shown up yet?"

"Yeah, she just went up a minute ago."

"Thanks, you're a dear." She darted into the elevator before he could say another word.

***

Helen loved the light this time of day. As the sun gently lowered itself toward New Jersey, the air turned luminous, the city golden. Eighteen stories below the penthouse terrace, Central Park unfolded in improbably lush greens. Tourists, glistening in the humidity, limped away from the Metropolitan Museum. Up here, a hesitant breeze was beginning to cool the afternoon. She raised the heavy crystal highball glass to her lips and took a long sip of cold vodka. She was already on her second drink, and her tolerance for alcohol wasn't all that high. But right now she felt that all the vodka in Mother Russia would not suffice to make this day dissolve.

Tom was on the phone with his father. He sounded tired but feisty. "I've got no idea....No, that's one thing I'm not worried about. The lawyers are good, the best. Among them, that team's got about a hundred years' experience at the SEC, they know everybody there. No, it's the publicity that concerns me....Yeah, it's time for the crisis management team to earn their keep. We'll have to watch them closely. We've kept those guys on retainer all these years but never had to use them....Yeah, sure. Okay, I'll call you back then." He hung up.

The doorbell rang.

Tom frowned. "That's funny. I didn't buzz anybody up." He stood and moved toward the door. "Let's hope it's the super and not one of the neighbors. If it's Mrs. Charlesfield, I may have to kill her."

Tom opened the door, but Helen couldn't make out the figure in the doorway. She heard him say, "Yes? Can I help you?"

***

The door swung open and Rebecca flashed her warmest smile. She hadn't expected Richardson to answer his own door, but there he was, backlit by the sunlight streaming in from the terrace. "You don't know me by sight, do you, Mr. Richardson? But Helen does."

Over his shoulder, she saw Helen stand up and freeze at the sound of her voice.

"I'm Rebecca Morgan. May I call you Tom?"

"You're...you're that...you've got a lot of nerve showing up here. How did you get past the doorman?"

She grinned, enjoying his spluttering outrage. "I'm a journalist, we're sneaky. Now, we can stand here chatting in the doorway all day, or you can invite me in...because you don't have the faintest clue what's really going on here, do you?"

Tom frowned, stepped back and sourly motioned her inside, then led her out to the terrace.

"I gather you two know each other."

Rebecca nodded. "Hello, Helen."

Helen stood pale and speechless. She looked as if someone had just puked all over her favorite Chanel suit.

Tom picked up a glass half full of whiskey and paused a second, looking pained. "Drink?"

Rebecca smiled, amused. Even now, his deeply bred manners asserted themselves. "No, no, thanks, I'm fine."

She could have sworn she could feel the heat of his glare toasting her skin. Only her lace-gloved hands were magically impervious.

He spat words at her. "How do you sleep at night? How can you print something like that? You must know it's a pack of lies, and I'll prove it too. Don't you realize that you're playing with people's lives?"

Rebecca laughed, savoring the moment. "And you don't, Mr. Billionaire? Oh, that's rich. Because, you see, that's exactly why this is happening. And I want you to know why. Of course, this conversation isn't really taking place. And don't ask me to tell you how. Take my word for it—there's a solid trail of evidence behind that story. When the SEC looks at phone logs, *The*

Magazine's computer backups…not a pretty picture. At least there's nothing on your computer. Have you checked it lately?"

Tom scowled. "There's something wrong with it."

"Your hard drive's been erased, overwritten." Rebecca beamed at him. "Of course, it'll look like you did it to destroy the evidence. Maybe some forensic computer team will recover a few fragments, but that'll just make things worse for you. You can shout out you've been framed, but really, who's gonna buy it? I'm your one-armed man, Tom." She giggled.

Helen finally spoke, a brittle edge to her voice. "What about Microfreq? And Cluster Node? They were mentioned in your story. How'd you plant evidence about them?"

Rebecca smiled at Helen, squinting in the sun. How interesting that Helen would focus on those. "You know, Helen, I've wondered about them myself. No, I didn't plant any evidence about Microfreq or Cluster Node, they're just mentioned in the story as gravy. Couldn't help notice some suspicious coincidences in the timing of some trades and some stories, so I piled them on. Why? Was the bastard really insider-trading? That would be too good."

Helen's face tightened. "No, I don't think so. Not technically, in the legal sense anyway." She gave Tom a look Rebecca recognized. She had seen it on a PBS nature show once, when a mongoose stared down a snake. "So you did short those stocks."

"Well, yes, I…"

"No, I understand now." Helen glanced at Rebecca. "He was just being a manipulative son of a bitch. He was just abusing my trust."

"Helen…" Tom took a step toward her.

"No. Don't. Don't even try."

His jaw clenched, twitched. "Okay. I guess I deserve that. But it took two to do that tango. You didn't have to pass on what I said."

Helen's eyes turned to ice. Flash-frozen to a temperature Rebecca had never seen before. "You counted on me to do just that. Which pretty much defines manipulation. That was calculated. You trash-talked those stocks to me, but you didn't mention you were shorting them."

A long, sweet, silent moment of pure tension. This was almost better than Rebecca had hoped.

Finally, Tom took a step back and turned to face Rebecca. "Why? Why are you doing this?"

"To pay a debt to a man you never knew existed. When you gutted Madsen—a particularly clumsy and pointless job of corporate butchery, if I may say so—you took away my father's life. Quite literally. The life of a better man than you could ever dream of being. A man who devoted himself, first, to his child, second, to his work. And in the end, they both let him down. The least I can do is avenge him."

Drunk with victory, she turned to Helen. "I hold *The Magazine* responsible too. Roberts used me like he used everyone else. And I played along…when my father needed me, I didn't hear. I was shutting out the world…to work on a story. A fucking story. So *The Magazine*'s gonna suffer some damage.

"And Helen. You were always good to me, back in the day. But you're consorting with the enemy, and for that, you'll go down too. I have to say, when I realized you were screwing this bastard…well, everything fell into place: Tom, you, *The Magazine,* even Kimmie…"

Helen blanched, her eyes suddenly fixed on something behind Rebecca.

The voice of an angry ghost lashed out. Kimmie's voice: "I fell into fucking place?"

***

Kimmie watched Rebecca spin around and go pale against her dark hair.

Kimmie stood in the open doors that led out to the terrace. Behind her, the door that led to the foyer and the elevator stood ajar. She had slipped through unnoticed, then stood and listened for a minute, rage building like pressure in her head. She had flashed on some of the things Rebecca had once said. "We'll be set for life, honey. All we have to do is keep quiet, show your Daddy-o the evidence and threaten to print it." Flashed on all the ways she had been seduced. Managed. Conned.

Now Kimmie spoke as she stepped out onto the terrace, her voice soft and ominous. "Why, you stupid, whiny, self-pitying cunt. You used me from the beginning, didn't you? So you throw it all away for a fucking story? For your self-involved, guilt-trip revenge? And you try to kill me. Twice.

"Oh, yeah. Very, very nice."

"Now, Kimmie." Rebecca's tone was smooth, controlled. Soothing. "Don't do anything rash. I can explain everything."

Kimmie shook her head. Did the psycho really think she could manage her way out of this? "No, you can't. I recommend that you don't even try. I've had about enough of you, bitch."

Helen stood rooted in disbelief as Kimmie pulled an enormous knife from her handbag, tossed the bag aside and charged across the terrace with a primeval battle cry.

The blade flashed in the setting sun. Kimmie seemed to be running in slow motion, her unruly waves of hair suspended in the breeze. Rebecca braced herself to meet the attack, knees slightly bent, eyes wide. Helen became conscious of the heft of the highball glass in her hand. With surreal clarity, she visualized Kimmie's trajectory up to the point where she would collide with Rebecca. Parabolas intersected in her head. She hurled the glass, still full of vodka.

For once, Rebecca was living in the moment, completely focused on Kimmie's attack and pretty much counting on adrenaline to help her dodge the blade. So it startled her when the crystal glass tumbled into her field of vision. It smacked hard off the side of Kimmie's face and shattered on the slate floor. The knife skittered across the terrace and Rebecca had a fraction of a second to appreciate her miraculous deliverance before she realized that she'd started to dodge in the same direction the glass had knocked Kimmie.

Off-balance, Kimmie plowed into Rebecca with the full force of her charge, catching her solar plexus with one shoulder, smashing the breath out of her. Rebecca flew backwards.

The small of her back smacked into something hard and the world turned upside down. She let go, weightless with the peace of the long fall.

Helen heard a muffled grunt, watched Rebecca stagger back a step and collide with the waist-high railing. Her momentum continued to push her back, lifting her feet off the ground. For an endless second her hands clutched at the air, her legs flailed through space. With a look of infinite surprise, she tumbled over and was gone.

Something struck Helen as especially odd about Rebecca's fall, but it took her a moment to figure out what it was: no scream. Perhaps Rebecca couldn't catch her breath. Just silence for a full second or so, then an echoing thwack. Helen walked to the railing and stared over the edge. Rebecca had caved in the top of a mammoth sports-utility vehicle.

She looked up. Tom stood in one corner, pale. He had picked up the knife. Kimmie sprawled on the floor, spitting out blood and a couple of teeth, her skirt tangled around her hips. Helen couldn't help notice that she wore no underwear.

"Goddamn, Helen," she said, "that's some right arm you've got there." She dabbed at her lip.

Helen could have sworn she saw a sudden glint in her eye, could almost see her synapses flickering, almost watch her soul calculate the next few moves.

***

Kimmie smiled ruefully. "Been a helluva day. For all three of us, I guess."

Helen stared at her. "What about Rebecca?"

Kimmie shrugged and tugged her skirt back into place. "All her fault anyway. Got what she deserved." She stood a little shakily, wiped her face with her sleeve. Damn, still bleeding. She hated having dental work done. Straightened up and segued into her pitch. "Hell. You know, maybe we can all salvage something out of this mess."

Tom seemed to snap out of a trance, gave her a sharp look. "What are you saying?"

She eyed him coolly. The man's antennae certainly twitched at any threat to his net worth. "I'm saying, I know we're all in shock right now, but let's try to focus. We don't have that much time before the cops show up."

"You know, Tom, I never wanted to ruin your life. I just wanted your money. We'd set you up, plant the evidence, then accept a fee to remain discreet about it."

"Basic blackmail, you mean," said Tom.

"Whatever. I'd rather call it reparation. We were gonna hit you up for ten million. Now I think I'll still take my half of that."

"For what?"

"For us all getting our stories straight before the police show up. Think about it. I can vouch for the fact that Rebecca was nuts. Crazed with guilt over her father's death. Tries to make you feel guilty too by leaping off your terrace. And it couldn't hurt your situation if she looks wacko. Or else I can tell how she came here to taunt you and gloat. How you tossed her off the terrace in a rage. You certainly had motive. How I tried to stop you, but Helen hit me with the glass." She fixed her gaze on the knife in his hand.

Reflexively, he glanced down.

Kimmie continued. "Think hard, Tom. The SEC is one thing. But there's nothing like a murder investigation to tarnish a reputation."

She gave the screw a final turn. "Of course, you can toss me after Rebecca. You've got the knife. But then, what would Mom think?"

Tom stared. "You really are a cold, ruthless little bitch."

Kimmie grinned. "Just my father's little girl."

A siren wailed from a few blocks away. Coming closer.

Tom surrendered. "What are your terms?"

Kimmie limped over to her handbag. She saw Tom tense and tighten his grip on the knife.

She laughed. "Don't worry, no more weapons." She straightened up with a slip of paper and her cell phone in her hands, relaxing now that she knew she had control. "This is the number of a bank account in the Cayman Islands. I want five million U.S. dollars wired into it by 9 a.m. tomorrow, New York time. I know you have accounts around the world, so don't give me any shit about the banks being closed. Personal funds, business funds, I don't give a damn where you get it. But when I wake up tomorrow, I'll call to check my balance. And if, having tried to protect my father, I break down and change my story tomorrow, that won't look too good."

She held out her phone. "Here, use my cell phone to make whatever calls you need to. It's one of those disposable phones, prepaid. They'll probably check your phone records, and we wouldn't want to leave a trail."

Stiffly, Tom reached out and took the phone, started punching numbers.

Kimmie turned to Helen, feeling as smooth as a social director on a cruise ship. "Why don't you go inside and call 911? For appearance' sake."

SATURDAY, OCTOBER 9, 1999

Susie Popitz watched her husband leverage his bulk out of the Adirondack chair, pour himself a fresh martini from the pitcher and glare westward, across their immaculately groomed expanse of East Hampton lawn. From up here, on the second-floor terrace, Susie could see over the tall hedge that bordered the property. An enormous white tent had been pitched on the grass beyond, and a platoon of underlings scurried about the yard next door. Like ants, she thought: Any given individual's motion seemed random, but there was an underlying order, an almost military sense of purpose. She found it irritating.

Popitz waved an enormous unlit cigar at the tent. "Well, they've lucked into a beautiful weekend for this extravaganza. Too much commotion. I come out here for the peace and quiet. Damn wedding's not till tomorrow, and look at them."

He turned and frowned at Susie. She could see his eyebrows bristling over the top of his opaque sunglasses. "You don't think there'll be helicopters? Paparazzi in the sky?"

She snickered. "Helicopters? What do you think this is? Maybe if Brad Pitt ever marries Jennifer. It's not Hollywood, Poopsie, it's just another billionaire."

"Hmmf. Just another billionaire." He shook his head and turned back toward the tent. "What's the world coming to?"

He paused to light his cigar. "One thing I'll give the son of a bitch, he didn't let a whiff of scandal disrupt his plans. Never let them see you sweat, that's the ticket. He understands that.

"You know, I almost feel a twinge of sympathy for the bastard, this whole Rebecca Morgan thing. Gives us something in common. Always knew that woman was loony tunes. Probably every word she ever wrote was a fucking lie."

Susie leaned forward and refilled her glass of Drambuie, offering him a fine view of her cleavage. As usual, it went to waste. "Well, she surprised me. I mean, I could tell she was wound a little tight, but this was crazy nuts. And jumping off his terrace? That's some psycho shit."

He nodded. "Yeah, psycho shit is right. And now I've gotta put up with psycho wedding shit. Maybe we shouldn't have come out this weekend."

She did her level best to burn holes through him with her eyes, but the back of his bald head remained infuriatingly uncharred. "Maybe not. You do realize why this wedding is so fucking annoying?"

He shrugged. "The noise, disruption..."

"Because we weren't fucking invited! The social event of the season, and here we are, the next-door fucking neighbors, peeking over the fucking hedge."

He sighed and sat back down, peering at her over his sunglasses. "And that bothers you. I would've thought you'd be used to that by now."

"I don't know if I'll ever be used to it."

"Fuck them," he said quietly. "Learn to live with it. Richardson's a snob, and I'm an *arriviste*, a self-made man. He'll never ask us over for tea and crumpets. Hell, half the reason I bought this place was I knew how much it would fucking irritate him. He'd probably like to back up that hedge with a goddamn moat." He smiled. "I'm surprised he hasn't thought of that."

Susie gulped down her drink and stood. Fury simmered inside her, and she knew if she didn't do something physical to relieve the pressure, it would boil over. "I'm going for a walk."

An hour later, having traipsed to the beach, sulked a while and wandered back, she was calmer as she started across the lawn. Still, the hedge drew her with its own gravitational pull. From ground level, she could hear but not see the bustle on the other side. The foliage was just too thick. She wondered if she could see underneath it. Feeling faintly ridiculous, she knelt on the grass and peered beneath the hedge. She could see ankles moving past.

Something glinted in the sharply angled light of late afternoon. Something close by, in her peripheral vision. She scanned the dirt and mulch beneath the hedge. There. Her hand scooped up a necklace.

She brushed it clean of dirt and studied it. A silver spiral on a disk of jade. It seemed familiar...

Her eyes widened as the memory rushed back. Rebecca Morgan. Of course, she'd worn it the morning they'd first met. Susie had admired it. Rebecca said it had once belonged to her mother. But how...?

My God, had she been spying on them, hidden in the hedge? Susie felt a sudden chill. But no...more likely she'd been spying on Richardson. Or maybe both? Jesus, more psycho shit.

She stood, a little shakily, and hefted it in her palm. It gleamed softly in the sun, a lovely thing. Was it bad juju?

Fuck it, she thought, Poopsie was right. Fuck everyone and the universe, too. Finders keepers.

She fastened it around her neck and smiled as she walked back to the house.

***

Helen drove slowly, carefully navigating the ancient Mercedes through the streets of East Hampton. Her grandmother had bought it back in the 1970s and had never seen any reason to trade it in for a newer model, despite the fact that it had clocked some 200,000 miles by now. Tatiana rode shotgun, making empty but animated chatter about the wedding preparations.

Helen let the talk wash over her without really listening. She should be excited, or nervous, or something. She felt as if she were trapped in a bubble, numb but for the tightening knot in her gut.

The last few weeks seemed unreal. The police investigation (mercifully brief, as Rebecca's death was ruled a suicide). The SEC investigation, which would probably go on for a few months. The fallout at work. And the wedding preparations, all at once. It was amazing she could still walk and talk.

In the end, she felt sure, Tom would emerge from all this only slightly bruised. *The Magazine* too. Rebecca had sustained all the losses. And to some extent, Preston. Llewellyn was keeping him on for now to avoid the appearance of admitting anything, but he had clearly lost confidence in his editor in chief. This had all happened on his watch. As soon as the SEC went away, Preston would be quietly forced out. She wondered idly whether Llewellyn would bring in an outsider or let Bruce run the show. Not that she cared anymore.

There was a sudden silence, and she realized her grandmother had asked her a question. Something about the caterer, she thought. She ignored it.

"Listen, Tatiana, I want to thank you for coming along."

"Well, of course, why wouldn't I be with my granddaughter today?"

"And for sending Mother off to deal with the florist and the cake. I...I just don't think I can deal with her today."

Tatiana chuckled. "That was clever of me, no?"

"Yes, inspired really. It's just...been such a difficult time."

"Of course." Tatiana nodded and grew quiet, studying her profile. "A time of madness. Tell me, whatever happened to that dear boy, Jack? Jake?"

"Jake. Good news there. Came out of his coma last week. They say he'll be all right."

"Ah, good, good. Such a dear, fun boy. And that other girl in all this, that Kimmie?"

Helen frowned. "Soon as the police were done with their questions, she vanished. I heard she moved to France."

"Really? Heard where? I mean, if she disappeared...?"

Damn, Helen thought, have to be careful. Tatiana's a sharp one. "Tom has his sources."

Tatiana nodded. "I see."

Helen wondered if she did.

"And you? Will you ever go back to *The Magazine*?"

Helen shook her head. "They've given me six months' paid leave, you know. Paid because it looks better. Officially, they're standing behind me, but it gets me out of the way. When the leave's over, I'll resign. That's part of the understanding."

"And how do you feel about that?"

Helen shrugged. "I don't mind. Relieved actually. Time to do something different. Thought I might try to write a novel."

"A novel!" Tatiana lit up. "How splendid, how artistic. A wonderful idea. Something of your own."

"Yes, I feel the need to find my own path."

"Your own path, but of course. You can do anything you want now."

Anything she wanted. Could she? Why, because she was marrying a rich man? Then why didn't she feel free?

Still a hundred yards short of Tom's driveway, Helen pulled over, stopping in the shade of the hedge that sheltered the estate from the road. She stared blankly into space, her breathing shallow, clammy hands clenching the wheel.

"Helen? Why did we stop here?" Tatiana sounded alarmed. "Helen, what's wrong?"

Helen's voice was soft, almost a whisper. "I don't know if I can do this. I don't think I want to."

"Do what?" Tatiana frowned. "Not the wedding?"

Helen nodded.

"Oh, nonsense." Tatiana chuckled nervously and waved a dismissive hand. "Just cold feet, it's normal. Every bride feels some of that."

Helen kept staring at the windshield as she shook her head.

Tatiana spoke sharply. "Helen, look at me. Look me in the eyes. Is it more than cold feet?"

Helen turned and felt Tatiana's gaze probing her face. She felt like a little girl caught in a lie.

Tatiana slumped back. "My God, you're serious. What is it, then?"

"I...I'm not sure I trust him anymore. Or if he trusts me. He can be devious, manipulative."

Tatiana nodded. "Go on."

"He...he has the resources to hire people to watch other people. Even me, he says it was an accident, but...I don't know if I want to live in his world. I don't even want to live in my world right now."

She blinked back tears. "Tell me what to do, Tatiana. I don't want to hurt him, let him down..."

"What nonsense. I can't tell you what to do. You must follow your heart. And Tom, he's a big boy. Of course his feelings would be hurt. If you do this, he'll be angry, embarrassed, his ego bruised. But he's a very handsome billionaire. It won't hurt him to stay single a bit longer, he'll do just fine."

Helen sniffed glumly. "Yes, I suppose he will."

"No, a more important question is this: If you do this, will he be heartbroken?"

Helen stared at her grandmother a long time, as if eternal silence could stave away her answer. "I don't think so."

Tatiana nodded. "Then he doesn't love you enough. Remember, you are my granddaughter. You are a Tyrkova, born with steel in your spine and fire in your blood. You deserve real love, real passion, a man who would die for you. A real man. Maybe you'll do better with one who hasn't been coddled by a family fortune."

Helen was startled. Tatiana had never spoken against inherited wealth before.

Tatiana nodded. "You look surprised. Yes, titles and money are all very well, but they make some people soft and turn others into idiots, full of themselves for no reason."

"But...my God, can I really do this?" Helen groaned. "Tatiana, the family estate in Russia, how can I..."

"Don't be foolish, Helen, do you really think I'd mortgage your happiness for a piece of land, ancestral or not? You would have inherited that soon anyway."

"Tatiana..."

"Besides, Tom presented me with the deed last week. Of course, I'll offer to return it to him. Being a gentleman and extremely wealthy, he'll refuse, I suspect. If not, that's life."

Helen stared blankly through the windshield. "What about Mother?"

"Don't you dare give her another thought, this is not her wedding. Don't worry, I'll take care of Alexandra. You can do anything you want."

"I don't know if I can face her..."

"Then don't. You can hide out with me, as long as you like." Tatiana brightened. "Stay with me and work on your novel, it would be such fun. We'll have a literary salon."

Helen almost smiled. "I don't know how much work I'll get done. But maybe I'll try that for a while."

"Wonderful." Tatiana sighed. "Too bad this is only an old Mercedes. We need a coach and horses to escape into the night properly."

She straightened and looked stern. "I'll deal with your mother, but there's something only you can do. And if you're going to do it, you should do it now."

Helen nodded and wiped her eyes. She checked herself in the mirror. Her makeup was a mess. To hell with it.

She started the car, slowly crunched up the long gravel driveway, stopped. "Will you wait here for me?"

Tatiana nodded. "I'll guard the coach and horses. Remember, steel in your spine."

Helen climbed out and spotted Tom in the distance, near the white tent. Her back straight as the horizon of the Russian steppes, she started across the grass, freer already.

ABOUT THE AUTHORS

Married for 22 years, Hugo and Kasia Moreno each have a couple of decades of experience working at financial magazines such as *Forbes* and *SmartMoney*. They currently run McParlin Partners, a thought leadership, strategic research and content firm, and live in Brooklyn.

63072761R10157

Made in the USA
Columbia, SC
09 July 2019